Tank Thornstone

A.R. Weston

Tank Thornstone
The Tablet of Rio de Monstros

BATB Publishing
Grimes, Iowa 50111

To Evelyn, Christian, and Hope. If no one else enjoys this book, if not a single copy is ever sold, if the only triumph from this endeavor is to hear you laugh, then it was worth it!

- Dad

Tank Thornstone – The Tablet of Rio de Monstros
Copyright © 2025 A.R. Weston
www.arweston.com

ISBN: 978-1-949439-15-1

Contents

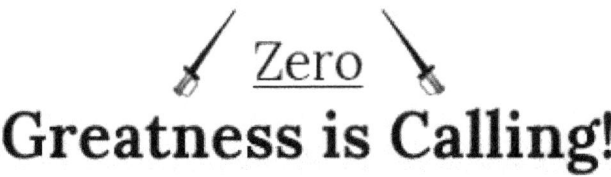

Zero
Greatness is Calling!

We have all heard the tale about the unlikely hero, the scrawny kid that defies all odds, the loser, the underdog, the wimp. It's cute to think about. The nerd evolves into the superstar, the geek transcends into the champion, and the little guy proves his self-worth. These stories are predictable, to say the least.

Thankfully, this is not *that* story!

In a small Kentucky town, the new kid at La Grange High School is about to learn the truth about his family's noble origins and save us all from global tyranny. He is not the average teenager. He is Tank Thornstone and greatness is calling his name!

This is *his* story...

One
Rise and Shine

Tank tossed and turned in his camo patterned sheets. Today marked the first day of school and boy was he dreading that alarm clock going off. Where has the summer gone? It felt like field day was yesterday and he had run to his mom's car shouting, "Hallelujah! No more school!"

If the last day of school was Tank's favorite, then the first day of school was the worst day of the year. Summer is all about swimming, playing ball outside, staying up late watching movies, and sleeping in till noon every day.

Then, in the blink of an eye, summer is over and it's time to go back to school. School is all about learning stuff, raising your hand, and worst of all, getting up early. Sometimes, Tank wondered if summer was a cruel prank that parents played on their children. Give the kids a taste of freedom and then take it away.

Every year it felt like summer was shorter and the school year was longer and longer. The parents and the teachers probably met secretly at P.T.A. meetings to discuss how they could eventually get rid of summer and make school all year round.

Tank rolled over again, grunted, scratched his tummy, let one rip, and then tossed around a little more. Glowing from the nightstand, his green LED alarm clock illuminated the corner of the room showing he had a little time until the alarm would go off. Tank kept his clock in military time because it reminded him of dad. There were exactly two minutes till the alarm went off, so he pulled up the blankets until they crept back over his head.

As the blanket covered his messy brown hair... **"beep, beep, beep, beep,"** the alarm clock filled the room with the most irritating sound on the planet. No rational human being enjoys the sound of an alarm clock, yet everyone has one. Alarm clocks are a clear example of self-inflicted torture for humanity. Within two nanoseconds, Tank extended his right arm, straightened his index finger like a medieval dagger, and stabbed the snooze button on the alarm clock.

"That ought to do it. Five more minutes is all I need," Tank yawned.

"ANDREW T. THORNSTONE!" yelled Mom from downstairs.

Tank's mom was no ordinary woman. In fact, he was quite sure she might be a superhero pretending to be a stay-at-home mom. Mom required little sleep, had superhuman strength to open any peanut butter or jelly jar, could detect even the smallest of lies, was the smartest person he had ever met, and she made the best food in the galaxy. Any mom who could hold down the fort with a rambunctious teenager like Tank while her husband was deployed overseas was undeniably a superhero. Mom had served in the military in the nutrition office when Tank was first born, but she had completed her service and was able to pursue her true passion of being a full-time mom.

Mom is 5'4, has a petite build, and has light brown hair that extends past her shoulders. She loves to wear workout clothes around the house and goes on early morning runs with her girlfriends as they prepare for upcoming races. Next month, Mom is set to compete in her first triathlon. Dad says Mom is "The perfect dime," but Tank is not sure what that means. Tank would tell dad that ten cents was an insult to explain what someone was worth.

Dad frequently described mom as "Fly," but as far as Tank could see, she did not have wings. When questioned about his unique vocabulary regarding mom, Dad clarified that "His wife was fresh!" Tank never noticed a body odor or hygiene issue with mom. Eventually, dad explained the expressions he was using simply implied mom was "beautiful and pretty." Tank would ask why not use the words, "bussin and snatched!" Dad had no clue what Tank was saying. It was as if they were speaking two different languages.

Getting past the communication challenges with dad, there was only one change to mom Tank would make. For years he had tried to figure out a strategy. Alarm clocks have snooze options, but evidently, Mom did not have this function, yet. Perhaps he would check the forums on the internet to see if anyone had figured out how to get their mom to let their child sleep five more minutes.

Tank chuckled. He had told dad that joke several times and it usually warranted a playful punch to the arm. To be funny, dad once printed off a manual to an alarm clock and pasted in a picture of mom. Mom did not laugh at the joke, but Tank sure did.

"Rise and shine, sweetie. It's time to get up, honey," hollered mom as she trudged up the stairs moments later.

Tank growled and tucked his head deeper under the blankets as Mom entered his bedroom. On her way in, she flipped on both light switches and swung open the curtains like a Broadway show was about to start. The first switch turned the ceiling light fixture on. The second switch turned on the freestanding lamp that stood next to the bed. Mom also had the audacity to pull the cord on the ceiling fan, eliminating the cool air that was blowing in the room. With the light shining through the blankets and the rush of cold air from the fan disappearing from above, reality sank in for Tank.

"Did you break wind a few moments ago?" questioned mom, sniffing the air.

"No, I did not break wind, but I may have cracked a rat," Tank laughed.

"Cracked a what? Andrew, that is nasty!" Mom fanned the air in front of her nose trying to disperse the smell.

Tank had heard one of his cousins in Colorado use the expression "crack a rat" to describe farting when they had visited last Thanksgiving. He had been waiting for the right moment to catch mom off guard with the expression to see her reaction. It was worth the wait. The first day of school was the perfect occasion to gross mom out.

"Mom, I don't want to get up. Can't I skip today? Everyone knows the first day of school is a waste of time." Tank passionately pled his case.

"You are so right," said Mom sarcastically. "Andrew, my love, your wisdom about life is undeniable."

"Think about it, Mom," continued Tank. "Everyone fakes being sick during the school year, but it takes courage to skip the first day."

"Uh huh, so skipping school is courageous?" Mom questioned.

"Yep, and doesn't dad tell me all the time that courage is the foundation of every man worth his salt?" smiled Tank.

"Nice try, Andrew." Mom pulled a nice pair of slacks and a blue button-down shirt from the closet.

"Mom..." he complained, "please call me Tank."

"The day you quit bellyaching about getting out of bed," razzed mom, "will be the day I will consider calling you Tank."

Tank leisurely pulled his head from under the blankets like a turtle out of its shell. He rolled over on his back, stretched his legs, and began to sit up. During the summer, Tank would sleep in every day. This was his first day getting up early in a few months. He wasn't necessarily against getting up early, but it was not something he enjoyed.

It wasn't like there was something exciting happening today. They weren't getting up early to go hunting or fishing, or better yet, go tailgating for a college football game. The only thing to get up for today was school and that never motivated anyone to do anything.

Dad would tell him fake motivation was better than no motivation. "Fake it till you make it" or "Fake the funk" as Dad would say when Tank didn't feel like doing a chore around the house. Remembering dad's advice, Tank sprang out of bed like lightning zapped him on the butt. One foot hit the carpet and the second foot struck the floor a few moments later.

"Ouch!" Tank yelled in pain.

Mom came darting out of the closet at record speed. Even world-class sprinters are jealous of Mom's quickness. One more thing about Mom that should be mentioned. She is the kindest and most loving person in the universe. Even St. Peter himself could take a lesson from Mom about caring for others, but, if there was even a chance that something or someone was hurting her child, then mom had no problem engaging in hand-to-hand combat.

There are the Green Berets, Seals, Pararescue, and Recon units. These groups are filled with tough men who do extraordinary things. If there is a problem in the world, they are ready to fight day or night. However, if you need an elite warrior to save the day, then there is no force on earth tougher than a mom who thinks her child is in distress.

Tank had thought about this in the past. If he had to choose between fighting a special forces soldier or battling mom when she was mad, he would take his chances with the commando because Mom would kick his booty for sure.

Mom swiftly arrived at the bed. Both Mom and Tank glanced down and noticed a little green toy soldier crumpled under his foot. Mom had been so focused on getting Tank out of bed that she hadn't noticed the mess in the room. Looking across Tank's room from left to right, there was a large brown bookshelf which doubled as a monster truck holder, but half of the monster trucks were scattered around the room.

The collection of monster trucks was something grandpa started buying as a tradition on Tank's first Christmas and every year he added a new one to the collection. A full-sized bed was near the center of the room and on each side of the bed stood a black nightstand. On the backside of the door hung a body-sized mirror that Tank used frequently to check for muscle gains in his biceps.

Posters of sharks, trucks, and sports cars covered the walls. On the other side of the bed, resting on the nightstand was his dad's 10x10 military picture in a frame. Scattered on the floor were at least a hundred toy green soldiers and a hundred toy tan soldiers. Fighter jets, armored convoys, and ground-to-air missile launchers were strategically placed throughout the room.

The only space in the bedroom that was not a declared war zone was the nightstand with his dad's picture. Tank always kept the nightstand clean and would use the drawer to store letters he received from dad. Reverence and respect for the military was something his parents instilled in him from an early age.

"What happened, Andrew?" asked mom.

"Ah man!" Tank lifted his foot showing the toy soldier sticking to the underside of his heel. "That was my favorite infantryman."

"Perhaps a good lesson," suggested Mom. "Pick up your room better and then you won't step on toys when you wake up."

"Mom..." sighed Tank. "These aren't toys."

Setting up strategic battle formations with his "toy" soldiers was one of Tank's favorite things to do. He didn't see any of his stuff as toys anymore because only little children played with toys. The toy soldiers and monster trucks were important training materials to study military maneuvers, or at least that is how Tank explained all the toys to people when he felt embarrassed about playing with them. Mom sighed, rubbed Tank's foot, and then patted him on the shoulder. There was no blood and only a tiny scratch on the bottom of Tank's heel. Tank sat there, as all young boys would, and soaked in a little empathy from mom.

"If you want me to call you Tank, then you are going to need to toughen up, honey," she giggled.

Mom walked out of the room and made her way downstairs. On the way down, Mom reminded Tank again that if he were to clean his room better then perhaps his "not toys" would survive longer. Tank sulked, trying to unbend the tiny, crushed toy soldier. He could hear singing downstairs.

She had a beautiful angelic voice. She danced into the kitchen and opened the oven. A few moments later a divine smell of breakfast casserole filled the whole house. Thinking about mom's comments about toughening up, he launched himself out of bed again.

"Toughen up. I am tough. I am the toughest kid in this town. That's for sure!" Tank smacked his chest a few times.

Tank took off his shirt, looked in the mirror at his muscles, and dropped to the floor to do his morning pushups like Dad taught him. Every morning when Tank woke up, he did pushups, sit-ups, and jumping jacks. Even though it was never fun getting out of bed, he liked to get in a quick workout early in the day. Dad would tell him *freedom isn't free* and neither are muscles.

Occasionally, mom would invite him to run a 5k race early in the morning which Tank enjoyed, but only because he loved competing with others. One of his goals before he finished high school was to not only complete a triathlon, but to win a triathlon. It was going to take some practice and pain, but he knew he could do it.

"Twenty-three, twenty-four, twenty-five..." Tank's breath grew louder as he finished his last set.

Tank laid on the floor thinking about dad for a moment. Dad was in incredible shape. In fact, describing dad as in shape was quite an understatement. There were professional athletes that wished they could do the physical things that Dad could do. Tank wanted dad to be impressed with his fitness when he came home in ten months. When Dad left to fight in the war, Tank promised him he would be the man of the house. Dad even made him raise his right hand and take the oath:

"I, Andrew Tannis Thornstone, do solemnly swear that I will support and defend my family against all enemies; that I will bear true faith and allegiance to the same; and that I will obey the orders of Mom. So help me God."

Dad had joined the military fresh out of high school as an enlisted artilleryman. An artilleryman can take a ninety-pound piece of steel and launch it over twelve miles in the air to destroy the enemy. Tank dreamt of the day when he was old enough to enlist and join the military.

When dad described his experience as an artilleryman, he would often refer to himself as a "gun-bunny." This made Tank laugh because he imagined the Easter Bunny covered in body armor and firing a cannon.

Being enlisted as a First Sergeant was something Dad spoke about with immense pride. After more than a decade of enlistment, he completed college and was commissioned as an officer. Dad never spoke about his job anymore, but Tank did recall seeing a certificate that said "counter-intelligence" a few years back.

Tank imagined his dad was a secret agent or something cool like that, but he was not sure what his dad did in the military nowadays. It wasn't because Tank never asked, but more so that dad would avoid the subject about his job and mom would change the topic when it came up. On dad's left arm, high up near his shoulder, was an inked tattoo that said "WARRIOR."

Three months ago, Dad was promoted to Captain and, along with the promotion, they received orders to move to Kentucky. Moving around is part of being the son of a military man, but that didn't make it any easier. Dad had left on deployment three times since Tank was born, but for the last five years had worked on base in Texas training new troops. Something felt different about this deployment for dad.

Tank was born on a military post in southwest Oklahoma and by the time he was two they had already moved to Texas. Texas was all that Tank could remember and was where his heart belonged. Between missing Dad, leaving Texas and his friends behind, and starting at a new school, he was struggling to find joy in life.

Most summers, dad would take him and mom on two-week long trips to exotic places. In the last five years, Tank had traveled to Australia, Greece, and twice to Brazil. During the trips, dad spent most of his day training for military reasons, but on nights and weekends they would travel the local areas. This year, they had planned another trip to South America, but it was canceled due to dad deploying.

8

Tank had spent time last school year trying to learn a little Portuguese in anticipation for their vacation, but it turned out to be a waste of time. Oh well, hopefully next summer, if dad didn't get his deployment extended, they could have a family vacation again.

Thinking about vacation would have to wait for a more cheerful day. For now, it was time to get ready for school or as Tank liked to call it, "Kid Jail!" As dad would say, using military lingo, it was again time to "Embrace the suck!"

Two
Dress for Success

The smell of bacon, eggs, cheese, and hash brown casserole wafted up the stairs and it was enough motivation to help Tank hurry up. Tank's mouth watered, his taste buds tingled, and his tummy rumbled. He took one more look in the mirror and flexed his biceps out in front of his chest. Tank walked into the closet and grabbed clothes for himself. Beads of sweat trickled down his forehead, so he hurried into the bathroom for a quick shower.

The clothes mom had picked out for him were neatly hung on the back of the bathroom door. After a two-minute shower and a serious attempt to pop an almost ready zit on his mid back, he covered himself with a towel. He marched the clothes mom had picked out for him back into the closet. Tank hid them far enough behind the other clothes in the closet hoping they would be harder for mom to find in the future.

"That smells wonderful, mom," yelled Tank as he finished buckling his belt. "I'm on my way down!"

"What in the world are you wearing?" Mom had a puzzled look on her face as she threw her hands up in the air. She looked at Tank like he had a baseball bat growing out of his forehead. "Didn't you see the pants and shirt I hung up in the bathroom?"

"Those weren't my style, mom," winked Tank. "This is my first day at a new school. I don't want to look like a dork. I am dressed for success!"

Tank had put on his finest pair of camo cargo pants. For a shirt, he had pulled out a gray one that dad bought last year. It had two black swords that crossed over each other with a cannon in the middle. On the back of the shirt the words "Field Artillery" were written in red letters. The best part of the shirt was the picture of the swords on the front perfectly matched the combat patch on his dad's military uniform.

Soldiers earn a combat patch when they deploy to fight in a war. Soldiers wear their regular unit patch on one arm and the combat patch on the other. In a strange way, wearing the t-shirt made Tank feel connected to dad. On his feet, Tank sported a pair of tan combat boots.

Yesterday, mom had given him a fresh haircut because Tank didn't want to "Look like a hippie," as dad would jokingly say when his hair grew long enough to touch his ears. Tank spent a couple of seconds in front of the mirror, fluffing up his bangs with hair gel.

Coming into the kitchen, Tank walked past their stainless-steel fridge and noticed his reflection. His arms looked good, his hair looked good, and his teeth were sparkling white. Mom laughed when she noticed Tank admiring himself.

Unlike past years, Tank would go to school without caring about his looks, but he cared a lot this year. Mom warned him about the perils of vanity a couple of times but figured worrying about his appearance was normal for someone midway through their teenage years.

Resting on the table, where Tank normally sat, was an envelope that had the words, "**Tank's First Day of School.**" The envelope didn't have a stamp on it and the words were written in mom's handwriting. Mom instructed Tank to put the envelope in his bag and open it when he arrived at school.

"I have a surprise," Mom smiled and pulled out her smartphone.

"What is it, mom?" asked Tank.

"Well, that's odd," mom mumbled. "Your father was going to try and video chat with us since it is your first day of school."

The thought of being able to talk with Dad brought a smile and delight to Tank's life. Mom explained that she had spoken with Dad a little earlier this morning and she thought he was preparing for a night mission. Dad never shared much regarding the details of his military operations. It was morning in Kentucky, but where Dad was likely deployed, it was nearing nighttime.

Mom tried to connect with the video chat once more and received an error message indicating the recipient was not online. Shrugging the issue off as nothing more than a connection glitch, mom apologized for getting his hopes up about video chatting and then encouraged Tank to get his plate ready for breakfast.

Tank was disappointed, but that didn't stop him from loading his plate with three heavy scoops of the breakfast casserole. Then, he opened the fridge and topped his plate with more cheese, a scoop of avocado, and hot sauce. For a drink he poured himself a glass of water.

"Not a bad way to start the day," he thought to himself.

Racing to see who could eat the fastest was a game dad had taught him from the military. Mom never felt compelled to compete in this silly game, but she did enjoy watching Tank obnoxiously stuff his face with food trying to finish first. Sometimes mom would pretend to participate by taking huge scoops with her fork and then chewing like a maniac for a couple seconds.

Despite the generous portion of food, Tank laid waste to the mountain on his plate within five minutes. Tank rinsed his plate in the sink and placed it in the dishwasher. Mom gently sipped the last of the iced coffee from her glass jar which had a matching glass straw and then leisurely took another bite of her freshly buttered whole grain toast. She enjoyed every delicious second.

Peeking down at her phone again, the connection error for video chat was still blinking. Hopefully, they could connect after school. Although connectivity issues were common, mom felt a bit uneasy knowing that her husband was out on a top-secret mission in the middle of nowhere. Dad was adamant to mom about talking to Tank before the first day of school, but the opportunity was slipping away. Mom tucked her phone into her purse, cleaned her plate in the sink, and did a final round of turning off lights in the house.

The kitchen was attached to the laundry room and the laundry room had a narrow hallway with a door which led to the garage. The cramped layout of the laundry room was one of the worst features of the house they bought in Kentucky because it felt cluttered.

Hung above the laundry room door was a silver horseshoe that Tank routinely reached up and slapped for good luck like his favorite college football team did before a game. Out in the garage and trying to be funny, Tank walked to the driver's door, plopped down in the seat, and gripped the steering wheel.

"Alright mom, I got this." Tank buckled his seat belt and put his palm out for Mom to hand him the keys.

"Okay, sweetheart. Please keep it under 75 miles per hour," replied mom.

"Really?" Tank responded with excitement and disbelief in his voice.

"Sure, honey! My purpose in life is to make you happy no matter what, so why not?" Mom shrugged her shoulders and dug through her purse looking for the keys.

"Thanks... Mom," Tank nervously responded.

"Andrew Thornstone!" scoffed Mom in a stern voice. "Have you lost your mind? Get out of the driver's seat."

Tank chuckled and unbuckled his seat belt. Mom had a good sense of humor, which Tank appreciated. He was excited to get his learner's permit next year, but until then, Mom had strict rules on him sticking to being the passenger only. Instead of stepping out, walking around the car, and then entering the passenger side like a normal person, Tank climbed from the driver's seat to the passenger's seat being careful not to drag his boots across the center console.

Mom sat, buckled her seatbelt, clicked the remote button on the sun visor to open the garage door, and then started the car. The leather steering wheel was equipped with several buttons and Mom used her fingers to turn the stereo to her favorite talk radio station.

Pulling out of their subdivision and onto State Highway 53, Tank reached out to turn the radio down. There was a question he wanted to ask, but during the summer, it kept slipping his mind to bring it up. The military base where dad was stationed was at least fifty miles away from La Grange and there were several other larger towns that were much closer to base than the place where they lived.

Looming in the back of his mind, he didn't quite understand the decision for moving to La Grange. Sure, the local pool was nice, there were a couple of good places to eat, and mom and dad had history here, but come on, this place wasn't practical at all for dad to commute back and forth every day.

"Mom, I get that you and Dad wanted to move closer to where you all grew up, but there are like five other towns closer to where Dad works. Why here?" inquired Tank.

"La Grange is a wonderful place to grow up. Your father and I have so many great memories here. I still remember the first day your dad moved to town from Arizona. He was so handsome. Did you know when we were kids dad's nickname was..." started mom.

"Yeah, yeah, yeah," Tank jokingly interrupted. "I know, mom. When you were a kid, you could buy an ice cream cone for a nickel and you walked backwards uphill five miles to school every day in the snow."

"Hey, I'm not that old, kiddo," smirked Mom.

Both Tank and Mom smiled and laughed out loud. Mom didn't answer the question as to why they didn't buy a house closer to the military base and deflected the conversation. She went on talking about nostalgic memories, such as going to football games, school dances, and her first date with dad. Tank was interested to hear about dad's "nickname", but he could tell when Mom was attempting to steer the conversation somewhere else.

It was like she regretted even bringing up dad's nickname from school and she kept trying to change the subject. Tank learned this evasive behavioral trait about mom a few years ago when he had interrogated her about whether the Tooth Fairy was real or not. She finally admitted the Tooth Fairy was fake after Tank set an elaborate trap and she ended up nearly falling down the stairs.

Tank probed with a few more questions, but mom still didn't answer the question about why not move to one of the other towns closer to base. Instead of pressing the issue, he took the high road and let it go. La Grange was great, and they had fun over the summer even though they hadn't done their traditional family vacation.

Reaching over he turned the radio back on. He switched the station to hip-hop music and turned the volume all the way up to ten. He cherished his last few minutes of freedom before they arrived at school and the misery would begin.

Three
The Kiss Blowing Incident

A sign appeared in the distance. Tank was familiar with this sign and he dreaded seeing it again. Regardless of the country, state, city, town, village, parish, or alien planet, children dreaded seeing this sign at some point in their life. It is a large white rectangle sign with bold black letters. Above and below the sign are blinking yellow lights. The sign "**SCHOOL ZONE**" seals the fate of every child who wishes they didn't have to go to school.

Nervous was not the right way to describe how Tank was feeling about going to a new high school. Overall, he was good looking, had decent grades, never had a teacher he couldn't win over, and he was known as an athlete during recess. Mom had shared with him multiple times how lucky he was to go to a middle school that still had recess, as with most places, recess was only for elementary kids.

In Texas, he felt like king of the castle at his middle school, but this was high school now. Harder classes, new teachers, and recess was probably a thing of the past. Over the summer, he hadn't made any new friends, and now, he was a little fish swimming in a new Kentucky pond. He felt as out of place as a dolphin trying to climb a tree or like a flamingo playing a drum set.

Pulling up to the front of La Grange High School, their car entered the student drop-off zone. School started in fifteen minutes and dozens of parents were in line dropping off their kids. For a small Kentucky high school, the school's appearance and landscaping was fantastic. The student drop-off looped around the front of the school and in the center was a large parking lot.

Older students who had their driver's licenses could be seen parking farthest out in the parking lot. It was like the faculty of the school were trying to say, "You may have your license, but you pesky rascals will still have to walk a mile to school." Teachers had assigned parking as there were about twenty spots marked with yellow numbers on the concrete closest to the building.

Buses were dropping off students on the side of the school. Across from the bus area, there was a large, grassy field with what appeared to be a football field and running track out in the distance. The two-story school building was made up of yellow stone siding with a navy-blue roof. Massive brown pipes, like gutters, hung from the top floor to the ground. Tank could see La Grange Middle School which stood across the street about a half mile away.

Tank noticed an exceptionally pretty girl with long dark hair and a pinkish backpack getting off a bus that had just pulled up. She wore black skinny jeans, a t-shirt, and had on a purple zip-up hoodie jacket. On her feet, she wore fashionable black jungle boots. Mom noticed Tank's head turn towards the girl as their car moved forward to the school's entrance. Tank turned around in his seat so he could look at the girl a few moments longer. Mom, noticing what was going on, laughed and shook her head from side to side.

"You are your father's son," mumbled mom.

"What? I like looking at all the pretty... buses." Tank pretended to casually look the other direction as if he had not been staring at the girl.

Their car inched closer to the front of the line for the student drop-off and mom put the car in park. A long line of cars was forming behind them, but Mom was taking her time saying goodbye. Out of nowhere, tears rolled down her cheeks. Tank could take apart the remote control and put it back together. He could drill, patch, and seal a flat tire on his dirt bike. If someone cut their leg and was bleeding to death, he could build the perfect tourniquet in thirty seconds flat, but he was not well-equipped to handle mom crying.

"What's wrong, Mom?" asked Tank with a concerned look on his face. Despite the traffic behind them, he hesitated to open the car door.

"Oh, nothing sweetie. I remember my first day of high school and this is such a big day for my little boy." Mom gave a loving smile.

Inside Tank's head, he kept thinking about what dad would do when mom cried. It didn't happen often, but there had to be a protocol to remember to help her stop crying. He gently put his hand on mom's shoulder. Mom looked up and another tear rolled down her cheek. Tank remembered a good question dad asked mom all the time. He kissed Mom on the forehead and the words tumbled out of his mouth.

"What's for dinner tonight, mom?" asked Tank.

"You are like your father." Mom wiped her tears. "We are having meatloaf, asparagus, and baked potatoes."

"I love you, mom," said Tank. "I am going to miss you today."

"I love you, too, Andrew," said Mom in a loving voice. "Oh, Andrew, wait... there is one more thing I need to tell you before you go to school."

"Yea, what's up, mom?" Tank noticed the line of cars behind them getting even longer.

Another parent, who had been patiently waiting, pulled their car out of the line and honked. Mom waved at the driver, mouthed the words, "I'm sorry," and paused for a moment. Crying caused her makeup to smudge under both eyes and Tank held back his laughter at her raccoon-like appearance. She looked like a pro football player who didn't know how to apply under-eye war-paint correctly. A serious look appeared on her face. Tank could tell mom was wondering if she should tell him what was on her mind. After taking a deep breath, Mom cautiously spoke.

"Dad wanted to speak to you this morning about something important, but I guess I will tell you instead. Several years ago, when your father and I went to school here, strange things happened. I need you to promise me you will not let curiosity get the best of you."

"When you say strange..." Tank raised his eyebrows as he opened the car door.

"Not kidding," declared Mom. "I am sure you will hear all sorts of rumors, but promise me you won't go looking for an adventure."

"I promise Mom. You know me," winked Tank, getting out of the car.

"Yes, I do know you," interrupted Mom with aggravation in her voice, "This is serious, Andrew! Children have gone missing and were never seen again."

Tank didn't know what to say as he closed the car door and walked towards the school. He was confused why Mom waited until now to bring this up. Mom was known to worry, but this felt different. Looking back towards the car, he put his left hand to his mouth and blew mom a quick incognito kiss, making sure that no one else would see. The last thing he needed was the reputation that he was the freshman who blew kisses to his mommy every morning.

17

Tank thought about the worst-case scenario if, heaven forbid, anyone would have seen the kiss blowing incident. Irrational thoughts spiraled in his head as he stood there thinking. Mom thought he was nervous to go inside the school, but that was not the case. Tank froze in place as he felt like the whole school was watching him. Because of his kiss blowing, the other students probably believed mom came over at lunch and spoon-fed him smooshed bananas as though he were a toddler.

Maybe they thought mom even filled up a bottle with warm milk and burped him over her shoulder. Of course, that was only if she wasn't too busy unbuckling him from his car seat to cuddle and swaddle him later. Let's not forget how mom had to routinely check his diaper in case he had an accident. Oh boy, this was bad! Tank did a quick 360° inspection of the area and was delighted to see that no one appeared to have noticed. Thank goodness!

"Remember!" yelled mom, getting Tank's attention. "No matter what you hear, let it go, my love."

Giving Mom a final wave, Tank heard the car shift into drive and the volume of talk radio increase as she pulled away. Tank stood there a few feet from the entrance casually fixing his hair before proceeding to the door. He watched Mom reach the stop sign and turn onto the highway. This was it, time to go inside.

Another student being dropped off was walking close behind Tank and they arrived at the door at nearly the same time. The guy was wearing a black, mixed martial arts hoodie, blue jeans, and white basketball shoes. His face donned thick framed glasses. Out of habit, Tank opened the door and stood to the side, allowing him to walk in first. Dad taught him from an early age that there was no excuse for not showing good manners.

"Thanks, bro," said the guy.

"No problem, dude," said Tank, in a cool tone of voice.

Entering the school, the guy Tank held the door for high-fived and began chatting with the same young girl that Tank had observed getting off the bus earlier. It was the pretty one that mom had caught him checking out. Tank wanted to say hello to the girl, but nerves got the best of him. What was he going to say... "Hey, I am from Texas, I am new here, you are hot, will you be my girlfriend, please?" Tank stood there mapping out his approach to talk to her, but eventually he chickened out.

While Tank was brainstorming, he must have blanked out because when he looked up, both students had turned the corner and were out of sight. Tank felt relieved and embarrassed at the same time. At least she smiled at him, but he wondered if she knew that he was a nervous wreck to speak with her. Oh well, there was still an entire school year for him to muster the courage to talk to her. Strung across the hallway near the administrative offices was a large banner. Tank commenced reading the sign to himself.

WELCOME TO LA GRANGE HIGH SCHOOL – HOME OF THE FIGHTING GENERALS – GO BIG GREEN!

"The banner is a bit much," whispered Tank to himself, "but at least the school's mascot is cool."

Tank remembered the envelope mom had placed on the kitchen table and pulled it out of his bag. It was a single piece of paper containing a map of the school. Mom had highlighted his homeroom class in yellow. A few days ago, Mom and Tank had visited the school's website to look for an interactive map of the school. Browsing through the school's entire website only took about five minutes because there was not much information available. They found a "map" of the school online, but it was pathetic and lacked any detail that would help someone navigate the school effectively. Tank had told mom it made more sense to do a simple internet search to see if a map existed, but mom adamantly opposed this idea.

Along with learning military battle formations, mom knew that studying maps was one of Tank's passions like his father. In secret, she must have dug through her old yearbooks and found a basic school outline she had photocopied on their printer. On the photocopy, Mom blotted out a couple of places and she waited until this morning at breakfast to surprise Tank with the envelope containing the map. The map was a pleasant surprise and better than nothing for sure, but it didn't give him much time to study it until now.

Both the first and second floor were nearly identical with their general layout. Three hallways formed an odd-shaped triangle and one of the hallways

19

extended beyond the others. The administrative offices were on the first floor at the front of the school. Classrooms were along the perimeter of the hallways and the library sat strategically in the center of the school. Lockers ran the entire length of every hallway. On the far-left side of the first floor, attached to a short hallway, was the gymnasium and across from the gym was the cafeteria. On the map, Mom had used a highlighter and put a mark on where Tank's first class was located.

Tank drifted off into a memory from a few years ago when his dad had taught him to read a map. Dad would say that any real man can do two things... "read a map and bench press his own body weight." Laughing to himself, Tank took another look at the school map and examined the layout carefully. First, he needed to find his locker to put his backpack away. Mom had bought him a new combination lock last week and he was excited to use it. He had even made up a jingle to remember the correct combination. He would sing, "1-1-2-1-8-9, six numbers that are mighty fine."

This was Tank's first time physically being inside La Grange High School. In Texas, the schools would invite students and their parents to tour the school before the first day for what they called an "open house". Students received their schedules, parents shook hands with the teachers, and the principal would give the typical elevator speech to students about staying out of trouble. The "open house" helped students feel a sense of ease about starting school in an unfamiliar environment.

Last week, La Grange High School had held an "open house", but they opted to host the event at a nearby hotel conference center. Oddly enough, zero teachers were present at the open house. They should have emailed the schedules to save everyone time. At the "open house", there were a few posters of random smiling students taped to the walls, a couple of pamphlets about joining academic groups, a long line to pick up student class schedules, and three security guards checking for ID before allowing anyone to enter. If the school administration was trying to appear awkward and sketchy, they sure had done a good job.

Waiting for those few extra moments with Mom in the car and studying the map may have been a mistake because now the minutes before class were winding down. Tank took a deep breath and focused. There was no way he was going to be late to any classes on the first day of school. According to the map, if he could find his first class in Room 114B, then his locker would be right around the corner. Of course, the only flaw in this strategy was the fact that the photocopied map he was using was over two decades old. Hopefully, the room and locker numbering system had not changed since then. Fingers crossed.

Holding the map in his left hand and with his backpack slung over his right shoulder, Tank meandered down the hallway. Other students were giving him strange looks like he was wearing a Halloween costume, but that didn't bother him. Occasionally, a cute girl would smile in his direction which put a little strut in his step. Also, every now and then, a guy would give him a "what's up" head nod. When you are the new kid, it is easy to see the negative and Tank made a choice to focus on the positive.

"There it is! I found it! Room 114B, oh yea!" Tank discreetly pretended to fist bump Dad.

Speakers mounted to the ceiling chimed three times and the busy hallway grew quiet. Students froze in place to hear what the speaker had to say. Pausing mid stride to hear the announcement, Tank prayed that this was a fire drill or a message sharing that school was canceled for the day. This may have been wishful thinking, but miracles do happen, don't they?

Could it be a snow day announcement? Before they moved, Mom had shared that Kentucky had snow days, a concept that Tank had never heard about in south Texas. Tank was not sure when or how snow became a threat, but it sounded exciting. Tank's imagination ran away with him. Maybe Tank would be calling Mom in a few minutes to tell her to come back to the school and pick him up. Then again, if it were viciously snowing outside, then perhaps the school would airlift the students by helicopter like he had seen on TV rescue shows.

Tank imagined himself harnessed into a helicopter as his legs dangled over the side while clouds were pouring down buckets of snow. Someone was trapped in the building and the school had no choice but for Tank to repel down a rope and save them. Oh no, who was trapped? It was the beautiful girl from earlier this morning desperately in need of rescue. With only one arm, Tank saved the girl, and they fell in love. All the students cheered for their newfound hero and the town threw a parade in Tank's honor.

Tank snapped back to reality as a nasally voice like that of a whistling walrus came onto the school's loudspeaker. Tank recognized the voice from the "open house" last week. The whistling walrus was literally the only person from this new school he had met face to face. No luck. The speaker didn't say anything about a fire drill, snow, or canceling school. Up until now, Tank had been in denial that school was going to happen. The message from the speaker was short and simple.

"Attention students! This is Principal Davis. Welcome back to school," said the speaker, "Classes start in one minute. Please make your way to homeroom."

There was no turning back now. Let the torment of the first day of school begin.

Four
The "T" is for Tank

"Uh oh!" said Tank to himself. "Guess I won't be putting away my backpack."

No time for dilly-dallying now. Tank power walked to the classroom like he was on a mission. Dodging students and side stepping the whole way, Tank's foot entered the classroom as the bell rang. The classroom was already filled with students and Tank was the last one to get there. A shot of anxiety erupted through his body as all eyes turned in his direction. He needed to play it cool and find an empty seat which wasn't too hard because there were only two left.

"Hey, sit over here," said a student, pointing to an empty chair.

Tank gave a slight wave pretending like he knew the kid and sauntered towards the empty seat. The room was way different than what he was expecting. In Texas, his middle school class felt normal. Granted he went to a small school in Texas, but still. In eighth grade, there were colorful posters all over the walls, a recess schedule was posted at the front of the room, and they had small individual desks that formed a rectangle. In his previous school's classroom, the teacher's desk, with the stereotypical apple on it, was at the front near the door.

This classroom didn't have desks at all. There were zero posters on the walls and much to Tank's despair, the recess schedule was missing. Small tables and chairs formed a rectangle around the room and there was an open space in the middle. One of the tables in the rectangle, the one that sat furthest from the door, also had an empty chair, but the table was slightly larger and thicker. The chair underneath the table was made of leather and had wheels on it.

In the far corner stood a handwashing station along with a first aid kit. On the outskirts of the room, there were waterless fish tanks lining the walls. Every fish tank had a different species of animal inside which included snakes, lizards, spiders, and scorpions.

"Sweet!" Tank thought to himself as he glanced at the animals in the room. He walked towards the student who had waved at him. Tank had a good imagination, but sometimes it was rather dark. He visualized that students came one at a time to the center of the room to do battle with one of the animals in the fish tanks.

The teacher would give the secret signal for the creature of doom to be released, and then she would hand the student a sword. If you defeated the creature, then you passed the class. If you didn't, then well, you died. Tank laughed loud enough that another student forcefully shushed him.

A short-haired woman strolled into the room as Tank approached the empty seat. She wore gray slacks and a green dress shirt outlined in silver stitching. The stitching formed an elegant design on the front of the shirt. Her shoes were black and had a thick bottom which made her look slightly taller. Mom had similar shoes, but Tank wasn't sure what they were called. It was easy to tell the woman was the teacher because all teachers have that "I am in charge" look to them.

Tank reached the empty chair and sat next to the kid who had called him over. Tank was pleased that he recognized him. It was the same dude that he held the door for this morning. Dad was right, manners do pay off. The teacher glanced over at Tank a couple of times, but she didn't appear to notice him sitting down after the bell rang. Since this was the first day of school, hopefully, she had mercy for new students.

"Hey, bro. I'm James." The student put his fist out.

"I'm Andrew Thornstone, nice to meet you." Tank disregarded his fist and positioned for a proper handshake.

Tank only used his formal name and handshake when introducing himself to someone new. This was something Dad told him was important. Luckily, James adjusted his fist bump into an open hand and the two firmly shook. Both James and Andrew stopped chatting as they noticed the teacher reach the front of the classroom or at least what looked like the front of the room. Tank didn't even get a chance to tell James the name he preferred to be called.

A small opening between the tables, near the slightly larger table, allowed the teacher to walk to the center. Ah, now the room's layout made more sense. The teacher was going to stand in the center of the room or perhaps she was going to fight the creature of doom first. Either way, Tank laughed out loud again imagining the woman pulling out a sword to fight one of the caged animals. James gave Tank a weird look. Apparently, his laugh was loud enough that it warranted another shush from the same student. The class became silent as the teacher prepared to speak for the first time.

"Good morning, class. I am Mara S. Sprinkle. You may call me Ms. Sprinkle. Welcome to ninth-grade biology and your homeroom for the rest of the year. Every day, we will begin class with roll call, the Pledge of Allegiance, and a lesson summary from the day before."

Ms. Sprinkle handed out the syllabus and started going into detail about all the exciting assignments for the year. The other students pulled out their journals to take notes. Taking notes for the sake of taking notes seemed silly. The syllabus was nothing more than a long set of notes and writing notes about the notes was a tad bit redundant. Tank whipped out his journal, but instead of writing notes about class, he decided to draw his favorite professional wrestlers instead.

Ms. Sprinkle finished explaining the final bullet point on the syllabus, which coincidentally, was about eliminating distractions in class. Tank finished drawing the final details on the portrait of his favorite wrestler barely in time to ensure no one saw that he was not paying attention.

An administrative assistant from the school's office tucked her head inside the classroom and handed Ms. Sprinkle a sheet of paper. The paper must have been a class roster because Ms. Sprinkle walked to the front of the room, looked at it, and declared it was time for roll call.

Tank wondered what responsible teacher forgets to print out their own class roster on the first day of school. Regardless, Tank sat there patiently waiting to hear his name as Ms. Sprinkle began. Thornstone was not exactly close to the front of the alphabet, so Tank was a veteran at waiting patiently during roll calls. Ms. Sprinkle continued to call the names in the class.

"James C. Cross," said Ms. Sprinkle.

"Here," James waved his hand in the air.

"Allison W. Dalman."

"Here," replied another student.

"Rebecca L. Foxx."

"Present," the rude shushing student across the room responded.

Ms. Sprinkle called fourteen more names. Tank was concerned when the final student she called had the last name "Washington." Maybe Tank's name was at the bottom because he was the new kid? Perhaps, because she hadn't called his name, he was free to go. Or maybe this was a test to see if Tank would be confident enough to speak up. Could it be that if he didn't say something, she would make him sit in the corner for the rest of the year and wear a silly hat?

"Alright class. I am going to lead us in the Pledge today," said Ms. Sprinkle. "Tomorrow, I will ask for a volunteer to lead."

"Excuse me, Ms. Sprinkle," said Tank in his most polite and respectful voice. "You didn't call my name."

"Let's see here. What is your name?" asked Ms. Sprinkle.

"My name is Andrew Thornstone," said Tank.

Ms. Sprinkle smiled, nodded, and looked at her clipboard as she studied the roster. A few times, Tank would see her eyes glance off the sheet and look at him. Figuring she was admiring his unique sense of fashion, Tank dismissed the random gawking from Ms. Sprinkle. Tank noticed her eyes moving back and forth across the page. She shook her head again, signaling that she was not able to find his name on the roster.

"Did your father go to school here, too?" asked Ms. Sprinkle.

"Yes," replied Tank. "He went to middle school and high school in town before he joined the armed forces."

"Oh, I thought I recognized the name Thornstone," said Ms. Sprinkle. "My fiancé got out of the military a few years ago."

As the other students waited and engaged in sidebar conversation, Tank and Ms. Sprinkle chatted for a few moments. She was excited to show off her diamond engagement ring. It was a gold band with a tiny diamond in the center. Tank tried to add to the conversation and mentioned that Dad had bought Mom a huge ring twice the size a couple of years ago. Ms. Sprinkle had several questions about Dad and what he did after high school ended. Ms. Sprinkle asked if dad was still married to Sara, which was mom's first name and his high school sweetheart. He confirmed they were still happily married.

Tank told her all about their time in Texas, their family vacations, and how the family moved back to town when Dad was promoted to Captain a few months ago. Suddenly, realizing she had a class to teach, Ms. Sprinkle returned to figuring out the roster situation.

"I don't see your name, but I am going to write it down and will make sure I update the roster for tomorrow," smiled Ms. Sprinkle.

"Awesome." Tank gave a thumbs up.

"What is your middle name?" asked Ms. Sprinkle. "I like to use middle initials in my daily roll call to make it feel more formal."

"My middle name is Tannis," mumbled Tank.

"I'm sorry." Ms. Sprinkle had a curious look on her face. "I heard you say the T, but what was the rest?"

"My middle name is Tank," he replied with confidence this time.

"Tank?" said Ms. Sprinkle, confused.

"Yes, in fact, everyone calls me Tank. That's what I go by," he declared. "The T is for Tank."

Ms. Sprinkle jotted down a note on the roster. Every now and then you find a person who insists on speaking the words out loud when they are writing and that is exactly how Ms. Sprinkle made her notes. Everyone could hear Ms. Sprinkle say, "Add to roster, Andrew T. Thornstone, aka Tank." Several students in the class were giggling and looking in his direction.

"To clarify, the middle name your parents gave you is Tank?" Ms. Sprinkle smirked.

"Yep, the "T" is for Tank!" Tank grinned.

The other students in the class were no longer giggling. Now, the students were wildly laughing and pointing at him instead. Tank's heart sank in his chest and his cheeks turned bright red. All the blood rushed to his head as he sat there waiting for the laughter to cease.

He was not trying to make an epic announcement or anything like that by asking to be called "Tank". One of the reasons the nickname, "Tank", was created was because a few years ago, he and his family had visited a military base that was known for giant oil tankers. Dad created the nickname for Andrew as a compliment to his muscles getting bigger and Tank was proud of it.

Tank took a couple deep breaths and played it cool. Ms. Sprinkle attempted to quiet the class, but even she was struggling not to giggle. James, the student sitting next to him, could tell that Tank was embarrassed. A few years ago, James had moved from Chicago when his dad accepted an engineering position for a mining company. James knew what it felt like to be the new kid. He looked at Tank, looked at the class who was still making fun of him, and raised his hand to try to get Ms. Sprinkle's attention.

"Yo, Ms. Sprinkle." James waved his hand wildly in the air.

"Yes, James?" replied Ms. Sprinkle. As she turned around the class grew quiet.

"Ms. Sprinkle, the "C" in my middle name stands for Cage and that's what I want to be called," said James.

"Cage?" snort-giggled Ms. Sprinkle.

"Yep, everyone calls me Cage." James pointed to his mixed martial arts hoodie.

Ms. Sprinkle paused and made another notation on the roster. The class was not laughing anymore. Tank took another deep breath and Cage patted him on the back. Cage held out his fist once more, signaling for another fist bump from Tank. Their fists pounded and the other students all looked at them. Gradually, the atmosphere of the classroom shifted. Now, the class was staring at them like they were the coolest kids in school.

"We have a Tank and a Cage," cackled Ms. Sprinkle. "This is going to be an interesting school year."

Ms. Sprinkle was still standing in the middle of the classroom. Apparently, she did not have a traditional desk. The larger table with the leather chair was her desk. The unique layout of the room made a little more sense. Tank guessed that since the teacher's desk was part of the group, she could effectively be part of class discussions without having to stand up.

Walking towards the empty chair, she put down the clipboard and picked up an American flag which was on a two-foot wooden pole. Extending her left arm slightly to raise the flag, Ms. Sprinkle covered her heart with her right hand and prepared them for the Pledge. As a class, they stood up and recited the Pledge of Allegiance. Once finished, Ms. Sprinkle sat in her chair to begin the first lesson. All the students sat, as well, ready to learn.

Tank's nerves had finally subsided as the class progressed. Ms. Sprinkle seemed nice and it was cool that she knew dad from back in the day. He had been thinking all morning about how he could get noticed at his new school. He wanted to make a name for himself as the funniest, boldest freshman in school. Who knew that the perfect opportunity was only a few moments away and Ms. Sprinkle would set him up for one of the most comedic moments of his life?

Five
Potty Protocol
& Secret Maps

A lot had changed in Tank's life this year. The state where he lived had changed. The school he went to changed. The house he had lived in changed. All his friends were back in Texas. Plus, Dad was gone for at least the rest of the year. There is an old military saying that "the only thing constant in life is change and change builds character." If this was true, then Tank must have built enough character for a lifetime. Tank tried to pay attention in class, but it was harder than he was expecting.

Unless there was action and excitement in school, Tank found most lessons rather boring. It also didn't help that Ms. Sprinkle's charisma and personality were drier than a bowl of dust in the Sahara Desert. Watching Ms. Sprinkle stumble through the first day of class was fascinating, to say the least. Maybe her teaching style was similar to watching grass grow on the football field. It was not the most exciting thing, but eventually, there was a lavish place to play the greatest sport in the history of civilization.

Ms. Sprinkle didn't seem well-prepared for class and she spent most of the remaining time talking about all the interesting topics the students would be focusing on during the year. When it was clear that she had nothing else prepared, she informed everyone about the rules of the classroom again. Tank wasn't quite sure why she went over the syllabus at all if she was going to cover the same information twice. It was too bad that mom had not packed him a pillow because his first class was turning out to be a real snoozefest.

The rules were easy. All students must listen, be respectful, raise their hand, and participate in group discussions. Oh, and if a student needed to use the bathroom, they must sign out. A hall pass was required to leave the room and must be presented to another teacher if they asked to see it. Tank doodled a picture of Ms. Sprinkle explaining the hall pass. He couldn't help but laugh when she shared the rules for needing to go potty.

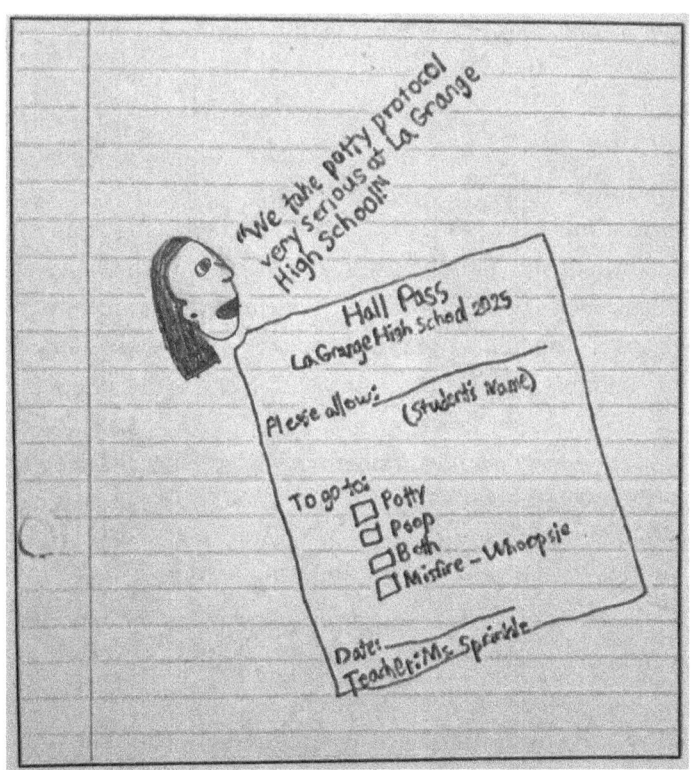

"Tank, is there something you want to share with the class?" asked Ms. Sprinkle.

"No," bluffed Tank, trying not to smile.

"Well, you laughed when I mentioned needing a hall pass," said Ms. Sprinkle.

Getting called out is never fun. But, come on, she was the one that brought up potty protocol. Tank thought carefully about what he would say next. Dad taught him how to play Blackjack and Poker a few years ago and he learned an important lesson. When someone calls your bluff, you can either fold or go all in. Ms. Sprinkle was calling his bluff. Folding is quitting and quitting was not in Tank's vocabulary. The class was silent as Ms. Sprinkle sat there waiting. It was time to go all in.

"Ms. Sprinkle, in Texas, we didn't have hall passes," Tank feigned an innocent look. "How does it work again?"

31

"Oh," paused Ms. Sprinkle. "That is understandable. If you need to go to the bathroom, all you have to do is pick up the hall pass and sign out of class."

Tank sat up a little higher in his seat and leaned forward. This was going terrific! The fact that he was the new kid gave him plausible deniability for asking any question, even a silly one, was okay.

Class was almost over and the bell was going to ring in a few minutes. Ms. Sprinkle told them she had one thing left to share with the class. She told the class it was a serious topic and they needed to listen carefully. When homeroom was over, the bell would ring and students would make their way to their next class, so it was important that Ms. Sprinkle had a chance to cover the information.

"What if I need to poop?" announced Tank. "What if I need to poop super bad?"

"Then you would need to get a hall pass!" Ms. Sprinkle was shocked at Tank's question. She stood there shaking her head.

The whole class erupted in laughter and one student snorted. James, or "Cage" as he preferred to be called, even dropped his pen and notebook. Tank kept a serious look on his face the whole time. Ms. Sprinkle didn't seem pleased with his question, but she kept calm. It was a good question though, right? A random question about pooping was not going to cut it. Tank wanted to see how far he could push the limit without stepping in it, no pun intended. The class paused from laughing long enough for Tank to ask more questions.

"Let's say the missile fails to launch," Tank showed a tiny grin this time, "or there is a malfunction and I make a mess?"

"That's gross," replied Ms. Sprinkle. "And yes, you would still need a hall pass."

"Does a single hall pass work for both number one and two?" asked Tank, "or would I need to do number one and then come back and get a new hall pass for number two."

"The hall pass works for both," responded Ms. Sprinkle firmly.

"Is it ever okay to use the classroom sink?" Tank resumed his serious face.

"Tank, that is inappropriate..." Ms. Sprinkle stood up from her chair.

"To wash my hands, Ms. Sprinkle," interrupted Tank. "May I use the sink to wash my hands?

"Yes! Now that's enough questions about the hall pass!" declared Ms. Sprinkle, annoyed at the conversation.

Ms. Sprinkle's hands were now resting on her hips and her posture had aggressively changed. Standing there, she was staring directly into Tank's eyes. The look on Ms. Sprinkles face was disbelief, disgust, and irritation. The laughter in the room had faded and now the other students were sitting in an uncomfortable silence. Tank did a quick look around the room and then sat there waiting for Ms. Sprinkle to speak again. Maybe he pushed it a little too far.

"Ms. Sprinkle," said Tank in a soft voice, "thank you for explaining the hall pass. I think I get it now."

Ms. Sprinkle shook her head, marched to the classroom door and locked it. On the far side of the room, glowed red numbers showing 9:29 a.m. on the digital clock which was located above the door. Students began standing up and gathering their things. Ms. Sprinkle raised her voice and firmly instructed everyone to sit back down. Tank's harmless hall pass questions had delayed Ms. Sprinkle enough to prevent her from sharing the important information with the class. The bell rang and students from other classes could be heard rushing about in the hallway, but everyone in Ms. Sprinkle's class sat there waiting to hear her speak.

Ms. Sprinkled dashed over to the other side of the room, took a few deep breaths and regained her composure. She wasn't kidding about having one more thing on the agenda before students could leave. Tank noticed that she had pulled out a key to open a locked cabinet and retrieved a large sheet of laminated paper. She was holding a detailed map of the school in her left hand. In fact, the map was almost identical to the one Mom had photocopied. The only difference was that this one was twice the size and instead of only showing the interior of the school, this map included the outside of the school grounds, as well.

Earlier this morning, when their car had approached the school, all Tank could see was the front of the school as they approached the student drop-off zone. In secret, Tank had attempted an internet search of the school trying to find the full layout of the grounds, but all the webpages were mysteriously

33

missing. Mom must have put a restriction on searching because nothing would come up without being prompted to enter a password. Oddly enough, even popular satellite imagery maps online didn't show the back or sides of the school. Ms. Sprinkle, displaying a map of the backside of the school, was interesting. Apparently, about a half mile behind the school was a small pond and large woods.

The map also confirmed that the football field and running track were across from the bus loading zone, not too far from where Tank saw the beautiful girl this morning. Ms. Sprinkle continued holding the map for everyone to see and then pointed to the pond. A serious look appeared on her face that reminded Tank of the same look Mom had made only an hour earlier when she was dropping him off at the front of the school. Ms. Sprinkle waited for everyone to be quiet before speaking.

Ms. Sprinkle spoke in a stern voice. "The Superintendent requires all teachers to remind students of the following: The back of the school, specifically the pond and woods, is off limits. Any student caught breaking this rule will face immediate disciplinary action including expulsion."

"Ms. Sprinkle?" Tank raised his hand.

"If this is another question about the hall pass" replied Ms. Sprinkle, "then I don't want to hear it."

"No, I get that hall pass thing, thank you," stated Tank, "But why is the back of the school off limits?"

"I am surprised *you* don't know," smiled Ms. Sprinkle. "Unfortunately, we are already a minute past the bell. Have a wonderful and glorious day. Tomorrow, we start our first lesson on the life cycle of amphibians."

Students stood up and began exiting the classroom as if Ms. Sprinkle hadn't said anything abnormal at all. Tank stayed seated, wondering why no one batted an eye about her strange comment regarding the back of the school. Her weird comment about being surprised he didn't already know made him wonder what that was supposed to mean. In Texas, Tank had spent most of his time outside fishing in the ponds and exploring the woods. Texas has rattlesnakes, mountain lions, scorpions, and wild pigs which are way more dangerous than any of the wildlife found in Kentucky.

Telling everyone to stay inside was a weird comment to make and especially the part about disciplinary action without any context as to why simply going outside would warrant such a harsh punishment. Wouldn't most schools encourage students to spend more time outside? The fact that she had to open a locked cabinet to access a map of the school grounds was outrageous. After showing the students the map, Tank noticed that she returned the map to the cabinet and locked it. "Oh well," he thought. He made a mental note of questions to ask Mom after school.

At breakfast, after Mom had handed him the envelope containing the map, she had also given him another piece of paper that she said would help him navigate his first day. At the time, Tank had smushed the paper into his pocket. He now reached in and pulled the crumpled piece of paper out. It read *Class Schedule 2025 – Andrew Thornstone.*

Unbeknownst to Tank, Mom had drawn hearts, flowers, and a nice note at the bottom wishing him a great first day of school. Tank smiled at the note while simultaneously making sure no one saw it. He browsed the class schedule trying to figure out where to go next. Between each class, students were given a ten-minute break to visit their locker and make their way to the next classroom.

"One class down and five more to go," whispered Tank, crossing Ms. Sprinkle's biology class off the list.

As Ms. Sprinkle's class finished, Cage had already stood up and was chatting with a couple of other students near the door. Tank wanted to thank him for being nice and speaking up about his nickname when the other students were laughing at him. Studying the map for a few moments, Tank was trying to cross-reference his current location in Ms. Sprinkle's room and his class schedule to figure out where to go next. Heading out into the busy hallway, without knowing where to go, was not an option. Tank looked up and noticed that Cage was already exiting the classroom. Saying "thank you" was going to have to wait till tomorrow.

"Later, bro." Cage waved over in Tank's direction.

"See ya, dude." Tank waved back at Cage.

Ms. Sprinkle's classroom was empty now. Even Ms. Sprinkle had rushed out of the room with everyone else. Maybe she should have used a hall pass if she needed to go that bad. When the room was empty, the fish tanks filled with bugs, snakes, and lizards gave the room a creepy vibe. There was something strange about La Grange High School, but he couldn't put his finger on it.

Tank kept thinking about the seriousness of Ms. Sprinkle's threat against exploring the back of the school. Being expelled for daring to walk outside to the back of the school didn't sound like something he wanted to explain to Dad on their next video chat. The other students must have already known the backstory. That was the only logical explanation for their lack of response. Whatever it was, it must have been a big deal.

Six
Tank Goes Boom!

Tank noticed that he only had three minutes left until his next class and he was still trying to figure out the overly complex class schedule which was written on a standard spreadsheet. Ms. Sprinkle strode back into the classroom and came towards him. Oh no, she was going to give him detention for joking about needing to poop.

Ms. Sprinkle looked different than she had a few minutes ago when class ended. Her entire face was covered in a tan-colored paste and she had applied a thick coat of red lipstick. Her cheeks had red blush caked on them and above her eyes was blue eyeliner with glitter.

"So does Drew ever talk about anyone from school?" asked Ms. Sprinkle.

The comment caught Tank off guard as he struggled to identify to whom she was referring. Dad's full name is Andrew Phillip Thornstone, but all his friends call him Drew for short. Mom would always refer to "Dad" as "Drew" when they were at home. Tank stopped telling people years ago that technically, his name was Andrew Thornstone Jr. because he didn't want everyone to call him "Junior."

In fact, one of the main reasons Tank appreciated the nickname "Tank" was because there was confusion around the house of who mom was talking about when she would say the name Drew. Mom, however, was not fully on board with the nickname yet.

Ms. Sprinkle was now batting her eyes and playing with her hair like a schoolgirl. She pulled out a chair and sat next to Tank. At first, he tried to ignore the comment and continued to study the map. The ability to read a map was something he took pride in but being distracted didn't help at all. Ms. Sprinkle sat there patiently waiting and told him that during middle school his dad and she had spent a lot of time together. There were so many stories she was sure his dad would have told him regarding their many adventures. He wasn't sure how to respond to her question and how she was asking made him feel uncomfortable.

"Dad tells me stories about his high school football buddies all the time." Tank tried to avoid the conversation.

"Does he ever mention any women?" questioned Ms. Sprinkle, blushing.

This was awkward. Tank glanced at the clock again and noticed that another minute was gone and he still was not sure where to go next. With only a few minutes left, he was desperate to end the discussion with Ms. Sprinkle, who was sitting there batting her eyes and waiting for him to respond. Trying to end the conversation politely, Tank mentioned that he needed to use the restroom and didn't want to be late for his next class. Ms. Sprinkle giggled and told Tank not to worry about being late for his next class. She offered to write an "excused tardy" note. His next teacher would understand.

Ms. Sprinkle's next group of students had already started filling the room for their next class. It was obvious that Ms. Sprinkle must have had a crush or previous relationship with Dad, but that was gross to think about. Mom and Dad are best friends and they have a solid marriage. Surely, Ms. Sprinkle was not thinking that Dad was single or that he was thinking about leaving Mom. Tank thought for a moment and chose his words carefully. It was time for Tank to "Go Boom," which was an expression he had coined for when he was about to use humor to stop a difficult conversation.

"You know what?" asked Tank. "Dad did mention this girl from school one time."

"Really?" asked Ms. Sprinkle. "What did he say?"

"Yes, I remember it clearly now," responded Tank. "Dad mentioned this girl named Mara during a joke he told at our family reunion last year."

"What?" Ms. Sprinkle leaned in closer. "What did he say?"

"Well," grinned Tank, "he said that she wore way too much makeup and looked like a rodeo clown."

"What did you say?" rebutted a startled Ms. Sprinkle.

"It couldn't have been you, though," smirked Tank. "Your makeup looks really, truly, absolutely great and fantastic. The joke was a huge hit. Everyone thought it was hilarious. We now refer to all clowns as 'Mara' in our family. "

Abruptly, Ms. Sprinkle stood up and aggressively shoved her chair under the table. Tank sat there and tried to study the map again. Two minutes was not much time to figure out where he was going next. Thankfully, Ms. Sprinkle was going to give him a note to excuse him for being a few minutes late. Ms. Sprinkle stomped to the other side of the room and grabbed her cellphone before Tank could ask for the note. Ms. Sprinkle, expressing the rudest look possible, while using one hand to text on her cellphone, turned sarcastically in his direction and waved goodbye.

Getting an excuse note was not going to happen, but that was okay. At least Ms. Sprinkle had stopped asking weird questions about Dad. Receiving a tardy was not the worst thing that could happen on the first day. Hopefully, that would be the last bit of adversity for the first day of school and he could move on to the next class. Several students were coming into the room and Tank quickly escaped to the hallway. Using his remarkable map reading skills, Tank successfully located where he needed to go next.

"Let's see. What's next, hmm, Phys. Ed.," said Tank, speaking to himself. "Boom! Oh yea, P.E class! I am on my way."

Tank never claimed to be the smartest kid in science. He was average, at best, in math, and English class bored him to tears, but P.E. was a subject that made sense. When it came to physical education, he was the sensei of sports, the guru of gym class, and a maestro at making fitness happen. Only one minute remained until the bell would ring and the gymnasium was on the other side of the school. Once again Tank found himself sprinting, dodging, and ducking his way through students to get to class.

The hallways were relatively empty compared to earlier, but he was walking so fast it was hard not to bump into other students. Apparently, all the other students felt it was necessary to be on time. Dad would say "If you aren't fifteen minutes early, then you are fifteen minutes late." Out of the corner of Tank's eye, he spotted Cage again. This time, he was at the far end of the hallway opposite the gymnasium.

Walking next to Cage was the same beautiful girl from this morning. The only thing at the far end of the hallway, where they were walking was a janitor's closet and a door with "EXIT" written above it. Tank paused and watched for a moment while Cage held the exit door open to leave the building.

Curiosity got the best of Tank. He turned around and lightly jogged to catch up even though it was in the opposite direction of where he needed to go. Perhaps, because he was new to the school, the gym teacher would give him a break for being late. Opening the exit door, he could see Cage and the girl walking at a fast pace towards the track.

Several teachers, who were preparing to close their classroom doors, observed Tank opening the door to go outside, but not one of them said anything, which seemed odd. He figured that seeing students escape would trigger the teachers to stop him, but no one said a word. Outside of the school, Tank sprinted to catch up. Within a few seconds, he was within yelling distance of Cage and the girl.

"Hey, are you all ditching class?" yelled Tank, jokingly, but in a semi-serious tone.

"No, we are on our way to P.E. class," the girl responded, looking over her shoulder at Tank.

"That's where I am headed, too!" Tank pointed at the map. "Isn't the gym in the school?"

"Mr. Jackson posted a sign on the locker room doors that class would be held outside at the track today," said Cage, as he waited for Tank to follow them.

Tank hurried to catch up. He was now jogging only a few feet behind Cage and the girl. Tank realized that his earlier thought about the girl being pretty good-looking was wrong. This girl was way more than pretty or beautiful, this girl was outright gorgeous!

There was not much in the world that made Tank nervous. He was confident in ziplining, climbing rock walls, and he felt comfortable wrestling people that were twice his size, but somehow this girl caused monkeys to jump in his stomach. He felt like a wreck trying to muster the courage to speak to her.

"Don't be a dork, don't be a dork..." Tank gave himself a pep talk.

The girl must have heard Tank talking to himself because she giggled as he got closer. Tank looked around and noticed that this was the far side of the

40

school near the bus drop-off area. That meant if they crossed the grassy field, they should, theoretically, arrive at the track within five minutes based on the map Ms. Sprinkle showed them in class.

Tank shuffled the last few steps until he was walking evenly with Cage and the girl. In the school, he could hear the faint sound of a bell going off indicating that class was starting. Being late to class was starting to feel like more of a trend, but, oh well. Unlike earlier when nerves got the best of him, this time, he was eager to talk to the girl. This was his chance to make a good second impression and he was not about to blow it like he did earlier.

"Howdy," blurted Tank in a thick Texas voice. "My name is Tank. What is your name?"

"My name is Rachel, Rachel Tran," she said.

"Great to see you again, Cage," exclaimed Tank.

"James, why is he calling you Cage?" asked Rachel.

"It's my nickname," replied Cage, laughing. "It's relatively new."

"Well then, I want to be called Ruby," declared Rachel, "since we are making up names we want to be called.

"Why do you want to be called Ruby?" inquired Tank.

"Because I'm as tough as a rock and never lose my shine," she definitively replied, showing a smile in Tank's direction.

"I don't remember seeing you in Ms. Sprinkle's class this morning. Where were you sitting?" asked Tank.

"Rachel, I mean Ruby, is in tenth grade," explained Cage. "P.E. class has all grade levels in it, but homerooms only have a single grade."

Tank nodded, smiled, and tried not to blush. This was different than last year when he went out of his way to avoid girls. Dad had warned him about stuff like this. He remembered some lesson Dad tried to teach him last year about a bird stinging a bee or something like that. Tank tucked his hands into his pockets and tried to act cool. Ruby was a year older than him and he had zero experience chatting with older women. They were still a little way from the track now and he wanted to make small talk with her.

"This is quite the hike," said Tank.

"I guess so." Ruby shrugged her shoulders.

"I mean, hiking is easy," declared Tank, trying to sound tough. "I could hike all day."

Ruby smiled a little bit, but she seemed distracted. Other than helping with introductions, Cage remained silent and Tank noticed that he had folded his arms across his chest. Earlier in Ms. Sprinkle's class, Cage was quite talkative and outgoing. They must have been talking about something serious before he showed up because Ruby also had a somewhat irritated look on her face. It was an awkward silence for sure and Tank felt uncomfortable.

"You never told me what you thought the truth was?" said Cage to Ruby.

"Yes, I did. My dad told me the truth about it the other day. It was a government coverup," whispered Ruby, in a voice soft enough that Tank could barely hear.

"My mom thinks aliens did it," replied Cage.

"Hey, not to be a blockhead here, but what in the blue blazes are you all talking about?" asked Tank.

Tank stopped walking and crossed his arms. Ruby and Cage also stopped walking and turned towards him. Honestly, Tank was not sure what exactly "blue blazes" or "blockhead" meant, but Dad would say cool things like that to make a point. When Dad's platoon buddies would come over, Mom would pretend to cough when one of them was about to say something "vulgar" as she would put it. Nevertheless, it was fun to quote Dad and somehow, he felt like it was honoring him to do so.

"You don't know?" asked Ruby.

"Know what?" Tank's cheeks turned red and he felt self-conscious.

"Have you been living under a rock, bro?" inquired Cage, sarcastically.

"No, I live over off Highway 53," quipped Tank, trying to lighten the mood.

"Well, where do you think they came from?" questioned Ruby.

"I have no clue what you are talking about," said Tank, now in a slightly frustrated tone.

Losing track of time, Cage and Ruby continued bantering about the origins of "something." At a turtle's pace, they meandered their way to the track. Tank was getting red in the face. He wasn't necessarily angry, but he felt semi-disrespected because they were not explaining what the "something" was. Ruby realized that Tank was growing aggravated and she turned in his direction to speak.

"We are talking about…" started Ruby, but she was unable to finish her sentence.

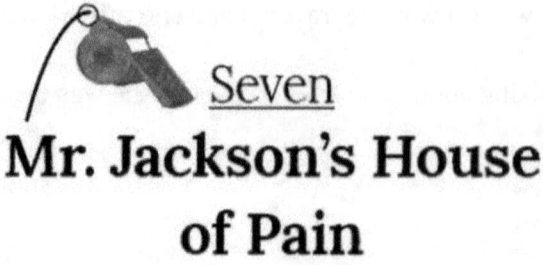

Seven

Mr. Jackson's House of Pain

Ruby's words were interrupted by the sound of a loud whistle. The conversation abruptly ended as a tall man wearing green basketball shorts and a gray t-shirt, sporting the school's logo, was standing there looking at his watch. Tank noticed several large veins that ran up and down both of his arms. The man's legs looked like two oak trees springing from the ground. A whistle on a green lanyard was hung around his neck. The guy's build reminded Tank of Dad. The man reached into his back pocket and turned away from them for a few seconds. When he turned around, a bulge of something tucked into his lower lip caused the man to spit.

"You're late," grunted the man. "I am Mr. Jackson and I have two simple rules. One: Be on time for class. Two: Come prepared to work hard."

Mr. Jackson stood a little over six feet tall and was a real man's man. He coached the basketball team, track team, football team, wrestling team, and the swimming team. If there was a team at school, you could bet that Mr. Jackson was coaching it. Mr. Jackson pointed at Cage, Tank, and Ruby. Other students were coming out of the restroom and had already changed into their gym clothes.

"You three," said Mr. Jackson.

"Yes sir!" Tank stood at attention.

Mr. Jackson pointed at the restrooms that were near the concession stand and ticketing gate and said, "Go change into your gym clothes and then take two laps around the track. Maybe that will help you remember to be on time!"

Mr. Jackson blew his whistle and started walking towards the rest of the students who were already waiting on the track for class to start. Uh oh, did Mr. Jackson give the order to change into gym clothes? Tank had not been able to visit his locker this morning and he was still carrying his backpack. Kneeling, he shuffled through the contents of his backpack. Tank noticed a tiny yellow note sitting on top of shorts, tennis shoes, socks, and a t-shirt.

Tank – I hope you have a wonderful first day of school. I packed you an extra set of clothes for gym class – hugs & kisses. Love mom.

"Hey, Mr. Jackson." Ruby tried to get his attention.

"Yes, young lady?" Mr. Jackson turned around.

"I don't have any gym clothes," said Ruby. "I do, but they are back in my locker."

"I forgot mine, too," said Cage.

"Let me guess," said Mr. Jackson. "They are in your locker?"

"No," replied Cage, shrugging his shoulders. "I figured that for the first day of P.E. we wouldn't need them."

Tank was still kneeling and was listening to the conversation between Mr. Jackson and his two new friends. In a few days, Tank was planning to try out for the football team. In eighth grade, Tank played quarterback at his Texas middle school near San Antonio and he was hoping to play the same position in high school. That would mean that Mr. Jackson would oversee the tryouts. The last thing Tank wanted to do was start off on a bad note with his future coach.

Earlier in Ms. Sprinkle's class, Cage had shown him friendship by sharing his nickname. Even when the other students were laughing, Cage went out of his way to make sure Tank didn't suffer alone. Regardless of what Mr. Jackson was going to say, Tank felt loyalty was more important, even to a new friend he had only known for less than a few hours. Tank stuffed his gym clothes down to the bottom of his backpack, pulled the zipper closed, and looked up at Mr. Jackson.

"I must have forgotten mine, too," said Tank.

"Well, isn't that magical," replied Mr. Jackson. "All three of you are late and unprepared."

"I apologize and accept full responsibility for my actions," said Tank, in a respectful tone.

For a few moments, Mr. Jackson stood there with his arms crossed as he spat brown goop from his mouth. Cage, Ruby, and Tank waited for Mr. Jackson to speak. In Tank's mind, a few scenarios of the punishment to come went through his head. For starters, Tank was pretty sure that corporal punishment was not permitted in Kentucky and certainly not for high school so, hopefully, that was not going to happen. Second, it was the first day of school and it didn't seem realistic for Mr. Jackson to fail them for the whole class based on the first fifteen minutes of the first day of school, could he?

Mr. Jackson paced for three steps, turned around, and paced in the opposite direction. Unfolding his arms, Mr. Jackson explained the two class rules again. On the underside of Mr. Jackson's forearm, Tank spotted a medium-sized tattoo. The tattoo was black and gray ink. It looked like an eagle with the word "Jarhead" written in the center. Tank immediately recognized the type of tattoo as someone who had served their country.

"You were in the military?" Tank's voice cracked as he grew in excitement.

"That's right, kid." Mr. Jackson pointed to his tattoo.

"My dad is in the military," said Tank. "He deployed again a few months back."

"What is your dad's name?" asked Mr. Jackson.

"Captain Andrew Thornstone," stated Tank, now even more enthusiastic.

"Oh yes, my fiancé texted me a few minutes ago to tell me that Drew's boy was going to school here." Mr. Jackson spat again. "I remember the guy. He graduated class of 2005, same year as me. He went to Oklahoma for boot camp and I went where real war-fighters go! I went to the Island. Yeah, buddy! Oorah!"

Mr. Jackson held up his cellphone to show Tank a smiling picture of Ms. Sprinkle displaying her engagement ring. Uh oh, this was not good. Ms. Sprinkle hadn't started to text until after the snarky rodeo clown comment. Tank tried to remain optimistic. He was thrilled that Mr. Jackson knew Dad and was also a military man. What were the odds of that happening?

Tank was sure that all would be forgiven for the three of them being late and not having their gym clothes. Dad would say that "Soldiers protect their own" and Tank was the son of a soldier so, hopefully, the rules would apply to him, too.

"I wonder what Captain Thornstone would think of his son showing up late and unprepared?" asked Mr. Jackson, crossing his arms again.

"It was a simple misunderstanding," stated Tank. "See, this is my first day and these two students helped me find the track."

"Let's add "making excuses" to the list," barked Mr. Jackson. "Reminds me of your dad."

Wow! This was something Tank had not prepared for at all. Tank stood there in shock. He wanted to punch Mr. Jackson. Who was this buster to insult his dad? Either Mr. Jackson was mad about what Tank had said earlier to Ms. Sprinkle or something must have happened between the two of them back in school. But how could he know for sure?

Over the summer, Mom had shared that back in the day, dad was the popular kid in school. Maybe Mr. Jackson didn't like dad because his fiancé had a crush on him when they were younger. Tank was confident that Dad could beat this dude up anyway, so who cared? Dad would say, "Haters gonna hate." Tank brushed off the rude comment about Dad and continued to show the utmost respect. Mr. Jackson unfolded his arms again and reached for his whistle. Holding the whistle in his hand, he yelled loud enough for the other students to hear.

"These three students," Mr. Jackson's voice bellowed, as he pointed at Tank, Ruby and Cage, "these three students showed up late and did not come prepared to my class. Let this be a lesson to everyone. I will not tolerate defiance."

"Mr. Jackson, please?" begged Cage. "It was an accident."

"If you give me a few minutes," pleaded Ruby, "I can run back into the school and get my gym clothes."

"You all have wasted seventeen minutes of my class," continued Mr. Jackson in a loud voice. "I want one lap around the track for every minute of class you have stolen from us. Do I make myself clear?"

"Yes, Mr. Jackson." Tank, Cage and Ruby responded as one voice.

"Oh, and son," Mr. Jackson pointed at Tank, "consider yourself lucky. I should bury you in the ground for insulting my fiancé. You don't want to enter Coach Jackson's house of pain, trust me."

Mr. Jackson shook his head again, turned away from them, and walked towards the other students who were still standing around waiting for instructions. Tank swallowed hard, took a deep breath, and tried to shake off

Mr. Jackson's comment. Running laps around the track was not the worst thing that could happen. Tank bent at the waist to stretch out a bit.

Seventeen laps is a little over four miles. It was no biggie, although getting sweaty in their regular school clothes and then going to their next classes was not ideal. Cage and Ruby stood there in disbelief hoping that Mr. Jackson would change his mind. Mr. Jackson turned towards them and aggressively blew his whistle.

"Are you three waiting for an invitation to start?" shouted Mr. Jackson. "Do I need to add laps?"

"I was born to run!" yelled Tank. "Thornstones can outrun anyone!"

"Calm down, hero," said Cage.

"What was that about?" asked Ruby.

"Did you insult Ms. Sprinkle?" questioned Cage.

"I may have suggested she looked like a rodeo clown, but it's a long story," grinned Tank, "I'll bring you up to speed during our seventeen laps."

Tank dropped his backpack on the side of the track and began jogging. Cage and Ruby followed. Compared to schools in Texas, this track was not all that bad regarding running. Texas schools had this hard-red concrete running track, but La Grange High School was more of a soft, black rubber track. Tank figured that in Texas the sun was so hot it would melt your shoes if you were not careful. This Kentucky rubber stuff wouldn't stand a chance of making it through the blistering Texas summer heat.

"Do you all want to sing cadence while we double time?" suggested Tank.

"Cadence? Double time?" asked Ruby, confused at what Tank meant.

Double time simply meant jogging and cadence meant singing. It was something Tank heard all the time when the troops went for early morning runs around the base. Most of his friends in Texas had parents who were in the military and it had never dawned on him that kids in other places wouldn't know about this stuff. A good cadence helps pass the time, builds comradery, and keeps everyone motivated. Tank tried to explain what cadence meant by singing a few classic running tunes.

"One, two, three, and a quarter,
somebody, anybody, get me some water..."

And...

"I can run, to the sun, just for fun..."

Or...

"Hey there, Captain Jack,
meet me down by the railroad tracks,
with some running shoes in your hand,
I'm gonna be a running man."

Tank sang his heart out trying to gain their interest. To say Ruby was laughing would have been an understatement. If Ruby had been drinking milk, it is safe to say it would have shot out of her nose by now. Cage shook his head from side to side showing he was not interested. Tank swallowed his pride, admitted defeat on the cadence singing, and the three continued their first lap around the track. Tank's mind kept flashing back to the conversation with Mom in the car earlier that morning. Also, the walk over to the track and the discussion between Cage and Ruby was bugging him.

Mom warned him to be careful about strange rumors being talked about at school. Now, the only two kids Tank had met all day were talking about strange things at school. Remembering the awkwardness of the walk over, Tank knew Ruby and Cage were obviously upset with each other about the topic. They seemed to have moved on from their argument since Mr. Jackson had punished them. The last thing Tank wanted to do was spark up a confrontation in what was already a cruddy situation.

They jogged until they reached the far side of the track. Tank noticed he was about fifteen feet in front of them and needed to slow down a bit. Running was something Tank did all the time. Last year, Tank had run a mile in five minutes and thirteen seconds and almost beat Dad. Cage and Ruby were breathing a little heavier, but they didn't seem like they were in bad shape. Tank imagined Ruby was into soccer and Cage obviously loved mixed martial arts. Both sports required a high level of fitness to compete. Tank slowed down until Cage and Ruby caught up with him.

"Yo, Cage," said Tank. "That thing you were talking about earlier, the alien's thing, what was that all about?"

"No one knows to be honest," replied Cage, as Ruby nodded her head in agreement.

"We have sixteen and a half laps to go," joked Tank. "Would you mind telling me what you do know?"

Cage and Ruby each explained what they knew. Years ago, the local game warden had caught several bizarre animals in the pond behind the school. No one knew how they got there or who put them there. The school put up a large fence around the pond and had placed barbed wire across the top. The school board had tried to drain the pond several years ago, but they stopped, and no one knew why. The parents, who had gone to the school when they were younger, avoided talking about it, but sometimes, in private, they would slip and share a strange story or detail.

"Animals in a pond?" replied Tank laughing. "Now that is bizarre."

"Why do you think Ms. Sprinkle threatened to expel anyone that crossed the fence?" challenged Cage sarcastically.

"I mean, who would possibly think that animals would live near a pond?" mocked Tank. "That's cray-cray if you ask me."

"Well, considering that the game warden caught two black caimans and a dozen piranhas, I would say that is significant," said Ruby as she put her hands on her hips.

"Caimans and piranhas?" gulped Tank in a disbelieving voice.

"They even think that two students were eaten alive," said Ruby.

Cage and Ruby went on to explain more of the eerie nature of the pond. Apparently, one of the contractors who was working to drain the pond was quoted in the local newspaper as saying the pond had no bottom. Like, it went on forever. The company that was hired for the job of removing the pond sent multiple scuba divers in to investigate and all of them but one mysteriously vanished. Then, some government agency came into town and arrested the only survivor and he was never seen again.

It wasn't that Tank didn't want to believe them, but the story did sound a little far-fetched. Tank's Uncle Darren would tell him these incredible stories about Dad when he was younger. All families have one person that tends to tell embellished stories. He remembered the story he had told Tank at a family reunion about Dad once fighting Bigfoot in the Australian Outback.

Uncle Darren worked for the government, but akin to dad's job, Tank was not sure what he did. He and dad got along fine even with Uncle Darren's unique sense of humor. There was only one time when Uncle Darren made a joke saying dad had voted for a democrat that Tank could remember them getting into a fist fight, but other than that, they were on good terms. When Uncle Darren would tell ridiculous stories about dad, dad would look at Tank and make a silly face. While Cage and Ruby were explaining the story, Tank probably made the same goofy face a couple times without realizing it.

They were still technically jogging, although it was more of a light shuffle now. Worried that Mr. Jackson would add extra laps, they jogged slightly faster, but not much. Ruby pulled a smartphone from her pocket and showed them a news article that was dated March 23, 2001. Tank was paying attention, but he was distracted. He couldn't believe Ruby even had a cellphone, let alone a smartphone.

The one time he had asked Dad for a cellphone, in case of emergencies, Dad had given him a couple quarters and wished him the best of luck. He asked Dad what to do with fifty cents and Dad instructed him to find a gas station with a payphone. When he asked what exactly a payphone was, Dad shook his head and said, "You're a smart kid. Figure it out."

The article on Ruby's phone indicated that three students were in a small canoe fishing on the pond after school. Their parents called the police after they did not return at sunset. A statewide search was conducted, but the students' bodies were never found. Investigators found ripped pieces of clothing with bite marks on them floating in the water, but they ruled that an animal

51

attack was impossible because none of the animals in Kentucky waters were capable of such an attack.

Ruby then used her index finger and flipped the screen to a screenshot of another news article dated August 5, 2005. This time, the article stated that the National Environmental Security Agency, abbreviated NESA in the article, had questioned two students who had allegedly disappeared for four days.

Since the students were under eighteen, the article excluded their real names. The two students were referred to in pseudo nicknames as "Phoenix" and "Spear." The article looked like it used to have more information in it, but several paragraphs had words smudged out in black marker making it difficult to fully read anything.

"I love the code names," joked Tank. "But most of this story is redacted, so who knows what it says."

"Did you see the part about the students disappearing for four days?" questioned Ruby.

"It's fake news," declared Tank. "Nothing to worry about. Probably a hoax started by a few kids looking for attention."

Distracted by the news articles on Ruby's phone, the three slowed down and walked as they began their second lap around the track. Continuing to scroll down the internet search screen, Ruby showed them dozens of similar news articles dated between 2001 and 2005 about strange occurrences happening near or around the pond. All of them were vague with information, some were redacted, and others, when clicked, would come up as **restricted access** only. The only noticeable recurring themes in the articles were the two names, Phoenix and Spear, but there was no specific information on what truly happened.

One of the articles posted on a popular conspiracy website mentioned that the La Grange occurrences were one of many government cover ups. The article made several ridiculous claims about wormholes, teleportation, and secret portals. There were even a few references to Bigfoot, aliens, Persian gods, leviathans, and a list of other geographic places in the world where similar events had happened.

Underneath the comments section were several anonymous bloggers who had shared that they had received incognito phone calls and were threatened with the charge of sedition if they tried to investigate the pond. One of the conspiracy theorists mentioned they were visited by two government agents who interrogated them for five hours. The blog included a screenshot of the badge the agents were wearing.

Ruby mentioned that her Aunt Leah went to high school in La Grange and had graduated around 2006 or 2007. Unfortunately, Aunt Leah only knew of the same rumors and stories that everyone else knew. If someone who graduated only a few years later didn't know the whole story, then figuring it out was going to require someone who was actually there.

Tank tried hard to remember the year books that were sitting in boxes in the garage. Mom was a year younger than Dad, but she graduated early from high school because of distinguished academic achievement. Dad just celebrated his birthday having joined the military when he was eighteen and he was born in 1988. Doing a little bit of math in his head, Tank realized it was possible that both Mom and Dad went to school in La Grange during the exact era of the mysterious news articles. Tank was looking forward to trying to video chat with Dad later that night and ask him.

The rest of the class was in the middle of the football field. Mr. Jackson was yelling at them about something and was not paying any attention to the track. Mr. Jackson never technically stated that they had to run every lap so walking a little didn't seem like a matter of life and death. Tank remembered the promise he had made to Mom of not letting curiosity get the best of him.

Dad once gave Tank advice at the dinner table when he said women sometimes say one thing and mean the complete opposite. In response to Dad's comment, Mom flicked Dad on the earlobe. Dad apologized to Mom for the comment, of course, but then Dad winked in Tank's direction a few seconds later. Using this logic, Tank wondered if perhaps Mom was really saying that she wanted curiosity to get the best of him. Yes, this had to be one of those situations, for sure.

Mr. Jackson stopped yelling and glanced towards the track. Ruby noticed and immediately put her cellphone away. Tank and Cage were still casually chatting, but they stopped when Ruby elbowed and shushed them. Noticing that Mr. Jackson may see them slacking on their laps, they all jogged in silence again. Tank daydreamed about what Dad would do to solve the problem of killer animals living in the pond behind the school.

Dad would grab his sniper rifle, order an airstrike, call for fire, rappel out of a helicopter into the pond while catching a caiman with his bare hands. Tank's mind continued to daydream about Dad saving the day. Mr. Jackson would run like a coward and Dad would have to save him, too. Mr. Jackson would have been more scared than a mouse checking into a cat motel. Tank laughed out loud, summoning a weird look from Ruby.

"So where is this pond?" asked Tank, breaking the silence.

"It's not that far away," replied Ruby.

"When we get to the far side of the track again, look to the left and you will see a creek at the bottom of the hill," said Cage.

"Sweet," said Tank. "I love creeks, especially catching crawfish in them."

"If you follow the creek for a little while, the pond should be right there," continued Ruby.

"*Should* be right there?" inquired Tank.

"I have never seen the pond," said Ruby. "I don't think anyone has in decades."

"Yeah, it can't be more than a five-minute jog to the fence," added Cage, "then the pond should be a little further."

"Challenge accepted," mumbled Tank.

Tank glanced back at Mr. Jackson and the rest of the students on the field. Mr. Jackson was counting while five other students did pushups as a punishment for something. Mr. Jackson even had his foot on one of the student's backs and occasionally let out a chuckle. What a jerk!

The rest of the class was divided into teams to start playing soccer. The only thing that was worse than playing soccer was watching soccer being played. Watching others play soccer was like watching paint dry or like watching water boil. Maybe being forced to do laps instead of being in class was the best thing that could have happened to them.

Eight
Danger – Keep Out!

Reaching the far side of the track, Ruby and Cage eagerly pointed to the creek at the bottom of the hill. Neither of them was thinking that Tank sincerely wanted to go to the pond when he said, "Challenge accepted." Ruby thought he was kidding around or trying to show off. Tank slowed down from a jog to a walk and surveyed the landscape.

The football field and track did not have a perimeter fence so sneaking off was not farfetched. Also, the hill was steep enough to provide the perfect cover. Mr. Jackson and the rest of the class had pretty much forgotten they existed anyway. All that Tank needed to do was get Cage and Ruby to agree to a little adventure.

"Let's go explore the pond," urged Tank.

"Are you cray-cray?" gasped Ruby.

"Look," said Tank, "the whole class is playing a game and Mr. Jackson is the referee. We can jog to the pond, look around, and run back without anyone ever knowing."

"I'm down," joked Cage. "We can say that we assumed we were supposed to do laps around the school if we get caught."

"The old playing the fool routine," chuckled Tank. "That's the spirit."

Tank did not wait for Ruby to respond and took off running towards the creek like a madman. The hill to get to the creek was steep enough that gravity took over. Tank was involuntarily sprinting and having a hard time not tripping over his own feet on the way down.

Near the bottom of the hill, Tank looked over his shoulder and could no longer see the track. Cage was halfway down the hill, running full steam ahead, and Ruby, shaking her head, reluctantly followed a few feet behind them. It took a couple minutes to reach the creek which was narrow and only a few inches deep.

Smooth, multi-colored rocks covered the bottom of the creek bed and with every step, Tank could see little crawfish darting under the rocks. He made a mental note to come back later with a bucket to catch a couple. The grass on the hill must have been recently mowed because it was short. Little pieces of green grass were sticking to the sides of his shoes and the smell of fresh cut grass filled the air. Up ahead, Tank could see that the grassy areas on the sides of the creek were not mowed, resulting in taller, thicker grass.

The rough outline of a fence appeared in the distance and was less than a football field away. Instead of running alongside the edge of the creek, like most people would, Tank decided to run down the center, being careful to pull his cargo pants up enough to avoid his pant legs from getting soaked. Cage laughed and did the same. From behind him, Tank could hear Cage stomping his feet in the water. Ruby kept to the edge of the creek and tried not to get her shoes wet.

Staying out of the water was not an easy task. As they got closer to the fence, the grass along the edges grew taller than Ruby! It was difficult for her to keep from stepping in the water while she ran. She looked like a tightrope performer from the circus trying to run along the edge of the creek.

When the water began to go over the top of his ankles, Tank decided it was time to stop running. Cage took a few extra steps to catch up with Tank and then walked, too. Carefully picking up their feet to avoid slipping, they moved along the inside edge of the creek where the water was shallower. By this point, their socks were soaked.

Walking together, Cage and Tank slowed down as they approached the fence. The grass growing on the other side of the fence and the enormous cattails in the creek made it impossible to see the pond. Looking back, they could see that Ruby was close behind them. They could no longer see the school or track at all.

The grass alongside the creek was way over their heads, but that was nothing compared to the fence standing in front of them. At well over ten feet tall, there was a rusted metal fence with two extra feet of barbed wire at the top.

The barbed wire looked like it was intentionally angled inward and not outward, which was an interesting feature. Considering that most fences were designed to keep people out, this fence was designed to keep stuff in.

"Okay, we made it to the pond. Time to go back," declared Ruby.

"Technically, we are only at the fence," said Tank pointing. "The pond must be up there."

"This is awesome," said Cage. "The fence is much bigger than I thought it would be."

"How do we get past it, though?" Tank looked for a way in.

"Yeah, wait, what?" questioned Cage. "I said it was awesome, not that I wanted to go further."

Climbing the fence was not going to be easy. Without something to cover the barbed wire, like a car floor mat or rug, they would surely cut their legs trying to get over the barbed wire. Going under the fence was a suitable and reasonable option. Although the fence went straight over the top of the creek, there was a small gap between the water and the fence.

Tank put his left hand on the fence to test how rigid it was and immediately his body violently shook! His whole body felt like he was being electrocuted! Cage yelled and Ruby screamed. Drool rolled out of Tank's gaping mouth and down his chin. Panic ensued from his friends as Tank put on an award-winning performance. Ruby reached for her phone to call for help, but right as she started dialing 9-1-1, a grin crept across Tank's face.

"Got ya!" Tank wiped away the drool.

"That's not funny!" shouted Ruby.

"Dude, what the heck, bro?" laughed Cage. "We thought you were being electrocuted to death!"

"The fence is not electric." Tank showed his hands. "It's only rusty and dirty."

Tank rolled his already damp cargo pants as high as possible and took a few steps toward the center of the creek. The water was almost to his knees. A frog was swimming across the top of the water and Tank scooped it up and tossed it at Ruby. Ruby screeched and threw her hands in the air.

Cage laughed, Ruby gave him the stink eye, and Tank put his hands down to grab the bottom of the fence. Using both arms, he flexed his biceps to bend the fence up until there was enough space for Ruby and Cage to comfortably crawl underneath.

"Come in a little deeper. The water is fine," said Tank.

"Umm, no," said Ruby.

"Are all Texans as nutty as you?" asked Cage.

"That's a fair question," chuckled Tank. "Now come on, bending this fence is not as easy as it looks."

Ruby, trying to impress Tank, rolled up her pant legs, stepped into the creek, and squatted down low enough and under the fence that her long hair nearly touched the water. Cage followed a few steps behind. Once Cage cleared the fence, Tank rotated his shoulders under the fence, too.

All three of them were standing on the other side of the fence in the middle of the creek in knee-deep water. Tank led the way as they maneuvered through the tall weeds and cattails. They could now see the pond. It was much smaller than Tank had envisioned in his mind.

The water had a green tint and the typical fishy smell that Tank remembered from fishing in Texas with Dad. Fortunately, the thick wetland plants did not come all the way to the edge of the pond so they could move forward a little easier. Around the edges of the pond lay a rocky shoreline and the ground was dry for the most part. The rocks were unique in their colors with little flecks of red, orange, and turquoise embedded in them. Ruby noticed that when the angle was right, the rocks glistened in the sunlight. Along the top of the pond near the edges grew copious amounts of green algae, but other than that, it was a stereotypical pond.

An old wooden canoe sat flipped upside down on the shoreline. Remembering the story about the three kids that went missing and were allegedly eaten alive sent shivers down each of their spines. Several rusty signs lined the perimeter of the pond that had bold printed words on them, **NO FISHING OR SWIMMING**. On the other side of the pond stood thick green and brown woods that covered the rolling hills and extended as far as the eye could see.

"Someone did a little overkill with the signs," laughed Tank.

"What do you mean?" asked Cage.

"There are thirteen of them," smiled Tank. "Seems a bit much, don't you think?"

"Maybe in case a Texan visits the pond," giggled Ruby, "they figure more signs will help get the point across!"

"Oh, you know that's not true," replied Tank. "You know Texan's can't read no good."

"Too funny, bro," laughed Cage. "I do agree though, whoever put up these signs was serious about staying away from the water."

"If I can throw a baseball from one side to the other," joked Tank, "then I doubt more than a dozen signs are needed to make the point."

"This is so cool," said Ruby, moving closer to the water's edge. "Since I was little, I have heard scary stories about this place, but it looks like a normal pond to me."

"My parents would ground me for months if they knew I was back here," added Cage.

"Okay," declared Tank. "What do we know about this pond?"

"Well…" said Ruby, "we know that we are not supposed to be back here."

"Exactly," declared Tank. "All we know is that the school doesn't want anyone back here. We also have information from a couple of old news articles and a conspiracy website."

"What's your point?" inquired Cage.

"My point is that the school is obviously hiding something," said Tank. "The fact that even parents don't know the truth is bonkers."

"Alright, this has been a lot of fun," declared Cage. "Maybe some other time we can pretend to be detectives, but we need to get back to class."

Ruby agreed with Cage, but she was trying hard to impress Tank. Up until this year, Ruby had considered all boys to be icky, but Tank seemed different. His Texas charm and rugged nature was unique. Trying to get his attention, Ruby put her hand on Tank's shoulder. She batted her eyes a couple of times while trying to coax him back to the school. They needed to get to class before Mr. Jackson threw another temper tantrum and added more laps or worse.

Tank noticed Ruby fluttering her eyelashes and wondered if maybe she had something in her eye. Years before, Tank had gotten a piece of rust stuck in his eye and he could empathize. Feeling like something is in your eye is one of the most awful things ever. Having something in your eye is worse than having a dentist accidentally sneeze into your mouth during a root canal, which according to Uncle Darren, happened to him last year. It never dawned on Tank that Ruby was trying to flirt with him. Tank gazed into the distance with his eyes fixed on the wooded area on the other side of the pond.

"Look at that," announced Tank. "I wonder what's back there?"

"Where?" shrugged Cage, turning around. He had recognized Ruby's overt attempt to flirt with Tank and was astonished that Tank did not get the hint at her intentions.

"Back that way," pointed Tank, "on the other side of the pond."

The fence nearest to the creek, where they had accessed the pond, was only about thirty feet from the water. In contrast, the fence must extend much further on the other side of the pond. In fact, they couldn't even see the top of the fence over there at all. The map in Ms. Sprinkle's class had shown a full perimeter fence. In the distance, there was also a patch of trees that didn't look quite right either. Reality didn't match what was printed on that map.

Near the trees, there was a small opening where sunlight was shining from the trees to the ground. Tank walked around the shoreline of the pond towards the woods on the other side. Entering the tree line, he put his hand up, waving for Ruby and Cage to follow him like he was a military commander.

Several years ago, Tank attended a summer camp on the military base where the instructors taught land navigation. Tank knew that an opening in the woods meant the ground must not be able to grow trees. Typically, this meant a change in terrain or possibly a sinkhole. Curiosity may have killed the cat, but it was not about to hurt a Tank. His first thought was that there must be a second pond or stagnant bog that nobody knew about, but without a closer look, it was impossible to know for sure.

Tank could hear Ruby and Cage crunching branches as they traipsed behind him. Tank had spent most of his time in the woods in Texas and this was like a walk in the park to him. As they navigated their way through the thick woods, Tank realized they were walking up a rather steep hill.

The ground was changing the farther they went. Near the pond, the ground was moist. As they entered the woods, the ground became firm and was covered in leaves. As they continued to walk, the ground changed again and they were walking on a mix of coarse pebble-sized rocks, some leaves, and loose dirt.

About a hundred feet in the distance, light was shining through the tree line and Tank slowed down. Ruby and Cage stopped moving as Tank went ahead to investigate. As the hill grew steeper, they could see a small opening in the hill that was only a few feet wide.

When Tank got within twenty feet of the opening, he could see another fence forming a circle around the opening. This fence was old and considerably shorter than the one near the creek. Thankfully, it didn't have barbed wire at the top. With a little jump, Tank was easily able to pull his body over the top of the fence.

Ruby and Cage approached the fence. Cage tried to jump over the top and promptly fell on his face, causing Ruby to laugh. Tank turned and held out his hand to help Ruby pull herself over. Ruby smiled at Tank and the butterflies fluttered in his stomach again. In front of the opening stood an old wooden sign bolted to a steel pipe that was hammered into the ground. The sign read "**DANGER – KEEP OUT**" in bold red letters. In addition to the sign, four large wooden boards were loosely stacked on top of each other, preventing anyone from entering the hole.

"I knew it! We found the source!" joked Tank, with a semi-serious look on his face.

"Hey Tank, bro," teased Cage. "You have a lot to learn about Kentucky."

"What?" exclaimed Tank. "I bet those animals came out of here."

Cage was still shaking leaves from his clothes after falling to the ground. Ruby was examining the old sign. There were words written in cursive at the bottom, but they were too rusty to read. As she focused her eyes on the small print, she could only make out a couple of words. Tank was busy trying to move the wooden boards so he could look inside the hole.

Long metal spikes were sticking out of the boards. They looked as if they were once used to fasten the spikes to the ground. Either the spikes naturally came loose over time because of erosion or someone had used a crowbar and pulled them out a long time ago.

Tank made a few more comments regarding his suspicion about the opening being the source of the strange animals found in the pond, but Cage was not so sure. Cage's dad had worked for a large mining company ever since they had moved to Kentucky. He had seen holes in the side of hills like this all the time when his dad would take him out to visit the jobsite. Cage didn't want to make Tank feel bad for not knowing about the hole's use. Instead of mocking Tank, Cage felt it was better to explain the origins of it instead.

"This was a miner's shaft used for coal expeditions," explained Cage.

"Judging by the looks of things, I am guessing they didn't find coal," added Ruby.

"No one looks for coal around here anymore," continued Cage.

"Why not?" asked Tank.

"Dad says there are too many caves around here," explained Cage. "Digging for coal is dangerous near caves because the mine can collapse."

"Danger-smanger," laughed Tank, continuing to move the boards that were laying across the opening.

Tank felt embarrassed for not knowing anything about coal miner's shafts or Kentucky for that matter. Also, if the school was hiding something, then what better place than this? Looking at Ruby, Tank couldn't get over how beautiful her lips looked as they sparkled in the sunlight. Ruby's whole demeanor was angel-like as she stood there.

Tank desperately wanted to prove to his new friends that he was rough, tough, and hard to bluff. His biggest ambition was to impress Ruby, though. Tank cracked his knuckles and popped his neck like action heroes do in the movies. Kicking the final board out of the way, he dropped to his hands and knees and high-crawled into the opening.

"I'm going to take a look around inside," proclaimed Tank, with a smirk on his face, and then he disappeared.

"Dude, come back!" yelled Cage.

"Tank, this is a terrible idea! What about class?" shouted Ruby. "We are going to head back, with or without you."

"We can't leave him in there alone," sighed Cage.

"I know that," replied Ruby. "But I don't want to go in there."

Cage freaked out a little bit and took two large puffs on his asthma inhaler which had been stored comfortably in his pocket up until now. Asthma attacks were something that Cage was all too familiar with and high stress situations seemed to make them worse. Ruby paced back and forth, hoping that Tank would suddenly pop out and say he was only kidding.

On top of being extremely claustrophobic, she also was not fond of crawling through mud which she could see lining the inside of the miner's shaft. Going into a dark hole in the side of a hill was not her idea of a good time. Ruby pulled out her cellphone and turned on the flashlight. A few minutes had passed since Tank disappeared.

"We go in, convince Tank to go back to class, and get out of there! Deal?" said Ruby.

"Deal!" Cage put away his inhaler.

"Yuck, I'm pretty sure a bunch of ducks pooped down here or something." Ruby's hand touched the goopy ground.

"Tank, dude, we're coming inside!" announced Cage.

Ruby's cellphone had an awesome flashlight on it and luckily, the sunlight was shining through the entrance at an angle where they could see inside considerably well. Using one hand to crawl, she held the cellphone up and out of the crud-covered ground to the miner's shaft. The shaft may have been narrow at the opening, but inside it quickly opened high enough where they could both stand up. Being able to stand up made Ruby extremely happy as she only had to drag her hands through the muck for a couple of seconds.

From the outside looking in, the entrance to the miner's shaft looked like a long tunnel, but thankfully, this was not the case. The entry was no more than a couple of feet long at best. Both Cage and Ruby rose to their feet to get their bearings. Ruby spotted Tank standing about half a soccer field away which was farther than she was prepared to go.

Walking farther inside felt like they were walking downhill as they moved towards Tank. Considering they were crawling into the side of a hill, this made sense. Stepping lightly to avoid slipping, they looked down and saw their shoes covered in nasty stuff.

They moved deeper inside the mine shaft to get closer to Tank. The sunshine illuminating through the entrance was still providing a decent amount of light. It was not enough light to see well, per se, but enough to where they were not in complete darkness. Ruby's cellphone helped them see a little better, as well. The ground near the entrance was disgusting, but as they ventured further, it transformed to a slick, wet clay. Walking carefully and trying hard not to slip, they were getting closer to Tank.

Ruby yelled out again, trying to get his attention. Tank waved his hand in the air acknowledging her, then motioned for them to come closer. Cage and Ruby walked painstakingly towards Tank and were about half a basketball court's distance to his location. Ruby was planning to scold Tank for recklessly going inside and was rehearsing a reprimanding soapbox speech in her head. She wasn't sure what to say, but it was not going to be nice.

"Cage, you ever seen a miner's shaft like this?" asked Tank, hearing their footsteps approaching from behind.

"No way, man! This is no miner's shaft!" replied Cage, now standing beside Tank. "This is a full-blown cave!"

Ruby shined her flashlight into the distance and the cave opened into what looked like miles of vast caverns. The air inside smelled moldy like a grilled cheese sandwich that had been left for weeks in the trunk of a hot car. Tank had not walked in a straight line once inside the cave, but his route veered left where there was a large piece of rock extending from the ceiling of the cave to the ground. One issue with not walking in a straight line was that the sunlight grew dimmer when not lined up perfectly with the entrance.

The large rock formed what looked like a freestanding wall because it stood vertically and was smoothly textured. Similar wall formations could be seen in the distance, but this one was much bigger. Tank stood in silence and stared oddly at the wall. Trying to capture his attention, Ruby pointed the light at Tank's face.

In the beam of the flashlight, Ruby could see that Tank had a fierce gaze upon his face and his eyes were focused intently. She was thinking about giving him a compliment, telling him that he looked like an action hero in the spotlight. However, her previous desire and plan to give him a piece of her mind about him foolishly crawling inside the miner's shaft made her rethink her praise. Cage interrupted before she could say anything.

"Oh my goodness!" exclaimed Cage.

"This is unbelievable!" said Tank. "I couldn't tell what it was, but with your flashlight I see..."

"What in the world?" interrupted Ruby before Tank could get his thoughts out.

Covering her mouth in disbelief, Ruby forgot about the compliment or lecture she had planned for Tank. Her flashlight quickly moved to the wall of the cave. Overwhelmed, she dropped her cellphone. Fortunately, the flashlight landed facing upwards and the light shined onto the wall. In silence, they stood staring at the wall and then looked at each other, baffled beyond belief. What was on the wall was like nothing they had ever seen before. Nothing could have prepared them for what was to happen next.

Nine

Phoenix's Letter

Ruby frantically reached down and picked up her cellphone. Wiping the muddy, sludgy clay off the purple case, she aimed the flashlight all around trying to see everything. She shined it across the top of the cave but even more so on the wall. It was like nothing they had ever seen before. Engravings, colored paintings, and etched drawings of bizarre animals were everywhere. Some of the artwork looked ancient as if it were created thousands of years ago although some of the artwork appeared to be only a couple decades old. The pictures looked as if monsters were coming out of the walls.

Each illustration of the creatures had similar, yet distinct features. Most noticeable similarities were the giant teeth, fins, enormous size, and sharp claws. Darker clouds moved across the sky in front of the sun making the light coming from the entrance to the cave grow dim. Ruby tapped a button on her cellphone labelled "light booster" and the flashlight got even brighter. Near the spot where they were standing, Cage could see the tail of a dark green snake.

"That's odd," said Cage.

"What's odd?" asked Tank.

"Well, this picture," said Cage. "I see the tail and part of the body, but where is the head of the snake?"

"Shine your light over here, Ruby," insisted Tank.

"This is getting dangerous, boys," replied Ruby. "We are already way too deep in this cave and my cellphone's battery is not going to last much longer."

"Challenge accepted," grinned Tank. "Let's find the head of the snake."

"Challenge, what challenge?" exclaimed Ruby. "Why do you keep saying that?"

Tank smiled out of the corner of his mouth, playfully snatched Ruby's cellphone from her hand, and then followed the body of the snake. Since he was holding the only good source of light now, Ruby and Cage didn't have much of a choice but to follow him. The body of the serpent stretched over one hundred feet and went around several corners into the dark cave. Walking closely together, they kept going until they spotted the snake's freakishly large green head.

The mouth of the snake was wide open and it had a slimy looking maroon tongue that slithered between thousands of sharp, yellow-stained serrated teeth. Each scale on the large reptile was as big as a man's fist. Worse than the drawing of the snake itself was the large painted pool of blood flowing down the wall seeping from the snake's mouth.

The artist, whoever it was, must have felt it necessary to scare the crud out of anyone that dared to look at the picture. Above the snake's head were words engraved into the rock. Cage read out loud, trying his best to pronounce the words correctly.

"Yacumama Serpente," Cage read slowly.

"Something about a snake?" guessed Ruby.

"Do all these paintings mean the stories about the pond are true?" asked Tank.

"This is graffiti," replied Ruby. "I don't think it proves anything."

"Not sure what it means," commented Cage, "but it makes the hairs on my arms stand up."

Ruby waited for Tank to drop his guard and then grabbed the cellphone out of his hands. She moved the flashlight back and forth, studying the head of the snake. They had followed the body of the snake far enough into the cave that her cellphone was literally the only source of light now. Even the dim light from the sun had disappeared as they went around corners following the body of the snake. To make matters worse, the battery warning light on Ruby's cellphone started blinking.

Under normal circumstances, the warning light meant there was about fifteen minutes before the phone would die. However, this was the first time she had used the "light booster" on the flashlight for an extended amount of time. It was anyone's guess how long they had until the cellphone turned off.

"Enough fun for one day," said Ruby. "We need to find the exit before my cellphone dies."

"Let's get out of here," added Cage. "I wonder if anyone knows we are even gone?"

"Nah, I doubt it," remarked Tank. "Mr. Jackson is too busy picking his nose and then yelling at his boogers for not following his two rules to notice we are gone."

Ruby giggled, then turned the cellphone screen towards Cage and Tank. Using her finger, she pointed at the battery warning light hoping they would see the seriousness of the situation. Then, she pointed her cellphone in the opposite direction of the snake's body. If they followed the snake's body back to the rest of the art they had seen on the wall, then hopefully, they would be able to see the light from the sun. They could get out of the cave and run back to class pretending like they had never left.

Mentally preparing herself to put her hands back on the nasty ground, Ruby started walking back, holding the flashlight at shoulder level. She kept thinking about the disgusting ground near the exit and had already been wiping the smelly, gooey stuff off ever since they first came inside. Cage followed right behind her. Tank paused in place, still trying to examine the head of the snake.

Ruby felt she had done a good job of impressing Tank by maintaining her composure inside the cave. One of her greatest fears was being trapped inside a dark room. Being inside the cave had almost pushed her over her daily anxiety limit.

Every time Ruby looked back at Tank, who was still trailing a few feet behind, she felt like he was overtly staring at her. Tank was not trying to be weird or rude. He liked the way she walked and he couldn't explain it. Up until about thirty minutes ago, he had not ever considered that other humans had unique walking styles, but something was oddly enjoyable about observing Ruby walk. Tank did a final look around and picked up the pace to catch up with them. He was trying to process the events of the day.

In less than a few hours, and since being dropped off at a new school, Tank had met one of the coolest guys and one of the most stunning girls ever. Plus, they had discovered a secret cave. Hopefully, when they had more time, and a couple of fully charged flashlights, they could come back to explore a little more. This was a good day and Kentucky was not that bad after all.

"Wait!" hollered Tank, after taking one or two steps. "There's a bag over there!"

Ruby paused, turned around, and shined her light in the direction Tank was pointing. Whoever had put the bag there must have been trying to hide it as it was tucked inside a small hole near another cave wall about twenty or thirty feet away. The only way to have ever seen the bag would have been to glance over at the right moment and have your eyes at the precise angle. It was a one in a million chance to notice something in the exact spot where the bag was sitting. To get to the bag, Tank needed to walk deeper into the cave.

Even from a distance, Tank recognized the brown, green, and tan pattern of the bag. It reminded him of a military rucksack. A rucksack is nothing more than an oversized backpack designed to hold a soldier's gear. The bag was tattered, torn, and the zipper looked busted. Along the top of the bag, there was a spot for two thick black plastic buckles, but one buckle was missing, causing the bag to hang open a little.

Sitting near the top of the bag was a thin silver necklace chain looped around the handle. On the chain, there were matching metal tags that had writing on them. Ruby's flashlight sparkled as the light reflected off the metal tags. Tank stood over the top of the bag while Ruby and Cage kept a safe distance, worrying that the bag might blow up or something irrational like that.

The tags had the initials, "P.T.", engraved on them. Ruby and Cage's curiosity must have been piqued because they came over to have a quick look, forgetting about the battery warning light.

"What are the shiny things on top?" asked Ruby.

"Those are dog tags," replied Tank, lifting his collar. "See, I have a pair, too. My Dad had them made on the base."

"Does that mean this is a soldier's bag?" asked Cage.

"Nah," said Tank. "I don't think so. These are more like souvenir dog tags that you can buy at the store. Real dog tags have a full name, blood type, social security number, and religious information."

"Oh," said Ruby. "I had no idea."

"My guess is that this must be a gym bag," said Tank. "P.T is a military term for physical training, you know, sit-ups, pushups, two-mile runs."

"Maybe, but I don't think so," said Cage.

"Why not?" asked Tank. "How do you know it's not a gym bag?"

"The initials P.T.," responded Cage. "That also could mean physical therapist or public telephone or anything else with the same initials."

Tank laughed at Cage for suggesting a physical therapist. He satirized the idea of a rogue physical therapist providing muscle therapy to injured patients inside a cave. Cage shrugged his shoulders, but he was certain that he was right about the initials not meaning "physical training."

Ruby held the flashlight over top of the bag while Cage and Tank debated for a few minutes regarding the meaning of "P.T." Both took turns pointing out flaws in the other person's opinion of what it meant. While they were busy debating the meaning, Ruby knelt to look inside and sift through the contents, being careful not to pull anything out of the bag.

Inside the bag was a pocketknife, rope, compass, a couple shiny rocks, and what looked like a large wooden tablet with what appeared to be words, symbols, and lines carved into the surface. The light from the flashlight reflected off the tablet, but even with the flashlight, it was difficult to see what the inscriptions on the tablet meant. Near the bottom of the bag, the two rocks reflected the beam coming from the flashlight. One rock was considerably larger than the other. Ruby's phone beeped and the battery icon flashed with a red lightning bolt.

"Cool pocketknife," commented Tank. "I was expecting shorts, t-shirt, and tennis shoes."

"I guess we can rule out physical training," joked Cage. "Tank, admit it. You were wrong."

"I can neither confirm nor deny your allegations," laughed Tank. "Fine, only if you first admit this is not a physical therapist's bag either," he bantered back.

"Unless you two can find three sets of night-vision goggles in the bottom of the bag," said Ruby, "we need to get out of here now."

Tank reached down, grabbed the bag, and slung it over his right shoulder. As he did, the wooden tablet fell from the bag and toppled to the ground. Using his left hand, he knelt, picked up the tablet, and cradled it under his armpit. Ruby's flashlight blinked on and off a couple more times indicating it was running out of power. The "light booster" that Ruby had turned on a while ago must have quit working because the flashlight was dimmer than before.

"Alright comrades," said Tank. "Let's march out of this place in double time."

"Not sure what that means," said Cage, "but let's get out of here."

Ruby, Cage, and Tank moved back to where they had been before seeing the bag and followed the body of the snake towards the cave's opening. Tank led the way, followed by Cage, and Ruby, who trudged behind them using her flashlight to light the path. The wet clay on the ground was like ice skating and they had to be careful not to fall on their backsides.

Cage and Ruby were dawdling slowly, but Tank was a little less careful as he power walked instead. It was only a matter of time before there was a wipe out. Tank's feet slipped out from under his body, and as his bottom struck the cave floor, there was a loud thud that echoed throughout the cave.

"Tank, you okay man?" inquired Cage.

"Yeah," grunted Tank. "I meant to do that. I was curious if the ground felt as hard for my booty as it does for my feet. Yep, it sure does."

Ruby gasped when Tank hit the ground and she rushed to his aid. Tank's pants were filthy and physically, he did not seem injured, but his ego was beat up. During the fall, the bag stayed on his shoulder, but the tablet tumbled into the air and landed a few feet away. This time, the side of the tablet with the engraved lines landed face down. Ruby noticed something taped to the back as it flew through the air. It seemed that Tank and Cage had not seen it. She decided not to bring it up because she was worried the boys would get distracted again, the flashlight would go out, and they would be lost in the cave forever.

The flashlight grew even dimmer, and Ruby swiftly pointed to the tablet, helping Tank find it on the ground. Tank picked up the tablet again and firmly tucked it under his armpit. The battery indicator on the cellphone showed a red lightning bolt with a red line slashing through it. It was only a matter of time until the phone turned off.

Ruby pointed the flashlight at the cave wall as they carefully rushed back, following the snake's body to where they had originally found the animal drawings on the wall. Thankfully, the clouds that were blocking the sun had gone away because when they got back to the tail of the snake, the sun was shining bright again, illuminating the inside of the cave.

When they could see the sunlight again, Tank slowed down and looked at his pants. He noticed they were covered in crud from having fallen and that was only the front side. Using his left hand, Tank wiped clay and sludge off the front and back of his cargo pants. Once he removed as much muck as possible from his pants, he wiped his hand on the side of his shirt. Ruby, feeling a bit more at ease from seeing the sunlight, teased him that wiping his hand off on his shirt defeated the purpose of wiping the crud from his pants. Instead of getting cleaner, he managed to simply spread the filthiness around. Tank winked at Ruby and she smiled back.

"Did you see there was something taped to the back of the tablet?" asked Ruby.

"What do you mean?" inquired Tank, holding out the tablet to look.

"When we get outside and back to class," urged Ruby, "we can take a better look."

Tank, who was not well-known for his patience, examined the details of the tablet. The outline of the tablet was not a perfect square. The right side was a right degree angle and the left side was tapered inward toward the top. For a moment, it almost looked like a massive piece that would fit to the bottom left side of a gigantic triangle-shaped floor puzzle.

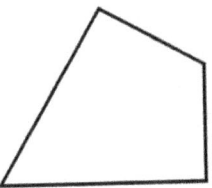

Even in the darkness of the cave, he could tell there was writing on the tablet, but it was impossible to know what was written given the cave's dimness. Attached to the back of the tablet with tape was an envelope tucked inside a plastic sandwich bag. Using his cleanest hand, Tank pulled the plastic bag off the tablet. The tape must have been old because it practically disintegrated with

73

little effort from pulling it. Tank yanked the bag off his shoulder and placed the tablet inside.

Using the one good buckle, he was able to secure the bag well enough to prevent the tablet from falling out again. Then he slung the bag back over his shoulder. In his hands, he held the plastic bag which contained the envelope. All they needed to do now was follow the sunlight to the exit, crawl out of the cave, and they would be on their way back to P.E. class. Ruby's phone had one percent battery remaining.

"Ruby, shine your light here for a second," gestured Tank.

"We don't have time right now," said Ruby. "There are only fifteen minutes left in P.E. class and we need to get back."

"This will take like two seconds," pleaded Tank. "Plus, we are not that far from the exit now anyway."

"Yeah," said Cage. "Let's see what is inside the envelope. Maybe it's money."

"Fine," said Ruby. "Then we sprint back before Mr. Jackson finds out we ditched class.

Cage moved closer and stood beside Tank as he attempted to open the plastic bag. Sunlight was helping them see, but Ruby's cellphone was still needed to see up close. The plastic sandwich bag, holding the envelope, was zipped closed and even with all of Tank's strength, he couldn't get it to open. Cage grabbed the plastic bag out of his hands and tried to pull the plastic locking mechanism apart. They were worried they might accidentally tear the envelope inside if they attempted to rip the bag open.

The exit was only a couple hundred feet away. Since they could see the exit in the distance and they could see the sunlight, Ruby calmed down about her phone getting ready to turn off. After all, even if the flashlight turned off, all they would need to do is follow the sunlight to get out.

"Hey, Cage," said Tank. "Can you grab the pocketknife out of the bag?"

"Yeah, bro," replied Cage, adjusting the buckle wide enough to reach inside.

The pocketknife appeared dark in color and had a brand logo that Tank did not recognize. Dad carried a red pocketknife that had multiple tools on it, but this one was more basic. The markings on this knife resembled a star with a

Spartan helmet in the middle. Shooting out of the star were eight bursts of light. The knife had a Greek or Latin inscription underneath.

The engraving said "Thárros." Being of Greek descent, Tank had seen the word before, but he had no clue what it meant. Cage held the knife in his left hand and pushed a small button on the side. Pressing the button released a spring inside the pocketknife and the blade flipped out. Ruby held up what was left of her dim flashlight, trying to help them see better.

"Dude," exclaimed Cage, holding up the knife. "Remind me to ask for a pocketknife like this for Christmas."

"You hold the bag and I'll cut it open," said Tank, putting his hand out for Cage to hand him the knife.

"No," replied Cage. "How about you hold the bag and I will cut it open?"

"Someone cut open the plastic bag, please!" shouted Ruby.

"Because I am much stronger, I guess I will hold the bag," teased Tank, holding it up towards Cage.

Cage sighed and pointed the blade of the knife towards Tank. Tank held the plastic bag with both hands making sure his fingers were far enough out of the way. He made a mental note that it's never wise to insult someone if they are holding a sharp knife. Using the pocketknife, Cage easily sliced open the plastic bag ensuring that he did not cut the paper envelope inside.

Being careful not to litter, Tank crumpled the plastic bag and slipped the trash inside his back pocket. On the exterior of the envelope were small words written across the part where the top of the envelope sticks to the bottom of the envelope. Across the seal was written the date, June 15th, 2005.

June 15, 2005

"That's the same year!" stated Ruby. "That is the same year and only a few months before one of those news articles we were reading earlier!"

"Oh yea," said Cage, "the one about NESA and the government coming to town to arrest someone."

"I don't think the government writes secret notes and leaves them to be found in caves," replied Tank.

Ruby paused for a moment and debated about telling Tank and Cage about what she had seen earlier. Before Tank had gone inside the cave, she had been trying to read the rusted sign at the entrance. When Tank crawled into the cave, she and Cage were so focused on finding him that she had forgotten to mention it. Now that Tank was holding an envelope dated 2005, it was time to share with them what the sign said outside the cave.

"Hey fellas," said Ruby. "Do you remember the sign outside the cave?"

"Yeah, the rusty one," replied Cage. "I didn't get a chance to look because I was wiping off leaves after falling on my butt."

"It didn't seem important at the time," said Ruby, "but the sign had NESA written at the bottom."

Tank, Ruby, and Cage warily looked at the envelope, discussing whether or not they should open it. The new information about the sign outside saying "NESA" left them on edge. The article did say that the person who NESA had spoken to was never seen again. What if the same happened to them? While they were discussing the sign and the letter, they were gradually meandering their way closer to the exit.

What was the worst that could happen to them by reading the letter? They were all a little too old to believe in fairy tales and it wasn't like opening an envelope was going to magically change their lives forever anyway. If a top-secret government agency was monitoring the cave, wouldn't they have busted in to arrest trespassers already? Tank used his thumb and inserted it underneath the side of the envelope, easily breaking the seal. Much to Cage's disappointment, there was no cash or gift card waiting inside the envelope.

The envelope contained a single piece of paper with a handwritten note. Ruby held the dim flashlight up close to the paper. It was impressive that the flashlight was still working at all by this point. The battery indicator was holding steady at one percent remaining. Ruby looked at the time on the cellphone. They only had ten minutes left of P.E. class. Cage pushed the blade of the pocketknife into the closed position and then shoved it back into the backpack which was still hanging from Tank's shoulders. Tank squinted his eyes and did his best to read the letter out loud.

> Dear Warrior,   2005
>
> If you are reading this message, then you found my bag. I couldn't risk bringing it with me as I suspect it would be confiscated. Despite my greatest efforts I was unable to return the Sacred Tablet of Rio de Monstros. We should have never taken it in the first place. On my last attempt to return it, several creatures followed me back and are now eating everything in the pond behind the school. Returning the tablet is the only way.
>
> Godspeed,
>
> Phoenix
>
> αολεμιστές τοα θάρρους

Ruby's battery light blinked once more, the phone vibrated, the flashlight turned off, and the power shutdown screen appeared. The shutdown process of the phone was surprisingly useful as the phone flashed bright colors, allowing a few extra seconds of light. Coincidentally, at the same time, a cloud must have rolled in front of the sun again because the entire cave grew darker.

Tank folded the letter, placed it back into the envelope and carefully stuffed the envelope into his front pocket. They didn't even have a chance to discuss what the letter meant or read it twice. The lack of sunlight coming from the entrance gave them all an uneasy feeling and collectively, they agreed that it was time to get out of there.

The power shutdown screen faded after flashing the cellphone company's logo a couple times, and then, the phone turned off. Ruby closed the purple cellphone case and tucked the phone into her back pocket. Sunlight was the only source of light now and it was considerably dimmer than it was before. Following the sunlight to the exit wasn't hard, but they had to tread carefully as the ground was still slippery. The exit was roughly fifty yards in front of them or about half the length of a football field away.

Something was wrong. The sunlight was shining through, but every couple of moments, the light kept getting slightly dimmer and they could hear a pounding sound echo throughout the cave. It sounded like a hammer hitting a piece of steel which sent goosebumps down their arms. The sound was terrifying! Looking towards the exit, they could see one of the wooden boards Tank had removed back in place across the front of the entrance. Tank remembered the steel spikes that were partially removed from the boards. They had looked like they may have been intentionally removed with a crowbar.

"Someone is closing the exit!" shouted Cage.

"Stop!" screamed Ruby. "There are people in here! Stop!"

Ruby and Cage were yelling so loudly, there was no way the person outside would not have been able to hear them. Tank wanted to join in, but he was trying hard to concentrate on the exit, hoping to identify the person committing the heinous act. Another wooden board was placed across the opening and they heard hammering again. When the hammering stopped, the noise changed to a scraping sound, like a shovel scooping up dirt.

When the scraping noise disappeared, the hammering would start up again. In the dim light, Tank could faintly see the forearms of someone and their hand holding a steel mallet. The hands and wrists of the person moving the boards appeared scrawny, but the overly powerful force of the hammer strikes suggested it was a sizable person casting the blows.

Tank started running towards the exit, but he only made it a few steps before falling to the ground. It was too slick to do anything but tread slowly. Another board was placed over the entry point and the sunlight faded again. They could barely see anything! The odd scraping noises began to make more sense now because simply hammering in the boards must not have been good enough. Whoever was out there made sure to use a shovel and tightly pack dirt against the boards, ensuring no sunlight was allowed into the cave. Once again, the hammer struck the steel spikes, locking another board into place.

"If the last board is hammered in," wailed Cage, "we'll be stuck in here."

"Keep walking," instructed Tank. "I need to get close enough to kick the boards out."

"Oh no!" sobbed Ruby. "The final board is being lifted up; he is getting ready to trap us in here!"

Seconds before the final board was placed securely on top and hammered in, the outline of a person's face appeared and two eyes looked in. The light was too dim to see their face and identify who it was, but they did notice an outline of a devious grin.

When it was obvious that the person had ill intentions, Tank's blood felt like it could boil. He lined up his body to face the boards. He was hopeful that by aligning himself with the exit, it would help them escape before the light was gone. The eyes vanished, the final wooden board was violently beaten into place, and dirt was packed on top.

Darkness spread through the cave. Not a single beam of sunlight seeped inside. They could hear whoever was responsible faintly laughing. An eerie silence filled the cave as the laughing suddenly stopped, indicating that the culprit had successfully completed their evil mission. Cage, Ruby, and Tank stood within a few feet of each other. Standing in complete darkness and with terror in their hearts, they stood there praying they might see daylight again.

Ten

A Beast in the Cave

Standing in a cave with no light is a unique experience. There is no sense of direction and every movement is nothing more than a guess. Anxiety punches you in the stomach. The first instinct is to scream, but screaming is pointless. Tank, Cage, and Ruby stood there in silence waiting for a miracle. Perhaps they were hoping this was only a practical joke and whoever boarded up the exit was simply playing around. Shocked and afraid, no one could find the words to speak.

Cage remembered that Ruby was standing close to his left side and he rapidly reached out to grab her shoulder. Feeling Cage's hand land on her shoulder caused Ruby to nearly jump out of her skin. Ruby attempted to move towards an out-of-reach Tank who was inching forward. Cage held onto Ruby's shoulder and followed her around as she swung her arms back and forth, trying to find the bag hanging on Tank's back. After several attempts, she finally touched the bag and hung on tightly as Tank led the way.

Their eyes started to adjust to the darkness, but only enough to see a few inches in front of their faces. The human eye is a remarkable part of the body. The pupil is designed to adapt in the darkness when there is no light. After a few minutes of meandering in complete darkness, Ruby could see the slight outline of Tank as he moved towards where he thought the exit was, but that was all she could see.

"Mr. Jackson has gone too far this time!" shouted Ruby, breaking the silence.

"You shouldn't have done it, Tank!" shouted Cage. "Why did you have to insult Ms. Sprinkle?"

"I don't think that was Mr. Jackson," replied Tank.

"Who else could it be?" questioned Ruby.

"Yeah," declared Cage. "Mr. Jackson said he wanted to bury you and trapping us in a cave underground is pretty much the same thing."

"Didn't you see the person's forearms?" asked Tank. "There was no tattoo and that means it couldn't have been Mr. Jackson."

Arguing about who trapped them in the cave was a moot point anyway. Getting out of the cave was priority number one. Priority number two was calling the police as soon as they safely got out to report attempted murders. Tank explained that he marked the exit in his mind before the final board was hammered into place. All they needed to do was walk in a straight line and everything should be okay or at least that was Tank's hope.

All sense of direction was lost and Tank couldn't tell if they were moving in a straight line or not. It was nice that Ruby was holding onto him, but she kept stumbling. Her sudden jolts caused Tank to slip several times and this made it difficult to move, in general. Tank tried to comfort his friends by reminding them multiple times that he lined up his body with the exit before it went dark. Even though deep inside his heart there was fear, he had to force himself to remain calm. Tank closed his eyes to concentrate as he tried to walk a straight line while also trying to zone out Ruby and Cage who were chattering about Mr. Jackson being an evil man.

Tank was getting irritated at the constant bickering and tried to interject insight into the conversation telling them that it was likely two people outside. Logically, it couldn't have been a lone suspect because two hands were visible holding the board at the same time as the hammering. Also, another board was added while the shoveling occurred. It was feasible that even if it was Mr. Jackson, there was an accomplice, as well. Despite his efforts, Tank's suggestion was ignored as Cage and Ruby were certain this was all Mr. Jackson's heinous plan to kill them.

They were still holding onto each other, moving cautiously, and trying not to slip. Without any prompting, Tank took the lead. It took them a few minutes, but they finally reached the place where Tank thought the wooden boards were located. Using both hands, Tank reached down and felt around trying to locate the spot where the bumpy cave-wall surface changed to smooth wood. Getting inside the cave required them to crawl before they could stand up again. This meant that the wooden boards would be closer to the ground.

Whoever trapped them in the cave must have known what they were doing because shoveling dirt against the exit prevented any light from coming in. In addition, the dirt must have filled in the gaps between the wooden boards, making it exponentially harder to feel the contrast in textures. Cage held on tightly to Ruby's shoulder as she continued to securely grip the bag hanging from Tank's back.

Forming a semi-straight line with their bodies, they used their free hands to feel around on the interior cave wall. If they found the boards, there was a good chance they could kick their way to freedom. Yes, long steel spikes were hammered into the hill holding the boards, but technically, they were only anchored into dirt. There was no way that Tank's strong legs wouldn't be able to kick them out. The only thing standing between freedom and imprisonment was a scavenger hunt to find the wooden boards.

No luck. They must have walked at least forty feet to both the left and the right, trying to feel their way to the exit. Walking near the wall of the cave was dangerous and tricky. The ceiling was significantly shorter near the exit, forcing them to duck down at times. Also, the interior cave walls were covered with random shards of protruding sharp rocks and the ground was still incredibly slick with sludge. Every step posed a risk of them falling and getting hurt. A serious injury down here could be fatal without emergency help available.

Tank's initial surge of adrenaline, mixed with panic, evolved into concentration. Confidence that they would quickly find the exit was starting to dwindle, but overall, he remained optimistic. His eyes were adjusting a little more to the darkness and it was only a matter of time until the boards covering the exit were found. All they needed to do was stay calm and keep searching. Tank was anticipating that the culprit responsible was still hanging around outside waiting. If this was truly attempted murder, then it was important to be prepared to fight when they got out. In his head, Tank imagined Dad showing up and giving the perpetrator a good beatdown.

Silence once again took the place of their conversation. All the bickering about who was responsible faded away. Perhaps the best they could do now was wait and hope, hope that someone would come looking for them. With any luck, the rescuers would bring a K-9 unit to smell their trail leading into the cave.

Cage let go of Ruby's shoulder and plopped down on the gross cave floor. Instead of encouraging him to stand up, Ruby and Tank sat next to him to rest for a moment. Getting off their feet felt great even though it required them to sit in the nasty muck. A bizarre sound prompted Ruby to break the silence. It sounded like a cross between a bathtub draining and a leaky faucet.

"Is someone crying?" asked Ruby.

"I'm not crying," asserted Cage.

"Soldiers never cry," joked Tank.

"It sounds like someone is crying," insisted Ruby, in a serious voice.

"I hear it, too," added Cage. "It's an odd gurgling sound."

"It sounds like an echo of water flowing," observed Tank, "but it must be far away!"

"Why didn't we hear it before?" asked Ruby.

"Maybe it started raining outside," replied Cage. "There were dark clouds in the sky when we got to P.E. class."

Struggling to sit still, Tank jumped to his feet to start searching again. Ruby and Cage remained seated cross-legged on the ground. The only chance of finding the exit was to carefully check along the walls of the cave, but at this rate, who could predict how much longer it would take? Ruby felt something brush her hairline and scolded Tank for playing around. Regardless of how much she liked him, this was no time to try and flirt with each other. Tank was busy trying to find the exit and was not messing around. Flirting with Ruby, though, would have been more fun than traipsing through a nasty cave.

Every two seconds, Tank noticed Ruby waving her arms around as if she were trying to swat a bug. Something must have startled Cage because his body suddenly jolted sideways. A loud screech came from one of them, but Tank was not sure if it was Ruby or Cage who made the sound. Tank, now standing fifteen feet or so away, kept reminding them that everything was going to be okay. All they needed to do was keep calm. Losing their minds, swatting at imaginary bugs, or flailing in panic was not going to help them get out of the cave.

Squeaking sounds echoed off the walls of the cave and a strong odor filled the area, leaving a chemical smell on their taste buds. The noises would last for a couple of seconds, then stop, start again, and stop. Tank recognized the smell of the odor. It was ammonia. Mom would use a cleaner that smelled like it to clean the bathroom floors when they lived in Texas.

Speaking of Mom, Tank kept wondering how she was doing and he regretted breaking the promise he had made when she dropped him off at school. He should never have led Ruby and Cage to the pond. Curiosity not only had gotten the best of him, but it also may have been the last of him.

Ruby and Cage were freaking out. The squeaking noises, smell, and the fact they were stuck in a cave started to drive them mad. Tank closed his eyes and tried to focus on all the lessons Dad had taught him.

A few years ago, during late winter when Dad and Tank were fishing, Tank, had fallen into the Raccoon River and was swept away in the frigid water. The only factor that saved him from drowning was a tree that had partially fallen into the river. Tank was barely able to hold onto the branches long enough before Dad had crawled on top of the fallen tree to pull him back to safety. The whole time, Dad had shown zero emotion and remained calm.

Once Tank was pulled from the rushing water, hurried to the nearest hospital, and treated for hypothermia, he asked Dad how he was able to remain cool in such a scary situation. Dad had explained that staying calm ensured that Tank did not panic. In addition, worrying about the outcome would not help make the situation better. Dad also said that "On the inside, it's perfectly fine to be terrified, but real leaders can keep it together even in the worst circumstances." Tank needed to try and do the same for his friends now.

The situation was tense. Ruby and Cage had gone from peacefully sitting down to aggressively laying on their stomachs covering their heads. One of Tank's gifts, other than being athletic, attractive, and a relatively good line dancer, was his ability to use humor to deescalate bad situations. Tank was the one who wanted to see the pond. He was also the one who had lifted the fence. He was the one who wanted to wander off into the woods and crawl into the entrance to the cave first. This entire predicament was his fault and he needed to step up and show leadership to get them out.

"Cage, that stinks man," said Tank. "I have heard of silent and deadly, but not squeaky and lethal."

"That wasn't me, bro," replied Cage slightly lifting his head.

"Ruby?" asked Tank, "What do you have to say for yourself?"

"Oh no," replied Ruby. "Girls don't do that."

Ruby laughed and Cage chuckled a little bit. It felt good to hear laughter and Tank made a few more fart jokes until they both were laughing. Some people say that toilet humor is the lowest form of comedy, but in a pinch, nothing works better to get people to smile. Sometimes cutting loose with fart jokes is the best recipe to dump a bad attitude. Wiping away your frown and flushing down your worries always works. Even when panic gives you the runs, you must plunge your mind of negative thinking. Stinking thinking should never clog the soul. Okay, enough with the puns.

Cage and Ruby were laughing as Tank rambled on with several jokes. They were laughing so hard they had all but forgotten that someone had trapped them in a cave and left them to die. It was hard to tell how much time had passed since they had left class. Ruby had been using her cellphone to keep an eye on the time, but now that wasn't helping either.

In the darkness of the cave, it felt like time didn't exist at all. Surely, someone would come looking for them. Then again, if Mr. Jackson, which Tank was still skeptical about, was responsible for trapping them, then he probably wouldn't go out of his way to help find them. Ugh, the smell of ammonia had grown even stronger and the squeaking noises came back. The laughing abruptly stopped.

"Ouch!" screamed Ruby. "Something just bit me!"

Tank stopped laughing, but it took Cage a few moments to stop chuckling. Neither Cage nor Tank realized that Ruby was being serious. At first, Tank wondered if Ruby had a weird sense of humor and maybe he was being rude for not laughing. What could possibly have bitten her? They were in a cave and it's true that bats do live in caves, but it's not like vampire bats lived in Kentucky.

The squeaking noises and ammonia smell were a dead giveaway that bats were living in the cave, but they were not physically capable of hurting them, right? Ever since they first started hearing the noises, Tank figured it was bats, but he refrained from saying anything because he didn't want to frighten anyone.

"Get them off me!" roared Cage. "They are biting at my ears."

"What are you talking about?" asked Tank. "Nothing is biting you."

"I think I am bleeding," moaned Ruby.

Tank could see the outline of Ruby holding up her hand, but in the dark, it was difficult to see any blood. He wanted to scold Ruby and Cage for making stuff up. It was one thing to try and swat imaginary bugs, but pretending that animals were biting you was different. Hopefully, Cage and Ruby were not taking a pit stop in fantasyland. Being stuck in this smelly cave was bad enough, but being trapped with two cray-cray people was only going to make escaping harder. A brush of air passed by Tank's face, tickling his chin and the smell of ammonia grew strong enough that he felt like throwing up.

"What was that?" yelled Tank. "Did one of you just wave your hand in front of my face?"

Fear swept through Tank's body when he grasped the reality of the situation. Cage and Ruby were not losing their minds at all. They were rolling on the ground using their hands to cover their heads. Tank was standing there watching the outline of their bodies flail around when he felt a sharp pinch on the back of his neck. Using his right hand, Tank felt the back of his collar where his t-shirt met his skin.

A warm liquid was dripping down the back of his shirt. Tank took a deep breath and tried hard not to panic. There had to be a logical explanation for the blood. It must have been a sharp rock hanging from the walls of the cave had scratched him. The sound of flapping wings echoed throughout the cave, wafting the horrid smell into his nostrils.

"Get up!" ordered Tank. "We need to move away from here!"

"Where do we go?" screamed Ruby. "All we can see is darkness!"

"We must have walked too far," replied Tank. "I don't know how or why, but these bats are biting us."

Cage jumped to his feet. Tank reached down and grabbed Ruby's hand. Even in this bone chilling situation, holding Ruby's hand made him feel warm inside. With great difficulty, the three tried to run away. The ground was so slick that they were falling down every other step while scraping their knees over and over. Their eyes had adjusted to the dark enough so they could see a couple of feet in front of their faces, but going any further resulted in total darkness all around them.

The sound of wings flapping followed their every step and the feeling of jagged little claws touching their shoulders spiked their adrenaline. Into the darkness, they hastily ran. Tank ran in front, holding Ruby's hand the whole time. Oddly enough, without the sound of Tank's dog tags jingling and the outline of the backpack bouncing up and down, Cage wouldn't have been able to follow without getting lost.

The further they ran into the expanse of the cave, the more they noticed the ground start to change. Fortunately, the slick wet clay was starting to feel a bit rocky and this made running much easier. Whatever was biting them seemed to be gone, too. The cave was quiet again, but they kept running in fear that the squeaking sound and smell would return.

Out of exhaustion, they stopped running all together and tried to catch their breath. Even Tank was hunched over from sprinting. Peace of mind didn't last long as Cage thought he heard another squeaking noise and collectively they took off running again. Tank darted ahead, followed by Ruby, and then Cage.

At least a mile away in the distance, they could see the subtle hint of daylight coming into the cave. The sunlight was obscured due to what looked like a mist of water falling from the top of the cave. For the first time in what seemed like an eternity, they had hope of surviving.

Earlier, they had heard water flowing and now the sound was more prominent than before. The ground was solid rock and they ran at a fast pace towards the light. Daylight meant there had to be a second exit to the cave. With any luck, the exit would not be too far from the school and they could easily walk back. Ruby was excited to get out and find a phone. That way she could call the police and report Mr. Jackson for attempted murder.

"Hallelujah!" cried Cage. "We're going to make it!"

"Keep moving!" urged Tank, as he picked up the pace.

"I can't wait to change my clothes." Ruby let go of Tank's hand.

"Hey, do you all want to sing a cadence?" joked Tank.

The smooth rocky ground felt great for running compared to the ice rink feeling back on the smooth clay. Once again, the ground changed and Tank could feel warm water seeping into his shoes. The water was only ankle deep and it reminded him of the creek they stomped in right before crossing the fence near the pond. When Ruby noticed the water, she slowed down as Cage easily passed her, splashing water into the air. Tank noticed he was a little too far ahead and slowed down to a light shuffle allowing both to catch up.

"Hey, y'all," said Tank, turning around. "This must be the other side of the creek."

"Thank goodness!" Ruby lifted her feet out of the water as she tried to avoid excess splashing.

Cage remained silent and was trying hard to breathe without needing to pull out his inhaler. Apparently, his asthma was not a major health concern these days as it had been years since he had a serious attack, but Tank did worry about him running too much. Tank told them that he was going to run ahead and see where the creek came out. Ruby began walking and Cage paused in place until she caught up and then he walked, too. Their steps were slow and purposeful as the water continued to rise.

Tank picked up the pace as he sloshed water all over his cargo pant legs. At first, the water was near his ankles. Now, he was splashing in knee-deep water. Obviously, the creek at this end of the pond was different from the creek they had followed to get to the pond. But who cared, they were close to getting out of the cave and that was all that mattered. A few moments ago, they had been running for their lives, dodging bats who were nipping at their every move and the glimmer of light in the distance had meant they were safe again.

"Watch your step!" yelled Tank, over his shoulder. "The water is getting deeper here."

"Can we stop and talk about this?" asked Ruby. "Where are we?"

Even Tank was struggling to effectively move in the water as it had risen to waist level. Ruby's question was terrific, but it was going to have to wait. The deeper the water got, the more they could feel a current pulling them towards the daylight.

Another puzzling observation Tank had noticed was the amount of humidity in the cave. Under normal circumstances, Tank would work up a slight sweat during a workout, but sweat was literally pouring from his head and creating a ring around his collar.

The nice part was that the closer they got to the light, the more they could see their surroundings. The water extended far and wide and they could see rocks forming a shoreline along the sides of the creek. It would have been possible to get to the edge and walk along the banks, but Tank kept this idea to himself. Tank didn't think Ruby and Cage would be strong enough to get to the side of the creek with the current growing stronger. The best option was to keep going straight.

Ruby and Cage were wading into the deeper water. Tank stopped in place and waited for them to catch up. The increased daylight also made it possible to see each other. The silver lining with the water being deeper was that their clothes were getting a good wash. They were not too far from the exit now, maybe a thousand feet or so. Tank stood there patiently and waved his arm in the air, signaling for them to catch up.

When they finally caught up with Tank, they held onto each other again as they kept moving towards the daylight. The water was getting deeper with every step. Cage was on his tippy toes and Tank and Ruby could no longer touch the bottom. As the current grew stronger, they were unable to hold onto each other. Tank was pulled to the left, Ruby was pulled to the right, and Cage lost his footing and was pulled under the water.

"Swim towards the light!" shouted Tank.

"Do you see Cage?" Ruby strained her eyes scanning the top of the water.

"He went underwater," panicked Tank. "I am going to save..."

As Tank finished his sentence, it was a relief when Cage's head came back to the surface. In his mind, Tank was getting prepared to dive under the water to try and find him. He was worried that Cage was sucked to the bottom and drowning.

Cage adjusted his glasses, which had amazingly stayed on his face after being dragged under the water. Ruby held her thumb above the water, gesturing to Tank that she was okay. Thoughts of getting out of the cave gave them hope. The sunlight was bright enough now they could see better.

The creek was about seven feet deep and the sound of running water was incredibly loud. It reminded Tank of a rapid-river-water ride at an amusement park except they didn't have a round rubber raft for protection. Tank was treading water and letting the current pull him towards the light. It was not that he couldn't swim; in fact, he was a fantastic swimmer, but he was way more worried about his friends than he was getting to safety.

Tank still had Phoenix's bag on his back which made it more difficult for him to swim. Suddenly, something unusual caught his eye as he glanced towards the far-right bank of the creek. A lone shadow was moving towards the water, but it was too far away to tell for sure what it was.

Ruby was doing a good job keeping her head above the water. Cage was struggling to not go under again. The exit couldn't be more than five hundred feet away. Small ripples appeared on the surface of the water which moved in Ruby's direction. Tank bobbed his body up and down. He would sink to the bottom, kick off, and then thrust himself upward to see better. Unfortunately, Ruby was so far away that she could not hear Tank yelling at her to swim away! Cage was oblivious and was flailing around in the water as he tried to stay afloat.

On the fourth time Tank bobbed up, he could see the tail of an eerie beast lurking across the top of the water. It had piercing eyes on the top of its head that sparkled in the sunlight. Black armored plating stretched down its back and it had dozens of long, pointed teeth around the head. The beast looked big from a distance, but it was hard to tell its actual size.

Ruby looked over her shoulder and saw the creature swimming towards her. She screamed and Cage looked over to see what was happening. This didn't make any sense! Tank was gazing upon an alligator-looking animal, but they were in northern Kentucky! There was no reptile like this living within eight hundred miles of here! Unfortunately, all of Tank's questions were going to have to wait. Right now, the only important thing was getting Cage and Ruby to safety.

Instinct kicked in and Tank jumped out of the water, splashing his arms, and making obnoxious crying noises. Ruby was going into shock as she furiously treaded water, barely keeping her head out of the water. Tank was pretending to be an animal struggling in the water and it was working! The beast's attention turned towards him as it rapidly swam in Tank's direction.

Tank could see the creature pass Ruby without noticing her. Cage was within yelling distance and Tank yelled at him to stay calm and stop splashing in the water. The beast ignored Cage, too. It was clear that Tank's diversion was working well. The only problem with his plan was that the beast was headed over to eat him!

"Try to swim over to Ruby," yelled Tank to Cage.

"I'll try!" bellowed Cage.

Adrenaline must have kicked in because Cage rocketed across the water towards Ruby like he was an elite swimmer. Tank was worried that Cage kicking in the water and making such a disturbance would trigger the beast to turn around. Tank continued to splash around in the water as the beast sank below the surface, holding its eyes just above the water to focus in on Tank.

Cage swam surprisingly fast and was already a few feet away from Ruby. Together, they treaded water as the current continued to pull them towards the light. Both turned their heads and tried to see Tank. Ruby was worried and she struggled not to scream.

The creek was much wider now and looked more like a river. The beast's body reemerged from the water and was only a few feet away from Tank. He could see Ruby and Cage's mouths moving like they were shouting something, but they were too far away. All he could hear were faint sounds coming from the distance.

"Watch out!" shouted Cage.

"It's going to eat you!" cried Ruby.

He had no choice. With the beast homing in on him, Tank was going to have to fight the beast and he had a plan! In Texas, he and Dad had gone fishing at this place called Three Rivers. One time, an alligator had sprung from the water and tried to bite him on the leg. Dad had explained that alligators do their hunting on the surface of the water. If Tank dove under the water and went to the bottom, then perhaps, he could surprise attack the beast. After all, struggling animals don't normally go under and lay on the bottom.

Bubbles rose to the surface as Tank plummeted to the bottom. Water splashed into the air as Tank kicked his feet on the way down. Ruby screamed again. She was positive the beast had just bitten Tank in half! Cage, on the other hand, made no sound and didn't move as if he were frozen in place. The splashing stopped. For Cage and Ruby, the sunlight and the exit of the cave were now only a couple feet away, but Tank was still hundreds of feet inside the cave!

The water was moving so fast that the source of the loud water crashing was obvious now to Cage and Ruby. Water was tumbling from hundreds of feet in the air, getting ready to smash them! They realized that they were at the bottom of a waterfall! Ruby and Cage were speechless. As they braced themselves for impact, they wondered if they would ever see their friend again.

Eleven
Mega-Waterfall
(Grande Cachoeira)

"Pain is fleeting, but triumph lasts for eternity." These were the words that dad would say when the chips were down and all hope was lost. Granted, most of the time dad was referring to a football game when he would mention this quote, but it was still a valid point. Tank laid on the bottom of the river and dug both hands into the mud. The current was strong, but his grip was strong enough to keep him in place.

Tank knew that trying to wrestle an alligator, crocodile, or whatever this thing was posed a serious health risk, but it didn't matter. All he could think about was doing whatever it took to keep this foul creature from going after his friends. Dad's voice played in his mind, "Nothing is impossible if we have the courage to fight for what we believe in." Under the murky water and with a predator lurking above, there was no room for second guessing the plan.

The average high schooler would have crumbled and broken in situations like this. Thank God, Tank was not an average high school kid. Tank was the son of Captain Thornstone and dad had taught him countless lessons over the years. For example, the trick to holding your breath for prolonged periods of time was to daydream and relax all the muscles in your body. Last summer, Tank was timed and was able to hold his breath for a little over two minutes.

Dad had not only taught Tank how to survive, but they frequently practiced survival skills together. Tank daydreamed about mom, too, and her soothing voice played in his head. She would sing weird rhymes around the house. He never thought those tunes would be lifesaving advice, but they made Tank smile. Rhymes such as, "If you want to make an alligator cry, then poke your fingers in its eye."

On the military base in Texas, Tank would listen to cadences the soldiers would sing as they ran five miles every morning. One of his favorites went like this, "If I should die in a combat zone, then box me up and ship me home." Wrestling a large reptile in muddy water was not exactly a combat zone, but Tank tried to think up a clever rhyme that he would be sure to share with mom if he made it home.

Waiting on the bottom for the beast to strike, he hummed the jingle, "If I should jump on this alligator's back, then I'll become a tasty snack." Tank laughed under water, causing bubbles to rise and break the surface.

Bubbles popping up on the top of the water triggered the beast to spin around to look hard for him. Daylight shining into the cave ahead penetrated the murky water and a dark shadow lurked above Tank's position. Waiting for the right moment to strike was essential. Tank laid patiently on the bottom and watched the large reptile swim back and forth. There was only going to be one chance.

It felt like forever, but it couldn't have been more than a minute since Tank had dived to the bottom. Letting go of the bottom, Tank put his right hand over the top of his left hand and pushed down to crack his knuckles. Popping his knuckles was a nervous twitch, but it also somehow relaxed him. He then rolled his neck back and forth a few times trying to loosen up. The current pulled him a few feet and he quickly dug his hands back into the muddy bottom to hold on.

Fear and worry resonated through Tank's mind and, for a couple moments, he wondered if he would ever get to see his mom and dad again. Tank wished he could tell dad one more time how much he appreciated him and tell mom she was an inspiration. The worst part about dying was not the dying part. It was the fact that mom and dad may never find him, especially if an alligator ate him. Love for his friends was the reason he had dived to the bottom and the reason why he must fight the beast. Thinking about Ruby and Cage getting to safety made him feel at peace with what needed to be done.

There were only two options when fighting a beast like this. The first option was to stick a hand down its throat while the creature was in the water. Push hard enough and far enough back, and in theory, water would flow into its lungs causing it to drown. Of course, the only problem with this strategy was that the person must put his arm in the creature's mouth with all the jagged teeth. If the person was willing to lose an arm, then it was not a bad plan, but Tank enjoyed having both arms.

The second option was to do exactly like mom said, which was funny considering it was a silly old nursery rhyme. Blinding the beast so it could no longer see allowed the person time to get away. Of course, getting poked in the eye was as fun for an alligator as it was for a human. If drowning the beast was off the table, then option two, taking out its eyes, was going to have to work.

The beast was still swimming back and forth above Tank's head. All he could see was its shadow. Tank got into strike position and counted down in his head. Rapid dominance was the name of the mission and it was time to make it happen. Ready, set, attack!

When the tail of the beast had fully passed again, Tank tucked his feet under his stomach and extended his legs like a frog jumping. Pushing off the bottom, he thrust his body up and out of the water as he came behind the beast. He grabbed the beast by the back legs and rapidly climbed on its back. Wrapping his legs around the rear portion of the beast, Tank clamped his thighs together with all his might. The beast attempted to turn around, snapped its mouth closed, then opened, then closed again. Hissing, roaring, and the sound of teeth gnashing together was louder than the water pouring down from what looked like a waterfall ahead.

The current was wicked strong and with the beast distracted and no longer swimming, the rush of water carried them both downstream. Tank held on and looked like a cowboy riding a bull at the rodeo. The beast was bucking, snarling, biting, hissing, and rolling, but Tank did not let go. He still needed to get closer to the head, but that was not going to happen until the beast calmed down a little bit.

Being on the back of the creature allowed Tank to see the unique features of the beast. Tank enjoyed watching nature shows on television and had a good eye for recognizing animals. It was only after crawling on top of the beast that identifying its species was possible.

The shape of the mouth, color of the body, and the size of the teeth indicated that this creature was a juvenile black caiman, which startled Tank a bit. The only conclusion he could come to was that this must be a rogue alligator that had swam up from Florida and was living in the Kentucky cave. Caimans, on the other hand, only lived in South America and they could never swim this far north. This was all wrong.

Knowing the particular animal species of the beast made a tactical difference. Alligators were relatively docile animals and were easy to scare. Tank had a little bit of experience with them from living in South Texas. Caimans though, especially black caimans, were a different monster. They were aggressive and it was common in the Amazon for them to eat people. Thank goodness this was not an adult and only about five feet long.

During their family trips to South America, Dad would warn him not to get too close to the riverside because of caimans. A cold shiver ran down Tank's spine as he wrestled to stay on top of the beast which was still violently thrashing in the water.

All crocodilians are cold-blooded and they run out of energy rather quickly. Tank rode on the beast's back for a while trying to wear it out and most importantly, stay out of its mouth. The current pushed them further downstream. Tank could see crashing water up ahead and it dawned on him that the creek was exiting the cave at the bottom of a waterfall. It all happened so fast. One moment, Tank and the beast were forty feet from the crashing water and the next second, the waterfall was right over their heads.

The waterfall was so powerful that both he and the beast were thrown several feet below the surface. Tank struggled to stay on top of the beast as it death rolled to throw him off. The bag they had found in the cave was still on Tank's back and fortunately, even with one buckle, it had remained closed. He could feel the tablet pressing against his back every time the beast did another death roll. The current was ridiculously strong now. When they rose to the top of the water, he and the caiman had already drifted far from the waterfall.

During the last death roll, water shot straight into Tank's nose and he struggled not to gag. The beast roared and snapped its mouth wildly back and forth. Driven mad with anger, the beast did another death roll. Only when the beast seemed to be running out of energy did Tank scoot forward while keeping his legs tightly clamped.

Tank successfully crawled towards the beast's head and was able to wrap his legs around its upper torso right behind its front legs. Looking down at the top of the beast's head, Tank paused for a moment and looked into its cold, dead red eyes. The targets were small, but Tank's aim was perfect. Using both fists, Tank plunged his hands into the beast's eyes, punching them multiple times.

The beast stopped thrashing for a few moments and swam towards the side of the river. As Tank and the beast moved farther away from the waterfall, the current became less aggressive. Tank vomited up water, which had started running into his lungs. It was a mixture of muddy brown water and green snot that came out of his mouth.

Tank's vomit splashed on top of the beast's head, which he thought was poetic justice. The beast had tried to kill him so being poked in the eye and puked on seemed well deserved. The beast swam towards the shallow water and Tank could feel the rocky bottom of the shoreline as the beast came to a sudden stop. The caiman was making yacking and whining sounds as if it were calling for its mother to assist in slaughtering Tank.

He needed to act quickly to make sure the mommy caiman did not hear her baby's plea for help. After catching his breath and wiping away the residual junk from his mouth, he realized that the exhausted beast had accidentally beached itself on the shore. Tank stood on the beast's back balancing like he was riding a surfboard. He picked up his right foot and crushed it downwards into the top of the beast's head, right between the eyes.

The beast thrashed wildly. Tank lifted his foot for the second time and crashed his heel between the eyes of the beast again. The beast tried to do another death roll but couldn't because Tank threw himself onto its back again like the famous crocodile wrestlers he had seen on T.V. This would never have worked on an adult caiman as Tank was barely able to overpower the juvenile.

The beast roared and hissed louder than ever. Tank noticed that the beast was bleeding from the eyes. One more kick and it was time to make his escape. Jumping to his feet again, Tank picked up his right foot higher as rage filled his heart. He lined up the final kick, but something stopped him. The beast was stunned and disoriented. It had finally stopped thrashing and was lying on the shoreline limp as a dishrag.

Wrath had lifted Tank's foot, but mercy and compassion caused him to gently lower it. The beast was defeated. After all, the caiman was only a teenager much like Tank. Who could blame the hungry caiman for acting like a hungry caiman? There was no need to end this majestic creature's life.

Tank took a deep breath, preparing to dive into the water again. He looked around as he tried to spot his friends. Standing on the back of the beast made it possible for him to see farther downstream. This was also the first opportunity Tank had to look back at the waterfall he had just crashed through.

The adrenaline rush of fighting a caiman left him feeling disoriented. The river had exited out of the side of a large mountain shaped like a horseshoe. Its size was incredible! Going from left to right, the river was approximately half a mile wide near the waterfall, but then narrowed after it passed the mountain.

A vivid memory sprang into Tank's brain. One spring, dad had been on a special assignment in New York State with a group of coalition forces. Dad was able to bring the whole family, and on that weekend, they had gone on a trip to Niagara Falls near the Canadian border. Compared to the waterfall Tank was seeing, Niagara Falls looked more like a cute splash pad. This was a real mega-waterfall. Tank snapped back to reality as he heard faint shouting in the distance.

Ruby and Cage had clung to a piece of floating driftwood. They had coasted farther downstream and they were still together, but Tank could not see them yet. Tank could hear voices screaming in the distance, but Ruby and Cage were nowhere to be found. Oh no! Was there a second beast out there eating them right now? Perhaps that is why the mommy caiman didn't respond because she was consuming his friends. Was Tank's attempt to save his friends all in vain? He was preparing to jump back into the water, but he decided to take one final look around.

Blood was dripping from the snout of the young beast and it was struggling to move. Tank said a quick prayer for the beast, hoping it would make a full recovery once they were far away. A little ways downstream, Tank could see a hand appear from the water, then another, and then another. Tank's joyful heart cartwheeled in his chest after seeing they were both okay. Ruby and Cage were gently floating down the river while yelling and waving their arms desperately to get his attention.

"Is Tank standing on the back of that thing?" asked Ruby incredulously.

"Holy moly!" cried Cage. "I think he is!"

"That's incredible! How did he do it?" Ruby was smiling from ear to ear.

Water splashed into the air as Tank jumped off the beast. In mid-air, he yelled "cannonball" like a little kid playing at the community pool as he jumped in. Ruby giggled. She was thrilled to see that Tank was okay! She let go of the driftwood and swam towards him against the current. Cage struggled, but he also started to swim.

Tank had been swimming underwater in their direction. With the help of the current, which was weaker than before, but still quite strong, it didn't take long until his head popped up a few feet from them. Treading water, Ruby and Cage were delighted to see their friend alive and well.

"Dude, that was raving mad!" declared Cage.

"You saved us!" exclaimed Ruby.

"Mom knew what she was talking about," joked Tank.

"What do you mean?" Ruby was confused at the comment.

"Oh nothing," smiled Tank. "I'll tell you about it later."

"Why would that beast be in a creek in Kentucky?" asked Cage.

"Bro, this is no creek. This is a river," said Tank. "I don't think we are in Kentucky anymore."

They were treading water and the current was pushing them farther down the river. The river was getting narrower. Ruby noticed that Tank was no longer smiling. He had a troubled look on his face, so she asked him what was wrong. A rumbling noise could be heard in the distance and Tank shared an important fact about waterfalls. Waterfalls are created when a river experiences a dramatic change in elevation, and those changes are typically followed by rapids.

"Oh man!" moaned Cage. "Rapids!" He shrieked!

The loudness of the river caused them greater anxiety. Tank tried to remain calm, but this worried him.

"What if it's another waterfall?" asked Ruby.

"It could be," replied Tank. "All I know is we need to get out of the water now!"

Cage and Ruby didn't need to be told twice to get out of the water. The current was pulling them much faster now and Tank's prediction of rapids was coming true. At best, the river was only forty feet from one side to the other and it was narrowing quickly. The rumbling noise of water sounded like a dishwasher on a heavy rinse cycle.

Getting out of the river was easier said than done. The shoreline to the left was much closer than the shoreline to the right. Tank was a strong enough swimmer that he knew swimming to shore could be done, but he was worried about his friends.

"We need to get to shore!" hollered Tank.

"I don't know if I can get to shore!" cried Ruby.

"Yes, you can!" Tank reached for the rope in the bag. "I will use the rope to help pull you to the shore."

"I think I can make it on my own." Cage puffed his inhaler, which was dripping water.

"Good stuff," smiled Tank. "I'll help Ruby and see you on the shore."

Cage and Tank fist bumped like they had done earlier in Ms. Sprinkle's class. Cage started swimming to shore. Tank, unable to get the rope out of the bag, pulled the bag off his shoulders. With great caution, and to ensure the tablet did not fall out, he snatched the rope from the bag. He tied a bowline knot around his belt and then tied a slipknot, wrapping it around Ruby's waist. Tank put the bag over his shoulders and swam with all his might towards the shore. Ruby, tethered to Tank, swam a few feet behind him. This was one of the worst days of her life, but she was glad Tank was here. Without him, it would have been much worse.

Swimming in the current felt like running a marathon... Left arm, right arm, kick, kick. Left arm, right arm, kick, kick. Tank reached the shore and used the rope to assist Ruby the last few feet. Along the banks of the river, there was only a few feet of rocky shoreline and then farther up the shore, it turned into an overgrowth of thick jungle.

Once Ruby was safely resting on shore, Tank sprang to his feet and looked for Cage. Standing there, he could see rapids forming not too far in the distance. A few moments later, Ruby also stood up and untied the knot from her waist.

"Cage! Where are you?" shouted Tank. "Cage, yell if you can hear my voice."

"I see him!" cried Ruby. "He's over there!"

Near the center of the river, Cage was perched on a boulder several hundred feet downstream. He had wrapped his arms around the boulder, but there was no way he could hold on for much longer. His eyes were filled with fear. The current must have been too strong for him to swim to shore. Tank still had the rope tied to his belt.

Beyond Cage's position, Ruby and Tank could see that the rapids were intensifying. Jagged rocks were sticking up from the river. The water near the rapids was not deep but had to be flowing at least fifty miles per hour. If Cage fell off the boulder, there was no way he would survive the rapids.

"I'm going to save him!" declared Tank. "But I will need your help."

"Anything," promised Ruby. "Just do it fast!"

"Follow me!" yelled Tank.

"Lead the way," replied Ruby.

Together, they sprinted down the shore, being careful not to fall into the raging water. The rope, which had been fastened to Ruby's waist, was dragging on the ground. As Tank ran, he pulled on the rope, looping it around his shoulder. Tank promptly found the end of the rope and started tying a lasso. Ruby was calling out to Cage, assuring him that everything would be okay. It didn't take long to reach Cage, but there were twenty feet of rapids standing between him and the shore.

"What's the plan?" asked Ruby, in a panicked voice.

"Have you ever seen an old western movie?" asked Tank, showing a quirky smile.

"Huh?" shuttered Ruby.

Stepping to where his feet were at the edge of the water, Tank leaned forward and swung the lasso over his head. The rope was swinging so fast that a whooshing sound could be heard even over the loudness of the water as it crashed over the rapids. All that was missing to make this the iconic moment from a Hollywood movie was Tank yelling, "Yee-hah!"

Tank threw the rope to Cage trying to get the lasso around his body, but it was a miss. He threw the rope again and Cage let go of the boulder with one arm as he desperately tried to catch the lasso which nearly caused him to fall into the raging rapids. Tank threw the lasso once more and it was a direct hit.

The lasso wrapped around Cage's neck and his right shoulder under the armpit. Tank pulled on the lasso, causing it to tighten securely.

"Hold on brother!" yelled Tank to Cage. "I got you."

"I can't hold on any longer!" shouted Cage.

Cage let go of the boulder and his body plummeted backwards into the rapids. The slack in the rope tightened and Tank was now playing tug of war against the current while Cage held on for dear life. With each pull, Cage moved a little closer to the shore. Something was wrong! Suddenly, Tank couldn't pull anymore.

A large rock was sticking out of the water and the rope had jammed underneath! This was not good. A tough decision had to be made. The only way to free the snag was to get back into the water and pull it free. Tank noticed that Cage had also lost his glasses in the rapids. Shoot!

"Follow the sound of my voice, buddy!" Tank declared to Cage. "He can't see us!" Tank exclaimed to Ruby.

"My glasses are for astigmatism!" yelled Cage. "I can still see you. My eyes have a hard time focusing when I read."

"He must have hit his head on a rock," explained Tank to Ruby. "He is making up big words because he is worried that we will judge him for not being able to see without his glasses."

Ruby shook her head at Tank's ignorance regarding how glasses worked, but whatever, she could explain it later. Tank instructed Ruby to dig her feet into the side of the shore as he handed her the rope. The rock causing the snag was supporting most of Cage's weight, making the rope feel artificially lighter than before. Tank's biggest fear was that the line would break from the sharp rock piercing it and then, "Adios, it was nice to know you, Cage" was a real possibility.

Tank quickly pulled out the pocketknife and took the bag off his shoulders. Using his left hand to hold the rope and his right hand to slice with the pocketknife, Tank cut the rope off his belt. Both of Ruby's arms were extended forward as she held onto the rope while Tank wrapped the rope around her waist and tied a knot.

"I need to pull the rope free," explained Tank, "and I can only do that if I get closer to where it's jammed.

"It's too dangerous!" cried Ruby.

"It's the only way to save him," said Tank. "When I yank the rope free, pull as hard as you can."

"Tank, wait!" shouted Ruby, putting her hand on his shoulder.

"Yes?" replied Tank.

"Be careful. I don't want to lose you again," said Ruby.

The rock snagging the rope sat approximately five feet out in the water, but going even one foot out in the water seemed like a death sentence. Tank took a few steps back from the water's edge before getting a running start. Poor Cage was still holding on for dear life. Tank jumped as far as possible and landed on a rock that hit him straight in the groin.

He yelled out, "Blue blazes, holy Toledo, mother manicotti, Ouch!" Crawling in pain along the top of the rocks, Tank was at the exact spot where the rope was stuck.

"Are you okay?" asked Ruby.

"Just peachy," replied Tank. "Once this is over, I am going to throw up again, though."

Tank gave a thumbs up to Ruby as he signaled for her to hold on tight. He reached into the water and pulled on the rope until it was unsnagged. Ruby pulled with all her might and hauled Cage to the edge of the shore. Cage held out his arm and Ruby heaved him up out of the water. Ruby looked back at Tank. He was still sitting on top of the rocks. She looked down to check on Cage and noticed he was struggling to breathe.

Cage reached into his front pocket and pulled out his inhaler. After taking a couple of puffs, Cage breathed normally again. Ruby could hear a faint splashing sound behind her. It was different from the sound of the rapids, but she figured it was Tank crawling on the rocks.

Ruby pulled the lasso off Cage and prepared herself to help Tank. She held the lasso in her hands and turned to the river, but Tank was no longer sitting on top of the rocks. He was gone! A cold shiver went down Ruby's spine. She stood on her tippy toes trying to find him in the river and thought she saw his shoes popping out of the water once, but that was it.

Cage stumbled to get on his feet, still trying to recover as he tucked the inhaler back into his pocket. Tears rolled down Ruby's face and Cage put his head down. Tank had survived the beast and saved Cage from the rapids, but now he was a victim of the river. The cruel sting of death had come for Tank and it pierced the hearts of Ruby and Cage.

Twelve
Rio de Monstros

Everybody deals with death differently and some better than others. Standing by the river, Ruby and Cage were alone. Their friend Tank was gone, crushed by the rapids and consumed by the river. Several minutes had crept by and they stood there in silence. Cage and Ruby were devastated. Occasionally, Ruby would look up as if she heard a voice wailing in the distance, but this was all her imagination and wishful thinking. Cage prayed under his breath for Tank as Ruby tucked her head into his shoulder trying not to weep.

"What do we do?" Ruby took a step back and untied the rope from her waist.

"I don't know," replied Cage. "We need to get back to school and explain what happened."

"School!" shouted Ruby. "Tank just died and you want to go back to school!"

"Calm down," said Cage.

"I'm scared!" cried Ruby. "We just crawled out of a river! And have you looked around lately? Where are we?"

Thick green jungle lined the outer shores of the river. Trees growing taller than one hundred feet towered over them, creating a dark shadow over everything. The river smelled like rotting fish guts. A slight breeze was blowing the mist from the rapids into the air and they could hear strange animal sounds coming from within the jungle.

Beads of sweat were starting to form on Ruby's hairline and Cage removed his already soaked hoodie. Under his hoodie, Cage was wearing a dark blue shirt with a red mixed-martial arts logo. The ridiculous humidity was causing him to feel dehydrated and nauseous. August in Kentucky was known for humidity so this was nothing out of the ordinary.

Ruby kept looking around and was rendered speechless at the incredible landscape. Right before Tank had bravely entered the water to unsnag the rope, he had taken off Phoenix's bag and dropped it to the ground. Cage walked over, picked up the bag by the broken buckle, turned it upside down, and shook it a few times. Water poured from the bag, forming a small puddle on the ground. Using the one good buckle, Tank had secured the bag by wrapping it around the top several times. When Cage yanked and shook the bag, he must have accidentally pulled on the buckle because all the contents within the bag fell to the ground.

"Why did you do that?" asked Ruby.

"I don't know," Cage frowned. "It seemed like a good idea at the time. I didn't think everything would fall out."

Ruby took a few steps closer and knelt to pick up the contents of the bag. The rope was laying on the ground and she tucked it back into the bag, rolling the rope around her elbow like a construction worker did with an extension cord. Cage squatted and grabbed the compass. As he did, he thought about the geography of Kentucky.

If the Ohio River was roughly fifteen miles northwest of the school, that would mean they would need to travel southeast to get back. Fortunately, there were a couple of small towns right off the river, and hopefully, they would have a chance to call their parents from there.

"We need to go that way," said Cage, pointing downstream. "Where is the pocketknife?"

"Tank put it in his pocket, and, oh my gosh!" shouted Ruby. "Are these real?"

"I doubt it," replied Cage, looking down at the shiny rocks. "Diamonds that big are worth millions of dollars. Why would they be in Phoenix's bag?"

"And the tablet," declared Ruby, pointing, "the engravings look like they are lined in solid gold."

"That's impossible," said Cage, urging Ruby to start walking. "Put that stuff back in the bag and let's get moving."

Ruby knew that Cage didn't know what he was talking about and Cage, likewise, knew that he didn't know what he was talking about. Ruby, however, complied and stuffed everything back in the bag anyway. She wrapped the strap and buckle around the bag like Tank had done earlier. Then, she put the bag on her back. They had been gone from school for at least two hours now and the sun was still high in the sky.

The town of Westport was right off the river and Cage was certain they were still in Kentucky. With a not-so-subtle nudge from Cage, they collectively agreed that Westport was their destination. The shoreline around the river was wide enough so they could walk together side by side. Every now and then, the shoreline would get so narrow they would have to tread carefully to keep from falling into the river. On the flip side, every now and then, the shoreline would get wide enough that an eighteen-wheeler truck, towing an alien spaceship, could have parked on it.

"I can't wait to see the look on Mr. Jackson's face when they arrest him for trapping us in that cave," said Cage. "He'll get attempted murder charges, for sure," he continued, listing out other likely criminal charges he remembered hearing from T.V. shows his parents watched.

"Don't you remember?" asked Ruby, still sobbing. "Tank said that he didn't think it was Mr. Jackson."

"I hope they use the stun gun on him," quipped Cage, still considering a punishment for Mr. Jackson.

Ruby laughed a little bit as she wiped her tear-stained face. Earlier, when they were trapped in the cave, Tank had used humor to help calm the situation. Cage tried his best to lighten the mood. He made his best impression of what Mr. Jackson would look like being stun-gunned and flopped around on the ground.

Ruby giggled at the sight of Cage pretending to be stun-gunned. She thought about Tank laughing, too, which caused her to tear up again. Even though they had only spent a little bit of time together, Tank's absence left an empty feeling in their hearts.

After they had walked for about an hour, Ruby and Cage noticed that the rapids had ceased. Walking along the shore of the river was creepy. The surface of the river was now calm and smooth. Birds they had never seen before were flying down and diving into the water. Every few minutes, large fish would spring out of the water and snatch one of the birds out of the air. The bird would flutter for a few moments and sink under the water as feathers and blood rose to the surface.

The darkness of the jungle was frightening too. Loud thudding sounds could be heard coming from beyond the tree line. Cage and Ruby figured out what was causing the scary noises when a tree crashed to the ground near them.

The river had more turns and twists in it than Cage was expecting. His dad would frequently take him to go fishing on the Ohio River by Louisville and it was interesting to see what the river looked like in the countryside. He kept thinking about Tank saying this was no longer Kentucky, but how could that be?

Cage excelled in math and calculated in his head the time they had spent in the cave and being stuck in the water. At max, they couldn't have traveled more than a few miles from school. Cage didn't know of any giant waterfalls in Kentucky either. In fact, he didn't know of any waterfalls like that in the United States at all! Perhaps Tank was right, but it didn't seem logical.

Up ahead, something moved on the shoreline. It was roughly six feet long and looked tan on one side and dark on the other. Ruby and Cage both froze in place. Ruby closed her eyes and held her breath, hoping it was only a figment of her imagination. Cage rose up on his tiptoes, trying to get a better look. Their greatest fear was sighting another alligator-monster-thing like the one that tried to attack them in the cave. Ruby opened her eyes one at a time, then suddenly tightened the straps on the bag and started sprinting down the shoreline towards the object.

"It's Tank!" shouted Ruby. "That's him!"

Cage raced down the shoreline, trying to catch up to Ruby. Tank's body must have washed up from the river. Ruby was smiling and laughing, but that instantly changed when she got within a few feet of his body. Tank was lying on his back, lifeless. Ruby used her index finger and checked to see if he had a pulse.

Three summers ago, she had taken a first aid class at the local community center before being allowed to help at her church's nursery. All she could remember from the class was mouth-to-mouth and chest compressions. Ruby did her best to assess the situation. Cage arrived a few moments later, out of breath, and was terrified when he saw Tank's comatose body.

"He must have drowned!" moaned Cage, in a somber voice.

"I can feel his heart slightly beating," exclaimed Ruby.

Ruby knelt, tilted Tank's head upwards, put her right hand under his neck, and then plugged his nose with her left hand. Cage stood there praying for his friend, but also checking around for danger that could be lurking from the forest and river. The sheer thought of another beast shooting out of the water terrified him and being eaten alive kept creeping into his mind.

Ruby leaned forward to begin mouth-to-mouth resuscitation. Her lips and Tank's lips connected as she blew air into his lungs. Tank's body fluttered a little bit at first, but then stopped. Ruby repeated mouth-to-mouth several times without any progress.

"I don't understand," said Ruby, standing up in frustration. "He has a heartbeat and I can feel his chest moving up and down."

"Hey," muttered Cage. "Where do you think all these footprints came from?"

The bottom of Tank's shoes were covered in mud and there were tracks leading from the water's edge into the jungle. He was also too far from the shoreline for the water to have pushed him there. Following the tracks, Ruby put her hands on her hips and let out a loud sigh. Cage stood there and looked down at Tank who was still laying there motionless. Maybe someone had pulled him out of the water and put him there.

"You should try mouth-to-mouth again," whispered a voice.

"I tried," yelled Ruby at Cage. "He must be in a coma or something."

"I didn't say anything!" exclaimed Cage.

"You told me to do mouth-to-mouth again," said Ruby.

"Wait a second. I have an idea," answered Cage, catching on to what was happening,

Cage turned his body around, away from Tank. Using his right hand, he bent down and took off his left shoe. Lifting his now shoeless foot off the ground, Cage brought his knee up to his stomach and then swung it back in the other direction like he was kicking open a door. Cage's foot struck Tank in the ribs. Tank groaned in a muffled voice and winced in pain, but overall, he remained motionless.

Ruby stood there with a puzzled look on her face. She couldn't tell if Cage was a genius for knowing some advanced first aid skill or if a demon had possessed him and he was simply kicking a wounded person for fun. Cage picked up his foot again and scooted a little closer to Tank, trying to get into a better position for what he audibly declared was "the kick of life" as he wore a sarcastic smile on his face.

"This time, instead of the ribs," asserted Cage, "I am gonna try for a headshot, but first I'll put my shoe back on."

"I'm alive! I'm alive!" shouted Tank, as he abruptly hopped to his feet.

"You jerk!" hollered Ruby. "We thought you were dead!"

"I'm sorry!" mumbled Tank. "I saw you all coming and I was simply going to jump up and scare you! But then you started kissing me."

"I wasn't kissing you!" replied a flustered Ruby. "I was trying to save your life!"

"Mission accomplished?" Tank humorously uttered as he raised his left eyebrow.

"Ugh... boys," sighed Ruby, relieved to see Tank alive and well.

"What happened man?" asked Cage. "You disappeared into the rapids."

"I know," replied Tank. "After I unsnagged the rope, I tried to swim back to the shore, but the rapids were too strong."

Tank went on and explained that the rapids pulled him down the river for what felt like an eternity. Pulling up his cargo pants and t-shirt, he showed them the many bruises he had endured from banging into the rocks. There was a gash above his left eye that looked like it had partially scabbed over.

Ruby and Cage also asked a couple of questions about the alligator from the cave, wondering if it may still be following them. Tank explained how he battled the raging monstrous beast like a heroic warrior and before it was over, the beast had begged for mercy.

The only downside to his altercation with the beast was that his dog tags had fallen off in the river. He lightheartedly laughed and declared that "He was willing to sacrifice his dog tags to save the day, of course!" Humility was not a talent Tank had fully developed, yet.

Ruby was furious. She crossed her arms and rolled her eyes the entire time Tank was speaking. She was glad he had survived, but pent-up frustration with him going into the cave, then having them think he was dead for over an hour, was causing anger to flood Ruby's mind.

Cage was listening intently to Tank's story of fighting the beast and tumbling down the rapids. All Cage needed was a soft couch, dim lights, and a bag of popcorn to make this the best story time ever.

"Why didn't you come find us?" yelled Ruby.

"I was going to," replied Tank, "but I was trying to figure out where we were first. I figured you all would keep walking down the river."

"We are heading down the river to the town of Westport," said Cage, trying to de-escalate the conversation.

"Yeah," said Ruby. "Thanks to your shenanigans, it's going to take us even longer to get there."

"Westport?" asked Tank. "Is that by chance in South America?"

"South America?" replied Ruby. "Why would you ask a stupid question like that?"

"Because that's where we are!" grinned Tank.

Ruby sighed again and started walking down the river shoreline. Cage wanted to stop and ask questions, but Ruby pulled on his arm, urging him to come along. As he looked back, Cage hoped that Tank was following them. Who did Tank think he was? First, he pretended to be unconscious so Ruby would kiss him and now he was making up a story about them being in South America!

Regardless of how heroic he was for fighting the beast in the cave, or his quick thinking to save Cage with a lasso, or how brave he was for going and exploring the jungle by himself, none of that mattered to Ruby. Even if it meant leaving Tank behind resulted in their impending doom, she was prepared to take that risk. Ruby was not having any more of this!

"Wait," said Tank. "I need to see the tablet."

"Why?" mocked Ruby, as she continued to dart ahead. "Will that teleport us to Africa?"

"No!" exclaimed Tank. "It will transport us to Mars. Then we will have to fight the intergalactic mercenaries of Jupiter."

"WHAT?" Cage was shocked by such a possibility.

"I'm kidding," laughed Tank. "If you want to survive, then let me see the tablet, please."

Ruby abruptly stopped walking. She was mad, but she was equally desperate to get home and she was willing to humor Tank a little. Dropping the bag off her shoulders and onto the ground, Ruby took a few steps back. Tank knelt, unbuckled the bag, and rummaged around until he found the tablet. At this point, the sun was hanging a little lower in the sky. If he had to guess, it was close to 1400 hours or two o'clock as a mere civilian would say.

Tank clenched the tablet between his armpit and chest, loosely re-buckled the bag, tossed the bag over his shoulder and started walking in the opposite direction of Ruby. He held the tablet out in front of his body with his arms fully extended. Cage followed closely behind, but Ruby scoffed and took a few steps back.

"Hey, Cage," whispered Tank. "Do you think Ruby is upset about the mouth-to-mouth kissing thing?"

"Just a little," said Cage, sarcastically. "What are you doing by the way?"

"That was my first kiss, bro. I hope my breath was okay," smiled Tank, as he looked towards Cage. "I am trying to put the tablet in direct sunlight."

"Why?" asked Cage.

"Because I wanted to kiss her," answered Tank, shocked by Cage's silly question.

"No!" exclaimed Cage. "Why are you trying to put the tablet in sunlight? Besides, I don't think that technically counts as a kiss! She looks like she wants to slap you!"

Tank took a couple more steps but couldn't seem to align the tablet with the sun. The jungle overhead was creating too much of a shade effect. To escape the shadow of the trees, they needed to get the tablet where the sun could illuminate it.

Tank knew what the answer was, but he wasn't sure Ruby would be willing to help. Honestly, it wasn't his intention to make her upset. Hopefully, she was willing to forgive him. Tank moseyed a few steps in her direction and prepared to apologize, but he never got the chance.

"That was despicable!" scolded Ruby, pointing her finger at Tank.

"I know, I'm sorry!" muttered Tank. "I wanted to kiss you since the moment I saw you getting off the bus today.

"You saw me getting off the bus?" asked Ruby.

"Yes!" replied Tank. "You are the most beautiful girl I have ever seen."

Ruby smiled and batted her eyelashes a couple of times. Oh no, the butterflies were flapping their wings in Tank's stomach again. Cage had grabbed the tablet from Tank and was attempting to find sunlight. He trekked up and down the shoreline and back towards where the jungle began, but no luck.

Cage then walked near the river and extended the tablet over the water. The reflection of the sunlight off the water lit up part of the tablet. Tank and Ruby were still actively chatting about what had happened earlier. After a few minutes of back-and-forth banter, Tank sincerely and humbly asked Ruby for forgiveness.

"I forgive you," said Ruby, with a smile. "I still think you are a jerk."

"That's fair enough," laughed Tank. "Now I need you to get on my shoulders."

"Wait, what?" asked Ruby, with a confused look.

"We need to get the tablet in direct sunlight so we can read the engravings," explained Tank.

The plan was weird, but Ruby played along. Tank knelt next to Ruby and heaved her up onto his shoulders. Carefully, Tank leaned out over the water's edge while Cage held onto his belt to keep he and Ruby from falling into the water. Ruby held the tablet out a little bit, but she struggled to keep her balance on Tank's shoulders. Half of the tablet lit up and sparkled in the sunlight.

"You need to hold the tablet out farther," said Cage.

"Extend your arms," ordered Tank.

"This is not as easy as it looks, fellas," cried Ruby. "I'm trying!"

Ruby was able to extend her arms enough so more of the tablet became illuminated. Tank pushed up with his calves and was balancing on his tiptoes as Ruby continued to reach upwards. Finally, the entire tablet could be seen. The tablet was magnificent!

The top layer of the tablet was plated in solid gold. Up until this point they thought the tablet was made of wood, but now they could see the body of the tablet was a piece of dark marble stone. Tank asked Ruby to read the golden engravings on the tablet so they could hopefully figure out how to get home.

"It's all in different languages," stated Ruby.

"I think some of it is Portuguese," said Tank. "Try your best to read it."

"Okay, I think it is a map of some kind," said Ruby.

"Maps are good," added Cage. "Does it tell us how to get out of this place?"

"I see what looks like a waterfall and it says Grande Cachoeira," explained Ruby. "On the river, it says Rio de Monstros. I don't know... it's a big area and the places all look small. It is hard to tell what is what!"

"Is that it?" asked Tank.

"No, there is a bunch of stuff on here," said Ruby. "I don't see anything that will help us."

"Okay," groaned Tank. "Let's get you down. Holding you up at this angle is killing my neck."

"Wait," commanded Ruby. "There are two deep craters in the tablet. One crater is bigger than the other."

The craters, per Ruby's description, looked like medium-sized holes in the surface of the tablet, but they were only surface deep because the back of the tablet was smooth. Cage recalled the two rocks from earlier that Ruby said were diamonds when he "inadvertently" dumped everything on the ground. He wondered if the rocks were part of the tablet and maybe had fallen off.

Tank had Phoenix's bag on his back and Cage determinedly reached inside. The force of Cage digging through the bag nearly caused Tank to fall over. Tank was confused as to why he was foraging through the contents of the bag as, up to this point, he was not fully aware of the significance of the mystery rocks.

Hopefully, Cage was not searching for the pocketknife. They had not had anything for lunch and Cage had mentioned a couple of times that he was hungry. Cage didn't seem like the cannibal type who would randomly murder someone so he could eat them, but a lot of strange events had already happened today.

"Try these shiny diamond-looking things in the craters," said Cage, holding up the two rocks.

"Oh, diamonds," replied Ruby, smirking. "I remember earlier someone saying they were absolutely and positively not real diamonds."

"I am guessing this is an inside joke?" asked Tank.

"Yeah," laughed Ruby. "An inside joke where the punchline is that Cage was wrong."

Cage reached up and handed Ruby the rocks he presumed to be diamonds. Tank, trying to win brownie points, made clear that he was one million percent on Ruby's side. These were diamonds, for sure. Tank went on to suggest that anyone who didn't think they were diamonds was out of their "blue blazing mind" and that Ruby was by far the smartest person he had ever met who had an intuition for solving the most complex mysteries of the universe. Ruby grinned at the over-the-top attempt by Tank to flatter her.

"Suck up," murmured Cage, as he pretended to cough.

The first diamond was roughly the size of a bottle cap and was about one fourth the size of the second diamond. When the first diamond was placed over the top of the tablet, it locked into place as Ruby exerted a little pressure. There was also a small burst of light around the area where the diamond fit into place, which both Cage and Tank noticed reflecting off the water. The second diamond was placed into the top of the larger crater, but it would not fit like the first diamond.

"This isn't working," said Ruby. "The second diamond doesn't fit."

"What about the first diamond?" asked Cage. "Why did the light shine brighter?"

"I don't know!" shouted Ruby. "The place where the first diamond is now says *Templo da Yacumama Serpente*. Also, on the bottom of the tablet a new word has emerged. It says *Zurvan*."

The earth started to shake, causing Ruby to fall off Tank's shoulders. Cage held onto Tank's belt tightly and they all tumbled backwards to the ground. Ruby dropped the tablet as she held a firm grip on the second diamond. The tablet shook uncontrollably on the ground.

As Ruby held the second diamond, it started to get warm to the touch. She loosened her grip as the heat from the diamond was too much for her palm to handle. The diamond in her hand broke free and shot like lightning into the tablet.

In a moment, the earthquake stopped. The tablet also stopped shaking. An intense light sprang forth from the tablet. Ruby, Tank, and Cage swiftly crawled away, worrying that the tablet was going to explode. As quickly as the light appeared, it vanished. Ruby and Cage both turned and looked towards the tablet.

Coming to his knees, Tank motioned the military command for "stop" by putting his fist up in the air. He wanted Ruby and Cage to stay in place while he took a closer look. Standing up, Tank took a few steps towards the tablet.

Instead of picking up the tablet, Tank stood over it and looked down. In the commotion of getting away from the tablet, they had moved close to the tree line. Shade from the foliage was covering the tablet, but the gold on the tablet was shining bright even without the help of the sun.

Several new inscriptions appeared on the tablet that seemed to have been activated by the second diamond. Also, whatever Ruby said after putting the first diamond in place had created an earthquake.

"Hey, Ruby," said Tank, looking over his shoulder. "What did you say right before we all fell down?"

"I think it was *Templo da* something," replied Ruby.

"Yacumama Serpente?" inquired Tank.

"That's what it said on the cave walls," shouted Cage, "right next to the giant green snake's head."

"You don't think it's real, do you?" asked Ruby.

Tank didn't answer. He picked up the tablet, cradled it in his arms, and studied the inscriptions. Ruby and Cage were on the breaking point of panic again. The tablet seemed to shine brighter as it was held towards one part of the jungle and dimmer when pointed in other directions. One of the new inscriptions was larger and shined so bright that Tank could not look at it without squinting his eyes. Ruby and Cage moved towards the tablet, trying to get a better look.

"Does that say O *Dourado*?" asked Cage.

"What does O Dourado mean?" asked Ruby. "Is it Spanish for safe passage back home?"

"No, I don't think it's Spanish," replied Tank. "It sounds like you are saying El Dorado... you know, the mythical city made of solid gold in the Amazon."

"Dude, we may have a map to a city made of gold!" joked Cage, fist bumping Tank. "We're gonna be rich, bro!"

116

Tank handed Ruby the tablet. He and Cage were busy high fiving, fist bumping, chest bumping, and dancing. Ruby, on the other hand, was searching the tablet to figure out how to get home. It wasn't like she was upset at the idea of finding the City of Gold, but who cared about riches when you were stuck in the jungle? She studied the map for several minutes, but it was difficult to understand the words.

Across the tablet, there were too many inscriptions to count. The majority was written in what appeared to be Spanish or Portuguese, while some were nothing more than random symbols and markings. There were at least six different languages used on the tablet. It didn't make any sense.

"What does *Rio de Monstros* mean?" asked Ruby.

"The word Rio means *river* in Spanish," said Cage. "I think Portuguese and Spanish are similar."

"*Monstros* sounds like the word MONSTER," said Tank.

"River of Monsters!" shrieked Ruby. "Why would anyone name a river *that*?"

"Because of THAT!" Tank swallowed hard, crouched down, and pointed.

Ruby stood still and watched as Cage dashed towards the jungle. Ruby shouted and instructed Cage to stop! He froze in place mid-stride.

A new threat stood on four paws with claws large enough to cut to the bone. Large teeth bulged from its mouth and its tongue was licking its lips. They heard growling and were about to find out why it was called the River of Monsters!

Thirteen
Jaguars Don't Swim!

"Everybody stay calm," instructed Tank.

"Okay," whimpered Cage. "I'll try."

"It can't see us if we stay still and don't move," said Tank. "Cats have poor vision and rely on movement to hunt."

"That was in a movie about dinosaurs," exclaimed Ruby. "Cats have incredible vision."

"Oh shoot!" muttered Tank. "You're right! That was an old movie that my dad let me watch. It gave me nightmares for weeks."

The large cat paced back and forth on the other side of the river's shoreline. It was a beautiful animal with a coat covered in black and gray spots. A long, smooth tail with the same coloration flicked back and forth as it paced. The ears were rounded and tucked upwards towards the sky. Razor sharp teeth protruded from the cat's jaw and they appeared strong enough to break through bones. Occasionally, the cat would growl in their direction, but it didn't seem to be interested in them. Tank, Ruby, and Cage deliberately backed away from the river and towards the jungle.

"I think it's a jaguar," said Cage. "You may be right, Tank. This could be South America."

"Thank goodness!" replied Tank. "Jaguars don't swim. They are terrified of the water. Hey gato, too bad there's a river!" Tank yelled out, mocking the jaguar.

"That's lions," whispered Ruby, taking a step away from Tank. "How do you know so much about nature and so little about cats?"

"I was always more of a dog person," smiled Tank. "Cats are gross."

"What do you not like about cats?" smirked Ruby.

"For starters, they poop in a box. Also, they rub on your legs and stick their butts in the air when you pet them," joked Tank. "I don't know, dogs are better."

"Ugh," replied Ruby, not happy with his comments. "Here I was starting to like you again," she joked.

"On second thought," declared Tank, "cats are cute. Oh, how I love playing with kittens. You get a string or laser pointer..."

"Can you all wait to flirt with each other when we are not about to die? What do we do?" asked Cage, interrupting Tank's obnoxious attempt to win Ruby's favor.

"We should be okay," replied Ruby, grinning at Tank. "It hasn't shown any signs of aggression. Don't make eye contact with it and stay calm. It probably came down to the river for a drink. Keep backing up into the jungle."

"Too easy!" replied Tank. "We can hide behind the trees until it skedaddles."

"Hey Ruby," muttered Cage. "What happens if we make eye contact?"

Tank and Ruby looked at Cage who had locked eyes with the big cat like he was having a staring contest with it. Cage's gaze was so fierce that he was practically staring into the cat's soul. To make matters worse, Cage tripped and fell backwards over a tree branch which caused a loud thud. Crouching down with its hind end sticking up in the air, the jaguar prepared to attack.

Cage was trying hard not to look, but come on, it was a jaguar. It wasn't like every day they saw a magnificent big cat from South America. The jaguar didn't make a sound at all and crept closer to the river's edge. Fortunately, the river was relatively wider now. There had to be, at minimum, one hundred feet the jaguar would need to swim to reach them. Tank pulled the pocketknife from his cargo pants and flipped the blade out.

"What do we do?" asked Cage, getting back on his feet.

"You two are going to run!" exclaimed Tank. "I am going to do battle with this kitten."

"Don't be ridiculous!" scolded Ruby.

"That's a terrible idea!" chastised Cage. "No way you can fight off a full-grown jaguar!"

"Look!" begged Tank. "I am the reason you both went into the cave and are here in the first place. This is all my fault. If dying is what it takes to keep you alive, then I gladly accept my fate."

"Stop it!" answered Ruby. "You didn't force us into that cave."

"Yea, bro," added Cage. "We both made our own decision to follow you."

"Wow!" smiled Tank. "You all are not mad at me?"

"No way, man," said Cage. "Friends forgive each other and drive on. Granted, in this case, we won't be driving on very long because a jaguar is about to kill us." He gave a half-cocked smile.

"Well," giggled Ruby. "I still can't believe you tricked me into kissing you. Also, you are wrong about cats. They are lovely creatures."

"It was a good kiss though, right?" laughed Tank, disregarding the cat comment. "Almost like you want to do it again?"

Ruby blushed and ignored Tank's remark about kissing. Tank was still holding the pocketknife out in front of his body. They had been moving backwards towards the jungle ever since they first noticed the jaguar and now, they needed to decide.

Ruby gave a few options of what they could do. They could stand their ground and the jaguar may get scared. She explained that it was possible that nothing would happen to them, but the worst-case scenario was that all three could get mauled to death. If they ran, however, they would trigger the jaguar's predatory instincts. The best case would be that two of them would survive, but one person wouldn't be so lucky. After sharing her thoughts, Ruby made a declaration to Cage and Tank.

"We have to stick together," said Ruby, holding out her hands to the side. "It's our best chance for survival."

"Right!" declared Tank, flipping the blade closed and putting the knife back in his pocket.

"I think so, too," said Cage.

Tank was standing on the right side of Ruby and Cage was on the left. Ruby gently laid the tablet face down on the ground and the three friends joined hands, forming a chain. Across the river, the jaguar remained motionless. The only part of the cat they could see moving was the tail which flicked back and forth in the air.

Holding hands and standing close to each other would, hopefully, make them look bigger. The thought process was that most predators, even giant jungle cats, can feel fear. Perhaps standing their ground and looking bigger would make the jaguar think twice about attacking.

When the jaguar growled and then leapt into the river, their hearts sank. Tank, still holding Ruby's hand, started yelling like a turbo-charged banshee flapping his free arm in the air. Cage looked over at him and was going to tell him to knock it off, but soon Ruby held up her arms, too. While still holding hands, they all started doing the same erratic movements.

The old cliché says, "If you can't beat them, then join them." or "When in Rome, do as the Romans do." Because of Ruby, Cage was swinging one arm wildly over his head while using his free hand to take a quick puff on his inhaler. Cage started yelling like a maniac, too. It must have been quite a sight to see. The cat was speeding across the top of the water in their direction.

"It's working!" announced Ruby, nodding her head at the jaguar.

"Keep making noise," added Tank. "We got this!"

"AAAAAH!" screamed Cage. "AAAAAAH!"

The jaguar had reached the middle of the river, but it was struggling to swim further. Their first thought was that jumping up and down like fools, yelling, screaming, and pretending to look bigger had made the cat think twice. Their second thought was that the current must have been strong, like before, causing the jaguar to swim slower. That didn't make a lot of sense, though, because the water was smooth and calm in this section of the river.

At least two minutes had passed since the jaguar had darted into the water towards them. It should have reached them by now. The jaguar's teeth may have been at a safe distance from them, but now the suspense was killing them as they continued to watch the slowing jaguar.

In the middle of the river, the jaguar was still struggling to swim. Finally, after a few more minutes, they noticed the jaguar had turned around and was trying to get back to the side of the river from where it had come. The jaguar was no longer growling but sounded like it was whimpering. Their plan must have worked. Ruby, Cage, and Tank cheered.

Victory felt good. They were relieved that they were not going to die a violent death from one of nature's finest killers. Ruby had let go of Cage's hand, but she was still firmly holding on to Tank's hand. She tilted her neck and shoulders towards Tank and kissed him on the cheek.

The jaguar was still in the water and only a few feet from the opposite shore. Hopefully, it would sprint into the jungle and they would never see it again. Suddenly, the cat went under water. Tank didn't know much about cats' swimming abilities, but it did seem odd that a jaguar could hold its breath and swim completely submerged. Cage was dancing and singing with joy. He was oblivious to what was happening in the water.

"Is that normal?" asked Tank, letting go of Ruby's hand.

"No!" replied Ruby in a panicked voice. "I think something is attacking the jaguar."

"Knock it off!" yelled Tank, as he punched Cage in the arm.

"Ouch!" hollered Cage, as he stopped dancing. "Why did you do that?"

Tank didn't respond to the question. Cage reacted by punching Tank in the arm, but Tank did not flinch at all. The jaguar's head rose above the surface of the water, creating a splashing noise. Cage finally looked over at the jaguar, too. All four paws were sticking out of the water. It was still kicking hard but the head of the cat was under the water! From a distance, it looked like it was wearing a large green belt around its middle.

Thrashing in the water, the jaguar rose above the surface one more time, but there was no head visible on the cat's body. Instead, a large green snake was tightly coiled around the jaguar's body, swallowing it head first. The snake was like the carvings in the cave. The jaguar's body had gone limp.

The snake was extending the muscles in its jaw and swallowing the jaguar whole from head to tail. The sound of bones crunching and breaking made Cage, Ruby, and Tank's stomachs queasy. Watching a snake eat is one of the nastiest things on the planet.

Ruby leaned over and grabbed her stomach as if she were going to vomit. Tank and Cage were watching as the back legs of the jaguar went down the snake's throat. As the tail disappeared, the snake slithered onto the opposite shore, pulling its body out of the water. Ruby stood up long enough to see the large bulge of the jaguar inside the snake's stomach and that was enough. She leaned over and dry heaved as bits of yellow stomach acid fell from her mouth.

Back in the cave, the snake that Phoenix had drawn on the wall was well over one hundred feet long. Phoenix must have exaggerated though; this snake was maybe twenty feet long. It was no bigger than the average large snake found in a local zoo. Not that twenty feet is not big, but compared to the giant anaconda drawing in the cave, this snake was relatively puny.

The snake's entire body was now resting on the opposite bank of the river. After a few seconds, the snake slithered off into the jungle and disappeared. Ruby spat one more time and then wiped her mouth using the backside of her hand.

"I guess at least the jaguar is gone," joked Tank.

"I say we head back towards the cave," said Ruby. "Maybe we can find a way out of here."

"You know that means getting back in the water," responded Tank. "That's the same water where a caiman tried to eat us and an anaconda just killed a jaguar, right?"

"We can stay on the rocky shoreline until we pass the waterfall," said Ruby. "Then we only have to swim a little distance."

"What about seeing where we are going?" asked Tank. "Even if we get past the water and into the cave, we won't be able to see anything."

"Don't forget about the current," added Cage. "No way we can swim against it."

Ruby sighed and knelt to pick up the tablet which they had forgotten during the chaos happening in the river with the jaguar and anaconda. Tank held out his hand signaling Ruby to hand him the tablet, but she held it closer to her body. She was shaking her head and mouthing the words, "No, No, No." Tank once again held out his hand for the tablet and Ruby continued to refuse to hand it to him.

"What's wrong?" asked Tank.

"If I give you the tablet," mumbled Ruby, "then y'all are going to want to use it to try and find O Dourado."

"Not me," interrupted Cage. "I want to go home."

"Same here," added Tank. "But don't you remember Phoenix's letter?"

Tank reached for his back pocket, searching for Phoenix's letter which he had found earlier while in the cave. When he pulled out his hand, the soggy remains of what used to be the letter came out as mush. Using both hands, he tried his hardest to unfold the piece of paper, but it was impossible. The water had destroyed the letter. Out of frustration, Tank wadded the soiled paper into a ball and chucked it into the river.

"Ah man!" declared Tank. "Phoenix's letter explained it all. Now the water has destroyed it!"

"If the water did that to the letter," stuttered Ruby, reaching to her pocket, "then what about my cellphone?"

Ruby pulled her cellphone from her pocket and shook it. Brown water poured to the ground. She held the cellphone closer to her eyes and could see that water had seeped all the way through the purple case and into the body of the phone. Ruby pressed the power button a few times, trying to see if anything would happen. The battery may have been dead, but in the past when the battery had died, the phone would still blink when the button was held down. The cellphone showed no signs of life.

"My parents are going to kill me," cried Ruby.

"It will be okay." Tank smiled. "I bet your parents will forgive you when they hear you were locked in a cave, thrown into a river, and almost attacked by a jaguar that was devoured by an anaconda."

"We can all put our money together and get you a new one when we get home," added Cage.

Ruby smiled. She placed one hand on Tank's shoulder and handed him the tablet. She then put her other hand on Cage's shoulder. Tank studied the tablet as he tried to remember the words in Phoenix's letter.

Cage moved closer to Tank and tried to help read the tablet. The tablet, with the diamonds firmly embedded into the surface, was still shining brightly. There must have been over one hundred inscriptions. It was at this moment that Ruby realized how lucky she had been today.

All the bad things that had happened during their adventure had been horrible. Someone tried to kill them by trapping them in the cave, a caiman chased them, they tumbled down rapids, they were scared, hungry, and lost. It was possible that all of them would never see home again. Somehow that didn't matter, though. Cage and Tank truly cared about her and together, as a team, they had already survived so much.

"I wish the letter wasn't ruined," said Tank. "I remember it saying something about returning the tablet.

"Me, too," added Cage. "That was right before the light went out and we had to make a run for it.

"I remember what it said," replied Ruby. "I have a photographic memory."

"You do?" asked Cage. "I didn't know that about you."

"That is so cool." Tank flashed a cheesy smile. "That is where you can draw pictures using your feet. I had an aunt in Omaha that could do that. You continue to impress me the more I learn about you."

"Thanks, I guess." Ruby hoped that Tank was joking. "Let me see the tablet. I will show you what Phoenix was talking about in the letter."

Tank handed Ruby the tablet and she held it up for all of them to see. They were standing in a semi-circle around the tablet with Ruby in the middle. Tank and Cage stood there while Ruby walked them through Phoenix's letter. She absolutely had a photographic memory! Ruby started at the beginning and pointed at key positions on the map. Granted, she was not pronouncing the names in Portuguese correctly, but they got the point.

"Hey, Ruby and Cage," said Tank.

"Yes?" replied Ruby, still looking at the tablet.

"Yeah, what's up, man?" responded Cage, lifting his head.

"I know today hasn't been the best," said Tank, "but I am so glad I met you both.

"Me, too," said Cage. "I am happy we survived our first day in the Amazon."

"I agree," said Ruby. "The day's not over yet, though. Hopefully, we are still alive for the rest of the day, too."

The heat and humidity were causing them to sweat uncontrollably. It had been since his breakfast with mom that Tank had anything to drink other than a little bit of river water he had swallowed earlier in the rapids. The sun was still high in the sky, but there was only a few hours before it would start getting dark.

Being near the river also left them exposed to hungry creatures who were looking for an easy meal. They needed to agree on what steps to take next.

125

In the back of Tank's mind, all he could think about was being stuck out here at night. When dad and he had gone camping, they would set up camp early and get a fire going. A good campfire kept curious predators away and also kept a person from freezing to death at night when it got cold.

Ruby motioned for Tank to turn around so she could put the tablet into the bag. Rustling noises could be heard coming from across the river again and Ruby whispered what she thought they needed to do. While Cage was bending down to tie his shoelace, Tank looked into Ruby's eyes and Ruby stared back into his eyes. How badly he wished that dad were here to give him some advice on what to do next. Dad would say "I love you" to mom, so that had to be the logical next step, right?

"Hey Ruby," said Tank, getting her attention "I love," he paused. "I love…"

"Alright," interrupted Cage, hopping up from tying his shoe. "Where do we go next?"

"You love what?" asked Ruby. "You said I love twice and then stopped. What do you love?"

"I love," hesitated Tank. "I love all kinds of things. I love water balloons and I can't get enough of them."

"Okay," interjected Cage. "Tank gets the most points for random comments today. Now where do we go?"

"We have to get over there," Ruby pointed to the other side of the river.

Cage jittered and fidgeted at the idea of crossing the river while his heart did a cartwheel inside his chest. Ruby took a few steps closer to the edge of the river and looked down. Tank instinctively stretched his legs like he would before starting a hard workout. Crossing the river was dangerous, but Ruby insisted that it was the only way to fulfill Phoenix's instructions in the letter. Trust is the foundation for friendship and both Tank and Cage trusted that Ruby knew what she was talking about. What happened next, though, was nothing they could have prepared for.

Fourteen
Single Rope Bridge

Hustling down the shoreline, Ruby didn't say a word. She was on a mission, but it would have been nice if she would have taken a few moments to explain the plan... a little hint, that's all. Obviously, she had figured out the tablet and Phoenix's letter. Tank and Cage followed closely behind. They were headed down the river and away from the waterfall. The only thing Ruby had told them was that they needed to cross the river, but then she started walking away from it.

The sun was hanging lower in the sky and fortunately, it was not beating down on them nearly as much. They had been swiftly walking in awkward silence for nearly thirty minutes and must have covered at least two miles in distance. The river was increasingly narrow, the shore was rockier than ever, and the current had noticeably picked up again. The water was not quite rapids, but it was not far off. Tank second guessed Ruby's plan as the noise of tumbling water grew louder and louder. Also, as the river grew more narrow, water was constantly splashing up on the shoreline, making it incredibly slick.

"Hey Ruby," said Tank. "Would you be so kind as to share with the class what we are doing?"

"Shouldn't we be heading back that way?" asked Cage. "We already reached our daily quota for rapids today.

"A little farther this way," said Ruby. "Keep going. Trust me."

"We trust you," asserted Tank. "Like my dad says, it's important to have faith, but confirm."

"There it is!" Ruby pointed downriver. "Like it shows on the tablet!"

Up ahead, about one hundred and fifty feet away, a small, single rope bridge strung across the river. Tank had seen this type of rope bridge all the time on the military obstacle courses at the base in Texas. The single rope bridge was tied between two trees about thirty feet apart and was approximately three feet above the water. They were still too far away to see the condition of the rope, but at first glance, it looked promising. With the help of a rope, crossing the river was going to be a much easier task. After walking a few more minutes, they were within a few feet of the rope.

"Do you want the good news or the bad news?" asked Tank.

"How about the good news first," replied Cage.

"Well," paused Tank, "the good news is this is Spanish braided rope. It is thick and tight between the trees. That should make it easier to use."

"What's the bad news?" questioned Ruby.

"Umm," grimaced Tank. "This rope looks ancient and appears rotted in the middle. Good chance it may break if we try to use it."

"Alright," said Ruby, without pausing. "Who wants to go first?"

"Wait a second," commanded Cage. "I am not climbing on a rope hung centuries ago without being told why."

Ruby walked behind Tank and reached inside Phoenix's bag. The sunlight was quite dim within the heavy shade of the jungle, but the tablet was shining increasingly bright depending on the position of the sun. With the tablet in her hand, Ruby marched closer to the river's edge as she looked at the opposite shoreline. As she moved, the golden surface of the tablet went dim. She slowly held out the tablet and gradually turned her body from left to right until she was facing Cage's direction. As she did so, the tablet grew so bright she could barely make out the inscriptions.

"This all makes sense now!" exclaimed Ruby.

"What is it, Ruby?" asked Tank. "Why is the tablet doing that?"

"Phoenix mentioned it in his letter," replied Ruby. **"The sacred tablet of Rio de Monstros must be returned."**

"Why is it bright as the sun one moment and then dim the next?" pondered Cage.

"I figured that out, too," replied Ruby. "When the tablet is facing O Dourado, it shines brighter. When it's facing away, it goes dim."

"But why does the tablet randomly blink with bright light when it's pointed back at the cave?" asked Tank.

"Yeah," replied Ruby. "I have not quite figured that part out yet."

128

Turning again towards the river, Ruby paused for a second. She was scanning the far side of the shoreline with her eyes focused on the jungle. On the other side of the river, a five-foot-wide hiking trail could be seen hollowed out from within the trees.

Tank was relieved to see the pathway because a trail meant that other people must be around. When he had gone on hiking trips in Yellowstone Park, dad would look for high traffic pathways because they were safer to use. There was a lesser chance of being attacked by a bear.

"Phoenix put in the letter that returning the *Tablet of Rio de Monstros* was the only way," said Ruby.

"But return it where and why?" questioned Tank. "Doesn't that seem vague to you?"

"To the temple, I am guessing," replied Ruby, pointing to the other side of the river. "The tablet says *Templo da Yacumama Serpente*, and according to the tablet, it's only a mile or so down that path. What better place for a tablet to be returned if not to a temple?"

"I still don't understand how returning the tablet gets us home," commented Tank. "How do you know it isn't supposed to go back to O Dourado or to one of the other hundred places on there?"

"Okay, so it's a wild guess," Ruby smirked. "So, who is crossing the bridge first?"

"Bridge?" laughed Cage. "This is a piece of rope stretched between two trees. Calling it a bridge is a tad generous."

"I can do it!" Tank moved closer to the rope. "I need you both to watch me carefully. Single rope bridges are tricky and dangerous."

While Tank prepared to cross the bridge, Ruby placed the tablet into the bag which was hanging on Tank's shoulder, making sure that it was secure and that the bag was closed tightly. Tank popped his knuckles and then grabbed the rope. This was one of the shortest single rope bridges he had ever crossed and it was not going to be an issue for him, but Tank worried about his friends. Even though the distance was short, getting friction burns on your hands and legs was a real possibility.

All his experience on military obstacle courses gave him an advantage. Crossing a single rope bridge can be accomplished in two ways. First, the person can crawl along the top of the rope, letting one leg hang down for balance. This is the best way for the experienced climber. The second option is to let your body hang under the rope and then grab the rope with your hands and cross your legs over it. This option was much harder, but it did get the job done.

"Watch me carefully," said Tank, climbing on top of the rope. "No matter what, it is important that you don't panic when you get out there over the water because you will lose your balance."

"Is the rope rotted?" asked Cage, as Tank advanced halfway across the bridge.

"A little." Tank crawled a little further. "I think we will be okay. We need to be careful."

"Wow!" shouted Ruby. "That was quick!"

Tank let go of the rope and set his feet on the ground on the other side of the river. It was great that Ruby and Cage thought his skills were amazing, but it was only thirty feet. It was not like he had crossed the Grand Canyon or something. He stood on the other side of the river, wiping his cargo pants and shirt free of debris from the rope. The worst part of crawling on the rope was that there were ants using it, too. Fortunately, Tank was quick enough that they didn't pose a problem as he crossed and he was able to avoid putting his hands directly on top of them.

The ants were further proof that they were in the Amazon rainforest. Each ant was the size of a wasp, but they did not have wings. They were reddish black in color and did not scatter to get away when Tank crawled over the top of them. Tank recognized the species right away. These were bullet ants and are a species that only lives in South America. Even though bullet ants have one of the most painful stings on earth, they didn't seem to be hostile towards Tank as he caused a vibration while climbing across the rope bridge.

Ruby didn't think twice about the ants. She pulled her body on top of the rope as she let one leg dangle to the side. Tank watched as Ruby performed a nearly perfect single rope crossing. When Ruby got close enough to dismount, Tank, like a gentleman, put his hand out and helped her get down. Cage mustered his courage and stepped closer to the rope. His left hand grabbed the rope first followed by his right hand.

Tank recognized the look on Cage's face. It was the look of needing to "prove himself." Tank knew exactly what that felt like because all too often dad and his military buddies had caused him to feel like that, too. Dad had pulled Tank to the side once and explained that "pride was a dangerous ride and to never let the need to prove yourself fog your mind."

Cage rolled his jeans up to the top of his calves and tried to pop his knuckles like Tank had done. He looked confident, but beneath the surface composure, he was scared to death! Tank could see it by the slight shake in Cage's arms. It wasn't the height of the rope nor necessarily the fear of falling into the water that caused Cage's anxiety. It was worrying that he could not keep up with his friends.

"No need to set any speed records," yelled Tank to Cage. "Take your time and go slow."

"I could cross this rope twice as fast as you even if it were twice as long," boasted Cage.

"Oh boy," whispered Ruby to Tank. "He is going way too fast."

Cage was holding steady as he navigated the rope until he got half-way across the river. For a moment, Tank wondered if maybe he had doubted Cage for no reason. Perhaps Cage had experience with single rope bridges, too. Ruby and Tank had crossed quickly, but the rope was steady the whole time. Cage, on the other hand, was moving too fast. His body was off balance and the rope was swaying back and forth.

In the twinkling of an eye, Cage lost his balance and fell to the side as he barely clung to the rope. He wrapped his legs crisscross on the rope and gripped the rope with both hands. Looking up at the sky, Cage was now going to have to crawl at a snail's pace on the underside of the rope, being careful not to lose his grip.

Holding on to the rope was only part of the problem. The commotion of violently shaking the rope had disturbed the ants enough that they went into attack mode. A long string of ants could be seen crawling on the rope towards Cage. The ants were still a good distance from Cage, but he needed to hurry up. This was bad! If the ants started stinging and Cage fell into the river, it may be game over.

131

If the rapids didn't kill him, then one of the monsters under the water would. Cage was panicking and breathing heavily like he was about to experience an asthma attack, but there was no way he could reach his inhaler this time. Fortunately, he could not see the ants coming towards him or that would have sent him over the edge.

"I know you are scared," said Ruby. "You have to keep moving."

"Move with a purpose!" yelled Tank. "Keep moving this way."

"I don't think I can hold on any longer," remarked Cage. "My palms and legs are sweating."

Tank took a closer look at Cage's hands. What Cage was interpreting as sweat running down his palms was tinted red blood. The same was true for his legs. Friction, from falling to his side, must have scraped the top layer of his skin off. Droplets of blood were steadily running down the back sides of his forearms. The ants may have awakened because of the vibrations of Cage falling, but now they were in full pursuit from the smell of blood. Once more, thankfully, Cage was oblivious to what was happening.

"Put your left hand three inches in front of your right hand," instructed Tank. "Now move your right leg forward three inches and keep going."

"Okay!" uttered Cage. "It's working."

"You got this!" shouted Ruby, "We have faith that you can do this!"

A single drop of blood, running down Cage's forearm, reached the tip of his elbow. The blood pooled there until it was the size of a penny. Time stopped for a moment as Ruby and Tank watched a single blood droplet fall from Cage's elbow into the rushing water. A few seconds passed and nothing happened. Then, another drop of blood fell into the water. Cage was sluggishly trekking across the underside of the rope. In a few more feet, they would, hopefully, be able to grab him in case he fell.

The more Cage moved, the more blood fell to the water. Cage was hanging upside down and would occasionally look down over his shoulder at the water. Small shadows of fish appeared swimming near the surface. The fish were relatively small compared to the other monsters they had already seen that day, but it still gave them an uneasy feeling. At first, the fish would swim to the surface and then scatter when they noticed Cage's shadow. But soon, they were jumping out of the water, coming only inches from Cage's backside. Cage let out a shriek when he noticed the blood seeping from his hands.

The swarm of bullet ants were marching on the rope, getting closer and closer. The ants had reached Cage's shoes and were moving towards his socks. Cage was only a few feet from reaching Tank's hand which was stretched out in his direction. One more final long reach and Cage would be safely standing on shore again. When one ant contacted bare skin on his calf, Cage, in terror, nearly kicked his shoes off.

The ant, unable to hold on with Cage kicking his leg wildly, released its grip and fell towards the water. A few inches from the surface, a fish leapt from the water and caught the large ant in mid-air. The fish did not swallow the ant whole, but instead, bit it into two pieces causing bug juices to splatter into the air. Ruby got a closer look at the fish when it sprang out of the water. It was only about eight inches long and had a red belly. The teeth of the fish snapped together several times, creating loud popping noises.

When Cage kicked his leg to knock the ant off, he lost his balance and his leg fell towards the water. Only one foot was wrapped around the rope and the other foot's shoe was skimming across the top of the water. A final stretch forward of Cage's hand on the rope was enough and Tank grabbed his shoulder. Ruby also reached out and was able to hold onto Cage's arm.

Ruby looked down and noticed that her hand was covered in Cage's blood. Normally, that would have freaked her out, but all she could think about was getting Cage off the rope to safety.

"I got you!" shouted Tank, pulling Cage to the shore.

Now safely away from the water, Cage laid on his back and used both hands to swipe the ants from his legs. Tank and Ruby helped Cage by removing the ants while trying to avoid being stung by the nasty little insects. The spot where the ant had stung Cage on his lower calf was already starting to fester with pus. Finally, able to reach his pocket, Cage grabbed his inhaler and took three large inhales until he was able to slow his breathing. The fish were still gathering on the surface of the water, remaining hopeful that the blood they had just tasted was only an appetizer.

"Are you okay?" Ruby looked at the wounds on Cage's hands and legs. She lifted her hoodie off her head, turned it inside out, and attempted to wipe away the blood.

"I shouldn't have tried to go so fast," sighed Cage. "What was up with those fish? Did you see the teeth on them?"

"I think they were piranhas," stated Ruby. "They had huge teeth! I am pretty sure they wanted to eat you."

"I think so, too." Cage nervously removed his shoe to show them the hole in the back of it from the piranha bite.

"Think about it this way," Tank had a sideways grin on his face, "we are headed to a temple to return a sacred tablet and you are now wearing a *holy* shoe."

Cage rolled his pant legs down and looked up at the trees overhead. The friction burns that were causing him to bleed were starting to scab up. He was physically exhausted from holding up his body for so many minutes on the rope bridge.

They could still hear the fish flopping in and out of the water, but they were moving away. Ruby knelt and wiped her bloody hands on Cage's pants which caused Tank to laugh. She figured since it was his blood, it made more sense than wiping it off on her own pants.

When most of the blood was gone, Ruby stood up and walked towards the path as she dropped her soiled hoodie onto the ground. Tank waited a few more moments because he wanted to ensure that Cage was okay. Tank, who had also been kneeling to help Cage, stood up and held out his right hand. Cage grabbed Tank's hand and pulled himself back to his feet.

"Hey bro," said Tank, in a quiet voice ensuring Ruby couldn't hear.

"I know man. You don't have to say it," replied Cage. "I know I shouldn't have been so stupid trying to show off."

"There is nothing wrong with being confident," reassured Tank, "but letting pride get the best of you can get you killed."

"I think I figured that out a few minutes ago," laughed Cage.

"No worries, man," replied Tank. "I feel like I learn that lesson every day. I am always doing stupid stuff."

Cage chuckled and fist bumped Tank. Ruby looked over her shoulder. She was glad to see that Cage was back in good spirits after his brush with death. Ruby stood in place, collecting her thoughts, and then started down the pathway towards the temple.

The sun was sitting lower in the sky which meant they were now in a race to return the tablet before it got dark. She had no idea what returning the tablet would do or why it needed to be done, but Phoenix felt it was important enough to risk his life. It was time to find *Templo da Yacumama Serpente*.

Fifteen
Templo da Yacumama 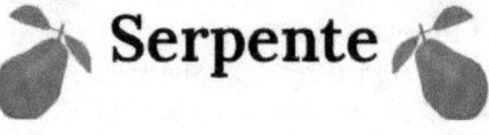 Serpente

The path to the temple was only a mile or two long or at least that is what the tablet showed. Tank couldn't help but notice the uncommon smoothness of the pathway. Grass, shrubs, and trees were literally everywhere, but this path was void of any plants.

There either had to be a lot of people using this path constantly and their feet had kept the surface smooth or something heavier had been used to keep it in this kind of shape. Tank imagined bright orange tractors with enormous heavy rolling pins, like the ones they use on construction sites, being driven along the path. He knew that even the hiking trails used all the time near the Trinity River in Texas were not completely vacant of vegetation or were this smooth.

Another thing that bothered Tank was the shape of the pathway. In all his years of hiking with dad, he had never seen a trail that looked like it was cut out of the forest. The center of the path was at least six inches lower than the sides. The pathway looked like a long slide you would expect to see at an outdoor playground. The only thing the path slightly resembled was a water runoff ditch, but that didn't make any sense at all because the path was dry. There were also several other signs that it had rained recently as evidenced by the water droplets on leaves and puddles on the ground.

Speaking of water, their unexpected journey through the jungle had left them increasingly thirsty. It had been since breakfast that Tank had anything to drink and he was sure it was the same for his friends, too. They found themselves carefully picking leaves off the trees that were close to the path and licking the small droplets of water from them to quench their thirst. It was not the most effective way to get fresh drinking water, but hey, it worked. As they walked, the pathway behind them looked like a bread crumb trail of shoeprints and leaves.

Now that they had crossed the river, Tank, Cage, and Ruby replaced their swift walking pace with more of a sluggish saunter. The events of the day had been particularly challenging. As they moved along, they heard an unfamiliar growling noise getting louder and louder as they trekked toward the temple. This growling noise was not a caiman nor was it another jaguar stalking them and it certainly was not an anaconda.

Gurgling and rumbling sounds continued as they walked towards the temple. They looked at each other and realized that the growling noise was coming from inside each of their stomachs! It was, undoubtedly, the scariest noise they had heard all day. The heat, lack of water, and hunger pangs were making them feel weak.

"What I wouldn't do for a slice of pizza right now," muttered Cage. "A slice of Chicago deep dish sounds delicious. Yum!"

"Oh yea," responded Ruby, "or a bacon cheeseburger with extra pickles and loaded with ketchup."

"Anything sounds good right now," said Cage, chewing on a leaf.

"How about a giant tortilla filled with barbacoa and covered in chipotle seasoned rice stuffed with a huge scoop of guacamole?" beamed Tank.

"Yuck!" Ruby pretended to spit in disgust. "What is barbacoa? Isn't guacamole that green gooey stuff?" Ruby's twisted face revealed her repulsion.

Tank was shocked by Ruby's comments and to add insult to injury, Cage was also shaking his head in disgust. A few moments ago, he was saying anything sounded good and now he was gagging at the idea of eating what Tank had suggested. Down in south Texas, guacamole is a staple in the daily diet. Mom had put it on everything from eggs, toast, sandwiches, and sometimes, even mushed it up in desserts.

As for barbacoa, Tank doubted that his two friends had ever had the opportunity to try it, but come on, it had to be one of the most delicious meats in the world. As Tank fantasized about a huge bite of delicious barbacoa, he caught sight of something unexpected. It was both coincidental and ironic.

"So, my friends." Tank pulled out the pocketknife. "If I were to offer you something delicious right now, would you eat it?"

"Oh boy," replied Cage. "Tank has finally lost his mind."

"Put the knife away," giggled Ruby. "We already discussed that we can't eat Cage..., yet."

"Yet?" chuckled Cage. "I hope you are joking."

Tank strolled towards Cage as he held the blade of the knife in his direction and licked his lips. Cage took a few steps back. The look on his face was priceless. When Tank was within striking distance, he grunted, turned towards the woods and wandered off the trail, disappearing into the bush. Cage sighed and flared his nostrils at Ruby to show his lack of amusement.

The vegetation was abnormally thick. There must have been thousands of different types of plants covering the jungle floor. The woodlands in Kentucky looked like a desert compared to the Amazon jungle. Occasionally, Tank would yell out to let them know that he was still alive while he foraged around for food.

As he went farther into the jungle, he noticed that the trees gave way to a plain displaying thick grass and rolling hills. It was somehow a relief to know that even the Amazon wilderness still had terrain that was a little more hospitable to travel through on foot, should it come to that.

Tank could hear Ruby and Cage yelling for him. As he listened, they sounded quite rude. Lack of eating had made them all a little hangry, but overall, each of them remained in good spirits. Getting some water from the leaves into their bodies helped ward off a little bit of their hunger pangs. At their insistence, Tank started walking back towards the path. He was about ten feet away from where Ruby and Cage stood.

"Catch!" yelled Tank, as he made eye contact with Ruby through the thick trees.

Ruby held out her hands like she was preparing to catch a baseball as Tank lobbed a green piece of fruit through the air in her direction. Cage held his right hand high in the air as Tank chucked a fastball in his direction, too. While Ruby and Cage could only catch the first few, Tank kept tossing the fruit even though they were no longer able to snag them out of the air. Green fruit, roughly the size of a pear, was raining down as Tank continued to fling them.

"Alright." Tank hopped back on the trail. "Let's eat."

"What in the blue-mazes are these things?" asked Ruby. "That's how you say it right? It's your little catch phrase when you don't understand something!"

"It's blue blazes!" declared Tank, laughing. "And these are avocados."

"Avo-whatos?" inquired Cage.

"Now they are not quite ripe yet," started Tank, "but if you cut them down the center all the way around and remove this little ball, then pull away the top layer of skin, ta da! You have dinner!"

Holding the green fruit to his lips, Tank opened his mouth wide and bit off a piece of the delicious avocado. Chewing for a second and then swallowing, he sighed in relief as his hunger began to be satisfied. Saliva formed on the roof of Cage's mouth and Ruby held out her hand for Tank to hand over the knife. Ruby sliced the avocado as she had seen Tank do, handed Cage half, and then took a bite out of her piece. Tank finished his first avocado and was patiently waiting for the knife so he could start slicing another one.

"This is unreal," commented Cage. "I love avocados! How have I not had this before?"

"I know," added Ruby. "I don't know if it's because I am hungry, but this has to be the most wonderful thing I have ever tasted."

"Who would have thought?" laughed Tank. "Both of you do love guacamole."

"Wait, what?" asked Ruby.

Tank laughed out loud, cleared his throat, and then laughed a little more. Ruby and Cage were slicing another avocado while Tank explained why he was laughing so hard. Neither of them could believe that guacamole was made from avocado, and ironically, that they had literally just scoffed at him for suggesting it. Next time, maybe they would keep a more open mind when trying new foods.

Regardless of their surprise at the enjoyment of eating avocados, they were stuffed and no longer hungry. Avocados are loaded with good fats that help satiate the appetite. Plus, it looked like fruit-bearing trees were everywhere. Tank had gathered a dozen avocados and put them in the bag so they would not be as worried about finding food later.

Feeling better from having filled up their bellies, their pace quickened towards *Templo da Yacumama Serpente*. The sun was quite low in the sky and Tank wondered if it was four or five o'clock in the afternoon. Out in the distance, they could hear thunder and a few darker clouds had appeared on the horizon.

The reality of their situation was starting to stare them in the face. It had taken them several hours to make it this far and getting back home at this rate did not look promising. Staying the night in the Amazon was not ideal and they were keeping their fingers crossed that reaching the temple would somehow teleport them home.

"That must be it." Ruby pointed ahead. "The temple is right up there."

"Let's talk this through before we get too close," suggested Cage.

"I agree," said Tank. "How do we know that the giant snake from Phoenix's drawing doesn't live there?"

"We already saw it, didn't we?" asked Ruby. "Remember it ate the jaguar at the river."

"That was a big snake," added Tank, "but it was small compared to the paintings in the cave. Let's be prepared to run in case we are wrong."

Finding the temple created a strong mix of emotions. Cage felt relieved and hopeful at the idea of returning the tablet so they could go home. Ruby was a bit disappointed at viewing the temple. In her head, she imagined this enormous, glorious, amazing, magnificent building, but this temple looked more like a single wide trailer that had been condemned.

The walls of the temple were made of sludge, sticks, and leaves. Sitting across the roof were old pieces of wood coated in mud. The temple itself sat in an opening in the jungle about the size of an acre where no trees had grown. There was nothing magnificent or glorious about it at all.

Tank's feelings about finding the temple were all over the place. For starters, he felt honored at the idea of completing Phoenix's mission even though he was not sure who Phoenix was or why it mattered. Secondly, he wondered why Phoenix struggled with returning the tablet. The mission was a little tough with the rapids, wild animals, and a single rope bridge, but it was not that difficult. Given time to prepare and the right equipment, Tank figured he could have returned the tablet in a few hours by himself.

Additionally, Tank was confused with how Kentucky and the Amazon were linked. Physically, it was impossible and magic is not real, trying to figure out what was going on was bugging him the most. The list of questions circulated in his head in no specific order:

1. Why did the government post warning signs and two fence barriers trying to keep people out?
2. Why were there weird drawings in the cave?
3. Who was Phoenix and why did he write that "returning the tablet is the only way?" What did that even mean, *the only way* to do what exactly?
4. Why did someone try to kill them by locking them in the cave?
5. Why did the tablet light up when the diamonds were attached and furthermore, why did they become brighter and dimmer?

And the most important question...

6. What in the Sam Hill was happening?

"What a dump!" exclaimed Ruby. "This doesn't look anything like a temple to me."

"Does anyone see a door?" asked Cage. "All I could find was this hole on the far side."

"I think that is the door," commented Tank. "Who wants to crawl inside and put the tablet back?"

"I'll do it!" Cage raised his hand. "Hand me the tablet."

"Are you sure that's a good idea?" questioned Ruby. "Maybe Tank should do this one."

Cage shrugged his shoulders, slouched his head downwards, and turned away. Tank shook his head and glared over in Ruby's direction. It was not that Ruby meant anything negative with her comment, but Cage had already tried and failed to prove himself once today. If putting the tablet back successfully was the only way to get home, she didn't want to risk Cage being in control. Ruby watched as Tank retrieved the tablet from his bag and admired it one last time.

The light shone brightest when it was pointed towards O Dourado but utterly dim when facing other directions. It was at that precise moment when Tank realized something interesting about the tablet. *Templo da Yacumama Serpente* and O Dourado sat in opposite directions on the map. Their current location near the temple was close to the right side of the tablet and O Dourado was on the far-left side.

The tablet was brightest when it was pointed towards one and dark when facing the other direction. Tank observed, however, that the tablet flickered when pointed towards some of the other symbols, as well. It seemed odd to him that the tablet would be devoid of light when facing the temple which is where they figured it was supposed to be when it was returned. While Tank was considering this, Cage was lamenting Ruby's comment about wanting Tank to put the tablet back. He had walked about fifteen feet away and was kneeling near the woods as he re-tied his shoelaces.

"Cage can do this!" Tank held out the tablet. "Here you go."

"I might mess it up." Cage finished with his shoe. "You both saw what happened on the rope bridge."

"Nah," smirked Tank. "What I saw on the rope bridge was a lad strong enough to hold up his body weight while being stung by bullet ants and having piranhas biting at his legs."

"When you say it that way, I guess it does sound pretty hardcore!" declared Cage.

"Yeah, man," nodded Tank. "You got this!"

"I am sorry I doubted you," apologized Ruby. "You are my friend. I have faith in you!"

Cage gave Ruby a giant hug and then fist bumped Tank. The tablet was now resting in Cage's hands while he positioned himself closer to the temple's entrance. The hole in the side of the temple was wide but only a few feet tall and located near the bottom so Cage had to crawl to get inside. Ruby noticed that storm clouds were getting closer and tried to encourage Cage to hurry up. Like the pathway, the entrance was smooth, similar in shape, and about the same width.

As Cage got into position, he regretted volunteering to take the tablet inside. What if that colossal snake painting was not an exaggeration? Perhaps all Cage had done was volunteer to be an anaconda's dinner.

"Wait!" shouted Tank. "Let's keep the diamonds. Phoenix's letter never said anything about them."

"I don't think that's a good idea," suggested Ruby.

"He has a good point," added Cage. "If we put the tablet back, then Phoenix's mission is complete. Also, when we get home, the diamonds will be proof that we were here, not to mention the fact, they are probably worth a lot of money."

"But the diamonds obviously go with the tablet," urged Ruby. "It's like the diamonds are the key to cause the tablet to shine. Wouldn't it make more sense that they would need to be returned, as well?"

"I guess you're right," sighed Tank. "It is too bad, though. Go ahead, Cage. Put the tablet back in the temple."

Cage got on his hands and knees. The ground was soft and had a spongy feel to it. The friction burns on his shins were quite sore. Earlier, when Tank and Ruby thought he was tying his shoes, Cage was trying to get a closer look at his lower legs. The wounds had scabbed over and were not deep, but there was a weird smell, like rotting flesh, that worried him.

A little bit of river water had splashed onto his body during the process of crossing the single rope bridge, not to mention the continuous sweat that was running down his legs into his wounds. Also, the scabs were a tad green in color and had a white pus forming under the surface. An infection out here could turn septic. The plan to return the tablet to the temple needed to work and it needed to work fast.

"What's it like in there?" asked Tank. "Is there a monster green serpent choking the life out of you?"

"Very funny," answered Cage. "It's dirty, really dirty in here."

A fair amount of light was shining through the small openings in the roof of the temple and after a few minutes, Cage was able to see reasonably well. There wasn't a whole lot to report to Tank and Ruby, though. Inside the temple, the ground had been rubbed smooth like the trail they were on. In the center, he could see a circular formation about twenty feet wide on the ground which looked like an indention in the soil. Along the perimeter of the circle, there were leaves, stones, branches, random pieces of clothing, and a couple of shoes that didn't match.

"I am not sure," shouted Cage. "I think I found the place where the tablet is to go."

"How do you know?" asked Ruby.

"Is there a sign or something?" inquired Tank.

"Yes!" replied Cage. "There is a huge flashing sign and a loudspeaker that says, PLACE TABLET HERE."

"Seriously?" Tank had a shocked look on his face.

"No man!" laughed Cage. "But someone graffitied the word '*gullible*' on the wall."

"That is bananas," responded Tank. "Why would someone write that?"

"I am messing with you," jested Cage, observing that Tank did not get the joke. "There is a spot in here that looks like an altar. I think the tablet would go towards the center of the circle."

"What do you mean? How do you know?" asked Ruby, losing her patience.

Cage explained the indention in the ground that he guessed was the border of an altar and the random items along the edge. He also gave a quick description of the interior of the temple from the left side to the right side, which didn't take long, because there was nothing else inside to describe. Holding the tablet firmly in his hands, Cage turned away from the altar towards O Dourado, which allowed the light from the tablet to illuminate the rest of the room. In the far corner of the room, he could see a jacket laying on the ground.

"I found something!" Cage picked up the jacket.

"Is it a satellite phone?" asked Tank, sarcastically.

"No, it's a jacket...," started Cage.

"Put the tablet back," interrupted Tank. "Quit fooling around in there so we can go home."

Overhead the sky was getting darker and the storm clouds were forming above them. Tank didn't know a ton about the Amazon jungle, but he did recognize a severe thunderstorm when he saw one. Cage put the jacket down and then held the tablet out and away from his body.

Kneeling on the side of the altar, he stretched out his body, placing the tablet as close to the center as possible. Lightning flashed across the sky and thunder roared over the jungle. Crackling lightning shot across the sky several times and the thunder grew loud, causing Ruby to cover her ears.

"What's happening?" shouted Ruby. "Did you put the tablet back?"

"Yes!" responded Cage. "I put it on the altar."

Rain started to pour on Tank and Ruby's heads, but other than that, nothing else spectacular happened. The wind was picking up and gusting in their faces. Little drops of hail, the size of pebbles, were crashing down. The hail was not big enough to cause serious injury, but the feeling was not pleasant. Inside the temple, Cage could hear the hail striking the roof, but inside he remained protected and dry.

Cage thought the sudden surge of the storm was because he had put the tablet back. He took a final look at the tablet, picked up the jacket, and prepared to exit the temple. On his knees again, he started crawling out only to be met by Tank and Ruby trying to get inside the temple.

"We need to stay in here for a while," groaned Ruby. "That storm is getting rough out there."

"Sorry, man." Tank pushed Cage to the side. "Until the hail and lightning stops, we are stuck in here.

"We put the tablet back!" insisted Cage, with desperation in his voice. "Phoenix's letter said it was the only way!"

"I don't know what to tell you, man," said Tank. "The tablet is back and we are still here. This storm is going to stop us from going anywhere tonight."

Cage grew furious and picked up the tablet from the altar. At first, he tried laying the tablet down in different ways. He turned it right, then left, then upside down. He tried to move it around on every inch of the altar's surface to find the right spot. Eventually, in frustration, Cage threw the tablet down and it landed facing up towards O Dourado.

Still enraged, he then sat on the ground next to the tablet and let out a big sigh. Tank sat nearby, took the backpack off his shoulders, pulled out another avocado, and handed the pocketknife to Cage. Ruby sat, too. They formed a small semi-circle around the tablet. The light from the tablet was like a campfire as they sat around it.

The inevitable moment had finally come. They had to face the fact they were stuck. Putting the tablet back in the temple was not going to save them and Phoenix's letter must have been nothing more than a sick hoax. Ruby wept and yelled a few words that weren't nice about Phoenix, whoever the chap was.

Seeing Ruby this angry reminded Tank of dad when he was bowling. Mom would say that dad's language would make a sailor blush with shame and

Ruby's vocabulary was not too far off. Cage calmed down from his angry outburst and put his hand on her shoulder.

Tank looked around the inside of the temple. The spot that had looked like an altar when they were standing now looked more like a nest when they were sitting down. The random articles of clothing and shoes scattered along the edge were incredibly chilling to think about. The garments were torn and shredded. The clothing being present meant people, but the clothing was still there and there were no people, so what happened to them?

Thinking about an animal that needed a nest this big gave Tank the creeps. The last thing he wanted to do was tell his friends about his terrifying observations so he kept them to himself. Trying to lighten the mood with humor, Tank pointed at Cage.

"That's a cool jacket," smiled Tank. "Is that leather or pleather?"

"What? Oh this?" Cage held up the jacket. "It feels like real leather, but it might be fake. I can't tell."

"Do you know how they make pleather?" asked Tank. "They take imitation fabric and pour cow pee on it. The "P" in pleather literally stands for pee."

"What?" chuckled Ruby. "Who told you that?"

"I just made it up!" smirked Tank. "It could be true. I don't know that it's *not* true."

"Cage, you should try it on." Ruby wiped her tears. "Let's see how it looks on you."

Tank had a way of getting everyone to laugh when they were feeling low. Thunder was still booming outside, the hail had stopped, the precipitation was still coming down hard, and fortunately, the roof of the temple was keeping most of the water out. Cage held the jacket up and admired it for a moment. He then looped his arms into the sleeves one at a time. The leather jacket looked like it was no more than a couple decades old and being inside the temple had preserved it nicely.

The collection of outfits was puzzling. There were fragments of modern digital camouflage uniforms and boots. However, some of the other clothes scattered around looked like they came from a movie based out of the early 1900's. Tank picked up a couple articles of clothing. They had the initials P.F.

146

sewn into the collar and a weird military looking insignia of a golden crown embroidered into it. Tank's mind didn't have the capacity to try and fathom a new mystery so he didn't give the random initials or emblems a lot of thought. Figuring out the clothing debacle would have to wait. Tank hoped he or she wasn't wandering around naked somewhere as all their clothes were here in the temple.

Oh well, the leather jacket looked awesome, although it must have belonged to someone a little taller and thicker than Cage because the sleeves were quite loose. Along the top of the left sleeve, there was a small pocket on the jacket which had something tucked inside. Cage reached in and pulled out a tiny square piece of metal which showed the logo of a star and an inscription.

"That symbol is the same as the one on the pocketknife," said Ruby. "It has the word *Thárros* at the bottom."

"This jacket may have belonged to Phoenix, right?" asked Cage.

"I wonder why he left it behind?" pondered Ruby. "What is the shiny metal thing you pulled out of the pocket?"

"It's a lighter," commented Tank. "My Uncle Darren has one like it. May I see it super quick?"

Cage handed Tank the lighter. As he flipped open the lid to the lighter, Tank held it up to his nose. The sweet, potent smell of lighter fluid tingled the hairs in his nostrils. Using his fingers and thumb, Tank flicked the flint a few times. On the third flick, the small wick inside the lighter sparked enough to allow a flame to pop up. Realizing there may be only a little juice left in the lighter, Tank shut the lid which killed the flame.

"Outstanding!" exclaimed Tank. "Now we can get out of here tomorrow."

"How is the lighter going to help us?" asked Ruby. "I don't think the flame is going to last long."

"We can build torches," replied Tank, enthusiastically. "That way we can see inside the cave. All these dry articles of clothing in the temple will work perfectly to serve as kindling for the torches."

Ruby wanted to feel hope, but despair was clogging her brain. Tank was always optimistic and thought up clever ways to conquer obstacles. She tried desperately to think positively and smile at Tank's plan to make torches tomorrow. Tank reached in the bag and then cut a few pieces of avocado before passing them around.

It was brilliant bringing extra food, especially considering they were stuck inside an old shack with a storm slamming the outside. Safely finding food in the dark jungle of the Amazon during a thunderstorm would be improbable.

Cage laid down on the floor without eating anything. He made a couple of comments about not feeling well and Tank could see that his wounds from earlier looked infected. Under normal circumstances, Tank would disinfect the wound, wrap it in gauze, and fashion a bandage out of sports tape. Out here, all he could do was pray for them to get back home tomorrow so Cage could get proper medical attention.

"I am going to lay down and try to get some sleep," yawned Ruby. "Tomorrow is gearing up to be a long day."

"Think about the adventure we can share with everyone at school tomorrow when we get back to Kentucky," smiled Tank.

"Kentucky!" Cage yawned. "I hope so. Oh, how I miss the Bluegrass State!"

"Who knows," giggled Ruby. "Maybe someone will write a book about this one day."

Raindrops, hitting the roof of the temple, provided a soothing sound like that of a car engine humming. Cage rolled over and was already asleep. Finding the jacket in the temple provided Tank with a little bit of relief. If the jacket had belonged to Phoenix that meant he had come to the temple and surely he had a good reason for doing so.

The plan for tomorrow was to build a couple of torches, walk back to the cave, and get back home. Ruby laid down and reached out to hold Tank's hand which caused the butterflies to perk up in his stomach again.

"Good night!" said Ruby, softly. "Tank, aren't you going to try and rest?"

"Sleep well," replied Tank. "I am going to stay guard tonight."

Ruby could not believe the valor, courage, and selflessness of Tank. She had never met anyone who cared that much about others in her life. Knowing that he was watching over them while they slept provided her with comfort. Today had been both physically and mentally exhausting for all of them, yet

Tank was willing to put his personal needs to the side for the sake of two people he met this morning.

Cage was snoring and sweat drops were forming on his brow. Ruby closed her eyes and with the help of the ambiance of the soothing rainfall, she drifted off fast. Tank sat up and focused his attention on the door of the temple. He had no clue if danger was headed their way or not, but he did know one thing; no matter what, he would die to protect his friends.

Sixteen
A Bloody Foot and Sweet Revenge

"What are you doing?" asked Ruby, her eyes fluttering open.

"Can you hold these for me?" nudged Tank, handing her something that looked nefarious.

Cage rolled over and covered his mouth with the jacket's sleeve. Clouds of thick smoke filled the inside of the temple, causing everyone to cough. The tent looked like the inside of a fancy cigar lounge, but there were no old men with stoic mustaches, plush chairs, or luxury top hats. Okay, so it was more like the inside of a rundown hookah bar, but potato, potata.

During the night, Tank had been busy building torches. He built a total of seven torches to help them on their journey home. Six of the torches were to take into the cave and the seventh, the one that was burning right now, was a test to see how long the light lasted. The smoke rose to the top of the temple and then billowed through the cracks in the roof and out through the entrance.

The torches were basic in their construction. Using the clothing scraps that lined the altar, Tank had taken six long sticks and smoothed down the rough edges with the pocketknife. Then, he had gathered a handful of the dry clothes and tied them around one end of the stick, being sure to make them as equal in material as possible. The shoes were cut up and the thick rubber soles were twisted around the bottom of the stick to form handles for the torches.

The final step was tying the shoelaces tightly around the clothing to help keep them mounted to the stick. Tank also repurposed a little bit of the rope from Phoenix's bag and cut short pieces from it. The small bits of rope served as wicks and helped the torches light properly while also extending their burn time.

"We will only get five minutes of light from each," said Tank, talking to himself. "If we take six torches with us, we should get thirty minutes total if we light them one at a time."

Realizing his error of lighting the torch inside the temple, Tank attempted to fan the smoke away. The single torch he had lit had fully burned out but still lay smoldering on the ground. Tank did his best to kick dirt over the torch to prevent more smoke from filling the room. Poor Cage's eyes were bloodshot and he must have used his inhaler three or four times in a short period.

Tank thought about the task ahead. They still had to hike to the cave. He also considered the option of trying to carry Cage all the way. Cage sluggishly rose to his feet. As Tank valiantly tried to fan the smoke from the temple, the final vapors of smoke cleared the room. In his fanning motions, Tank mixed in a variety of classic dance moves, even going so far as to do the "lawn mower, sprinkler, and shopping cart" to get a giggle from Ruby. Up until this point, Cage had not said a word.

"Good morning, sunshine," smiled Tank, getting Cage's attention. "How did you sleep?"

"Not too bad." Cage tucked his inhaler away. "Thirty minutes is not much time to get to the other side of the cave and my legs are killing me."

Cage lifted his pant leg and showed them the infected wounds that had swollen during the night. The pus-filled scabs were greenish in color and smelled horrible. He had not slept well at all. The pain in his legs was excruciating, causing him to toss and turn all night.

Cage kept thinking about the physical requirements of the journey home and having to navigate the cave. Trying to get back home meant using his legs a lot, including going over the single rope bridge again and swimming in a nasty river with caimans. The thought of having to wrap his legs over the rope gave him relentless worry.

"I think you should leave me here." Cage looked deep into Ruby's eyes. "Get back home and send help to get me."

"Cage!!!" exclaimed Ruby. "We are not leaving you in the Amazon!"

"Yeah, man," added Tank, trying to help. "What if another jaguar comes and eats your face!"

"Nice!" Ruby's eyes rolled as she looked at Tank. "Real nice!"

"I'm only kidding," smiled Tank. "If Cage stays here, who is going to wear this harness that I made for the single rope bridge?"

Whipping his head in Tank's direction, Cage was confused when he saw what looked like a seat tied out of rope. As Ruby covered her mouth in surprise, Tank tossed the harness to Cage. The harness was a single piece of rope that was tied into an elaborate Swiss seat, the same kind that soldiers used to repel down mountains. Cage could put both of his legs through the openings in the harness and then tie the other end of the harness to the single rope bridge. The harness would prevent him from falling into the water and from needing to wrap his legs around the rope.

"You're the best, man," nodded Cage. "What does this loop do?"

"Once I get you secured to the rope bridge," explained Tank, "I will tie this end of the rope to the loop in your harness and then I will cross the bridge. That way I can pull you to the other side."

"What about the river?" inquired Cage. "With the waterfall, I don't think my legs are up for the journey."

"I thought about that, too," winked Tank. "Please know that you are in good hands. I know a trick that will help when we get to the river."

"You always know a trick," smiled Cage.

"Breakfast, anyone?" Ruby snatched the last three avocados from the bag.

"I am falling less in love with avocados," laughed Cage.

"Me too!" agreed Tank. "Three meals of it in a row is a bit too much. Also, it looks the same coming out as it does going in."

Sitting inside the temple, they sat in a circle around the tablet as they ate their breakfast. Given the circumstances, it wasn't too bad. At least they had a little food in their stomachs to start the day. Small water puddles from the rain had formed in low spots throughout the temple and they used their hands to lap up the water to satisfy their thirst. The sun was shining through the cracks in the roof, allowing the damp ground to start drying. There didn't appear to be a rain cloud in the sky. None of them spoke as they silently ate their breakfast.

Closing her eyes, Ruby imagined she was sitting in a cottage off the shores of the Mediterranean Sea. At any moment now, a butler would bring in a lovely cup of warm tea and then she would go and lay on the beach. Tank was daydreaming, too. He was dreaming that dad was there and this was a fishing trip in Alaska. Going outside, he would go and snag salmon out of the streams. Cage daydreamed about two things. Hugging his parents again was at the top of his wish list. He also desired that he could go to the emergency room and get a shot of antibiotics.

"Y'all ready to go home?" Tank jumped to his feet. "By my estimates, we are a solid half day's walk from the cave entrance."

"What are we going to do with the tablet?" asked Ruby. "Should we take it with us?"

"Leave it here," stated Cage. "If we end up dying on the way home, at least we completed Phoenix's mission... whatever that's worth."

"Do you all smell that?" asked Tank.

"No more fart jokes, please," laughed Ruby. "It's way too early in the day."

"Did you hear that?" Tank had a concerned look on his face.

"Seriously dude," snickered Cage, "way too early and not funny."

Tank wiped avocado remnants off the blade of the pocketknife. Something had seriously provoked him to go from easy-go-lucky to ready for war. Holding up his hand, he held his finger over his mouth, instructing Ruby and Cage to be quiet. He could hear footsteps coming from outside the temple. It was hard to tell if it was a single person moving or multiple people. Whoever was outside was obviously trying to keep their presence a secret and this further put Tank on edge.

"Come out, come out," yelled a man's voice from outside the temple.

"Stop!" whispered Tank to Cage and Ruby. "I will go out! Stay in here!"

"I know three of you are in there," said the voice. "Don't make me come in and get you."

Tank threw the bag over his shoulder and tucked the knife carefully into his pocket, making sure the blade was still open. They had no choice but to exit the temple and hope for the best. Tank went first, tucking the torches under his arm. Ruby followed and Cage walked closely behind.

The outline of a tall, muscular man was standing directly in front of the sun. Holding up their hands to shade their eyes, they could not see his face because their eyes had not yet adjusted to the brightness. It was not until the man spoke again that he revealed his identity. Even before the man made another sound, Tank recognized the smell of chew.

"You're late to my class again," the man said mockingly. "I guess the laps around the track didn't teach you a lesson after all."

"Mr. Jackson!" shouted Ruby, recognizing the voice. "I knew you were the one that shut the entrance to the cave! Wait until my parents find out about this."

"Why would you do that Mr. Jackson?" asked Cage. "You could have killed us."

"Take it easy," laughed Mr. Jackson. "It wasn't my idea to trap you in the cave."

"You're a liar!" yelled Ruby. "You left us to die!"

"No, my friends." Tank shook his head. "He is telling the truth. It wasn't Mr. Jackson's arms I saw yesterday."

"Then who wanted to kill us?" asked Cage. "If it wasn't Mr. Jackson, then who?"

"She did!" Tank pointed to the side of the temple. "She is the reason for all of this!"

Coming from behind the far side of the temple, another familiar face appeared. It was Ms. Sprinkle and she was pointing a pistol at them. The pistol Ms. Sprinkle held was a nickel-plated revolver which she held at waist level. It was most likely a small caliber similar to a Thirty-Eight Special. Tank pondered the rationale for Ms. Sprinkle shooting him. Was it all because he "hinted" at her clownish appearance yesterday? It wasn't that he didn't want to get shot. He simply didn't want to suffer a bullet which came from such a wimpy pistol. Why couldn't she shoot him with a 45 ACP or a 50 BMG or something sweet like that?

Both Mr. Jackson and Ms. Sprinkle were wearing clothes designed for wilderness hiking. They must have known about the link between Kentucky and the Amazon. Mr. Jackson was wearing tan cargo pants and a short-sleeved digital-camo shirt. He was also carrying Ruby's blood-soaked hoodie that she had left near the single rope bridge yesterday. Ms. Sprinkle had on black shorts and a green tank top. Across Ms. Sprinkle's and Mr. Jackson's waists were bulky water canteens.

Cautiously, Ms. Sprinkle walked towards them, being careful not to make any sounds with her footsteps. She even went so far as to correct the excess sound Mr. Jackson was making as he smacked his lips together before he spat chew on the ground. Tank found this behavior odd. She and Mr. Jackson already had the element of surprise. Whispering and tiptoeing around while trying to keep down the noise seemed a little unnecessary.

"It was your idea to trap us in the cave," said Tank. "You knew the only other way out was through the river."

"Well done!" cackled Ms. Sprinkle. "When I saw you walking towards the exit of the cave, I was only going to make sure you were all expelled from school, but when I saw Phoenix's backpack, I couldn't pass up the opportunity."

"Why do you care about Phoenix's backpack?" asked Ruby.

"That's none of your business," taunted Ms. Sprinkle, cocking the hammer of the pistol and loosely pointing it in their direction. "Now hand me the bag!"

Tank reluctantly pulled the backpack from his shoulders and tossed it on the ground. Mr. Jackson noticed the dog tags hanging from the bag. Disrespectfully, he put his foot on the backpack and pulled on the small silver chain until it broke. He then shoved the dog tags into one of his cargo pockets and laughed.

The rope harness Tank had built for Cage was partially hanging out of the back of the bag and was dangling on the ground. Ms. Sprinkle took a few steps closer and handed Mr. Jackson the pistol. The hammer on the pistol was still in a cocked position as Mr. Jackson tucked it into the front of his pants under his belt. Tank wondered why a skilled military man would ever point a cocked and loaded gun at his groin like that. What if the trigger slipped? *Ouch*, Tank thought to himself.

Ms. Sprinkle knelt in front of the bag and started scavenging around like she was looking for something. The longer she searched and rummaged through the bag, the more frustrated she became. Tank joked to himself that maybe she was looking for another 10 lbs. of makeup for her face. This internal thought caused Tank to smirk and let out a meek laugh.

"Where is the tablet?" shouted Ms. Sprinkle. "I saw Phoenix put it in this bag right before he hid the bag in the cave."

"What tablet?" smirked Tank. "All that was in the bag was a rope."

"He's lying! If the tablet isn't in the bag, then it's in there!" Ms. Sprinkle pointed at the temple.

Mr. Jackson walked over to the hole in the side of the temple and prepared to crawl inside. Pulling a small flashlight from his pocket, he lifted his shirt and brandished the gun to remind them that he had a weapon. He also pointed to his tattoo reminding Tank that not only was he armed, but he was also skilled with firearms. Ugh. Tank wished that his dad were here. Dad would have undoubtedly put Mr. Jackson in a "gooseneck" submission hold until Mr. Jackson was shedding tears like a babbling brook.

When Mr. Jackson's back legs disappeared into the temple, Cage gave a nod to Tank as if he wanted to battle-charge Ms. Sprinkle. Cage kept on mouthing the word "knife," gesturing towards Tank's pocket. It was clear that Cage wanted Tank to use the knife and try to regain control of the situation. Although not a bad plan, Tank was certain that any attempt to fight back would result in gunfire.

"Are those torches?" Ms. Sprinkle asked as she winked at Tank. "That's too cute! You are like your father."

Ms. Sprinkle assumed that Mr. Jackson was out of earshot. However, as he prepared to grab the tablet, Mr. Jackson must have overheard the comment about the torches. He let out an angry sigh at the idea of Ms. Sprinkle mentioning Tank's father. Within a matter of moments, he was holding the tablet and was hostilely exiting the temple.

Tank noticed the bitter glare on Mr. Jackson's face as he exited the temple. Ms. Sprinkle was still going on and on about Tank's dad being clever. Listening to his fiancé talk about another man seemed to make Mr. Jackson increasingly irritated.

Once Mr. Jackson crawled out of the temple, he marched over to Tank and aggressively grabbed the torches from under his armpit. He couldn't help but admire the workmanship of the torches. Mr. Jackson handed the tablet to Ms. Sprinkle. She held the tablet close to her chest at first but then extended her arms so she could admire the golden glow which resonated from the surface. She lifted her arms and pointed the tablet towards O Dourado.

"This is it, honey," asserted Ms. Sprinkle. "This is the tablet I was telling you about. This is what Phoenix and I found all those years ago."

"Why is it all shiny?" asked Mr. Jackson.

"The tablet is a guide," explained Ms. Sprinkle. "When the diamonds are in place, the lost city of gold, O Dourado, glows bright!"

"Phoenix left a letter," shouted Cage. "It said that the tablet had to be returned..."

"Did he now?" Ms. Sprinkle interrupted Cage. "Where is this letter?"

"It got destroyed in the river," declared Tank. "It's nothing but mush now."

"That's convenient," smiled Ms. Sprinkle. "I don't doubt it. Phoenix was paranoid about people using the tablet to find O Dourado. Your father did everything he could to keep the tablet away from others, as well."

"What does my dad have to do with this?" questioned Tank.

"You don't know, do you?" grinned Ms. Sprinkle. "Your dad moved from Arizona to Kentucky for a reason."

"Yeah, and our football coach gave him the nickname 'Phoenix' on the first day of Spring practice when he learned he was from Phoenix. He was such a smug showoff," added Mr. Jackson.

"And all the girls called him Phoenix because we thought he was *hot*," giggled Ms. Sprinkle.

"His own son doesn't even know anything about him," teased Mr. Jackson.

Ms. Sprinkle went on to explain that Tank's dad, Drew, had brought her to the Amazon several times when they were younger. She even went so far as to say that dad's first kiss happened on one of their adventures. They decided they would use the tablet to travel all over the world, only the two of them. They were in love!

"You're a liar!" shouted Tank.

"Believe whatever you want, sweetie," laughed Ms. Sprinkle. "If it weren't for that bimbo, Sara, ruining everything, we would still be together."

"Hey," grimaced Mr. Jackson. "I thought you said you broke it off with Drew after that caiman showed up in the pond behind the high school and the Feds got involved."

"I did honey," responded Ms. Sprinkle. "Now I am with my sugar bear, my handsome sweet Ricky. I am so glad I have you, baby!"

Mr. Jackson smiled at Ms. Sprinkle's empty flattery and pandering. It was so obvious that she was a bag full of hot air, but Mr. Jackson, the dolt, was eating up the turd-pie Ms. Sprinkle was serving. She blew him a kiss and he pretended to snatch it out of the air like a lovesick puppy.

"It wasn't meant to be anyway, Phoenix and I," added Ms. Sprinkle. "After those kids went fishing and disappeared, the suits from the government got involved. Fame-chasing reporters wrote those articles about us which caused my parents to never let me go out with Drew again."

"Does that mean that you are..." asked Cage.

"That's right," Ms. Sprinkle winked again at Tank. "My middle name may be Sandra, but you can call me Spear. The 'S' is for Spear!" She had sarcastically mocked Tank from the first day of school saying 'the T in his middle name stood for Tank.'

"Kid," Mr. Jackson chuckled. "You are what we call in the infantry ten up and two down. Do you know what that equals? Eight up, get it? You are ate-up!"

Tank turned away from everyone. The sarcastic grin on Ms. Sprinkle's face was too much to bear. Mr. Jackson was laughing ecstatically like it was the funniest joke he had ever told. Granted, Tank figured that Mr. Jackson laughed at his own farts, used crayons to pick his nose, and likely spent his Saturday mornings watching cartoons while munching on marshmallow cereal like a toddler. Sincerely, maybe it was the funniest joke Mr. Jackson had ever told.

Dad never told Tank that he went by the nickname 'Phoenix' or that he had an adventure in the Amazon jungle when he was in middle school. How could he keep something like that a secret from his own son?

Did mom even know about dad's journey to the Amazon or his past relationship with one of Tank's new teachers at La Grange High School? Either she was intentionally keeping it a secret, or worse, she didn't know either. Cage and Ruby remained silent, but their faces revealed a level of disbelief.

Tank could see that Cage and Ruby were struggling internally with this news. They probably felt the same way Tank was feeling about dad or they were thinking that Tank was hiding this information from them. Either way, they must have felt a little betrayed because Tank sure felt that way.

"I guess you won't be needing these torches anymore," said Mr. Jackson.

"Wait," pleaded Ruby. That's how we are going to see in the cave so we can get home."

"Home?" Ms. Sprinkle waved her finger in the air, mocking Ruby. "Who said you all are going home?"

"Cage is injured! Look at his legs!" cried Ruby. "Tank, do something!"

Mr. Jackson pulled out a lighter from his pocket, spat the chew out of his mouth, and then lit one of the torches. He then put the rest of the five torches together, creating a large fireball. Tank turned around and noticed the sadistic look on his face as he tossed the glowing fire sticks onto the roof of the temple. He heard Ms. Sprinkle whisper "idiot" as she stared at Mr. Jackson. With her left hand, she signaled to Mr. Jackson that they needed to get away from the now burning temple. Once again, Tank noticed a concerned look on Ms. Sprinkle's face which he had seen earlier. She was attempting to be suspiciously quiet.

"Walk!" ordered Ms. Sprinkle, pointing down the path.

"Wait," urged Mr. Jackson. "We have extra rope in the bag. Let's bind their hands to be safe."

Ms. Sprinkle didn't hesitate to agree. Tank was not sure what Mr. Jackson was planning after they were tied up, but it probably wasn't good. It was doubtful this story was going to end with "then they were tied up, taken to the fair for cotton candy, and they all lived happily ever after." She pulled the rope harness out of the bag first and looked confused as she wondered what it was.

Mr. Jackson put his thumbs up and congratulated Tank on tying together a perfect Swiss seat as Ms. Sprinkle nodded understandingly. Although it was a sarcastic comment, Tank took it as a compliment. If they got out of this alive, Tank would be sure to bring Mr. Jackson a coloring book for his generous compliment regarding the Swiss seat when he was in prison. The Swiss seat was tied tightly and required excessive effort to untie it. Losing her patience, Ms. Sprinkle gave up on the harness and pulled out the remaining strip of rope that had been tucked into the bottom of the bag.

In frustration, Ms. Sprinkle shoved the Swiss seat into the bag and tossed the remaining rope to Mr. Jackson. From his left pocket, Mr. Jackson pulled out a pocketknife and cut the rope into three equal parts. Ms. Sprinkle paid little attention as she continued to intently study the tablet. The temple was still burning strong but now was almost unrecognizable. Ms. Sprinkle walked into the distance staring at the tablet as if she was hypnotized or something.

"Put your hands together and in front of your body," barked Mr. Jackson.

"Do you really need to tie our hands together?" Tank tilted his head sarcastically. "I mean, we are kids and you are a military veteran."

"What do you mean?" Mr. Jackson began tying Cage's hands together.

"Never mind," mocked Tank. "I get it, you are nervous that you are not up to the challenge of battling teenagers. That makes total sense."

Mr. Jackson swiftly lifted his right arm in the air and backhanded Tank across the face. When Mr. Jackson's arm made contact, it felt like a tidal wave had struck him. Tank fell back several feet and landed flat on his butt. The impact of the hit opened the scab on Tank's face and blood gushed down. Tank thought about professional wrestling on TV and what he had often seen. It was time to practice his taunting skills. Tank jumped to his feet as he concocted a plan. All he needed now was to execute his tactical strategy!

"Wow, that tickled a little bit!" declared Tank. "I think the wind blew me over."

"Oh yeah? You need another, huh?" Mr. Jackson promptly responded.

"This time can you see if Ms. Sprinkle can hit me? That way it might hurt." exclaimed Tank. "And what sort of fellow open-hand slaps another dude?" continued Tank.

Not getting the joke, Cage jumped in, "I thought only wusses slapped each other and winners threw punches!"

Tank smirked as he laughed. Mr. Jackson was now enraged. It reminded Cage of the classic cartoon scene where smoke comes out of the villain's ears. Ruby stood there watching Tank, thinking he was a mad man for provoking Mr. Jackson like that. Mr. Jackson stepped closer to Tank and grabbed him by both shoulders. Lifting his right knee, he jammed it into Tank's stomach, knocking the breath out of Tank as he fell to the ground. This was all part of the plan, but it sure did hurt.

"Sugar plumb!" Tank stood back up. "You take my breath away, sweetie pie. I bet you are fantastic in pillow fights!"

Calling Mr. Jackson "sugar plumb and sweetie pie" escalated things to the next level and it also caused Cage and Ruby to both giggle at the same time. Mr. Jackson grabbed Tank by the shoulders again and lined up another knee to the stomach. Although the first time was a hard hit, this time, the look in Mr. Jackson's eyes was different. This time his goal was to seriously damage Tank.

There is a moment in movies where time lags and it is like the scene is happening in slow motion. The director of the movie does this to show the reactions of the characters. Well, this was not a movie, but it sure felt like it to Tank. When Mr. Jackson stepped closer to Tank again, it felt like time had all but stopped.

Tank could see small sweat beads forming on Mr. Jackson's head. He could smell the chew and mild body odor coming from his armpits. With both of Mr. Jackson's arms now fully on Tank's shoulders and the incoming of the knee, Tank had to land his strike perfectly. As Mr. Jackson's knee went up, Tank's fist went down and was right on target. Mr. Jackson fell to the ground like he was doing a bellyflop at the pool.

"You hit me in the..." screamed Mr. Jackson.

"Ouch!" Tank interrupted Mr. Jackson before he could finish his sentence. "That looks painful!"

Mr. Jackson rolled on the ground for a few moments as he winced in pain. He looked like a toddler who had accidentally run into an open door at full speed while chasing a bouncing rubber toy ball. Ms. Sprinkle was so far out in the distance and infatuated with the tablet that she didn't appear to notice what was going on. Mr. Jackson was done messing around. He was more than mad! He was ready to kill!

Putting his right hand into his belt, he grabbed for the pistol, but he had forgotten that the hammer was already cocked because what happened next was more than a tad ironic. In his rage, Mr. Jackson attempted to pull the pistol from his waistband and instantaneously, there was a loud BOOM!

The percussion from the gun going off was so loud that Ms. Sprinkle began running towards them. Ruby and Cage both hit the ground and covered their heads. Tank didn't budge, even with the loud pop of the gunfire. He strategically stood a couple feet away from Mr. Jackson and carefully watched.

161

Blood was pooling on the ground. Mr. Jackson had managed to shoot the top of his own foot while pulling the pistol out of his waistband.

"Nice shot!" Tank stepped towards Ruby and Cage. "Looks like you just visited Coach Jackson's house of pain! Better luck next time, pumpkin!" He mocked Mr. Jackson.

Mr. Jackson rolled around on the ground, his groin aching from Tank's punch, his foot bleeding, and his pride curled up, weeping in the corner. Ms. Sprinkle was sprinting towards them and closing in fast. Tank asked Ruby to pick up the bag and for Cage to grab the Swiss seat. Tank took a few steps towards the sobbing Mr. Jackson and knelt down to pick up the pistol.

"Don't shoot him!" pleaded Ruby.

"I have never held a gat," fibbed Tank, aimlessly pointing the pistol towards Mr. Jackson. "Which end do the sharp pointy things come out of?"

Tank casually held the revolver at waist level, being careful not to point the barrel at Ruby and Cage. Not only had Tank held a pistol before, but he was a pretty darn good shot. Dad had taken him to the range tons of times and he generally felt comfortable with firearms. In fact, Dad had bought Tank his first rifle when he was only six years old and he had been shooting consistently ever since.

"Hey, Ms. Sprinkle," hollered Tank. "Did you know your fiancé is a highly trained sniper? He can hit a twelve-inch target at point blank range without even trying!"

Ms. Sprinkle stopped running when she noticed Tank holding the pistol. Tank cocked the hammer and carefully handed the gun to Cage. Unlike Tank, Cage had only fired a gun a couple of times and never a pistol. Cage reluctantly agreed to hold the pistol and shook nervously while Tank moved closer to Mr. Jackson.

"Stop moving!" commanded Tank to Mr. Jackson. "Hey grunt, you are losing a lot of blood!"

Tank unwound his belt and knelt down to get a better look at Mr. Jackson's hemorrhaging foot. He pulled off Mr. Jackson's tennis shoe and observed a small entry hole on the top where the bullet had gone in. The bottom of his foot looked like a horror movie inside of a butcher's shop. The mix of burning gunpowder, smoldering flesh, and incinerated rubber from the shoe

162

wafted a disgusting odor into the air. Using his belt, Tank wrapped it around Mr. Jackson's mid-calf muscle and then pulled as tight as he could. It wasn't the perfect tourniquet, but it would suffice for now.

Ruby was holding the backpack, Cage was holding the pistol, and Tank was tightening the pull string on his now beltless pants to prevent them from falling down. He didn't want the lack of having a belt to mean he was flashing everyone his underwear a million times. A flashback went through Tank's head as he remembered the time when he was in a movie theater, holding a large popcorn and mega drink, and his pants had fallen down around his ankles while he was walking. No sir, that was not going to happen today!

"Give us the tablet!" ordered Ruby to Ms. Sprinkle.

"No!" replied Ms. Sprinkle.

Cage pointed the pistol towards the sky and pulled the trigger. The loud BOOM caused Ms. Sprinkle to throw the tablet at Tank's feet. Cage would have looked cool if he had not let out a noticeable shrieking sound after the crack of the gunpowder went off and he dropped the gun after shooting it. In his defense, it was rather loud and it was his first time shooting a pistol. Ruby stooped down, picked up the tablet, and secured it in the bag.

Tank swiftly picked up the pistol and opened the cylinder. There were six rounds loaded and two of them had been fired. Using his left hand, Tank emptied the remaining four rounds into his right palm. It was time for Ruby, Tank, and Cage to scatter. Ruby's adrenaline must have been on full blast because she was yelling at Mr. Jackson and Ms. Sprinkle to "leave us alone and do not follow us." She kept repeating herself over and over. He was not sure if it was the numbness in his ears from the two loud gunshots, but Ruby sure had some pipes for vocal cords.

Holding the four bullets in his hand, Tank used his other hand to toss the pistol into the center of the burning temple fire which had been reduced to nothing more than a bed of hot coals. Moving the bullets to his right hand, he wound up his throw like a major league pitcher and launched them deep into the forest. He could hear the faint sound of them landing far in the distance.

"Good luck finding them out there," Tank mumbled under his breath.

"Are you okay to run?" asked Ruby to Cage regarding his injured legs.

"Yes, running away sounds wonderful. Let's get out of here!" Cage responded, with hesitant optimism in his voice. The look of fear filled his bloodshot eyes.

With the tablet vigorously bouncing around inside the backpack as Ruby carried it on her shoulders, the three friends booked it back down the path towards the river. Mr. Jackson had been immobilized and they could hear Ms. Sprinkle frantically yelling at him to get back up. Although the three friends didn't know where to go next, they were, at least out of immediate danger... or so they thought. As they ran, they could hear screaming behind them.

Seventeen
What Puppies?

Tank, Cage, and Ruby ran faster than they had ever run or at least it felt that way. Even with the wounds on Cage's legs, he was booking it down the trail, making his running style a bit interesting to watch. Tank imagined an ostrich being forced to put on tight pants and then envisioned three-dozen rabid chipmunks biting at the ostrich's bum. That was the best analogy Tank could think of to describe Cage's running style. In any other circumstances, the jokes would have been pouring out of Tank, but in this case, the lad was injured and at least he was trying his best to run.

A few minutes had passed and Cage had taken the lead doing his extravagant, shuffling, silly, chaotic running technique. Tank was a few feet behind him and Ruby was about five yards back. With the heavy awkwardness of the backpack, Ruby was forced to take shorter strides. She also commented that she felt like the bag was growing increasingly heavy as they moved farther away from the burned down temple. Surely that had to be all in her head.

"You're bleeding!" shrieked Ruby, as she grasped for another breath.

"Yeah," replied Tank, also breathing heavily as he looked over his shoulder. "Mr. Jackson opened the scab on my face with his weak slap."

"No, your leg!" Ruby pointed at Tank's leg.

Cage, hearing the conversation taking place behind him, slowed down to more of a walk. The adrenaline was starting to fade and his infected wounds were throbbing. Tank also slowed to look at his own leg. Sure enough, there was a fair amount of blood near the pocket area.

Darn! Tank had left the blade open on Phoenix's pocketknife just in case he had needed it in the temple. He carefully pulled out the pocketknife, closed the blade, and put it back into his pocket. The wound from the open blade was shallow but appeared to be nothing more than scrapes as a result of his legs moving up and down while he was running.

Cage stopped and promptly sat on the damp ground. Tank walked over to Cage and sat down, as well. Seconds later, Ruby joined them. Mr. Jackson and Ms. Sprinkle were far enough away so they could no longer be seen nor heard. It also helped that the trail to the temple was constantly curving and winding throughout the jungle. Dad would say "out of sight, out of mind," which was cliché, but an accurate way to describe the current situation.

"What happened to your leg?" asked Cage, pointing at Tank's pants.

"Oh, I was saving ketchup packets and one must have busted while I was running," replied Tank.

"Ketchup packets?" questioned Cage.

"Yes, of course, ketchup packets!" declared Tank in a convincing tone of voice. "I love ketchup! I am the ketchup king. Soy el rey loco del ketchup!"

"Oh, stop messing with him," whispered Ruby. "That is blood on your leg."

"Oh, I am not messing with him. How dare you!" Tank winked at Ruby. "You all don't keep random ketchup packets in your pockets in Kentucky? I keep ketchup in one pocket and mustard in the other in case I need them. What do you all do if someone offers you a hot dog? Do you seriously eat it with no ketchup or mustard? I guess Texans are better prepared and superior in their approach to life!"

Tank kept a serious, yet stoic look on his face for about two seconds and then they all busted out in glorious laughter. It felt so good to laugh and joke around again. Even if it was only for a moment, at least they were not thinking about their pending doom in the Amazon. Of course, it was blood, but the concept of a ridiculous Texan walking around with ketchup and mustard packets in his pockets for no reason was the slapstick humor they needed at that moment. Although funny, a hotdog slathered in ketchup and mustard did sound marvelous.

The hilarity didn't last long as Ruby's face went from happy giggling to sobersided intensity again. They could hear what sounded like screaming in the distance. The sound was high pitched like a whistle, but then the sound would fade away. A couple moments later, the sound returned.

This was no ordinary "I am scared of the dentist" scream. This was the scream you would hear when the out-of-control snowplow was about to hit the school bus. Furthermore, the school bus was stuck on the railroad tracks and a train was reaching 100mph, but then you come to realize the school bus is filled with hundreds of adorable puppies that are up for adoption. This screaming was the real deal!

Tank slipped into another daydream as he saw himself on a mission, driving an armored combat vehicle to stop the out-of-control train and snowplow from murdering the puppies. Driving the snowplow was Ms. Sprinkle and wearing a 1920's conductor uniform and donning a tall top-hat was Mr. Jackson. Ms. Sprinkle cackled, "Kill them all! Get those puppies!"

The daydream continued as Mr. Jackson stood on top of the main train engine. He grunted and stuck his pointer finger into his belly button. Tank jumped out of the armored combat vehicle as he used a tow strap to tie a grapevine knot to the frame of the bus. Tank pounded his chest and then pulled with all his might on the strap as he heaved the bus out of the way right at the last moment. His efforts were nothing more than brute strength and sheer determination.

"Save the puppies! Thou art your savior this day!" shouted Tank.

"WHAT PUPPIES?" a panicked and confused Cage cried as he jumped to his feet.

"Sorry," answered an embarrassed Tank. "Sometimes my inside thoughts come out of my mouth. There are no puppies."

Ruby's face showed that she was not surprised at Tank's randomness anymore. She let it go. The screaming started again, this time a little louder as if whomever was making the obnoxious noise was getting closer to them. Tank motioned for Ruby and Cage to get off the trail and hide in the thick shrubs which were about ten feet away. Normally, Cage and Ruby would have protested, but Tank was adamant that he would jog back down the trail and check out what was making the noise.

Generally speaking, hearing screaming should ignite a fire inside of everyone to run away, but not so much with Tank. His mind went to yesterday when he promised mom not to let curiosity get the best of him, but now here he was running down a trail in the Amazon jungle towards a bloodcurdling scream. He most likely would be eaten by a creature straight out of Hades! But hey, mom would understand that stuff happens, right?

Ruby helped Cage get off the trail. Cage's adrenaline rush was gone, his wounds were now starting to take their toll, and he winced in pain as they crouched behind a fallen tree. Tank continued running towards where the temple used to stand. By now, hypothesized Tank, it would be nothing but ashes. He was not super concerned about seeing Mr. Jackson or Ms. Sprinkle given they were now unarmed. Hopefully, Mr. Jackson was still enjoying that large piece of humble pie he was served from the escapade of shooting his own foot.

In Tank's head, all he could think about was dad and why he never mentioned any of this when they had moved to Kentucky. The dots had finally started to connect when mom had attempted to share dad's nickname when they were in the car yesterday. Tank, like a fool, had interrupted her. It didn't matter, though. Dad was the best man Tank had ever met and he trusted that if he was kept out of the loop, there was a good reason. Also, there was not an ounce of deceit in mom's heart. There had to be a logical explanation for her lack of transparency.

Tank jogged down the trail until he could see the small smoke cloud coming off the ruins of the temple. No Mr. Jackson, no Ms. Sprinkle, and no sign of where the screaming sound may have originated. Well, this was a pickle and not a delicious dill pickle either. This was that dreadful bread and butter pickle your grandma serves on the vegetable platter at Thanksgiving. Only sick and demented people enjoy bread and butter pickles. Sweet pickles are the same. Only demons consume those.

Did Mr. Jackson and Ms. Sprinkle go off the trail and try to navigate the jungle? There was only a single trail towards the river and trying to navigate the vast jungle would have been a death sentence for sure. Mr. Jackson was not the brightest bulb in the pantry nor was he the sharpest tool in the shed, but he was not a complete ignoramus either. No way was Jackson trying to freestyle the path to the river to return to Kentucky.

Tank scoured the area, trying to find a trace of the dynamic duo of Mr. Shoots-himself and Ms. Cakes-on-makeup. Mr. Jackson was undoubtedly hiding somewhere in the jungle finishing a coloring book and Ms. Sprinkle was likely looking for a mirror to admire her slightly below average facial features. Perhaps

Mr. Jackson was even coloring in the lines this time, but that was probably not the case.

The area was clear of any human life, but something was making that awful screaming sound. There was no way Mr. Jackson and Ms. Sprinkle had just vanished into thin air. Out of the corner of Tank's eye, he spotted little droplets of blood on the ground which led off the trail. This was going to be like tracking an animal during archery season. Follow the blood drops and the trophy deer would be at the end of them, except, in this case it was not a deer but a six-foot-tall meathead with a gunshot wound to the foot.

"Hey, get over here!" yelled a masculine voice from the thick jungle.

Tank was not usually flustered, but the ghostly voice alone caused him to nearly jump out of his own skin. Hearing the voice, Tank sprang into what looked like a martial arts fighting stance. His hands came up to protect his face and one leg went back as if he were preparing to kick someone round-house style to the face. The last thing he wanted was for Ms. Sprinkle to try and surprise attack him with the old, "hey, look over here" routine. Even worse would be Mr. Jackson hobbling over and then tripping over his own shoelaces, which Tank assumed he was not able to tie himself without adult supervision.

"Get over here!" This time a feminine voice called out from the thick bush.

"Who is that?" Tank pivoted on his foot to better position himself towards the sound.

"It's Mr. Jackson! Who do you think it is?" asked the male voice, sticking his head out for Tank to see.

Tank immediately recognized the face of Mr. Jackson as he peeked his head out of the jungle overgrowth. He could also see Ms. Sprinkle's face a couple feet away from where Mr. Jackson was crouching on the ground. This didn't look as much like a surprise attack as it looked like two people who were terrified of something or they had lost their minds? It was one of those options.

"Prove that it is you. The last time I saw you," yelled Tank, "what were you doing?"

"I was lying on the ground," Mr. Jackson promptly replied.

"Why were you lying on the ground?" inquired Tank.

"Because I got shot in the foot!" replied Mr. Jackson.

"Who shot you in the foot?" Tank said with a smirk.

"I shot my own foot, you little turd. Now be quiet and get over here!" Mr. Jackson snarled back.

Tank marched towards the tree line, being careful to watch for any sudden movements from either of them. Under his breath, but still loud enough for Mr. Jackson to hear, Tank uttered, "I bet you learned your marksmanship skills at the Island where real men go to the military."

Neither Mr. Jackson nor Ms. Sprinkle was even looking at Tank as their gaze was intensely focused on the place where the temple used to be. Mr. Jackson appeared to no longer be bleeding and Ms. Sprinkle was clutching her hands to her chest. Something had seriously frightened them.

"Okay, I am over here!" shouted Tank. "Why are you all acting so weird?"

"Keep your voice down and look over there," whispered Ms. Sprinkle.

Tank looked out in the distance where the temple used to be and he saw a squirrel darting through the low hanging branches in the jungle. Likewise, there was a small troop of monkeys frolicking around high in the trees. Other than the occasional random jungle sound out in the distance, Tank could not see anything else out of the ordinary.

"Okay, then," Tank said in a soft sarcastic voice, not seeing anything nefarious or of concern. "I am going to go back with my friends and you all are on your own."

"Don't you see it?" Ms. Sprinkle asked in a terrified tone of voice.

"It's more horrible than I imagined!" Mr. Jackson winced in pain while pointing towards the smoldering temple.

Tank took another good look around, trying hard to see whatever had startled them both. On a relatively low hanging tree branch sat a momma bird feeding a nest of baby birds. Not necessarily one to think something was cute nor precious, Tank shrugged his shoulders. Mr. Jackson and Ms. Sprinkle's face and body language indicated that they were about to make a run for it, or in Mr. Jackson's case, a "hobble" for it.

"It's going to eat us! I told you it was real!" stated Ms. Sprinkle.

"I didn't know, baby. I thought he was full of crap! He was constantly making up goofy stuff, trying to scare everyone," replied Mr. Jackson.

"Hey cray-cray people," interjected Tank. "I don't think it's big enough to eat you. It's only a bird. Also, to my knowledge, Amazonian squirrels are vegetarians, so chill!"

It was no more than a nanosecond after Tank had uttered the word "chill" that the mystery was solved. An enormous snake slithered from where the temple used to stand. It was Yacumama Serpente! The drawings in the cave were slightly exaggerated, but not by much. Then again, Yacumama was still far off in the distance. Maybe it was like looking up at an airplane flying at thirty-seven thousand feet. From the ground, it looked like a tiny dot moving across the sky. In this case, perhaps up close, Yacumama was a monster bigger than the picture in the cave.

The snake hissed and moved with haste down the trail in their direction. While Tank was watching the snake in both fear and amazement, Mr. Jackson and Ms. Sprinkle stood up to start running away.

As he was getting up, Mr. Jackson positioned his uninjured foot behind Tank and then gave him a shove, causing Tank to fall to the ground, landing on his buttocks. Yacumama was much faster than Tank expected and was closing in on his location. The snake did not appear to be interested in either Mr. Jackson or Ms. Sprinkle because its two black eyes were trained solely on Tank. Tank sprang to his feet and raced into the jungle, moving like a torpedo in corn syrup.

The terrain had changed significantly as he ran farther away from the trail. What was once a thick jungle had now morphed into an open, grassy plain with rolling hills. For a split second, it almost felt like he was back in Kentucky. He kept looking over his shoulder, checking to see if Yacumama was still following him.

In the distance, there were several creatures grazing. One of the animals looked like a pig but had the nostrils of a seal. Although it was totally an inappropriate time to think about food, Tank's stomach rumbled as he craved something delicious to eat. He looked at the grazing pig-seal and daydreamed about crispy bacon that was seasoned with sweet maple salt.

A strange thought entered Tank's mind. Here he was running through the Amazon and he had randomly noticed an animal that reminded him of a delicious food. Coincidentally, an enormous snake had noticed *him*...

"I *am the crispy bacon seasoned with sweet maple salt!*" Tank rationalized.

Tank's pace transitioned from all-out sprinting into fast-paced running. His brain needed to "digest" the reality of the situation. He took another quick look to check if Yacumama was still in hot pursuit and did not see the snake anywhere. He could hear what sounded like something moving in the grass, but it was hard to tell if that was all in his head.

Dehydration and exhaustion were impacting his judgement. Likewise, his emotions were all over the place. His heart kept whispering to him, "you got this, keep going," and his brain kept shouting, "give it up kid, you're going to die!" Tank slowed down to a brisk shuffle to process his thoughts.

Talk about daydreaming at the wrong time! He wondered if Yacumama Serpente would eat him raw or if he would cook him first. Then again, snakes don't have arms, so cooking would prove problematic.

Did Yacumama have venom or was he more like a boa constrictor that would squeeze him to death? If there was venom, would it kill him quick or knock him out because the snake preferred its food living during the feast? Then again, perhaps the venom would turn his insides to mush. Who could blame anyone for desiring to tenderize their steak before they dug in?

Tank's daydream surged into another daydream of dad explaining how to cook a steak... Long story short, the explanation included a tutorial from dad that the only proper way to eat a steak was medium-rare and that anyone that ate a steak well-done could not be trusted. Granted, dad's comment was a playful jab at grandpa who would always overcook the steak, but come on... dad did have a point, right?

Tank snapped back to reality as he nearly tripped over a field rock that was sticking up from the ground. It was hard to explain, but Tank accepted the fact that he was about to die. The daydreaming was nothing more than a way to get his mind off the most likely outcome. There was no way he could outrun Yacumama for much longer. Death seemed inevitable!

Eighteen
Sniper on the Hill

In an attempt to flee, Tank had swayed, swerved, and shifted his direction dozens of times, zigzagging like a madman. Tank assumed that Yacumama had given up the pursuit because he had not seen the serpent since he had first sprinted away. In that moment, Tank felt confident that he was out of immediate danger. His next move would be to find the trail and, hopefully, locate his friends.

His brain continued riding on an emotional roller coaster. There was no way he would be able to find the trail before it was dark again. Simply put, something was going to eat him out here! Tank wondered if perhaps a snake was not the worst way to go and maybe he had fled Yacumama needlessly.

He considered the options... Option one: Devoured by a snake. Option two: Slaughtered by a jaguar. Option three: Murdered by a caiman. Option four: Killed by 'input random animal name' here. All the options returned to the same conclusion, which was his pending death.

Even with his high level of endurance, Tank was running out of steam. He reckoned he had gone at least two to three miles by now. He maintained a slow shuffle, with bursts of intermittent speed when he thought he heard the sound of Yacumama in the grass.

Hopefully, Cage and Ruby were able to follow the trail back to the cave, and with any luck, a rescue crew would eventually find them. After all, they both had loving families in Kentucky and surely their families would try to find them. Moreover, Mr. Jackson, who likely was not hugged as a child, still conceivably had a mother who would wonder what happened to her baby.

Then again, maybe not.

173

Tank laughed out loud, envisioning Mr. Jackson, sucking his thumb, while his own mother explained why she, herself, did not like him that much. Would she even be surprised that he shot himself in the top of his own foot or would she say, "Well, that's my baby-boy!" It was a mean thought, sure, but still funny to imagine. As Tank contemplated that thought, he nearly fell over laughing as he imagined that Ms. Sprinkle would indeed, and without a doubt, be rescued.

When people are lost, it is common for them to shoot flares into the air. A flare burns at two-thousand degrees and is bright red or multi-colored. The purpose of the flare is for anyone and everyone searching for the lost person to see the flare, and then "abracadabra" like magic, the lost person is found. Ms. Sprinkle had been wearing twenty pounds of bright colored makeup, brighter than a flare. Tank figured that a search and rescue crew located on Mars would be able to see her face.

This would be the first rescue mission where the police would call the International Space Station to help spot the lost person. The directive to the space station would read... "Start looking for the eccentric circus lady." That would be all the direction the astronauts would need to locate Ms. Sprinkle.

"Enough running away," Tank turned around and faced the opposite direction.

For a split second, he felt optimistic that perhaps his tremendous athletic abilities were too much for Yacumama to handle. Playing the position of quarterback for the football team in Texas had taught him about escaping and maneuvering away from obstacles. In his mind, he spiked the football, but as he imagined his greatest victory, his rejoicing was cut short as the grass parted and the devil, in serpent form, came into view. Yacumama rose high above the grass, forming a classic snake "S" attack shape with its body.

"Holy mackerel! Holy Mother Teresa! Holy banana-butt!" Tank took a few steps backwards.

The serpent was a legit gargantuan leviathan, worthy of its legendary status. Tank could logically grasp why Ms. Sprinkle let out a blood-curdling scream earlier when she had first seen the thing. Although, out of fairness, Yacumama may have been the one that screeched when glancing and seeing the Makeup Queen.

Tank couldn't help the mean-spirited thoughts that kept popping into his head. Unfortunately, they came at the most inconvenient times. But, hey, "the Lady of Perpetual Cosmetics" did have a fiancé that insulted dad. She had personally aimed to steal mom's husband and there was the whole trying to kill them thing, too. Let the jokes continue to fly...

Gazing upon Yacumama, Tank could more than understand why whoever had drawn the picture in the cave of Yacumama went into detail to illustrate its disturbing features. Earlier, when Tank had spotted the serpent creeping from behind the temple's ashes, the size of the snake was not overly impressive, but that was all an optical illusion.

In the distance and in the direction from where Tank had run, he could see Mr. Jackson and Ms. Sprinkle staring at him. They were slouched down and were trying to keep a low profile.

Tank stared into Yacumama's eyes and Yacumama stared into Tank's eyes. He shifted his left foot, slightly moving forward, and Yacumama violently thrashed towards him, just out of striking range. Tank jumped back forcefully and paused in place. Yacumama rose up higher and more menacing than before.

Swiftly, the giant serpent took another swipe at Tank's body, only this time, Tank could feel Yacumama's foul breath penetrate his nostrils, pass deep into his sinuses, and land squarely on his taste buds. It was a mix between a rotting fish smell and that of raw sewage. It smelled worse than a pig taking a bath in contaminated hot goat cheese.

There was not much Tank could do nor was there any plan or strategy popping into his mind. Oh, how he wished dad were here to save him, but it wasn't going to happen this time. It was time to accept his fate. He had seen plenty of documentaries about snakes and, at least, he imagined it would be a quick way to go. Yacumama would bite him, wrap him up, and then eat him headfirst. Eventually, he would be a pile of poop somewhere in the Amazon jungle. Maybe Mr. Jackson would step in it! Speaking of Mr. Jackson, at least he and Ms. Sprinkle were about to get a good show of Tank being devoured by Yacumama.

Tank tried with all his might to think of something comical, but the best he could do was to imagine Yacumama giving him a friendly hug and kiss. He also remembered his Grandma Rae, pinching his cheekbones together and saying things like, "I could eat you alive," whenever she would greet him. Maybe, once he arrived in heaven, Tank would be able to tell grandma that Yacumama beat her to the punch. A slight smirk came across Tank's face as he boldly took a step forward to get closer to Yacumama's gigantic body.

There was only one thing left to do. Closing his eyes, he prepared for the inevitable incoming bite. Tank took one more step towards Yacumama. He could hear hissing, as if Yacumama was getting angrier at the sheer audacity of Tank inching closer.

Suddenly, across the plain, two enormously loud pops rang out, followed by two more loud bangs. The sound was certainly coming from a rifle. Tank knew the sound was not your granddaddy's peashooter. This was a sniper rifle, blasting and spraying bullets across the plain. Tank opened his eyes and watched as Yacumama rose up and faced the explosive sounds coming from the rifle.

Tank's ears were ringing and his head was spinning. What had happened? Amid the incoming gunfire, Tank had thrown himself to the ground faster than a burrito goes through a sumo wrestler. Covering his head with both arms, he sprawled out and buried his face into the dirt.

"Wasn't this lovely," he thought to himself. His four likely predictions were all wrong. He wasn't going to be eaten, he was going to be sniped!

There must have been a dozen shots fired and then the gunfire momentarily stopped. Granted, Yacumama was not some garden snake meandering through a pumpkin patch, but it was going to take some serious

176

gunfire to take this monster down. Yacumama was not going to roll over and die without putting up a fight.

As Tank lifted his head to look around, the shots rang out again. He could hear the bullets whizzing above his head.

What would dad do right now? Tank dug deep into his memories. Tank recalled a story that dad had shared about a combat drill he had done during training in Oklahoma. Dad said that to pass boot camp, the soldiers had to do a night infiltration combat mission where they had to crawl under barbed wire while the sergeants launched fifty-caliber rounds above their heads. The story dad told sounded thrilling, but now with bullets literally flying overhead, the thrill was gone.

As Tank remembered the story, dad had said that the secret to survival when being fired upon was all about staying low. "Move with a purpose and stay calm," dad would say. Tank made a split-second decision that he needed to move, albeit he was not sure where he was going to move to, but anywhere was better than in the line of fire of a trained sniper who was armed with a high-powered rifle.

As Tank considered his options, he contemplated people making lists of activities they liked to do. The list might include going out to dinner, watching a movie, or eating their favorite ice cream. Heck, they may even include going to a haunted house and encountering a guy in a mask who would chase them with a chainsaw! Tank knew the one activity not on the list would be crawling across the muddy Amazon plain while bullets flew over their head!

Tank kept his head low as he inched his body forward. His speed was pretty good considering he was crawling like a geriatric turtle walking backwards through peanut butter. Other than that, his speed was fantastic. After a couple moments of practicing his form, he was able to speed up a bit. He could feel sharp rocks scraping across his torso which went from the top of his collarbone down to his belly button. It hurt, but it was still better than small pieces of lead coming 3,000 feet per second from the barrel of a rifle.

Not only could Tank feel the spray of bullets overhead, but he also experienced heavy gusts of wind like a hurricane. An all-black helicopter gunship flew towards him, causing him to stop his low crawl and bury his head deeper into the ground. His head was buried in the topsoil to the point he was practically French kissing the core of the earth.

For a moment, Tank slightly lifted his head and opened his eyes. The helicopter flew low and fast as it zipped across the Amazon plain. The blades on the helicopter were moving faster than a blind dog chasing a squirrel covered in gravy. The noise coming from the gunship was like that of the Krakatoa volcano eruption.

The helicopter was armed with two large cannons on each side and a six-pod payload of air-to-ground missiles. An even bigger gun was attached below the pilot's seat. Tank could hear and see the helicopter as it fired the larger gun. It was moving towards Yacumama. Gigantic chunks of dirt were being ripped from the earth as bullets struck the terrain. The pleasant fragrance of gunpowder filled the air.

The helicopter made another pass, Tank closed his eyes, and prayed it would end soon. Even with the deafening gunfire and the sound of helicopter blades splitting the air, Tank could still hear the giant serpent hissing and growling. The helicopter switched from gunfire and launched a pair of air-to-ground missiles. The missiles whistled by as they tore through the atmosphere towards Yacumama.

The explosions sent such shockwaves across the area that it felt like a small earthquake. Once again, the helicopter came back around, but this time it did not fire any shots. It continued flying until the sound of the helicopter faded to nothing more than a mild hum in the distance. Enough was enough! Tank needed to abandon his prone position and see what was happening.

Seizing every bit of courage he had, Tank forced himself to lift his body off the ground. The horrendous noise had made his ears hurt, making the inside of his head feel like an old school steam engine was passing between his ears and into his brain. He came to his knees first, peeking up only enough to see above the tall grass. Yacumama was nowhere to be seen and the helicopter was no longer in the air. Tank couldn't determine if it was his ears playing tricks on him because he couldn't see the helicopter, but he thought he could still hear it.

It was time to stand up even though Tank thought doing so could be the end. If the sniper was still out there, then Tank would surely be an easy kill.

Despite his trepidation, Tank stood up. He was surprised to see, well, nothing. The sniper was gone, but all that gunfire had not gone to waste.

Tank walked toward the area where he had last seen the snake. As he got closer, Tank could see the outline of Yacumama laying on the ground. Blood was everywhere! It looked like a giant hot dog that had been drowned in a pallet's worth of jumbo ketchup containers. The smell was atrocious and the flies were already falling in love with the horrid corpse.

The sun hovered lower in the west, indicating that dusk was not too far around the corner. Seeing Yacumama's lifeless body was both encouraging and surprisingly depressing. The terror of the great serpent sent chills down Tank's spine, but the thought of the magnificent creature being slain was also a dreadful shame. Tank was thankful that he and his friends were safe and that Yacumama was dead, but dying from spraying bullets which descended from a death chopper was a terrible way to die.

The seconds felt like minutes and the minutes felt like a lifetime as Tank contemplated his next move. His priority was to try to spot the sniper and avoid being shot. His second priority was to keep from being demolished by a helicopter gunship. Tank oriented himself to the landscape and deduced the most likely place a sniper would be positioned. There was a single hill about 800 meters to Tank's left. One of the most beneficial tactics in combat is to seek higher ground. Tank rationalized that any clever sniper would make that area their shooting perch.

Much to Tank's surprise, he didn't have to look hard for the sniper. A large man, wearing a dark green camo uniform, a full-face mask, and a helmet, stood up and stared straight at him. Tank's first intuition was to fall back and kiss the ground again, but the sniper did something odd. He lowered his rifle and motioned for Tank to come closer.

What in the blue-blazes was happening? Tank wondered if maybe the sniper had been sent to save him. Maybe he was wrong to be fearful. It had been a full twenty-four hours since he and his friends went missing and perhaps this was someone from the rescue team.

Tank bolted across the plain in the direction of the sniper while avoiding getting too close to the body of Yacumama. He had seen too many horror movies where the monster was only pretending to be dead. When the victim got too close, the monster would jump up and attack. This didn't seem likely in this case because Yacumama had pretty much been torn in half from the gunfire.

If the sniper was a good guy, then Tank had no time to spare getting him to help find Cage and Ruby. For all he knew, they were being attacked by another heinous creature. An even worse scenario was that Ms. Sprinkle had captured them and Mr. Jackson would be torturing them.

Over the last day, Tank had physically exerted himself more than he had ever done in such a short period of time. With the energy he had left, he sprinted towards the sniper's location. The sniper remained still as he watched Tank running towards him, however, that all changed as Tank got within yelling distance.

Suddenly, the sniper turned around and started running away! Tank was fast, but compared to this chap, he felt slower than a snail in molasses. The sniper bolted away from Tank.

The intense sound of the helicopter seemed to come out of nowhere. A rope was thrown from the helicopter, suspended a couple feet off the ground. The sniper threw his rifle over his back, grabbed the rope, and attached it to a harness. Once he was securely connected, the helicopter took off.

It all happened so fast that Tank was having trouble putting his thoughts together quick enough to grasp the situation. The conflicting thoughts in his head were challenging to process. The sniper was clearly not there to hurt him or Tank would already be dead. It seemed that the sniper was trying to save him, but why save him only to leave him stranded in the Amazon? None of this made any sense at all.

The helicopter performed a turning maneuver and flew straight over Tank's head. It was flying low enough that the energy from the downforce of the helicopter blades threw Tank forcefully to the ground, causing him to roll several times across the hard rocky surface.

The speed of the helicopter was astonishing, as well. This helicopter was on a mission. As Tank looked up, he could see the sniper holding on with one hand to the rope and pulling a pistol from a holster which was mounted to the side of his hip with the other hand. Where could he be going? As Tank wondered about the intentions of the sniper, his thought ended prematurely as the helicopter slowed to a crawl.

Tank could see the sniper pointing to the ground and shouting at something or someone. At that moment, Mr. Jackson and Ms. Sprinkle stood up as the helicopter approached and the sniper dismounted from his harness. Tank had figured that with all the gunfire, those two would have fled with their tail between their legs. Now he wondered if they had been waiting and watching to see if Tank would meet his Maker and were so amused by the thought that they had forgotten to run away.

As the sniper approached them, Ms. Sprinkle took off running towards the rainforest. Mr. Jackson picked up a stick and was swinging it back and forth as if he were trying to get the candy out of a piñata at a birthday party. A platoon of eight men, holding rifles at the ready, charged from the rainforest in Ms. Sprinkle's direction. They were too far away for Tank to hear what they were yelling at her, but he watched as Ms. Sprinkle's hands went above her head and she surrendered to the soldiers.

To his credit, Mr. Jackson tried his best to fight off the sniper by using the stick, but his stick-fighting skills were about as impressive as his shooting skills. With the foot injury, Mr. Jackson looked like an angry one-legged pirate wielding a wooden sword.

The helicopter flew a short distance away and landed on the plain. As the sniper got close to Mr. Jackson, Tank assumed that he was ordering Mr. Jackson to give up, but again, to his credit, Mr. Jackson refused to waive the white flag of defeat.

Tank continued to watch the fiasco, eagerly waiting to see what would happen next. When the soldiers got within an arm's distance of Ms. Sprinkle, they zip-tied her hands behind her back, placed a bag over her head, rushed her to the helicopter, and tossed her headfirst into the chopper. Mr. Jackson, the one-foot warrior, kept swinging the stick.

The sniper stayed a safe distance away to avoid being struck. As the sniper watched Mr. Jackson's prowess at stick swinging, the sniper did something that Tank was not expecting. He tilted his head to the side and then holstered his pistol.

"No way," uttered Tank to himself. "No way Mr. Jackson frightened off an armed sniper with a tree branch."

181

The sniper took a few steps towards Mr. Jackson and paused. Mr. Jackson, more belligerent than ever, spat half-chewed brown snuff towards the sniper and then waved his fist in the air. Mr. Jackson kept barking "Oorah!" The sniper took a few more steps towards Mr. Jackson and paused again.

Mr. Jackson started taunting the sniper by pointing at him and mouthing foul words. The sniper shook his head a couple of times as Mr. Jackson continued to pursue confrontation. Even with his face hidden by the mask, Tank imagined the sniper thinking, "Who does this joker think he is?" Tank was wondering the same. Maybe Mr. Jackson was tougher than he had thought.

Nope! The sniper may have paused momentarily, but it was not because he was afraid of Mr. Jackson. The sniper reached into his cargo belt and pulled out a different handgun. This one was smaller, was black, and had a yellow plastic grip. The sniper was yelling at Mr. Jackson, but he was done requesting that Mr. Jackson comply with his instructions. The sniper proceeded to fire a single shot at Mr. Jackson. His aim was flawless.

The pistol didn't fire bullets, but from the barrel sprang two wires that emitted sparks. It was a "stun-gun!" Tank cheered as the wires contacted Mr. Jackson's face. One wire stuck to his left cheek and the other to his right cheek. It was almost cartoonish to watch Mr. Jackson's body flail as he fell to his knees. Tank wished that Cage could be here to see this! Ever since they had been trapped in the cave, Cage had made at least a dozen comments about Mr. Jackson being stun-gunned.

The sniper held the button on the stun gun, ensuring that Mr. Jackson was getting the shock of his life. Because of the turbulence of Mr. Jackson's convulsions, one of the canteens, which was attached to Mr. Jackson's belt, had accidentally opened and water began to pour down the front of his pants. Five of the soldiers that had snatched Ms. Sprinkle and hurled her into the helicopter came running towards the sniper.

As they came closer, one of the soldiers took his rifle, turned it backwards, and hit Mr. Jackson on the back of the head, causing him to fall face first to the ground. The sniper then approached Mr. Jackson and proceeded to pull a liquid-filled syringe from his load-bearing vest pocket.

The sniper released the wires from the stun gun and secured it back into the holster. Mr. Jackson had ceased shaking and a soldier promptly put his foot on his upper back. The sniper held the syringe with his left hand and inserted the needle into Mr. Jackson's neck. One soldier proceeded to grab Mr. Jackson by the feet while another soldier grabbed him under the shoulders, picking him up like a sack of moldy potatoes.

Mr. Jackson could be heard sobbing and groaning. The two wires, still sticking to his cheeks, dangled on the ground. The water stains on his crotch made him look like he had wet his pants. The soldiers transported him back to the helicopter and lobbed him into the cargo hold. This was not the best moment for Mr. Jackson's dignity nor his pride.

Tank stood there and continued to observe. Certainly, the soldiers realized that he was watching all the commotion. Even so, the helicopter lifted off the ground as the final soldier buckled himself into the seat. The sniper looked directly at Tank and locked eyes with him. He continued to shake his head like he was attempting to communicate something to Tank.

The helicopter flew about fifty yards from Tank, reduced its elevation, and hovered close to the ground. Three of the soldiers unbuckled and leapt out. Oh no! Maybe they had changed their minds about coming after Tank! Tank watched as the soldiers unexpectedly sprinted away from his location. It was as if they were on a new mission. But why? What were they running towards?

Tank could see a young girl near the jungle where the tree line and the plain merged together. She was wearing an olive-green camo backpack that was slung across her shoulders. Beside her was a youthful looking man wearing a leather jacket. Tank's heart sank deep into his chest as his worst fear was played out in front of his eyes. Ruby and Cage must have become impatient as they waited for him near the trail to the temple. Now they were in plain sight!

The soldiers held their rifles at the ready as their crosshairs focused on Cage and Ruby! One of the soldiers went left, one soldier went right, and one soldier raced to get behind their location. Once the soldiers were in place, the helicopter rose high in the sky and flew away in the opposite direction. Tank could think of only one option to try to help them. Before proceeding, he knew that there was likely nothing he could do to stop the commandos from reaching them, but he could possibly delay them enough to figure out a better option to aid in their escape.

The soldier that was veering left harnessed his weapon behind his back and pulled a stainless-steel canister from his vest. When the soldier pulled the pin, he threw the canister like a javelin towards Cage and Ruby. He proceeded to throw a second canister, then a third canister, then a fourth. With the help of the wind, smoke filled the area, making the entire plain foggier than a goldfish with amnesia.

The breeze swiftly moved the smoke towards the rainforest. Nothing and no one could be seen. As Tank's adrenaline shot through his body, he forgot about being tired and gained his second wind. Tank moved across the plain towards his friends like a greased pig fleeing a butcher shop.

Cage and Ruby had to be disoriented and frightened. Tank was hopeful that they would fall to the ground and try their best to hide in the tall grass. At a bare minimum, he hoped the soldiers would have to play a round of hide-and-seek for fifteen minutes before capturing them. Flashlights attached to the underside of the soldiers' rifles were illuminating the smoke. Cage and Ruby sprang to their feet and darted onto the plain. Their lungs ached from smoke inhalation.

Tank was furious at the sniper who had motioned for him to run towards the hill. All along, the sniper and his troops were plotting a cunning plan to capture Cage and Ruby. By coercing Tank to run towards the hill, the soldiers had been able to separate him from his friends. Tank wondered why they had let him escape the mouth of Yacumama. The snake could have eaten him and they could have saved the bullets and accomplished the same thing.

As Tank peered through the smoke, he realized that Ruby and Cage had split up. Whether this was intentional or by mistake, Tank did not know for sure. The soldiers were yelling commands for them to "Get on the ground now!" Fortunately, no shots were fired... yet. Ruby had managed to successfully flee and she ran straight into Tank's open arms. Her face said it all. She was terrified! The smoke was still heavy but was starting to fade.

"Tank!" Ruby wrapped him in a bear hug.

"I thought they had captured you!" exclaimed Tank. "I thought you were gone forever."

"They have him!" cried Ruby "I saw them tackle Cage!"

Tank pointed towards the smoke and declared, "Then who is that?"

184

Ruby smiled as she saw Cage come limping towards them through the smoke. The wounds on his legs had severely diminished his ability to move. Tank considered it a miracle as both he and Ruby hurried to him. Cage was hollering incoherent words and waving his arm as if he were trying to make them aware of something, but they could not make out what he was saying.

"It's.... A.... Trap....!" gasped Cage, but it was too late.

The three soldiers had them surrounded. Tank only had a split second as he whispered to Cage and Ruby.

"Please don't tell them about the name Phoenix; please don't tell them about my dad."

Ruby nodded, affirming that she heard Tank's statement as a soldier kicked Cage in the back of the knee and he fell to the ground. Another soldier wrestled Ruby to the ground, forcing her head into the dirt. The third soldier pointed his rifle at Tank. It was game over when the soldier made the following proclamation.

"Surrender or we kill them both!" commanded the soldier.

Tank fell to his knees and put his hands above his head. The battle may have ended, but Tank was ready to go to war to save his friends!

Nineteen
Commando Interrogation

The soldiers grabbed Tank first. Before he could get a close look at the soldiers, he had a dark bag placed over his head. He almost puked as the bag was not clean and the inside smelled rancid like a skunk's backside. He could hear Ruby and Cage having the same done to them. Once the bags were securely over their heads, the soldiers searched their pockets, confiscating Ruby's cellphone and Cage's inhaler. Oddly enough, the soldiers did not touch or search the backpack that was still dangling from Ruby's shoulders.

When they got to Tank, they reached into his pocket and pulled out Phoenix's pocketknife and the lighter. A long, unexplained silence followed. One soldier ordered them to move, but it wasn't like they had a choice as other soldiers came from behind and grabbed them by the shoulders, forcefully shoving them forward. The sound of the helicopter had disappeared into the distance and it didn't appear that it was circling back to pick them up any time soon.

Walking in a single file line as soldiers walked adjacent to them, Tank, Ruby, and Cage had no idea where they were going. Cage was struggling to walk at the desired speed so a soldier picked him up and fireman-carried him the rest of the way. Tank could hear Cage groaning as the soldier brutishly carried him along. Tank could hear the soldiers speaking to each other, but they were communicating in what seemed to be military code speech.

Tank listened attentively as he tried to figure out what they were saying, but they were being intentionally quiet with their communication. Occasionally, a soldier would give an update on their location via the radio and the person on the other end of the radio would respond with "Roger."

Tank recalled a memory where dad had explained that the military used phrases like "Roger" when they talked to each other. Of course, dad made up a

186

story telling Tank about a soldier named Roger. They could never find Roger because he had to "take a leak" as dad would put it. Mom would say, "Stop it," and giggle at dad's comments. Dad would then double down and say, "It's not my fault Roger had a tiny bladder" as he smiled at Tank.

The story dad had told made no sense, but that was the point of the story. It didn't have to make sense. It was all to get a laugh using cheap toilet humor, nothing more, nothing less. Eventually, dad would follow up with the actual explanation. Military members say "Roger" to tell the other person they have "received" their message. In Tank's mind, however, dad's "potty explanation" was way more entertaining.

Other than stumbling a few times because of the rugged terrain, the walk was uneventful. Prior to the bag being placed over his face, Tank had a couple of moments to observe his friends. Ruby and Cage were in a state of shock with what was happening to them. Tank was almost certain they were still walking behind him, but with the bag over his head, it was hard to tell.

Coincidentally, Tank remembered yesterday morning when they were despairing they may never see another human being again. When Mr. Jackson and Ms. Sprinkle had showed up, they thought "Anyone but these two doofuses." Now that they had encountered gun-wielding commandos and gunships, the doofuses didn't seem all that bad.

Looming in Tank's head was the fear that the soldiers were leading them somewhere to be executed. As he considered this, he reasoned that because the accents of the soldiers were American, they surely would not do such a thing and that helped to put his mind at ease. Of course, it was possible, Americans could be villains, but it didn't seem likely in this case.

These commandos did not stumble upon Tank and his friends by chance. They were ordered to be there. For all Tank knew, these guys were dad's buddies and he, Ruby and Cage were being taken to safety. Perhaps the whole "surrender or we kill them" comment was all a big misunderstanding. The thought, however, did enter Tank's mind that his assumption could be wrong.

The walk continued for what seemed like another hour. There were no breaks, no talking, and no water. When the soldier that sounded like he was in charge gave the order to "halt," all the other commandos stopped at once. Up until the soldier in command ordered his men to "halt," Tank could hear the soldier's feet slapping the ground in harmony as they marched, their feet collectively stopping at the same time. A new voice emerged from the distance, barking instructions at their group.

There is something about the armed forces where the tone of voice and sentence structure indicate the hierarchy of the person speaking. Tank had noticed this military characteristic over the course of several years from being around soldiers of both higher rank and lower ranks. Whoever this new guy was, he was considerably higher ranking than the troops who had placed the bags on their heads. Tank figured he was likely an officer, which was verified a couple moments later when the soldier nearest to them said the name, Colonel Grimes, while greeting the strange voice.

"Sergeant Woodbine, are these the three I heard mentioned over the radio?" asked Colonel Grimes.

"Roger, these are the three," replied the commando.

"Get those bags off their heads and bring them inside the FOB," ordered the Colonel.

Ruby let out a breath of relief when the bag came off her head. Cage was next, and then finally Tank. Looking around, Tank was surprised to see that the soldiers had brought them back to what appeared to be a special forces outpost. A few moments ago, the Colonel referred to this place as an FOB, which stands for "Forward Operating Base." The outpost was nothing more than a couple of tents and three guard towers which wielded machine guns that were set up strategically around the perimeter.

Razor wire had been tactically positioned about twenty feet outside the boundary. Additionally, twenty feet farther from the boundary were bulges in the terrain that appeared to be landmines. Tank assumed the commandos had planted them into the ground for extra security. There was a single entry point and a path, which they had just walked, leading to the FOB.

Near the tents lay a huge pallet of bottled water and near the center of the FOB was a helicopter landing pad. There was no sign of a helicopter. The helipad was made of concrete and elevated off the ground. The Colonel and his Sergeant approached them, while the other troops strolled back to their tents. Tank noticed only a dozen soldiers or so occupying the FOB.

"You all must be thirsty!" The Colonel motioned for them to grab a bottle of water from the pallet.

The Colonel's voice was calm and soothing. Colonel Grimes was taller than an average man and had short gray hair. He had several wrinkles across his face, particularly around his eyes and mouth. His mustache was neatly kept and he wore a beret on his head that was perfectly folded over his right eye. Sergeant Woodbine, by contrast, was a noticeably shorter man and had darker hair. He was clean shaven and, instead of a beret, was wearing a military style camo baseball cap.

The three friends didn't think twice as they each snatched and chugged a couple of one-liter water bottles. Nothing had ever tasted that good, that was until Sergeant Woodbine pulled out a handful of protein bars from one of his cargo pockets. Cage, Ruby, and Tank walked toward the helipad, sat down, and started devouring the protein bars.

The mere fact that the helipad was concrete meant that the FOB had been there for a while. The uniforms of the soldiers were unmarked. There were no insignias, no patches, no flags, and no rank indicators on their chests.

"How long have you kids been out here?" inquired Colonel Grimes.

"Since yesterday morning." Ruby filled her mouth with a chocolate chip cookie dough protein bar.

"Yeah," added Cage. "We crawled into a miner's shaft near our high school in Kentucky and ended up in this wild place."

When Cage mentioned the miner's shaft, Tank observed the Colonel motion his hand in the air towards one of the guard towers. Inside the guard tower, on the east side of the FOB, Tank could see a soldier picking up a radio and relaying a message, but to whom the message was sent was unknown.

The roof of one guard tower housed a sizable satellite dish. It was similar to satellite dishes that were used to get extra TV channels in homes. Tank hadn't noticed before, but there were two different types of all-terrain vehicles parked behind the guard tower. Each had multiple red spotlights mounted on the back. The smaller vehicles looked like four-wheelers. Tank also observed other large vehicles that looked like hybrids, resembling a four-wheeler and a boat. The situation made Tank feel uneasy as something didn't feel right about the soldiers or the entire layout.

Colonel Grimes cracked a joke about the three smelling like spoiled avocado and musty garbage. He asked Ruby about the origins of her backpack. Ruby responded by walking him through what had transpired inside the cave and how they had happened upon the backpack. She was careful to ensure no reference of Phoenix was mentioned in the details.

The pace of Ruby's explanation was lengthy and thorough. Colonel Grimes interrupted her multiple times as he asked clarifying questions, specifically regarding the contents of the bag. He grew more and more impatient as she continued.

There was a bizarre curiosity intertwined with the Colonel's questions. Ruby failed to take the hint that the Colonel could have cared less about her story and only wanted to know what was in the bag. She spent the next five minutes sharing how scared they had been and how she wanted to go home. Tank remained quiet and tried his best to show zero reaction in his facial expressions.

"That is an interesting story, kid," replied the Colonel. "May I please see the backpack?"

Ruby hesitated but complied with the Colonel's request. Colonel Grimes put his hand out to retrieve the bag as Ruby passed it to him. Promptly, the Colonel handed Sergeant Woodbine the bag and Woodbine unbuckled the strap that was securing the contents inside. Woodbine gently placed the bag on the ground and both he and the Colonel knelt to scour the contents. Sergeant Woodbine held out the compass for a moment but discarded it to the side like it was trash.

The Swiss seat Tank had crafted in the temple was knotted up and remained in the bag. Colonel Grimes let out a sigh and he tossed the rat's nest of rope to the side as his hand moved through the empty bottom of the bag. Ruby was not sure what he was looking for, but his attitude was rapidly shifting from easy going to raging malevolence the longer he spent searching the bottom of the bag.

Colonel Grimes picked up the bag and shook it three or four times. In his anger, he turned around and dropkicked the backpack like a professional football kicker attempting a record breaking sixty-seven-yard field goal.

"Where is the Tablet of Zurvan?" shouted Colonel Grimes. He nodded his head and gave an incognito command that only Sergeant Woodbine appeared to understand.

Sergeant Woodbine hollered a command in the direction of the tents and immediately, multiple soldiers rallied to the helicopter pad. The sergeant and a couple of the soldiers ordered Cage, Ruby, and Tank to their feet and pushed them forward causing the water bottles to be knocked out of their hands.

"Mr. Jackson and Ms. Sprinkle took the tablet!" exclaimed Ruby. "We were waiting on the trail to the temple for our friend to return. That's when they ambushed us and stole the tablet."

"Who are they talking about?" uttered Colonel Grimes to Sergeant Woodbine.

"The two adult civilians we reported, sir," responded Sergeant Woodbine. "We have them in custody and have already searched them. I can personally confirm they do not have the tablet. They are on their way to A.D.X. Millard as we speak. We found this on the male." He pulled out the dog tags that had P.T. carved into them.

"Interesting!" Colonel Grimes smiled. "The top brass will be excited to have a little chat with Phoenix when he gets to A.D.X. Millard. We have been trying to find that buster for years. I would hate to be him when they learn his identity, especially after all the headaches he has created for our commander."

"Warriors of Thárros? It's more like the Gutless of Thárros!" A soldier scoffed and laughed in a mocking way.

"Sir," declared Sergeant Woodbine, pointing at the three, "we tracked these three teenagers for several hours yesterday. Our hidden cameras and satellites viewed them entering the GAP in Kentucky. Near the waterfall, our surveillance team observed them using the tablet when they exited the river. We know for certain they had possession of the tablet."

"Why would we lie to you?" rebutted Ruby. "Mr. Jackson and Ms. Sprinkle took the tablet."

"Yeah!" Cage threw his hands in the air. "Those two are the reason we are here in the first place. They already knew about O Dourado and wanted the tablet from the start. You should ask them about O Dourado."

191

Colonel Grimes regained his composure. For a moment, Tank was worried that he was going to pull his pistol from his hip holster and start blasting. Colonel Grimes looked like he could chew on nails, drink gasoline, and crap lightning bolts considering how angry he was getting.

Tank kept looking forward innocently and was careful not to speak. Dad had shared with him some basics of interrogation and the importance of not voluntarily providing information to anyone that may have malicious intentions. When it came to interrogations, dad taught him that "less is more."

"Why would we care about O Dourado?" scoffed Colonel Grimes.

"It's why you want the tablet, isn't it?" asked Ruby. "Treasure is all you and your men care about."

"I am sure our leaders wouldn't mind the financial gain of a city made of gold, but that's small compared to what that tablet is worth," responded Sergeant Woodbine.

Sergeant Woodbine made it crystal clear that they could care less about O Dourado and the potential riches the City of Gold may yield. As Colonel Grimes paced back and forth, Ruby kept locking eyes with Tank. Tank kept locking eyes with Cage and Cage kept locking eyes with Ruby.

The way their eyes moved back and forth was slightly comical because they all knew what was on each other's minds. How were they going to get out of this? Since they had arrived in the Amazon, they were asking the million-dollar question... *What in the world was happening?*

"Sergeant Woodbine, take a platoon of your men and scavenge the area for the tablet. If you don't find it by 0800 hours, then terminate the captives, except this one!" Colonel Grimes commanded, as he pointed at Tank. "Put this stud on the first transport to A.D.X. Millard. We need to have a little chat with him about the symbols on that pocketknife and lighter that we found in his possession."

"Why do you all want the tablet so badly?" yelled Cage, digressing to the tablet. "You all want the tablet so badly that you are willing to execute a couple of kids if you don't get it?" he continued, incredulously .

Colonel Grimes chuckled a bit. "Well, it's simply the fact that you already know about one of the tablets. That knowledge seals your fate. We must kill you. Those are the orders we have received directly from D.C. Of course, if you are willing to serve your country and help us find them, things could get a lot easier. If not, things could get a whole lot worse. Well, will you serve your country?" asked Grimes. He studied Cage, Tank, and Ruby's reaction to the question. Their faces said it all.

"No, I didn't think so." Colonel Grimes turned his back to them.

Sergeant Woodbine strolled off towards the tents and most of the soldiers followed him. He could be heard providing details of their plan to search for the tablet as they made their way back to the temple. Mr. Jackson and Ms. Sprinkle must have hidden the tablet when they noticed the soldiers coming in their direction. What did it even matter though, especially after Colonel Grimes' pronouncement about their fate. They were going to be executed, regardless.

Soldiers clutched Ruby, Cage, and Tank by their hands and moved them away from the helipad. Near the water pallets, a steel pole projected out of the ground. The pole was almost eight feet tall, resembled a metal light pole, and was anchored to the earth in thick cement. The pipe was hollow and had four shower heads which pointed in different directions. This must have been where the soldiers showered after being out in the field all day.

As they neared the area, the soldiers zip-tied Ruby's hands around the pole. Cage struggled against the soldiers, but, eventually, his hands were also securely fastened around the pole. Tank did not contest being zip-tied and on his own volition, put his hands around the pole. At this point, Tank had not made a sound.

The soldiers walked away as Colonel Grimes casually strolled over to their location. He was smiling from ear to ear and was amused to see the three kids zip-tied to the pole. The Colonel was gearing up for Round 2 of the interrogation and Tank was worried that his friends may unintentionally provide him with too much information, like their home addresses or names of their family members. He didn't want to risk the Colonel trying to gain leverage over them.

Ruby wept and Cage was at a loss for words. Tank looked aimlessly into the distance trying his best to keep a fierce gaze on his face. An idea unexpectedly popped into his head, but it was nutty and a long shot should it work. He needed to distract and discourage Colonel Grimes from continuing his questions. This called for something out of the ordinary, something risky... something on the brink of utter ridiculousness.

"We are expecting a big storm in a couple of hours," jeered Colonel Grimes. "The forecast is for baseball sized hail and severe lightning. I am glad I am not the one strapped to a steel pole. You can make this end, you know. All you must do is tell me where to find the tablet and I will order my men to release you unharmed."

"Helicopter blades spin really fast," Tank said casually, his voice in movie theatre volume as he continued to stare into the distance. "But do they go left or right? Around and around they go, where they stop, nobody knows..." As he uttered this last statement, his voice transitioned into a creepy, whispering voice.

Tank turned his head and stared at Colonel Grimes like he was a unicorn wearing a prom dress. Ruby and Cage were dumbfounded by Tank's bizarre behavior. On a scale from one to ten, Tank had reached nutty level eleven. Clicking his tongue against his cheek, Tank clicked, clacked, and clopped his mouth as he made a variety of noises. Colonel Grimes tilted his head and looked at Tank. He then cocked his head and looked at Cage and Ruby as he tried to make sense of the situation.

"There once was a little helicopter that thought he could fly, he spun, he sputtered and he flew away like my uncle Dan." Tank continued to utter incoherent nonsense as he went cross-eyed.

"What's wrong with this kid?" asked the Colonel. "Is he one glazed donut short of a baker's dozen or something?"

"Yes, as long as I have known him," declared Ruby.

"He does this sometimes," added Cage. "He is from Texas if that helps explain things."

"I be from the state starting with "T". I like pickled yams and pumpkin cakes! Pour me some sweet tea and slap my knee partner..." Tank began to shuffle his feet like he was two-step dancing. He then shouted a big Texas "Yeehaw!."

Colonel Grimes was beyond confused as he scratched his head. He looked at Tank, who was dancing like a fool. Ruby and Cage looked at each other seriously pondering whether Tank had genuinely lost his marbles this time.

When Tank bellowed, "Giddy up, giddy up, giddy up you curly wolf," a couple of soldiers poked their heads out of their tent to see what all the commotion was about. Colonel Grimes shrugged his shoulders and started walking away. What hopes he had for continuing the interrogation seemed to have been aborted.

Tank stopped dancing when the Colonel turned away. Acting like an outlandish fool was the only clever idea that had bounced through his brain. If he could perplex the Colonel enough, then maybe he would give up asking them questions. The silly idea was working perfectly until the Colonel whirled around and faced them again.

"You know." The Colonel performed an exaggerated pause. "I have a better idea. I have changed my mind should we not find the tablet."

"You're not going to kill us?" whimpered Ruby.

"No, I have thought of a better solution," stated Colonel Grimes. "See, tomorrow the locals are going to catch wind that their precious snake is dead and they are going to look for someone to blame. You three brats will take the responsibility."

"We didn't kill Yacumama!" Ruby cried. "We are only teenagers! They will know you are lying."

"Oh, they won't ask any questions," quipped Colonel Grimes. "Three outsiders are roaming around their territory! The locals will connect the dots on their own and you will be held responsible."

"We will tell them the truth," postulated Ruby. "Then they will come after you."

"That is a cute thought," winked Colonel Grimes, as he laughed. "Did you know Yacumama is considered a deity to them? After they torture you, they will likely skin you, roast your carcass over a fire, and then eat you for dinner. I guess in a weird way I should thank you all. I have wanted to slaughter that bloody snake for years and finally got approval. Once the head honcho heard the tablet was at risk of being damaged, he gave the order to kill it."

When Colonel Grimes had stopped chuckling, Tank announced, "Polar bears and daffodils, they both smell pretty and wear fancy leotards, but don't pet the hippo or he will slap your pony."

Colonel Grimes shook his head as he sneered at Tank. Part of Colonel Grimes wondered if this strange boy was messing with him, but Tank kept up the charade. Next, Tank bobbed his head like a chicken. On his final bobbing motion, Tank puffed out his chest and vocalized a yodel. He hit most of the musical notes with gusto and bravado.

Upon completion of the yodel, Tank held out his hand to Colonel Grimes and asked him to "help him make music to honor Yacumama." The Colonel was not sure what to make of Tank's peculiar behavior. Moreover, Tank, pretending to be bonkers, was throwing Grimes off his interrogation game. Colonel Grimes met Sergeant Woodbine halfway as Grimes was walking back to his tent and handed him a quarter-filled glass of whiskey.

The sun was going down and several overhead spotlights illuminated the area. As Colonel Grimes got to his tent, he turned one more time to look at the three captives. Seeing the Colonel staring once more, Tank used his hands in the gloom of the lights to create shadow puppets. Colonel Grimes could be seen muttering, "Oh, forget it!" as he opened the slit in his tent to go inside.

The commando interrogation was over and hopefully, Colonel Grimes was lying about a thunderstorm in the forecast. One of the machine guns on the guard towers swiveled around and was pointed at them. They needed to produce a plan to escape or tomorrow would be their last day on earth.

Twenty

Drive it Like You Stole It!

"Cage, are you okay, brother?" asked Tank, speaking softly.

"Just peachy, bro!" Cage grunted as he sat with his hands zip-tied around the pole. He carefully lifted his pant legs up for his friends to see.

The wounds on Cage's legs had gone from bad to worse over the last few hours. Tank didn't want to tell him what he was thinking, but he wondered if Cage would have to have one or both of his legs amputated because of the infection. The wounds were seeping pus and smelled horrendous. It looked like two pieces of hairy French bread sticking out of his torso and moldy cottage cheese was oozing out. For how bad it looked, the smell was twice as horrible.

Ruby sat and tried to move closer to Cage. With her hands also tied around the pole, she tried her best to comfort him. If her hands had been free, she would have gladly wrapped him in a big hug and told him that everything would be okay even though she feared it might not be. Although it was not the most comfortable and not much space was available, Tank also sat closer, trying his best not to bump into Cage's festering legs.

"We need to wait a couple of hours for the guard on that tower to stop paying attention. Eventually, he will need to go to the bathroom, right?" whispered Tank.

"Don't even say it, Tank," interrupted Ruby. "There is no way we are going to escape this one." She wept as she continued.

"I wish I could see my mom one more time. I wish with all my heart I could tell her how much I love her just one more time." Cage hung his head as he also sobbed.

"There is always a way to escape," urged Tank. "Don't you all ever watch movies or professional wrestling cage matches?"

"Ugh, this isn't an action movie nor is it some silly cage match on TV," Ruby exclaimed, with frustration in her voice. "We are going to die. You know escaping is impossible."

Tank looked at his friends and then glanced up at the guard tower. The soldier in the tower had a machine gun, which looked like a fifty caliber, aimed in their direction. Maybe they were right to give up. There is an old saying, "A person can survive anything as long as they have hope, but once hope is gone, despair is all that is left." Despair is treacherous as the person's will to fight vanishes, and once the will to fight disappears, then death is sure to follow.

"Oh, come on," declared Tank. "Hope may be hard to see sometimes, but trust me, it is not gone. Think of all we have already been through."

Ruby tilted her chin up to give Tank a small grin, but she was struggling to be optimistic.

Occasionally, Colonel Grimes would pop his head out of his tent, yell something random, and look over at them. His body language and speech indicated that he was thoroughly enjoying his bottle of whiskey. Sergeant Woodbine and a small dispatch of troops could be seen gearing up for their mission to search for the tablet. Tank figured they would be heading away from the FOB momentarily.

Escaping was going to be problematic. The pole they were attached to had shower heads that were sticking out about eight to ten inches. The zip-ties were snug on their wrists. If they were able to somehow climb on each other's shoulders, then perhaps they could finagle their hands around the shower heads.

If they could free their hands, then theoretically, the person on top could jump down. Once they were down, they could put the next person on their shoulders, and so on until all three were freed.

Trying not to draw attention, Tank leaned back and put his feet on the pole. He used his legs and pushed with all his might while simultaneously pulling his arms in the opposite direction. He tried his best to act like he was casually sitting there. He even yawned a couple of times to illustrate to the guard in the tower that he was not trying to escape. The zip-ties were only half an inch thick, but the plastic was strong and resilient. He tried for about thirty minutes to break the zip-ties. There was a reason why the military used them to restrain people and Tank was figuring that out the hard way.

The sun gave way to the moon and night set in. The stars in the sky were beautiful as they illuminated the jungle. Not a single cloud could be seen and the wind was mildly blowing a cool breeze. Animals of all sizes and types could be heard frolicking around in the forest. Colonel Grimes must have been lying about the severe storm coming their way in an effort to panic them so they would share more information about the tablet's location.

Integrity is important in the military, but during an interrogation, the person trying to gather intel is prone to lie. While this did not surprise Tank, he was ultimately glad that the Colonel was lying about the storm. Lightning hitting the pole would have turned Tank and his friends into human shish kebabs.

Tomorrow, Ruby and Cage were going to be turned over to the locals and Colonel Grimes had cynically informed them that they would be eaten. Tank had heard that cannibals still existed in the Amazon, but hopefully, that was false, too. Moreover, the Colonel also mentioned that Tank would be transferred to some place called A.D.X. Millard. He was not sure what that meant and he sincerely did not desire to find out.

The Colonel had used the word "*Zurvan*" to describe the tablet. He had also referred to the tablet in plural form as if there was more than one. Hopefully, the government was prepared to be disappointed as Tank had no clue what they were talking about. Regardless of the consequences, he was not going to answer any of their questions about Phoenix's pocketknife or the lighter because that would lead them to his dad.

Struggling to keep his eyes open, Tank drifted off to sleep. As he slept, his head would tumble downwards and his body would jerk forward, waking him up. Ruby had already fallen asleep and was snoring like a chainsaw revving. If it were not for Ruby sawing logs in her slumber, Tank would have already passed out. Tank looked over at Cage who was asleep, as well.

Trying to get comfortable while your hands are zip-tied around a pole is impossible. Ruby had leaned forward and her left shoulder was tightly pressed against the pole. Cage's body had collapsed towards Ruby and her right shoulder was supporting his head. Sporadically, Cage's body would start jittering uncontrollably from the infection ravaging his immune system. Tank leaned forward and placed his head on the pole, trying his best to close his eyes. He needed to get at least a couple hours of sleep for he was past the point of exhaustion.

As Tank finally slept, he dreamt. In an instant, he was out of the Amazon Jungle. Colonel Grimes did not exist, Yacumama was not real, and mom was picking him up after his first day of school. He jumped into the car right as she turned down the talk radio station. Mom asked him how his day had been and he responded with nothing more than a shrug of his shoulders.

In the dream, mom asked him how he felt about his dad being Phoenix and if he had successfully returned the Sacred Tablet of Rio de Monstros. Tank looked at her and started yelling, "Why didn't you tell me, mom? Why didn't you tell me, mom?" She started crying and replied with "I wanted to sweetie, but your father is a..."

The dream ended abruptly as a semi-loud pop, followed by a foul odor, filled the FOB. The series of thuds across the FOB were louder than a BB gun, but quieter than a typical gunshot. Tank's head came off the pole and he looked up trying to figure out what was happening. Because of the intensity of the dream, he was experiencing a cold sweat and the weight of his body, pushing against the pole, had left a red indentation on his face that was sore when he touched it.

He must have slept for a minimum of two to three hours. Ruby and Cage also woke up and were rattled. They tucked their heads down out of instinct. The machine gun mounted to the guard tower was still pointed at them, but the soldier manning the station was slouched over and unconscious.

Subtle popping noises could be heard around the FOB. Gradually, the noises disappeared and a lone soldier appeared, exiting Colonel Grimes' tent. Ruby and Cage lifted their heads as the eerie silence had aroused their curiosity. The lone soldier was not Colonel Grimes! The soldier moved towards them. He was wearing a similar, yet unique, uniform from the troops they had seen earlier near the helipad. Another soldier, who was stationed at the FOB, came charging out from one of the tents, but he was taken to the ground. In a flash, he was put to sleep via hand-to-hand combat. The new guy, whoever he was, was certainly not a friend to Colonel Grimes and his unit of commandos.

Tank bounced to his feet and tried his best to shield Ruby and Cage with his body. The new soldier tenaciously made a beeline towards the shower pole where the three friends were detained.

Tank barked, "Stay back, stay back, get away from us!" The soldier did not slow down and reached into his pocket. He was on a mission, but what that mission was they did not know. Tank took a deep breath and watched as the soldier pulled out a knife and prepared to skewer them to death.

"I'm sorry," moaned Tank to Cage and Ruby. "I am sorry I could not protect you."

"We know, we know." Ruby and Cage nodded their heads, understanding Tank's sentiment for apologizing.

They closed their eyes and held each other as the soldier held out the knife towards their bodies. The knife cut deep, but it did not cut flesh. Cage felt something he did not expect. The soldier had sliced through the zip-tie and freed his hands from the pole! He then proceeded to cut the zip-ties from both Ruby and Tank's hands. When Tank opened his eyes, the soldier had stood up and was already taking a few steps back. The soldier lifted his wrist to his mouth and like a classic spy movie scene, spoke to his watch saying, "The package is free, repeat, the package is free."

"Who are you?" questioned Tank.

The soldier did not reply because his attention was on Cage's legs. Strung across the soldier's back was a green medical bag. He wasted no time treating the wounds on Cage's legs. Cage laid down on his back as the soldier gave him a firm nudge to do so. The soldier started by pouring a clear liquid on his legs which caused Cage to wince in pain. Once the liquid was bubbling up, the soldier patted both his legs dry, covered them with gel, and then wrapped them in gauze and bandages. He was quick, super quick, with his treatment.

"I am going to give you two shots in the arm." The soldier pulled out a syringe. "One shot is a powerful antibiotic and the second shot is for the pain. The medicine will take about fifteen minutes to kick in."

Cage did not protest. What was he going to say, "No sir, please don't save my life?" Besides, the soldier had single handedly taken down a special forces outpost filled with well-trained commandos. Tank watched as the soldier administered the two injections into Cage's arm. He had so many questions for the man that was saving them, questions that he wanted answered.

"Which GAP did you all use to get here?" asked the soldier. "Was it the GAP of Caverna de Morte?"

"Who are you?" asked Tank. "Who are you?" Tank asked again.

"Why are you helping us?" added Ruby.

"My name is Elias. Now tell me, which GAP you used to get here!" spoke the soldier in a stern voice.

"What is a gap?" questioned Cage, sitting up as he waited for the pain to subside.

Elias was in a rush and overly paranoid. He continuously gazed upwards at the guard tower. Tank noticed that Elias was carrying a gun filled with tranquilizer darts. That was why the sounds of the shots they heard earlier were quieter than normal. The dart gun also explained why he was obsessed with watching to make sure the soldier on the guard tower did not regain consciousness.

Cage, who was already starting to notice the pain in his legs subside, engaged in conversation with Elias. Tank put his hand up to Cage, motioning for him to remain quiet. Ruby, who was both appreciative and desperate for Elias to help them, put her hand up to Tank and scolded him for shushing Cage.

"What is your problem?" uttered Ruby to Tank. "Elias is here to rescue us. Why are you being so rude to Cage?"

"Have you all seriously never watched any war movies?" insisted Tank. "How do we know Elias is legit, if that is even his real name? How do we know it is not one of Colonel Grimes' men?"

"What? Didn't you see him battle that dude laying on the ground over there?" Ruby pointed at the soldier who had still not regained consciousness. "He totally kicked that fella's butt a few minutes ago. He is a good guy."

Elias stepped away as a voice transmitted over his radio. The volume of his wrist radio was low and they observed him holding his palm near his ear. Ruby attempted to adjust her head so she could try and intercept what the person on the other end of the radio was saying. Unfortunately, Elias was aware of Ruby's eavesdropping and he moved even farther away. Elias' face indicated the significance of the message he was receiving.

While Elias talked into the radio, Tank took the opportunity to challenge his friends on their willingness to trust this new bloke and he explained his concerns.

"This Elias guy, I don't trust him! It is the oldest trick in the espionage book. Colonel Grimes is not a dummy or an amateur. I bet this Elias chap is one of his men sent as a double agent. He helps us escape by cutting the zip-ties, wins our trust by curing Cage's legs, and then his mission is for us to help him locate the tablet. But don't worry. If we help him locate the tablet, there are three pieces of lead he will eagerly plant in our skulls."

Elias came charging back towards them as they continued to banter back and forth on why or why not to trust him. The guard on the tower was twitching and fidgeting as the sedative was wearing off. Likewise, the unconscious soldier that Elias had tossed like a ragdoll a few minutes ago, had rolled over onto his back and was coughing. The foul odor they smelled earlier turned out to be a chemical sleep grenade. Elias had deployed it into one of the tents on the FOB. The sleep agent was starting to subside.

"There are eight bogie combatants inbound to our location." Elias turned away as he checked the perimeter. He twisted around and shouted, "Now tell me which GAP you used! I will help you get back."

"Elias," Ruby spoke. "Elias, what do you mean when you say gap?"

"Sir?" Cage softly said. "We don't know what a gap is."

"You got here somehow, right?" declared Elias. "The Geo-Accelerated-Portal! Which one did you use?"

"Hey, buddy," said Tank, sarcastically. "We were in a cave in Kentucky one moment, and the next, we were floating down the river with a caiman after us. How about you do us a favor and you tell us what Gee-Excelsior-Potato we used."

"Sorry, Elias," Ruby said softly. "Our friend here is under the impression that you are only pretending to help us so we will help you find the tablet and then you will kill us. You're not a double agent, right?"

"Oh, great question," Tank mocked her. "Like a double agent would tell us he is a double agent."

Tank and Ruby started bickering back and forth. Ruby said, "You are such a jerk." And Tank followed up by saying, "Well, you're naïve." That prompted Ruby to respond by shouting, "Well, you're stupid!" Not to be outdone, Tank exploded by yelling, "Well, you're stupider." Not being one to back down, Ruby derided Tank saying, "Well, you're the stupidest."

Ruby lifted her hand as she was preparing to slap the lips off Tank's face. This was not going to be some puny smack either. This was going to be a colossal slap comparable to a category five hurricane. With this hit, she was going to give Tank flashbacks of being in diapers again.

Thankfully, Elias jumped in and set them both straight. "Hey, you're both right and acting equally stupid towards each other! You, girl," he pointed at Ruby, "don't be naïve. What if I am a bad guy and tricking you? Don't be so quick to trust."

Elias continued, "Hey, boy!" he shifted his finger towards Tank. "Lighten up and stop being such a pompous jerk to your friends. I am on your side. Listen, we have already secured the Tablet of Zurvan you all had in your possession. So, please chill!"

Cage laughed out loud because the whole conversation was considerably comical to observe. Elias looked over at Cage and winked at him. It was funny, but Cage was giggling harder than the situation required and he was acting equally strange. Both Ruby and Tank realized how silly their argument had been. They both gave a slight grin towards each other. Ruby giggled and Tank chuckled.

Elias spoke like dad, being both direct and firm. Tank appreciated his candid interjection and his comment about whomever he was affiliated with already acquiring the tablet. Knowing they had the tablet gave peace of mind. Elias dug around in one of his other cargo pockets and pulled out Phoenix's pocket-knife and lighter.

"Your full-bird Colonel friend in there had these on his table." Elias held out the items. "I am guessing Phoenix's pocketknife and lighter are yours?" He pointed at Tank and placed the pocketknife and lighter in his hand.

"I didn't think I would ever see those again," responded Tank.

As Tank extended his hand to reclaim the lighter and pocketknife from Elias, joy grew in his heart. Elias knew Phoenix. Phoenix was not some abstract character from a story. Phoenix *was* dad and dad *was* Phoenix. The lighter was in dad's jacket, the jacket that Cage was now wearing. The lighter was dad's when he was a boy and there were probably a thousand stories behind the pocketknife.

One day, when Tank was able to talk with dad again, oh, the questions he had for him about his adventures in the Amazon. He also remembered a gazillion far-fetched stories that Uncle Darren had told him. What were the chances they were all true or at least some of them?

"You ought to be more cautious hauling around something with that symbol on it," Elias added, "unless you have a death wish or something. I am half surprised the Colonel didn't tar and feather you for bringing these onto his FOB."

"What does this symbol and word mean?" Tank's voice was filled with anguish. He desperately desired to hear the truth about dad's past.

"It means..." Elias hesitated to answer Tank's question. "It means..." He then yelled at the top of his lungs, "**INCOMING!**"

A deafening, whistling sound could be heard as an explosive ordinance flew through the FOB and landed near a tent about seventy-five feet behind their location. Three seconds after the object hit the ground, there was a **BANG!** Shrapnel split through the air and demolished one of the tents. The only saving grace for the shrapnel not hitting them was the pallet of water that absorbed most of the blast. Instead of tiny pieces of metal wrecking their bodies, they were, fortunately, covered in a large splash of water.

Sergeant Woodbine and his troops were returning from their hunt for the tablet. Woodbine and his men were riding green four-wheelers that sported oversized tires. They had parked in a tactical formation about two-hundred meters away from the FOB, flanking the front side which had the only entry point. An individual soldier could be seen holding an M203 grenade launcher and he was reloading. Elias yanked two smoke-bomb canisters from his cargo belt. He underhand lobbed them towards Sergeant Woodbine's platoon in front of the FOB. A thick cloud of smoke filled the air, making it difficult to see. Elias crouched down on the ground and then ordered Cage, Ruby, and Tank to follow him.

"Do you all see that Amphibious Assault Truck behind the tent over there? It's that truck-boat looking thing?" Elias pointed. "That A.A.T. is our ride. We need to get to that truck and then get you kids to the GAP of Caverna de Morte. That will get you back to Kentucky."

"Roger," replied Tank.

"What does a guy taking a leak have anything to do with this?" Elias winked at Tank.

The three friends bear crawled and followed Elias behind the tent where a fully armored bullet-proof amphibious assault truck was parked. Cage was giggling while he meandered through the smoke. Apparently, the medication that Elias had given him was working well, very well. Cage's legs were free of any pain, and he was humming and whistling. At one point, Cage stood up, abandoned his bear crawl, and pretended to disco dance in the smoke as he pointed his finger up and down. Tank grabbed him by the waist and pulled him down to the ground.

"Tank and Ruby," Cage blurted out. "That truck has wheels on it and looks like a dingy boat, but can it shimmy and shake like me, baby?"

Tank ignored the strange commentary from Cage. He was just grateful that his friend was no longer in agony. Elias opened the door to the truck and he, Tank, and Ruby crawled inside, except Cage. Tank took the front seat and Ruby was in the back with an empty seat next to her. The sound of four-wheeler engines screamed as half of Sergeant Woodbine's platoon roared into the FOB, including the soldier with the grenade launcher. One soldier got out and closed the steel gate behind them, blocking off the best escape route.

Cage continued acting like a befuddled buffoon and started practicing his golf swing as he hollered, "Fore, fore! Watch out for my ball!" He transitioned from imaginary golfing to acting like he was reeling in a large fish, as he yelled, "Fish on! Fish on! Oh Lordy, it's a big one."

"Get in the truck!" commanded Tank.

"My friends, the pain is gone!" Cage hopped onto the hood of the truck and seamlessly performed an interpretive tap dance.

"No," responded Ruby. "The pain in your legs may be gone, but now it is you who are being the pain! Please get in the truck! The commandos are coming!"

The commandos dismounted from their four wheelers and came storming towards the truck. Lasers mounted to the bottom of their weapons penetrated the remaining smoke. It looked like a scene from a war movie. Red dots, stemming from the lasers, were streaming across Cage's body. If it were not for Elias kicking Cage's legs out from under him and then forcing him into the backseat of the truck, there was a good chance Cage would have been nothing more than a sponge for the commandos' bullets.

Elias slammed the door as the commandos started firing upon the vehicle. The armor of the amphibious truck was thick and repelled the bullets like a golden retriever's coat repels water. Sparks were flying as bullets bounced off the sides of the truck. Elias punched the gas, launching the vehicle backwards, to avoid running over the commandos. Elias drove twenty feet in reverse and then stopped as he ran directly into a tree. The incoming fire from the commandos stopped and they were shouting "Get out of the truck! Show us your hands!"

When Elias put the truck in park and started opening the door, Ruby about had a heart attack. Tank was yelling, "What in the blue-blazes are you doing?" Elias took a step out as the commandos continued forward with their weapons ready. He placed his hands on his head and then turned around with his back to the soldiers. Was he giving up? No, Elias was pretending to surrender only as a ploy to get the soldiers to move away from their four wheelers.

Like greased lightning, Elias dove back into the truck, threw the gearbox into "drive," and accelerated forward like a spring-loaded foot-trap on steroids. The soldiers leapt out of the way as the truck Elias commandeered plowed ahead. The four wheelers were large, but the truck-boat thing Elias had picked for their escape was not something with which to trifle. Like a tin can being stomped on by an obese elephant after a pie eating contest, the four wheelers crumpled and were smashed to pieces.

With their four wheelers destroyed, the soldiers opened fire, but their small caliber ammunition was not strong enough to penetrate the armor of the truck. Elias was smiling as he crashed through the front of the FOB. He put the pedal to the metal. Once they were reasonably far away, he performed an impressive whip-around driving move that spun the front of the truck towards the FOB. Sergeant Woodbine and his remaining troops were waiting for them to get closer before starting their pursuit.

"Cover your ears!" yelled Elias.

Elias pulled a handheld detonator from his pocket. There were two buttons on it with an antenna sticking out. The remote itself could not have been more than four or five inches long. He pressed the first button and then the second button. **KABOOM**! Every landmine that had been planted by Colonel Grimes' unit detonated at the same time. The initial sound was loud, but the shockwave was like nothing Tank, Cage, or Ruby had ever experienced. It felt like being punched in the chest by a heavyweight boxing champion.

Sergeant Woodbine looked in disbelief as he realized what was happening. The FOB was all but destroyed. Not a single tent was left standing. Tank observed Elias looking back and forth across the FOB. He was checking to ensure there were no fatalities. Elias almost gave Tank the impression that while he was not on the same side as Colonel Grimes, he also didn't have any desire to hurt any of the commandos.

Near the gate, a commando was laying on the ground as he had been too close to one of the landmines. His leg had a jagged piece of shrapnel protruding through his thigh. Elias opened the door to the truck and stepped out. He stood there and gave Tank instructions.

"See that man over there?" asked Elias. "He is critically wounded and needs help. I have already inputted the coordinates for Caverna de Morte into the onboard satellite mapping system. There is a specific point on the waterfall called Grande Cachoeira. You must pass through the right spot to get back into the cave."

"Elias," uttered Tank. "I have never driven before. My parents are strict about it, but I think I can figure it out on the fly."

"Move over!" Ruby suddenly crawled over the center console. "I have my learner's permit and have completed driver's education."

"You know all that stuff you learn in driver's education?" asked Elias, "You know, be courteous, use your turn signals, come to a complete stop and look both ways." He continued regurgitating all the common clichés associated with safe driving.

"Yes, of course!" Ruby nodded her head. "Keep your hands at ten and two. Defensive driving is always the best option!"

"Yeah, forget all that garbage and drive it like you stole it!" Elias grinned at Ruby.

Elias ran towards the wounded soldier as the sound of gunfire commenced again. Elias was incredibly brave and bold to help the wounded soldier. Granted, he was the reason why the landmines had all blown up, but as they say, "You win some, you learn some," right? He managed to avoid being shot and reached the wounded comrade, pulled medical equipment out of his bag, and tried to stop the bleeding. Ruby put her foot on the gas pedal and sharply turned the truck toward the trail leading away from FOB.

She tried her best to push the pedal through the floor. The tires on the amphibious assault truck spun wildly as dirt flew into the air. Sergeant Woodbine was not going to let them get to the cave without a fight. Tank could hear Ruby whispering under her breath, "Bring it on, jerk-face! Let's dance, little sergeant!"

Twenty-One
Mysteries Out the Wazoo

In all high-pressure situations, it helps when there is a high level of confidence. As dad would say, "Confidence is the key to success and faith is the foundation for survival." It wasn't like adversity didn't exist, but all things considered, there was a lot of room for optimism. For starters, one of the biggest challenges they faced was getting back to the cave. That meant going into the river again and there were miles of vast wilderness to drive in order to get to the cave. They had already had enough near-death experiences with the river of monsters to last a lifetime.

With the help of the amphibious assault truck, the journey to the cave was no longer a problem. It was unlikely that a caiman, anaconda, jaguar or any other wretched monster of the Amazon would be able to penetrate the armor.

Likewise, Sergeant Woodbine and his men were likely going to chase them and would be within striking distance in a few minutes. The weapons the soldiers were carrying were small and weak. It was going to take some real firepower to break through the armor of the vehicle. They should be able to drive to the cave without any real interference.

Once they got into the cave, they would have no way to see where they were going. The inside of the cave had jagged edges lining the interior, vast caverns that went for miles, and although they never saw them the first time, there were likely steep drop-offs into the abyss.

Yesterday, they were going to attempt the journey through the cave with do-it-yourself style torches. This amazing truck they were driving had several lights mounted to the roof, grille, and rear bumper. Furthermore, knowing that Ruby had experience driving was icing on the cake. Tank tried to make small talk as Ruby sped down the trail towards Sergeant Woodbine and his troops.

"I didn't know you had your learner's permit," said Tank, sitting in the front seat next to Ruby.

"Yes, I turned sixteen on Thursday of last week," replied Ruby.

"And you have already completed Driver's Education? Impressive!" added Tank. "The age is fifteen in Texas, but then we moved to Kentucky. Now I have to wait another year. Darn Bluegrass State!"

"Well," hesitated Ruby, "I completed the online portion of Driver's Education."

"Wait, so how many times have you physically driven a car?" inquired Tank.

"Tons of times," Ruby assured Tank. "My mom let me drive around in our empty church parking lot the day I got my permit and on Sunday, my parents had me back out of the driveway. I mean, they moved the other cars first and my dad sat next to me holding the wheel the whole time."

Tank swallowed hard and kept his internal thoughts to himself. Ruby had driven before; it was a true statement, but the devil was in the details. His confidence in escaping Sergeant Woodbine and his soldiers fell a bit. Ruby was smiling, Tank was grimacing, and Cage was drooling because he had passed out in the backseat of the truck.

It was outstanding to see Cage resting. Right before he fell asleep, he had removed his shoes and socks. He then recited, "This little piggy went to market. This little piggy stayed home." Fortunately, Cage had only made it two stanzas into the nursery rhyme before he went night-night.

Sergeant Woodbine and his gaggle of remaining troops were parked on their four-wheelers waiting for them. The commandos had observed Elias use the amphibious truck to plow through their fellow soldiers' four-wheelers at the FOB and he had ordered his men to move to the side of the trail.

Using the tiny side mirror, Tank looked back at the FOB to see if anyone was following them. The sun was playing peek-a-boo over the horizon which allowed them to see their surroundings better. When Tank and his friends had been brought into the FOB, the bags on their heads had prevented them from knowing their whereabouts.

Now they could see the path leading to the FOB cut through the jungle which had originated on the Amazon plain. It made sense that the soldiers would follow the plain for easier travel and then shelter in the forest for better cover at night. The path on which they were leaving the FOB was not long and Sergeant Woodbine's group was parked off to the side near the end.

The vehicle they were in did not have a rearview mirror as the armor and shape of the vehicle blocked the view. The dashboard did, however, have an impressive display of cameras which showed multiple angles. Tank pressed the buttons on the touchscreen and checked out all the unique camera views.

If a person did not know better, then all logic pointed to the conclusion that this vehicle was designed specifically for caves, and not just any caves, but caves with an entrance that stemmed from a river system.

In the center of the screen, a blue line showed the route and a red arrow indicated their position on the map. Once they got off the short pathway to the FOB, they could drive on the plain which was parallel to the river. The final part of the journey would require a quick trek through the jungle back to the waterfall. The onboard navigation further proved Tank's inference that Colonel Grimes had attempted to use the amphibious truck to enter the cave.

Scrolling through the saved previous destination's list, there were longitude and latitude coordinates that perfectly matched Caverna de Morte and Grande Cachoeira. Surprisingly, there were also coordinates at the top of the list, with corresponding labels, that routed to O Dourado, Paso de Uluru, and some place called Pico de Neblina.

There must have been twenty additional locations on the list and not all of them were in Spanish and Portuguese. Oddly enough, some on the list appeared to be on different continents as the names were Greek, Scandinavian, and Mandarin sounding names.

Tank clicked out of the previous destination list to allow Ruby to see where she was going on the satellite imaging system. Mounted to the side of the onboard navigation system was a sophisticated radio identical to the one that Colonel Grimes had prompted the soldier in the guard tower to use. Tank had seen something similar in the military vehicles in Texas but never this technologically advanced.

The mystery as to whether Colonel Grimes had survived the explosion on the FOB was solved as his voice came through the radio. Tank increased the volume on the radio to hear what Grimes was saying. He knew the tricky part about military encrypted equipment was getting the technology to connect to the other.

Once the radios were linked with an encrypted code, it was significantly harder to prevent outsiders from listening in to classified conversations. Tank only knew this to be true because he remembered this guy called "Sparks" who was from dad's unit telling him about it.

In this case, Colonel Grimes needed to communicate with his men. Ironically, his only option was to use the radio system which was also installed inside the vehicle of the people he was trying to pursue. The truck that Ruby, Cage, and Tank were in passed Sergeant Woodbine and his men.

The commandos did not move. Colonel Grimes could be heard on the radio telling the troops to stand down and regroup at "Rally Point Echo." Tank, being a relentless smart aleck, blew a kiss in Sergeant Woodbine's direction and waved both hands like a goof as they passed the other troops. They glared back in disbelief.

Sergeant Woodbine and his troops could be seen racing down the pathway towards the FOB. Tank presumed they were going to pick up Colonel Grimes and other survivors. They would then meet as a group at "Rally Point Echo," whatever that meant. Hopefully, Elias had been able to help the soldier with his injuries and then made a clean get-away. It was doubtful that the Colonel would forgive Elias for attacking his troops and then blowing up his FOB.

Ruby was acting strange. She explained that she was nervous and that she doubted Colonel Grimes was going to give up. Tank encouraged her to know that everything was going to be okay and for her to think about positive things. She tried her best.

"What are those?" asked Ruby, pointing to a medium-sized box on the ground near Tank's feet. "Are they smoke-grenades?"

"These are incendiary grenades," responded Tank. "They have a five second delay and burn at 4,000 degrees Fahrenheit. They are stainless steel canisters, waterproof, and have an internal core made of white phosphorus."

"Wow!" shouted Ruby. "How did you know that?"

"What can I say?" Tank smirked and raised his eyebrow at Ruby. "I am quite extraordinary. People say that about me all the time! I don't say it, people say it. You are truly blessed that I allow you to sit this close to me."

"And you are modest about it!" Ruby rolled her eyes. "I bet you are also the best at humility and meekness, too." She looked away in disgust.

"Ruby," whispered Tank as she ignored him. "Ruby," said Tank a little louder while she continued to ignore him. "Ruby!" Tank yelled. "I am only messing with you! The side of the box says incendiary grenade and has a bunch of details written on the container. I had no clue what they were! You should be proud of me. I can read the big words. You know I am not that smart."

Ruby giggled. For a moment, she started to get quite upset with Tank for his bullish attitude which was rooted in arrogance. She was glad he was only kidding about being a know-it-all and he was only slightly an egomaniac. To Tank's point, the sidebar conversation did help take her mind off the fact that at least half a dozen angry commandos were regrouping and likely going to massacre them.

The trip to the cave was relatively quiet and dull. There was no sign of Colonel Grimes or Sergeant Woodbine. The sunlight was a game changer in relieving their nerves. According to the navigation system, there was another hour of driving before they would get to the turn headed toward the river and then another fifteen minutes until they would see the waterfall. There was going to be a little bit of off-roading required which normally would have sounded like fun, but it made them both anxious to think about.

Looming in the back of Tank's mind was the massive size of the waterfall and what Elias had said about entering at the right point. Hopefully, they would know specifically where to go.

Cage was getting restless in the backseat. The bandages on his legs, antibiotics, and pain medicine was exactly what he needed. Ruby, being alone with Tank, took the opportunity to discuss what had transpired at the FOB with Elias and what she had been wondering regarding Phoenix.

"Thank God for Elias!" Ruby tried to spark conversation. "Do you think he really knows Phoenix? I mean do you think he really knows your dad?"

"Look," replied Tank, defensively, "I didn't lie to you about anything. I don't know what is going on. I didn't know Ms. Sprinkle was Spear. I didn't know she and dad had dated. I have no clue who Elias is or what is happening!" Tank took a deep breath, preparing for a verbal fight.

"No, Tank! I didn't mean anything bad by asking," assured Ruby. "I think it is awesome that your dad is a hero!"

"My father is not a bad guy!" Tank slammed his hands on the dashboard. "Wait, did you say hero?"

"Yes, he hid the backpack in the cave all those years ago to keep the Tablet of Rio de Monstros safe," explained Ruby. "He was trying to keep the tablet out of the hands of people like Colonel Grimes. I am sure he had a good reason!"

Tank let out a sigh of relief. He had been dreading the moment when his dad would come up in conversation. Tank had been rehearsing over and over in his head what facts he knew. All his game planning on how he would talk with Ruby and Cage on the topic was rooted in him defending dad. He was certain that Ruby, for whom he cared deeply, would hate his father for being Phoenix. Thankfully, she thought dad was a hero and so did Tank. Cage's head popped up as Tank and Ruby's conversation was taking place. Tank sighed and then spilled his inner thoughts.

"I appreciate you saying that, Ruby," shared Tank. "Dad is the best man I have ever met. I don't know why he kept his identity as Phoenix a secret, but I am sure he had a good reason. If he wanted the Tablet of Rio de Monstros returned, then he must have known why and where it needed to go. I trusted him before all this happened and I trust him still."

"You mean the Tablet of Zurvan," announced Cage from the backseat. "Elias called it the Tablet of Zurvan. Colonel Grimes called it the same thing, too."

"Welcome back!" snickered Ruby. "Cage, you sure were having a good time before you fell asleep."

"I had this dream that I danced on top of a car." Cage scratched his head. "Glad it was only a dream."

Tank and Ruby burst out laughing, recalling Cage's shenanigans back in the FOB. Cage did have a point, though. Elias had said Tablet of Zurvan, yet Phoenix had written Tablet of Rio de Monstros in his letter. Who was right and

215

who was wrong? Perhaps they were both right and the tablet had multiple names.

Tank pulled the lighter from his pocket and looked at the symbol and writing. Ruby kept her eyes focused forward and her hands fixed tightly on the steering wheel. She was getting more and more comfortable with driving as their trip progressed. By Tank's calculation, this was only her third time driving a vehicle, but her learning curve was exceptionally good.

"Elias had mentioned in the FOB that this symbol and writing meant something," declared Tank. "My dad not only had the pocketknife, but he also had a lighter with *Thárros* inscribed."

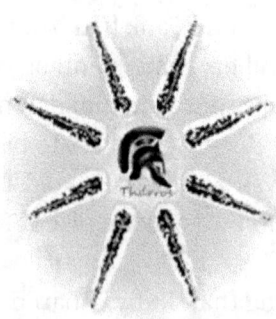

"What do you all think Thárros means?" asked Ruby.

"No idea!" Cage changed the topic back to the tablet. "Didn't the tablet say Rio de Monstros on it?"

"Yes," replied Ruby. "The river said Rio de Monstros, but after the second diamond was connected, the bottom said..."

Tank interrupted, "The bottom had *Zurvan* chiseled into the surface, but it only showed up *after* the second diamond was attached."

"Do you remember the earthquake?" asked Cage. "We all thought it happened because Ruby had said Rio de Monstros, right? What if it was because she said *Zurvan*?

"Maybe?" Tank intentionally changed the topic back to his dad. "It all happened so fast. All I know is that if my dad said he was a Warrior of Thárros, then so am I."

216

"So, Phoenix, I mean your dad, is a Warrior of Thárros," started Ruby. "He called it the Tablet of Rio de Monstros because that is what the river is called. Colonel Grimes said Tablets of Zurvan, as in plural. Maybe the tablet we found in the cave is the Tablet of Rio de Monstros, but the multiple tablets together are called the Tablets of Zurvan. Elias, however, who we also presume is a Warrior of Thárros, said *Zurvan* to describe the single tablet we had found. Does that make sense at all? Am I missing something?"

"Mysteries, mysteries, mysteries!" exclaimed Cage. "I feel like my brain is doing mental gymnastics.

"We have mysteries out the wazoo!" declared Tank.

"Out the what?" asked Cage, chuckling.

"The wazoo!" replied Tank. "You know, your keister... Your fanny... Your tushy... Your moon caboose... Your toot-cannon! We got mysteries out the wazoo!"

After regaining their composure from laughing at Tank's bum references, the three friends started kibitzing. They spent the next 45 minutes discussing a variety of hypotheses on what could or might be happening. Tank proceeded to share a recent epiphany with them.

When Yacumama was preparing to consume him, the sniper on the hill could have easily killed him. Tank almost got the impression that maybe the sniper was trying to help. However, he also seemed to be targeting Ruby and Cage by misdirecting Tank to run toward the hill. Once Tank concluded his story, they collectively agreed that the sniper was simply trying to separate them from each other because he thought Ruby and Cage had the tablet in the backpack.

"Do you all remember yesterday near the temple?" asked Cage. "Ms. Sprinkle said that she and Tank's dad used the tablet to travel all over the world."

"I remember! It is way too gross to think about!" Tank shook his head, repulsed at the idea of Ms. Sprinkle with dad. "Hopefully, after he kissed her, he brushed his teeth a million times, gargled with kerosene, and then burned his clothes."

"Elias asked us what gap we used to get here." Ruby changed the topic as Tank looked like he was going to barf. "He said GAP stands for Geo-Accelerated-

Portal. We never got to hear more about how gaps worked because at the time, Tank was throwing a tantrum about trusting him," she teased.

Tank laughed out loud. Ruby giving him a hard time was well-deserved and funny is funny. Dad would say, "Don't dish out what you can't take." Cage also added a couple of sharp jabs. He revealed that he had seen Tank blow a kiss to his mom the other day as he was entering the school. Cage rocked his arms and pretended to comfort an imaginary baby. He was clearly indicating that Tank was, in fact, the baby Cage was swaddling in his arms. Tank kept laughing. Funny is funny!

There was still no sign of Colonel Grimes and his men. The navigation system blinked, indicating that it was time to turn off the plain and go back into the jungle. There was the outline of a pathway that had been used by other vehicles, but it was tight and overgrown with vegetation. The speaker on the dashboard beeped a couple of times and verbally instructed them to turn left. As Ruby slowed down to make the turn, the radio emitted static and they heard a familiar voice.

"Please be advised." Colonel Grimes' voice transmitted over the radio. "I repeat, please be advised. Stop the vehicle immediately and get out with your hands up. This is your first and last warning! Please acknowledge that you will comply."

"What do I do?" panicked Ruby. "Should I stop?"

"No way!" replied Tank. "Listen, do you hear that? I can hear the waterfall. We are not that far away from the cave."

Tank picked up the handset on the radio and answered. "Hey, Colonel Grimes, you dog-faced pony soldier, how about you and the rest of your little boyband come and make us get out and put our hands up. Please don't send Sergeant Woodbine. I don't think he is tall enough to reach the doors of our truck. Stop us if you can, you popcorn fart!"

Tank slammed the handset into the plastic mount on the side of the radio. Cage sat back in his seat and tightened his seatbelt as Ruby pressed firmly on the accelerator. The trail toward the river was bumpy. The shocks on the amphibious truck were working well which reduced the bounciness, but it was still an unpleasant ride.

There was a black lever between the driver and the passenger seats that had an illustration of a boat propeller on the top. Next to the lever, there were simple instructions showing how to convert the truck into aquatic mode. They needed to drive into the river to ensure the wheels were fully submerged, shift the gearbox to neutral, and then pull the lever all the way back.

"Keep your eyes peeled." Tank barked instructions to Cage and Ruby. "Colonel Grimes will likely use the four-wheelers to try and run us off the road. God only knows what they planned for us while they were regrouping at Rally Point Echo."

"I can see the river!" exclaimed Ruby. "We are going to make it!"

Ruby punched the gas even harder and the amphibious truck drove directly into the river, causing a massive wave to launch across the side. The waterfall was very close. Ruby used her right hand and cranked on the gearshift to place the truck in neutral. Then, Tank promptly pulled the lever and they could hear the wheels turning upward and the propeller striking the water at the rear of the truck. Ruby once more hit the gas and they crept forward towards the waterfall.

"How do I know where to go?" asked Ruby.

"Umm, I don't know." Tank shrugged his shoulders. "Where is Elias when you need him?"

The excitement of reaching the river was gone. Suddenly, a familiar sound arose with earsplitting intensity over the sound of water crashing. Near the waterfall and blocking the river, the helicopter gunship that had demolished Yacumama was descending. Colonel Grimes had not planned to attack them with four-wheelers at all!

The gunship's doors were open and it was filled with a half dozen commandos. A rubber skiff, which was mounted under the gunship, was being lowered to the water and the troops were preparing to repel a ladder rope. Ruby eased up on the throttle and the amphibious truck came to a halt.

"At least I think I know where the entry to the cave is," uttered Tank. "The gunship didn't fly to that spot by chance. They are trying to keep us from entering the cave.

Two four-wheelers were parked on the shoreline near the waterfall where Colonel Grimes and Sergeant Woodbine waited. They were standing together and Sergeant Woodbine had a large rifle, similar, but different from the one the sniper had brandished yesterday. The gunship was fully restocked with air to ground missiles and hovered a few feet above of the water. Colonel Grimes picked up his radio.

"You have ten seconds to acknowledge and comply," ordered Colonel Grimes. "In ten seconds, my gunship lights you all up like the Fourth of July! Ten, nine, eight...," he started an exaggerated countdown.

"Can those missiles get through the armor of this truck?" asked Ruby.

"No way; he is bluffing," assured Cage. "Am I right?" he asked Tank.

"Those missiles are designed to take out bunkers," sighed Tank. "We don't have any choice. I am going to respond and tell him we surrender."

Tank picked up the radio handset as Colonel Grimes continued to count down. "Four, three, two." When Tank began to speak, the Colonel stopped counting. Sergeant Woodbine lifted his hand, giving the halt signal to the gunship. Colonel Grimes held his hand up in the air gesturing Cage, Ruby, and Tank to get out of the amphibious truck. After a few moments of waiting, he waved in their direction and then pointed to his watch as if he were losing his patience.

"Alright," shrugged Tank. "Alright, let's get out and head over to Colonel Grimes."

"Be careful," reminded Ruby. "Let's not forget this is the same place where we first encountered the caiman. Also, the current is quite strong here."

Cage unlatched his door first, but slammed the door shut when he noticed the helicopter moving erratically. The gunship abruptly swerved to the right and then veered to the left. Cage could see the pilot shifting the joystick and moving his legs up and down. Because of the turbulence, one of the troops who had already unbuckled his harness fell from the gunship into the water.

In the skiff, and covered by what looked like a black tarp, something moved. A man wearing a camo uniform was hiding! He sprang up from his position and climbed the rope ladder. In the meantime, the pilot was trying to maneuver the gunship to prevent the man from reaching the cargo hold. It was Elias! He was back and ready to fight!

Twenty-Two
Caverna de Morte
(Cave of Death)

Elias climbed the rope ladder and reached the cargo hold of the helicopter. He dispatched the troops by throwing them, one by one, into the river. Like clockwork, he continued to disarm the special forces commandos. His fighting skills were superior in every way. With ease, Elias detached the soldiers from their harnesses, even as they tried to fight back. He threw punches, elbows, knees and headbutts. He dominated every single one of the soldiers in hand-to-hand combat.

When the final commando was tossed into the water, Elias pulled out a switchblade and cut the rope which held the skiff. The pilot steadied the gunship, unbuckled his four-point harness, and attempted to overtake Elias. With a single strike to the face, Elias hurled the pilot out of the gunship and into the water. With blood spurting from his nose, the pilot fell into the river.

Treading water beneath the helicopter, the troops swam towards the rubber skiff which was being carried with the current down the river toward the amphibious truck. The soldiers were disarmed, disoriented, and desperate to get out of the river.

A school of piranhas were leaping out of the water as they moved toward the soldiers. They must have smelled the blood of the soldiers from over a mile away and what looked like nine bulky, brown logs were also floating toward the soldiers. As the troops struggled to get away, the "logs" submerged towards their target.

Three of the commandos had reached the skiff and climbed inside. Using their hands, they desperately paddled to get closer to the remaining soldiers. The soldiers were shouting to their comrades to swim faster.

"Are those what I think they are?" asked Ruby, incredulously.

221

"Yes!" Tank nodded his head. "Those are exactly what you think they are... caimans!"

Elias buckled himself into the pilot's seat and elevated the gunship high above the water. When he was high enough, he did one of the most impressive aviation moves imaginable. He pulled on the joystick sending the gunship vertically into the air with the nose of the helicopter pointing towards the river.

"Is Elias going to blast the soldiers out of the water?" shrieked Ruby.

"He is going to send them to kingdom come!" hollered Cage, as he watched over the center console.

Elias pressed the trigger and started hailing bullets into the river, but he did not hit a single soldier because they were not his target. Cage, Tank, and Ruby put their hands over their ears as the noise of the gunship reverberated through the air. The explosive sounds from the gunship were deafening.

Elias swept the machine guns back and forth at the caimans' bodies which caused plumes of water to splash into the air. The rounds were landing near the soldiers, but Elias' aim was true. He was trying to save the commandos from the hungry pack of caimans.

The remaining troops scurried into the skiff as the dead caimans floated away. Elias had a huge smile on his face as he waved to Tank, Cage, and Ruby. The transmission over the radio resonated with the welcome voice of Elias.

"Attention," joked Elias. "This is your gunship captain speaking. If you could kindly look out your front window at this lovely cave, your safe passage home will be right this way."

Elias turned the helicopter towards the cave and shot a series of tracer rounds from the gunship which directed them to the entrance of the waterfall. The tracer rounds illuminated the daylight with magnificent red light. When the final tracer round was shot, Elias turned the helicopter towards them. With a salute of his hand, Tank motioned to Elias. Elias returned the salute.

"Long live the Warriors of Thárros!" declared Elias over the radio, as he pulled on the joystick and prepared to fly away.

"Warriors of Thárros forever!" declared Tank into the radio. He covered his heart with his right-hand, showing respect.

As Elias flew away, Tank glanced towards the commandos. They were desperately paddling towards the shore, but the ferocity of the current was preventing them from exiting the river. As Tank looked at Colonel Grimes, he saw that he was holding the scope of the rifle to his eye. He was pointing the rifle at the helicopter! Tank could see a cruel smile on his face. Suddenly, an ear-splitting gunshot rang out.

The glass on the front window of the helicopter shattered. Colonel Grimes had used the rifle, shooting Elias directly through the heart! The gunship violently spun around multiple times as its blades came dangerously close to the water. With a final spin, the gunship crash landed on top of the skiff killing every commando that had sought refuge from the river.

"No!" screamed Ruby.

"He killed him!" cried Cage. "Colonel Grimes killed Elias!"

Tank was speechless as he watched in horror. His brain could not process what had just happened. Colonel Grimes, who had killed Elias, had also inadvertently killed his entire unit. There was no remorse as he observed Grimes and Sergeant Woodbine laughing. Elias had cared more about the Colonel's platoon than he did!

"Warriors of Thárros. What a joke," scoffed Colonel Grimes over the radio. "I guess he didn't live as long as he thought he would."

Colonel Grimes slowly lifted the rifle and zeroed in on the amphibious truck. The barrel of the rifle was aimed at Tank's face! Tank's adrenaline spiked as he lifted his entire left leg over the center console and jammed his foot on the accelerator. The amphibious truck leapt forward as Colonel Grimes' first shot struck his window. The bullet-proof glass nearly crumbled.

Projectiles struck the outside of the truck as small holes appeared in the armor. Daylight showed through the door where the armor was struggling to repel the bullets. God forbid Colonel Grimes hit the same spot twice as the bullets could easily pass into the cab of the truck!

Tank steered the amphibious truck and sped to where Elias had aimed the tracer rounds. Water, crashing from the waterfall, had semi-submerged their vehicle and was creeping through the cracks at the bottom of the doors as the propeller struggled to maintain power.

As he maneuvered the truck, Tank gripped the steering wheel with his left hand while his left foot was firmly planted on the gas pedal. Ruby, who was still in the driver's seat, was now a passenger along for the ride. Bullets continued to spatter the back of the truck as they plowed through the waterfall and into the cave. The water hitting the windshield made it almost impossible to see.

Acting out of panic, Ruby pushed one of the many buttons on the dashboard as she tried to get the window wipers to work. She managed to find every button except for the wipers. Instead, all the lights mounted to the amphibious truck turned on, including the interior lights.

As she found the right switch for the window wipers, the truck narrowly missed the sharp rocks which rose above the surface of the water. Tank yanked the wheel sharply to the left to avoid the rocks. As they drove through the cave, Ruby grew tired of Tank commandeering the amphibious truck. She shoved Tank's leg off the gas pedal and his hand from the steering wheel. Reluctantly, Tank let her drive.

"What is that smell?" asked Ruby.

"It smells like a freight truck or tractor has been in here," added Cage. "Did it smell like that before?

"That is JP8 diesel fuel," answered Tank. "Colonel Grimes shot the back of our truck and he ruptured the gas tank to slow us down."

Ruby peered at the fuel gauge. Tank was right. When they first commandeered the amphibious truck, the fuel gauge showed full and they had only used a quarter of the tank driving to the cave. The fuel tank was now barely above a fourth of its capacity and rapidly falling.

"Get to the shore," hollered Cage. "We need to get out of the river!"

"What about the caimans?" cried Ruby.

"Would you rather be stuck in this truck in the middle of the river or on land?" shouted Cage.

Tank remained silent. The emotion from seeing Elias die was weighing heavily on his mind. Ruby steered toward the shore as she kept her foot firmly on the throttle. Getting out of the water was simple. Once the truck came to a stop on the rocky shoreline, Ruby placed the truck in neutral. She pushed the lever with the propeller decal into its original position, the wheels lowered, and she shifted into drive.

The low fuel indicator light appeared and the smell of diesel was incredibly strong almost to the point of gagging. Their eyes and noses watered from the overwhelming fumes. Ruby did not stop but continued to drive down the shoreline until they were past the point where the river began.

The amphibious truck was on its last leg. The fuel light started blinking and then beeped. The truck's engine idled roughly for a few seconds and the wheels rolled to a stop. When the engine quit, the lights on the vehicle slightly dimmed as they ran solely on battery power.

Ruby opened her door and stepped out. Cage and Tank crawled out, as well. Tank placed his hand over his face and cried. Ruby and Cage were also overcome with emotion and wept uncontrollably. They were now far enough inside the cave that the sound of the waterfall was present, but not overwhelming. In fact, they could no longer see the waterfall crashing into the river. As they recovered, the radio came in at full volume and emitted a broken, staticky voice.

"Congratulations!" It was Colonel Grimes. "You survived my gunship, but now you are all alone in the Cave of Death. There is nowhere you can go where we can't find you." He finished his antagonistic rant by saying "Ordo Orbis Terrarum!" and then grunted.

The lights on the radio turned off and only a couple of exterior lights remained. Tank wiped away his tears. Sadness flooded his heart, but he could not let Elias' sacrifice be in vain. The mission was to get back to Kentucky. It was time to lead the way!

"What are we going to do?" Ruby moved towards Tank. "We have no way to see and there is nothing but darkness ahead."

"We have these." Tank opened the truck door and pointed at the box of incendiary grenades near his feet. "They burn at 4000 degrees, remember?"

Tank picked up the box. With the help of the incendiary grenades, seeing would not be a problem, but they would need to use them sparingly. Under the box was a brown carrier bag that looked like a glowing pillowcase. What a strange item to find inside an armored amphibious truck.

"What is that?" Ruby pointed at the bag.

"I don't know!" answered Tank. "It is shining!"

Tank jumped out of the truck fearing Colonel Grimes had hidden a secret explosive device inside. Tank pondered the comedic nature of surviving a giant snake, escaping a gunship, and evading a psycho colonel with a rifle only to finally meet his doom by getting blown sky high by a pillowcase laced with dynamite. Cage reached inside the truck and picked up the bag as Ruby and Tank took several steps away from the vehicle. Cage carefully grabbed the brown bag and unfolded the top.

As he opened the bag, the light grew brighter and they were amazed by its contents. It was the Tablet of Rio de Monstros! Even in his death, Elias had managed to outwit the stupendous Colonel Grimes. Tank and Ruby fell to their knees in disbelief.

The tablet was brighter than ever. In the FOB, Elias had mentioned that they had already secured the tablet, but he never told them he had hidden it in the truck which they would use to escape! Cage handed Ruby the tablet as she glanced at it and admired what she was holding. She slowly handed it to Tank.

Tank took the tablet and held his arms up towards the ceiling of the cavern. The entire cave illuminated in magnificent light. It was like the tablet had power over the cave! At the temple, the tablet had only glowed with this intensity when pointed towards O Dourado. This time, the tablet intensified its light as it was pointed into the cave. A clear pathway appeared in the distance, laden in golden, sparkling light.

"The tablet is showing us the GAP," declared Ruby. "This is why Colonel Grimes wanted the Tablet of Rio de Monstros so badly. Imagine what the military could do with this? Entire armies could cross oceans and continents with ease. With the tablet, you could control the world.

"You mean *Tablet of Zurvan*," Cage corrected Ruby.

At the mention of the Tablet of Zurvan, the ground began to shake! Phoenix had called it the Tablet of Rio de Monstros, but perhaps he had avoided referring to it as the Tablet of Zurvan because simply uttering the word "*Zurvan*" caused the earth to violently shake. This was the Tablet of Rio de Monstros and judging by the shape of the tablet, there were at least two more tablets out there that could be connected to it.

"Let's not say that word again," ordered Ruby.

"Yeah, a little bit of pee ran down my leg when you said that!" joked Tank.

"Where do you think the other tablets are?" asked Cage.

"I don't know," answered Tank. "I fully understand why my dad decided to keep this tablet a secret and hide it in the cave."

A beam of light flashed across the tablet and shot far into the cave. It was like a shooting star had erupted and cast a spotlight where they needed to go to get home. It was obvious that the tablet was not of this world. It was something that defied the laws of physics and scientific understanding.

"Let's go home!" declared Tank.

"We need to be careful," said Ruby. "They call this place Caverna de Morte. This is the Cave of Death."

"I don't think that will be a problem." Tank motioned his eyes toward the tablet. "We have nothing to fear now that we have the tablet and the diamonds are in place. Watch this!"

A single caiman was resting on the shore near the river. Tank had noticed it laying there when he first stepped out of the truck. Tank held the tablet, pointed it at the beast and the beast scurried away. Likewise, in the distance, a small group of vampire bats were hanging upside down. Not only could they be seen, but the ammonia smell of their urine was wafting through the air. When Tank pointed the tablet in their direction, the bats bolted in the opposite direction, fleeing from the light.

"Without the tablet, this *would* be the Cave of Death," uttered Tank. "With the tablet we can rename the cave "Caverna de Sunshine and Lollipops!"

Tank handed the tablet to Ruby and shoved a few of incendiary grenades into his cargo pockets. In haste, the three friends charged down the pathway. The magnificence and wonders of the tablet were revealed as they walked the pathway of Caverna de Morte. There were miles and miles of caverns, twisting pathways, ceilings taller than skyscrapers, and walls covered in pure gold, accented with diamonds and rare gems.

Occasionally, they would look over their shoulders to see how far they had come. As they grew more excited about getting to Kentucky, the outline of a jaguar appeared behind them. There was no reason why it should be in the cave, but it must have tracked them inside. The growling jaguar showed his teeth and started sprinting in their direction. As quickly as their confidence had grown with the use of the tablet, they found themselves running away like a turkey on the day before Thanksgiving. The jaguar did not seem to care that they were holding the tablet.

Ruby, followed by Tank and Cage, took off down the pathway. The trail they were on was narrow and the glowing light from the tablet outlined a safe passage through the cave. Along the sides of the pathway were steep drop-offs and sharp rocks. It was remarkable they had managed not to die three days ago when they were running from the bats in the dark.

Tank and Cage followed closely behind Ruby as they raced to escape from the cave and into Kentucky. Regardless of their best efforts, there was no way to outrun the jaguar. They abruptly stopped running when they heard the imminent paws striking the ground just a few feet behind them. They turned in unison to face the vicious cat. They were going to die!

Ruby and Cage ducked their heads and prepared to be attacked. Tank, however, puffed out his chest as the jaguar suddenly froze in place and stared into Tank's eyes. At any moment now, the cat was going to lunge at Tank's neck, grab him by the jugular vein, and strangle the life out of him.

"Good kitty," said Tank softly, as he pulled the pocketknife out. "That's a good kitty. I truly do hate cats! I want you to know that! I needed to get that off my chest before this thing kills me," he said, as he glanced at Ruby and braced for impact.

Ruby lifted her head, stood up tall, and held out the tablet in front of the jaguar as it initiated a pounce. The jaguar immediately halted its attack, whimpered as if the tablet was inflicting it with pain, and darted away as fast as it had appeared.

"That was a close one," said Cage. "Why didn't we pull out the tablet to start with?" he laughed, nervously.

"Totally kidding about hating cats." Tank made eye contact with Ruby. "I don't hate them. I love them less now."

"Sure, you were!" teased Ruby. "Look up ahead; it's the exit."

Less than two hundred feet ahead, they could see the outline of wooden boards laying across a small opening near the floor of the cave. The ground evolved from rock into sludgy, gooey, clay and was a dead giveaway that they had arrived closer to the entrance. Oh, how Ruby was dreading putting her hands back onto the goopy ground. Even with the light, they had to slow their steps to avoid slipping.

Parallel to where they were standing on the pathway, there stood the large interior wall where they had first seen the painting of Yacumama. To their amazement, the paintings were not only on a small portion of the cave, but continued on several of the walls for what looked like miles of caverns. Ironically, the wall nearest to them had an image of a jaguar eating a man. They chuckled in unison realizing the death they had escaped.

The smell of duck poop and the stink of a fishy pond filled the air. The smelliness inside the cave would even make a buzzard stick an air freshener up its nose. Besides the memorable smell of the entry to the cave, there was another nefarious smell in the air. The scent, however, was faint and subtle.

They were so close to freedom, but something seemed terribly wrong. They were being followed! Tank motioned for Cage and Ruby to stop. Behind them, they could see the outline of a man. Maybe it was one of Colonel Grimes' commandos. They needed to get to the exit and they needed to get there fast!

The man was running toward them and seemed to be throwing rocks in their direction. Up ahead, they could hear the sound of a prybar and sledgehammer. The boards across the entry to the cave were being removed. Someone was outside the cave trying to help them escape! Only fifty more feet and they were back home. Out of nowhere, the three friends began to feel dizzy as if they could pass out. The slickness of the cave floor caused them to walk at a turtle's pace. Fifteen more feet! They could almost touch the exit. Ruby dropped the tablet and it tumbled to the ground.

"Hey, are you all feeling okay?" Tank struggled to take another step. "My head feels heavy."

"I feel weird!" Cage froze in place. "My legs and arms feel like they are about to fall off."

"Is the world spinning?" Ruby looked towards her friends. "Tank, why do you have two heads?" She fell to the ground.

Tank stood there for a few moments and tried to keep his balance. His head was woozy and he was struggling to lift his arms. Cage fell to the ground near Ruby and then Tank plummeted to the nasty floor. The Cave of Death had claimed three more victims.

229

Twenty-Three
The National Environmental Security Agency

"Where am I?" Tank blinked rapidly and opened his eyes.

"You are safe," replied a voice. "I am Agent Calvin Locke with The National Environmental Security Agency. How are you feeling, son?"

Tank lifted his head from the stainless-steel table and looked around. The chair he was sitting in was bolted to the ground as was the table. On the table was a steel circle-hook that looked like it was designed to secure handcuffs. Tank observed another chair, made of wood, sitting on the opposite side of the table, but it was not attached to the floor.

The room was roughly ten-by-ten feet with yellow painted concrete walls and a single opaque window. Adjacent to the window was an oversized thick, wooden door with four black hinges. A water pitcher and two red plastic cups sat in the middle of the table.

Tank's memory was fuzzy and he had a mild headache. He could not recall how he got there. The last thing he remembered was someone following them in the cave, a chemical smell, feeling dizzy, and a vague memory of his face hitting the mud. After that, it was lights out!

Agent Locke was a well-dressed man who wore a black suit and black tie. On his collar, he wore an American flag pin. His slightly greasy black hair was parted to the left. He stood on the other side of the table and allowed Tank a few moments to collect his thoughts. Tucked under the agent's right arm was a tan folder. When the agent adjusted his arms, Tank could partially see a logo near the center of the folder, but he did not recognize the emblem.

"Where are Cage and Ruby?" asked Tank. "Where are my friends? What is going on? Where am I?"

"They are safe. Both are perfectly safe," assured Agent Locke. "Their parents have already come to get them. Once our meeting is over, I will give you my phone and you can call them yourself to verify."

"Where is *my* mom?" asked Tank, elevating his voice.

"Oh, Sara?" responded Agent Locke. "I just got off the phone with her. She is on her way here now. She asked me to tell you that she is excited to see you and can't wait to give you a hug."

Agent Locke went on to explain to Tank that three days ago, a man named Richard Jackson had contacted the police and reported seeing three students ditching school and boarding a bus to Chicago. Tank's mom had driven to Chicago, but after hearing the news that Tank had been found, she was on I-65 headed to Louisville. She was still a couple hours away.

"Sara mentioned taking you to a pizza place for dinner. She said it was your favorite," added Agent Locke. "Someplace near Main Street, if that means anything to you?"

The agent was referring to one of the best places in town to eat. The last food Tank had was a protein bar on the FOB with Colonel Grimes. Mom was on her way to get him, his friends were safe, and in a few hours, he would be devouring a meat-lovers pizza with extra cheese and marinara dipping sauce. This was terrific!

"Who did you say you worked for?" asked Tank, his head still blurry.

"The National Environmental Security Agency. We call ourselves NESA," responded Agent Locke.

Tank sprang to his feet and backed up to the door. Agent Locke placed his hands up in the air in a non-aggressive manner and kept saying, "Calm down. Calm down. It's okay, son."

When Tank's back hit the concrete wall, he put his fists up and guarded his face, indicating to Agent Locke that he was ready to go fisticuffs. Agent Locke pulled the chair out from the table and sat. He reached forward and grabbed the pitcher of water, taking one of the plastic cups. He calmly poured a cup of water and took a few sips as he motioned for Tank to sit down.

"I am not here to hurt you," insisted Agent Locke. "We are on the same team."

"You are on the same team as Colonel Grimes!" yelled Tank. "We are NOT on the same side!"

Agent Locke smiled and took another sip of water. He shared that Colonel Grimes and his rogue group of commandos were wanted for treason. Tank and his friends had managed to take down an international fugitive from justice. With his troops gone, Colonel Grimes' compound was seized by NESA and he was being arraigned in Gitmo as they spoke.

"Why should I trust you?" uttered Tank, suspiciously. "I know what you all do. I have seen the news articles about NESA."

"Why do you think I am here?" asked Agent Locke. "I didn't come to Kentucky to see all the lovely horses. I came here to give you this."

Agent Locke laid the folder on the table and pulled out a single piece of paper. Tank took a few steps closer to get a better look as Agent Locke began reading it out loud. While reading the subject line, Locke deliberately paused and placed emphasis on key words. He would say a few words, look at Tank's face, and then continue reading. Tank realized that Locke was attempting to read his reactions, which is common practice in interrogations.

Tank tried his hardest to maintain a straight face and keep his eyes forward. His effort to maintain his composure was valiant, but a lost cause. Everything seemed too good to be true.

Agent Locke continued to read...

Office of the Director

The National Environmental Security Agency

Official Memorandum

Subject: Special Award Nomination

Dear Andrew Tannis Thornstone,

This memorandum is a notification that you have been nominated to receive The Homeland Security – Gold Medal of Freedom. Your valiant efforts and determination in protecting the environment and the United States of America are a true inspiration.

Please be advised: Your nomination for this award is currently under review as we continue to determine potential compensation for your noble acts.

Thank you for your service,

HMP

Hilary Mandell-Pike
Director of Operations
Washington, D.C. 20515
N.E.S.A

NESA FORM: 1221970

Agent Locke turned the memorandum around and pushed it to the other side of the table. Tank lowered his fists, traipsed over to the table, and sat to read the letter. The letter was on official letterhead, was personally signed by the director, and appeared to be legitimate.

"You are a hero, kid," Agent Locke flattered Tank. "Your dad is so proud of you!"

"My dad!" exclaimed Tank. "He knows what happened?"

"Knows about it?" asked Agent Locke. "His son brought down an infamous criminal. Do you know what? I bet your dad will even be promoted to Major because of his son's unwavering devotion to the country."

Tank smiled and joyfully grabbed a plastic cup. As Agent Locke poured him some water, Tank held out the cup and initiated a "cheers" to Agent Locke and NESA. All the events, all the mystery, all the danger of the river, and all the adversity, had resulted in a happy ending. Life was good!

"Yes! Cheers!" smiled Agent Locke, toasting Tank. "Now we need to figure out a couple of things so the director can confirm the nomination with Congress. Afterwards, we can start the promotion paperwork for your dad. With your willing cooperation, I bet a check for millions of dollars will be yours soon."

"You name it!" responded Tank. "Can you see if my mom can order the pizza now? That way it is ready when we get there."

"Sure, in a moment. But first, I have a couple more questions." Agent Locke nodded his head in agreement to call Tank's mom.

Agent Locke motioned towards the door and another agent came into the room holding a laptop bag. Agent Locke referred to the new guy as "Agent Sauceda" and thanked him for bringing the bag and promptly dismissed him.

"You had some interesting stuff on you when we found you in the cave," said Agent Locke, pulling out three incendiary grenades from the bag.

"Yes," responded Tank. "I took those out of the amphibious truck so we could see in the cave."

"And you didn't use them?" asked Agent Locke. "How did you all see to get back?"

Tank hesitated. The answer to the agent's question was that the tablet had guided them back, but there was no way he was going to tell the agent. At least he was not going to share yet, for he was not sure if he could trust him. Agent Locke pulled the tablet from the bag and gently placed it on the table in front of Tank.

"We also found this." Agent Locke pointed at the tablet. "Tell me about this."

"Oh," bluffed Tank. "That is a useless thing we found in the jungle. We figured it was some tribal artwork. You can throw it in the trashcan. It's not important at all."

Agent Locke readjusted his position in his seat, frowned, pulled out his cellphone and started to type a message. With the agent distracted and the tablet sitting there, Tank examined it and noticed that both diamonds were missing. The two craters were empty!

"Sorry, I was on my phone. I needed to take some notes and document your answer with our D.C. office," said Agent Locke. "You know, it's typical boring government protocol. Walk me through how three teenagers navigated a pitch-black cave from Kentucky to the Amazon Jungle and back again? Full respect to you, kid, but you hear how ridiculous that sounds, right?"

"What you just said sounds ridiculous," added Tank, sarcastically. "Going from Kentucky to the Amazon through a cave is impossible. Right?"

Agent Locke remained calm and assured Tank he was only there to get the facts. He reminded Tank again that this was simply the final step before he would receive an award and money. He needed to answer the questions truthfully and they would be set. Tank calmed down and tried to level with Agent Locke.

"I don't know," declared Tank. "We were trapped in the cave, we went to the Amazon, and then we came back. I am having a hard time remembering the events."

"When we were removing the boards from the entrance, the inside of the cave appeared to be bright," stated Agent Locke. "We have already established you didn't use any incendiary grenades and you didn't have any flashlights, so how did you see? It's a simple question."

"You see, you see," Tank stuttered his words. "We could see because we could see."

"You used the tablet," interjected Agent Locke. "You are not on trial here, kid. Say you used the tablet. We already know that is what you did. Stop stressing about it!"

Tank was not sure what to say. He simply nodded his head in agreement that they did, in fact, use the tablet to see in the cave. There was awkward silence as Tank stared at the tablet and Agent Locke waited patiently for him to respond. When it was clear Tank was not going to reply, Agent Locke began speaking again.

"See," said Agent Locke, "that was not hard. You used the tablet. Hey, I would have done the same thing. How does it work, though?"

Agent Locke shared with Tank that he and a few agents from NESA had gone back into the cave after they had rescued them. The tablet was laying a few feet from their location. Part of their investigation of the pond and the cave was to get a better understanding about the tablet and its potential threat to the United States. Once Tank shared more details about the tablet and its abilities, then NESA would be on their way back to Washington. He assured Tank that after his questions were answered, he could have his reunion with his mother and friends. After all, NESA had bigger and better things to do than explore some backwoods cave in Kentucky.

"You know I have been investigating this cave on and off for the last twenty years," joked Agent Locke. "In fact, I've spent so much time away from my wife and kids over the years, I would appreciate your cooperation in this so I can get back to my family. I sure miss them. You are going to have pizza with your mom here soon. It would be perfect if I could have pizza with my kids later tonight, too. Please share with me the way the tablet works."

"I promise you!" Tank slammed his hands on the table. "I don't know how it works. It just works!"

"Alright," groaned Agent Locke. "That is fair. No pressure. Maybe with some rest it will all come back to you. I am going to need you to sign this before your mom comes to get you."

Agent Locke pulled out another piece of paper from the folder and handed it to Tank. He explained that this was a national security issue and it was standard process to have civilians sign a "Classified Attestation Disclosure," as it was critical that no one else know about the tablet or the cave.

Agent Locke assured Tank that he had already spoken to Sara, Tank's mom, regarding the disclosure Tank needed to sign. She was in full agreement and ensured Agent Locke that it would be no problem. She had given verbal permission over the phone for Tank to sign without an attorney or legal guardian present.

"You know," replied Tank, "I am sorry for being so rude to you earlier when I heard you were from NESA. I assumed you were the baddies, but you have been a real stand-up guy. My dad would like you."

236

"We get that sometimes," laughed Agent Locke. "Having to keep secrets at times gives us a bad reputation, but we are patriots doing our job. We are all about service and love of country!"

Tank read through the document that Agent Locke had placed on the table. It was standard and non-specific to anything regarding the tablet or cave. The form mentioned that events, which had happened and any known government-related activities, would be kept confidential. The final section of the document referenced possible penalties for failure to adhere to the attestation. Agent Locke handed Tank a pen.

"What does *this* mean?" Tank pointed to the bottom of the document.

"Oh, that is the NESA motto," replied Agent Locke. "When I studied your profile, I noticed you grew up on a military base. I am sure you have been around the government enough to know that all groups have their own corny Latin mottos," he laughed.

"Ordo Orbis Terrarum?" asked Tank. "What does it mean?"

"It means New World Order," answered Agent Locke. "Through protecting the environment, we are creating a better world for all mankind."

Tank signed the document and passed it back to Agent Locke. Agent Sauceda stepped back into the room and retrieved the signed form. He must have been watching through the double-sided mirror because his entrance immediately followed Tank signing the paper. Agent Locke picked up the tablet, tucked it into the laptop bag, got up and walked towards the door.

"Agent Locke?" asked Tank. "I am worried about my friend, Ruby. How are the wounds on her legs doing?"

"She is doing great. Her parents took her to urgent care. All is good," responded Agent Locke. "Ruby told Agent Sauceda to let Andrew know that she was doing much better."

"That's weird," exclaimed Tank. "Cage was the one that had wounds on his legs and Ruby would never refer to me as Andrew. She only knows me by the name, Tank."

Agent Locke walked over to the table and chuckled. He apologized for the confusion regarding Ruby's legs and told Tank that it was "a simple Freudian slip of the tongue." Agent Locke mentioned that he had been up for several days worried sick about three missing children. He was desperately trying to save Tank and his friends. His misspeak was because he was tired and nothing else.

"We both need to get some rest," stated Agent Locke, as he read a text on his phone. "I think with a good night's sleep your memory will be refreshed. Unfortunately, the recent text I received was from your mom. She has had some car trouble and will not be here until tomorrow morning. She wanted me to let you know she was sorry and that she loves you."

"How long have you and Colonel Grimes worked together?" asked Tank, grinning. "You both must have gone to the same school; that is, "The School of Bad Liars.""

"I am not sure I understand," replied Agent Locke. "You saw the letter from our director. Why would I make that up? My ask has been simple. I need to report to my superiors and give them the information about the tablet and its capabilities. Why are you making this so difficult?"

"You are one of them!" yelled Tank. "You and Colonel Grimes are in this together!"

"Did you hit your head when you fell in the cave?" Agent Locke raised his eyebrows. "You are delirious, kid. You need to calm down."

Agent Locke walked to the door and out of the room. Tank stood up and paced back and forth. All the blood in his body was rushing to his head. This Agent Locke guy was a fraud and his whole story about an award, money, and his dad being promoted was all a farce! Agent Locke opened the door and walked back into the room. His demeanor continued to be calm and relaxed.

"Let's go ahead and end our conversation for today," said Agent Locke. "We can pick back up tomorrow morning when you are rested. With your mom still away, and for your safety and protection, we are going to keep you in custody tonight. I mean, I suppose we *could* drive you to meet with your mom tonight, but you would need to tell me about the tablet first."

"Even if I told you about the missing pieces," Tank threw his arms in the air out of frustration, "I still have no clue about the tablet!"

"Missing pieces?" uttered Agent Locke. "What missing pieces?"

Agent Locke motioned for Agent Sauceda to come back into the room. He instructed Sauceda to have agents return to the cave and do another check to see if there was anything near the place where the tablet was found.

"How big are the missing pieces?" asked Agent Locke.

"I don't remember," responded Tank. "They were either the size of a hamster or like the size of an elephant. Have you ever seen a freshwater turtle?"

"A freshwater turtle?" Agent Locke started to lose his cool. "Yes, I know what they look like!"

"Yes, well," replied Tank, "the missing pieces looked nothing like a freshwater turtle."

Agent Locke slammed his fists on the table and sighed. Even with his well-polished nice guy routine, his temper was starting to flare and he looked like he was ready to snap. Before he could speak again, Tank beat him to it.

"Magic wands!" Tank pretended like he was waving a wand and casting a spell.

"What about magic wands?" Agent Locke had a serious look on his face. He was genuinely buying the magic wands add-on.

"There are two magic wands," declared Tank. "To activate the light, two people dressed in black robes must point the magic wands at the tablet, say a spell, and grimace at each other like they are constipated."

"Are you serious!" snapped Agent Locke.

"No, that would be super dorky!" snorted Tank, amused. "Could you imagine?"

"Tell me what the missing pieces are or I will make you wish you were never born!" yelled Agent Locke.

"If I knew where the missing pieces were," quipped Tank, "I would tell the Warriors of Thárros and they could destroy you and all the dirtbags at NESA with your new world order fantasy."

Agent Locke took a deep breath. It was impressive how he was able to instantaneously control his anger and restore his composure. Judging by how he was responding and able to manipulate others, he was a well-trained government agent. After an exaggerated pause and a smile, Agent Locke began speaking again.

"Let's take a quick walk," stated Agent Locke. "I think there is something you need to see."

"No, thanks," grinned Tank. "I am quite comfortable here in this splendid concrete room."

"If you don't want to pick out flowers for a funeral," stated Agent Locke, "then you will follow me now!"

Startled by Locke's comments, Tank reluctantly got up from his chair to follow him. Agent Sauceda opened the door and Tank and Locke walked out. As Tank walked into the main building, he noticed several police officers. Some of the cops were sitting at desks, some were walking the hallways, and there were a few making copies at the copy machine. Not one of them batted an eye at Tank or acknowledged his existence. Agent Locke led Tank to a window on the far side of the building.

Tank could see mom's car in the parking lot and in the driver's seat sat his mother! She was crying. Agent Locke told Tank that his mom had already been notified of her son's body being found. It was a shame that Tank was not willing to share vital information about the tablet and its missing pieces. Agent Locke would love to update his mom that Tank had, in fact, survived. They could clear everything up and she would start crying tears of joy instead of tears of sorrow.

Tank shook his head and mumbled the word "No" at him, refusing to share more information about the tablet. He thought about Elias' sacrifice and the consequences of sharing about the diamonds. Agent Locke motioned towards two officers who proceeded to open the door and walk outside. One officer walked to his mother's car, pulled out his sidearm, and demanded that she exit the vehicle.

Tank's mom got out of the car as the second officer forcefully pulled her arms behind her back and latched handcuffs on her wrists. Tank could see the officer saying, "You are under arrest."

"You monster!" Tank grabbed Agent Locke by the collar.

"Restrain him!" ordered Agent Locke, as several officers rushed to control him.

"Your mom is being arrested for the assault and kidnapping of a James Cross and Rachel Tran," said Agent Locke. "Poor kids have still not been found. Maybe we will add a murder charge, as well! Killing two teenagers, she will most likely get the chair!"

"You said they were with their parents!" hollered Tank.

"I lied!" laughed Agent Locke. "Tell me what the missing pieces are and you have my word. I will release your mom to you right now and I will also order your two friends be released from A.D.X. Millard."

A memory flashed into Tank's brain of dad teaching him how to play poker. Oh, how he wished it were time to double down or go all in. If only dad knew what was happening, he could certainly fix all of this. A single tear rolled down Tank's cheek. It was time, unfortunately, to fold.

"They are diamonds!" screamed Tank. "There are two diamonds that attach to the tablet. That's what the missing pieces are, I swear! That is how the tablet works!"

Agent Locke smirked and gave a directive to Agent Sauceda. "Get Colonel Grimes on the radio and tell him we are looking for two diamonds. Have him search the cave near Grande Cachoeira and our agents will search Caverna de Morte near our side of the GAP."

"What about the boy and his mom?" asked Agent Sauceda.

"Put them both on the next plane to A.D.X. Millard," ordered Agent Locke.

Tank was placed in handcuffs. Through the slits in the window, he could see his mom being placed in the back of a squad car. He struggled against the police officers, but three on one was too much, even for Tank.

As Tank realized his fate, something miraculous happened. A tall, slender man wearing a suit entered the police station. It was Uncle Darren and he was walking toward Agent Locke! The look on his face was relaxed but determined. He must have seen Tank's mom being arrested in the parking lot, although he was not showing any emotion.

"Hand that boy over to me right now," ordered Uncle Darren, displaying a badge to Agent Locke.

"The boy is wanted for conspiracy against the U.S. Government," replied Agent Locke, in a snarky tone of voice. "And, I have a warrant for his mom's arrest right here."

"That young man is a minor and that arrest warrant has nothing to do with him," declared Uncle Darren.

"Here is a signed copy of the Classified Attestation Disclosure the kid signed." Agent Locke pulled out the document. "Since signing, he has mentioned the tablet multiple times and violated the agreement. Foolish kid even waived his right to legal representation."

Uncle Darren glanced at the document. He then informed Agent Locke that if he had not obtained an arrest warrant for Tank, then he would personally ensure congress was informed regarding the lack of due process. He also reminded him that Tank was a minor which would not sit well with anybody.

"Fine, fine," replied Agent Locke. "Take the kid, but I will have a warrant for his arrest in a few hours. Don't get too comfortable. I will have one for you, as well, Agent Thornstone," he said, pointing at Uncle Darren.

The officers who were restraining Tank removed his handcuffs as Agent Locke shoved a bag towards Tank. It was his school bag that he had left at the track before Mr. Jackson had them start running laps. Uncle Darren did not say a word but simply grabbed Tank by the arm and dragged him to the exit door and into an unmarked SUV.

"Keep your mouth shut, Junior!" ordered Uncle Darren. "There are ears and eyes everywhere."

"What are you doing?" yelled Tank. "They have my mom."

"For goodness sakes," exclaimed Uncle Darren. "Be quiet if you want to get your mom back alive."

They drove across town and onto Highway 53. Tank realized they were on the street going to his house. They sat in silence for the rest of the car ride. As they drove, Uncle Darren grabbed Tank's backpack and tossed it out the window onto the side of the road.

When they got to Tank's house, Uncle Darren drew his pistol, got out of the SUV, left his keys on the driver's seat, and proceeded to go inside through the front door. He was checking the house to ensure no one was there. Tank sobbed as he slowly got out of the car and entered the house through the garage. He passed through the laundry room and into the kitchen.

As he walked through the laundry room and into the kitchen, Uncle Darren shouted, "Watch out!" Tank jumped and saw Uncle Darren with his pistol extended and ready to fire.

A man dressed in full camo and holding a rifle was standing in the kitchen. He had on a full mask and only his eyes could be seen. It was the sniper

242

that had killed Yacumama! He was aiming his rifle at Uncle Darren! Colonel Grimes must have sent him to finish Tank and his family off.

"Holy manicotti!" Uncle Darren lowered his weapon. "Drew, you scared the blue-blazes out of me. Watch what you are doing next time, Phoenix. I almost shot you in the head!"

"Drew?" whimpered Tank. "Phoenix? Does that mean?"

The sniper lowered his rifle and removed his mask. It was dad! Tank's eyes poured tears, greater than the flow of the Amazon River itself. He was overtaken with emotion and grabbed his dad in the biggest bear hug possible. His dad wrapped his arms around him and said "It's okay, Tank. I am here now! Dad is here."

"They have mom!" wept Tank. "They have my friends! They have the tablet!"

"It will be okay, son." Dad pulled something out of his pocket. "Your mom will be okay. It will take more than a couple rent-a-cops to keep that woman in custody. We will get your friends back, too. Also, they don't have these." He smiled and winked, showing Tank the diamonds.

"Elias is dead," shared Uncle Darren, solemnly to dad. "Grimes shot him!"

Dad mumbled a few choice words under his breath. You could see the grief on his face and his despair at hearing about Elias' death. Once he recovered his emotions, dad roared, "Mark my words. Before this is over, those scumbags at NESA will know they should have NEVER messed with the Warriors of Thárros!"

"Never mess with the Warriors of Thárros!" bellowed Tank. "And definitely, never mess with the Thornstone Family!"

"Get ready, son!" grinned Dad. "This adventure is not over. It's only getting started!"

Appendix A
The Warriors of Thárros

In 334 B.C., Alexander the Great, King of Macedonia, Son of Phillip II, began his vicious military conquest to rule the world. One by one, empires, nations, and all free peoples of the realm fell to the sword, spear, and iron fist of his impenetrable Greek armies.

Conquering first the Persian Empire, he set his sights on world domination. Egypt, The Indus Valley, Thebes, and Asia Minor submitted to his authority. After a decade of cruelty, malice, and havoc, his armies grew weary and frustrated at their king's ambition to establish a new world order.

His men could not fathom the true depths of Alexander's ambition. Alexander was searching for something, an ancient power of the Persian orient. That power was a way to seamlessly cross oceans, mountains, and expand his empire. Alexander lusted for the Tablets of Zurvan, yet he did not grasp the consequences of using the tablets for King Darius of Persia had warned Alexander that to join the three tablets together would bring about the end.

By joining the three tablets together, Alexander believed he would surmount a power equal to that of the gods. He believed that Zeus himself would kneel at the throne of his global Greek kingdom. General Thárros, a loyalist to Greece and of Spartan descent, opposed Alexander's plan to use the tablets. A small company of courageous men, led by Thárros, obtained information of Alexander's secret plot to seize dominion over all the earth and they opposed him.

The historian Plutarch, who was paid 15 Minas by the ancient Greek government to distort the truth, reported that Alexander had died of an infectious disease in Babylon in 323 B.C. This was a lie. Thárros, aware that

Alexander "The Accursed" planned to exploit the tablet's abilities, assassinated King Alexander and confiscated the tablets.

The Tablets of Zurvan remained a secret for nearly 200 years until the reign of Julius Caesar of Rome in 49 B.C. Caesar had been told about the legendary tablets and their magnificent powers. To keep the tablets out of Roman control, the offspring of Thárros fled Roman expansion and settled in Lusitania, which is now known as modern-day Portugal.

In Portugal, the tablets, still guarded by the children of Thárros, remained hidden as all knowledge of their abilities were known by few that lived. It was not until 1807 A.D. that Napoleon of France invaded Portugal and learned the Persian myth of the tablets was true.

Napoleon's advisors informed him that by joining the three tablets together, he would be invincible and harness a power the earth had never seen. The children of Thárros decided to use the tablets sparingly as it was the only way to avoid world-wide destruction.

Kariagos, a descendant of Thárros, and a nobleman of Portugal, ordered his blacksmiths to grind down the front of the tablets and re-inscribe them in three different foreign languages. Altering the tablets was accomplished at great cost for they grew unstable and unpredictably released their energy.

Precious stones and gems from ancient Persia were embedded into the tablets to subdue their power. Furthermore, Kariagos vanquished the tablets to the far corners of the earth to ensure that the tablets never could be rejoined together.

In 1913, a British explorer reported encounters with unimaginable monsters while he traveled through the Amazon jungle searching for El Dorado, the legendary city made of gold. He found the city but only took one piece of treasure and that was The Tablet of Zurvan. Although he did not know it at the time, he had found something with power far beyond his ability to comprehend. He never made it home and was never seen again for the mighty serpent, Yacumama, devoured his body and seized the tablet.

Possessing one of the tablets, Yacumama was worshiped by the local tribes as a deity. A temple was built, and human sacrifices were offered to the beast. It would not be until 1988 when the United States Government would, by chance, rediscover the tablet's existence. Under the guise of protecting the environment, a new agency was established to locate all three tablets and bring them to Washington D.C. where they would be harnessed as a means to create a new world order.

Once again, the descendants of General Thárros would be called upon to save the world from the apocalypse. These courageous men have protected the unknowing masses from certain death and global tyranny. These men are known as the Warriors of Thárros.

Thárros
Πολεμιστές του Θάρρους

Appendix B
Shape of the Tablet(s)

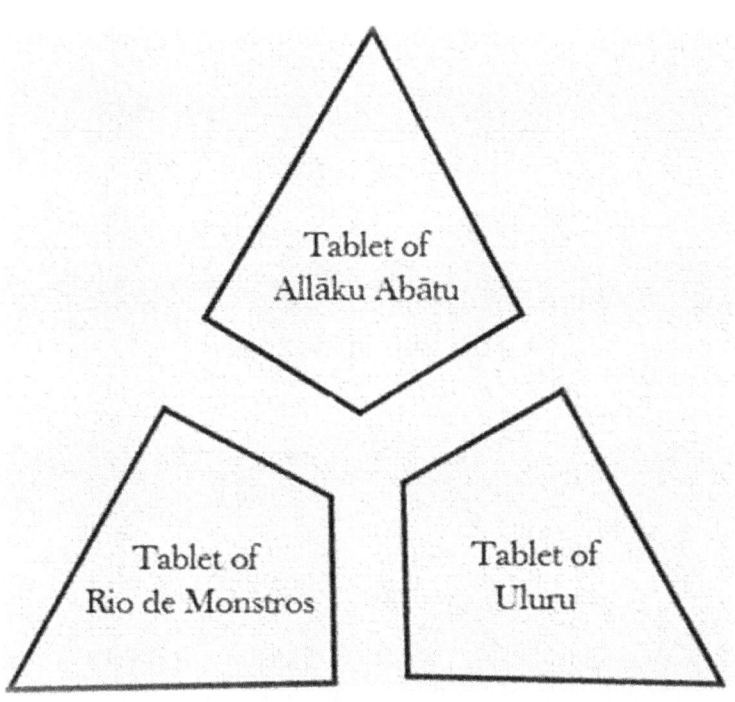

This book ends here. If you choose to leave an honest review on Amazon, thank you!

www.ingramcontent.com/pod-product-compliance
Lightning Source LLC
Chambersburg PA
CBHW071143170626
46809CB00002B/753